STAR

Also by Danielle Steel

ZOYA
KALEIDOSCOPE
FINE THINGS
WANDERLUST
SECRETS
FAMILY ALBUM
FULL CIRCLE
CHANGES
THURSTON HOUSE
CROSSINGS
ONCE IN A LIFETIME
A PERFECT STRANGER
REMEMBRANCE
PALOMINO
LOVE: POEMS
THE RING
LOVING
TO LOVE AGAIN
SUMMER'S END
SEASON OF PASSION
THE PROMISE
NOW AND FOREVER
PASSION'S PROMISE

DANIELLE STEEL

STAR

THE DELACORTE PRESS
LARGE-PRINT COLLECTION

Published by
Delacorte Press
Bantam Doubleday Dell Publishing Group, Inc.
666 Fifth Avenue
New York, New York 10103

Library of Congress Cataloging in Publication Data
Steel, Danielle.
Star.

I. Title.
PS3569.T33828S7   1989   813'.54
88-3975
ISBN 0-440-50072-9
Limited edition 0-440-50172-5
Large-print edition 0-440-50170-9

Manufactured in the United States of America
Published simultaneously in Canada

March 1989
10 9 8 7 6 5 4 3 2 1
BG

**This Large Print Book carries the
seal of approval of N.A.V.H.**

To the only man
who has ever brought
thunder and lightning
and rainbows
into my life.
It happens once,
and when it does,
it's forever.
To my one and only love,
with all my heart,
beloved Popeye.
I love you.

Olive.

STAR

CHAPTER
1

The birds were already calling to each other in the early morning stillness of the Alexander Valley as the sun rose slowly over the hills, stretching golden fingers into a sky that within moments was almost purple. The leaves on the trees rustled gently in the barest breeze as Crystal stood silent in the damp grass, watching the brilliant sky explode in shimmering colors. For brief moments, the birds stopped singing, almost as though they, too, were in awe of the valley's beauty. There were lush fields, rimmed by rugged hills where their cattle wandered, grazing. Her father's ranch cov-

ered two hundred acres, its fertile earth yield-
ing corn, walnuts, and grapes, with the cattle
they bred bringing in their greatest profit. The
Wyatt Ranch had been profitable for a hundred years, but Crystal loved it not for what it
brought them but for what it was. She seemed
to commune silently with spirits only she knew
were there as she watched the tall grass rustle
softly in the breeze, and felt the warmth of the
sun shine down on her wheat-colored hair, as
she began to sing softly. Her eyes were the
color of the summer sky, her limbs long and
graceful as she suddenly began to run, pressing
the damp grass beneath her feet as she headed
toward the river. She sat on a smooth gray
rock, feeling the icy water dance over her feet
as she watched the sunlight reach the rocks.
She loved watching the sun come up, loved
running in the fields, she loved just being there,
alive and young and free, at one with her roots,
and with nature. She loved to sit and sing in
the quiet mornings, her full voice billowing
around her, magical even without music. It
was as though there was something special
about singing then, with only God to hear her.

There were ranch hands who herded her
cattle, and Mexicans who tended the corn and
the vineyards, her father overseeing all of it.
But there was no one who loved the land as

dearly as she, or her father, Tad Wyatt. Her
brother, Jared, helped him after school, but at
sixteen he was more interested in borrowing
her father's pickup and going to Napa with his
friends. It was a fifty-minute drive from Jim
Town. He was a good-looking boy with his father's dark hair, and a knack for taming wild
horses. But neither he nor her sister, Becky,
had Crystal's lyrical beauty. Today was
Becky's wedding day, and Crystal knew that
her mother and grandmother were already
busy in the kitchen. She had heard them as she
slipped away to watch the sun come up over
the mountains. Crystal waded out into the
stream, the water rushing to her thighs as she
felt her feet go numb and her knees tingle, and
she laughed aloud in the summer morning,
pulling her thin cotton nightgown over her
head and tossing it onto the bank. She knew
there was no one to watch her as she stood
gracefully in the stream, totally unaware of
how startlingly beautiful she was, a young Ve-
nus springing forth from the stream in the Alexander Valley. From the distance she looked
every bit a woman, as she stood holding her
long pale blond hair on top of her head with
one hand, as the curves of her exquisite body
were swallowed slowly by the icy water. Only
those who knew her well realized how young

she was. To a stranger she looked full-grown, eighteen or twenty, her body ripe, her eyes huge and blue as she looked up at the early morning sun and squinted happily at the sunshine, her shimmering nakedness seemingly carved out of the palest pink marble. But she was not a woman, she was a girl, not yet fifteen, although she would be fifteen that summer. She laughed to herself as she thought of them looking for her, coming to her room to wake her so she could help them in the kitchen, her sister's fury to find her gone, her grandmother clucking in toothless irritation. As usual, she had escaped them. It was what she liked best, fleeing from tedious obligations and running loose on the ranch, wandering through the tall grass, or into the woods in the winter rains, or riding bareback singing to herself as she rode clear over the hills to the secret places she had discovered on long rides with her father. She had been born here, and one day, when she was very old, as old as Grandma Minerva and even older than that, she would die here. Every inch of her soul loved the ranch, and this valley. She had inherited her father's passion for the land, for the rich brown earth, and the lush green that carpeted the hills in the springtime. She saw a deer standing nearby, and she smiled. There were no enemies in Crystal's world, no dangers, no secret terrors. She belonged here, and never doubted for a moment that she was safe here.

She watched the sun rising in the sky, and walked slowly back to the riverbank, stepping over the rocks easily with her long legs, until she reached her nightgown and pulled it over her head and let it cling wetly to her body as her mane of pale blond hair fell far past her shoulders. She knew it was time to go back, they would be furious by now. Her mother would already have complained to her father. She had helped make twenty-four apple pies the day before, she had baked bread, dressed chickens, helped to cook seven hams, she had stuffed fat ripe tomatoes with basil and walnuts. She had done her share, and she knew there was nothing left to do except fret and get in the way, and listen to Becky shout at her brother. She had plenty of time to shower and dress and get to the church by eleven. They didn't need her, they only thought they did. She was happier roaming the fields and wading in the stream in the morning daylight. The air had already grown warmer and the breeze was dying down. It was going to be a beautiful day for Becky's wedding. 15

She could see their house in the distance as

she heard her grandmother's voice calling shrilly for her from the porch outside the kitchen. "Crysstalll! . . ." The word seemed to reverberate everywhere as she laughed and ran toward the house, looking like a long-legged child, with her hair flying out behind her.

"Crystal!" Her grandmother was standing on the porch as she approached. Grandma Minerva was wearing the black dress she wore when she had serious work to do in the kitchen. She had a clean white apron over it, and she pursed her lips angrily as she saw Crystal gamboling toward her, her white cotton nightgown glued damply to her naked body. There was no artifice to the girl, there were no wiles, there was only that staggering natural beauty she was still unaware of. In her own mind, she was still a child, and aeons away from the burdens of being a woman. "Crystal! Look at you! You can see right through that nightgown! You're not a child anymore! What if one of the men sees you?"

"It's Saturday, Grandma . . . no one's here." She smiled openly into the weathered old face with a broad grin that evidenced neither embarrassment nor contrition.

"You should be ashamed of yourself, and you should be inside getting ready for your sis-

ter's wedding." She muttered disapprovingly
as she wiped her hands on her apron. "Running around like a wild thing at sunrise.
There's work to do here, Crystal Wyatt. Now
get inside and see what you can do to help
your mama." Crystal smiled, and ran around
the wide porch to climb easily into her bedroom window, as her grandmother slammed
the screen door and went back to helping her
daughter in the kitchen.

Crystal stood alone in her room for a moment, humming to herself as she peeled off her
nightgown, and tossed it easily into a damp
heap in the corner, as she glanced up at the
dress she would be wearing to Becky's wedding. It was a simple white cotton dress with
puffed sleeves and a little lace collar. Her
mother had made it for her, as simply as she
could, with no frills, no added adornments to
enhance her already striking beauty. It looked
like a dress for a child, but Crystal didn't
mind. She could wear it to church socials afterward. They had bought plain white pumps in
Napa, and her father had bought her a pair of
nylon stockings in San Francisco. Her grandmother had grumbled disapprovingly over
those as well, and her mother had said she was
too young to wear them.

"She's only a child, Tad." It always annoyed

Olivia when he spoiled their youngest daughter. He was always bringing her treats, or something foolish to wear from Napa or San Francisco.

"It'll make her feel special." Crystal was the child he had adored since she was born, there was a place in him that ached each time he saw her. As a baby she had had a halo of platinum hair and eyes that looked right into his as though she had something special to say to him and no one else. She was a baby born with dreams in her eyes, and a magical quality about her that made people stop and stare. They had always stared at Crystal. People were drawn to her, to some quality deep within as well as to her beauty. She looked like no one else in the family, she was unique, and she was the music in her father's heart. It was he who had chosen her name the first time he had seen her nestled in Olivia's arms only moments after she was born. Luminous and perfect. Crystal. The name suited her to perfection, with her bright clear eyes and the soft platinum hair. Even the children she had played with as a child had known she was special, different in some intangible way. She was freer and brighter and happier than they were, never governed entirely by the rules and limitations set on her by others, like her nervous, always complaining mother, or her far less beautiful older sister, or the brother who teased her mercilessly, or even the stern grandmother who had come to live with them when Crystal was seven, when Grandpa Hodges died in Arizona. Only her father seemed to understand her, only he knew how remarkable she was, like a rare bird one had to allow to fly free from time to time, soaring high over the ordinary and the mundane. She was a creature delivered to him straight from God's hand, and he always broke the rules for her, gave her little gifts, made exceptions for her, much to everyone else's annoyance.

"Crystal!" It was her mother's sharp voice outside her door, as she stood in the room she had shared with Becky for almost fifteen years. The door opened before she had time to answer, and Olivia Wyatt stood glaring at her in nervous disapproval. "Why are you standing there like that?" She was naked and beautiful, and Olivia didn't like to see it. She didn't like to think of her that way, already well into womanhood, yet with the innocent eyes of a child as she turned to look at her mother, in the blue silk dress she was going to wear to Becky's wedding. She had covered it with a clean white apron, just like Grandma Minerva's. "Cover yourself! Your father and brother are up!" She eyed Crystal sternly, and pressed the door closed behind her, as though they were standing just outside, waiting to see Crystal's naked young body. In truth her father would only have admired her, startled to see her as more of a woman than she truly was, and Jared would have been, as always, indifferent to his sister's striking beauty.

"Oh Mama . . ." She knew how angry her mother would have been if she could have seen her standing naked in the stream only moments before. "They're not going to come in here." She smiled with an innocent shrug, as Olivia scolded.

"Don't you know there's work to do? Your sister needs help with her dress. Grandma needs help carving the turkey and slicing the hams. Don't you ever make yourself useful, Crystal Wyatt?" They both knew she did, but seldom to the women of the house, and always to her father. She preferred riding the tractor with him, or helping him herd the cattle when he was short of men. She worked tirelessly in brutal rainstorms bringing stray calves in, and she had a gift of gentleness with all their livestock. But that meant nothing to her mother. "Get yourself dressed," and then, glancing at the clean white dress hanging on her closet door, "wear your blue gingham till we leave for church. You'll get your dress dirty helping Grandma in that."

As her mother watched her, Crystal slipped into her underwear, and pulled her old blue gingham dress over her head. For an instant, it made her look like a child again, but her womanhood was already too advanced to be denied even by the faded gingham. She hadn't buttoned it yet, when the door flew open, and Becky exploded into the room, chattering nervously and complaining about her brother. She had brown hair like her mother's and wide-set brown eyes. There was a handsome plainness to her face, and her body was long and slim not unlike Crystal's, but there was nothing remarkable about her features, and her voice was pitched in an anguished whine as she told Olivia that Jared had soaked all the towels in the ranch's only bathroom.

"I can't even dry my hair decently. He does it every day, Mama! I know he does it on purpose!" Crystal watched her silently almost as though they had never met. After living side by side for almost fifteen years, the two girls were more strangers than sisters. Rebecca was cut in her mother's mold, the brown hair and brown eyes, the nervousness, the constant complaining. She was marrying the boy she had fallen in love with when she was Crystal's age, and she had waited for him through the war. Now almost exactly a year after he had come home safely from Japan, she was marrying him. And at eighteen, she was still a virgin. "I hate him, Mama! I hate him!" She was referring to her brother, as her long brown hair hung damply down her back, and tears stung her eyes as she looked angrily at her mother and sister, berating Jared.

"Well, you won't have to live with him anymore after today." Her mother smiled. They had had a long talk the day before, wandering slowly past the barn, as her mother explained what Tom would expect of her on their wedding night in Mendocino. Becky had already heard about it from friends, several of whom had gotten married within months of their sweethearts' return from the Pacific. But Tom had wanted to find a job first, and Becky's father had insisted that she finish high school. She had accomplished that five weeks before, and now on a bright, sunny day in late July, her dreams would come true. She was going to be Mrs. Thomas Parker. It sounded very grown up, and more than a little scary. And secretly, Crystal wondered why her sister was marrying him. With Tom, Becky would never go farther than Booneville. Her life would begin and end right there, on the ranch where

they had grown up. She loved the ranch, too,
far more than the others did, and she wanted
to settle here one day after she'd seen a piece of
the world. She dreamed of other places, other
things, [other people than the ones she had
grown up with. She wanted to see just a little
bit more of the world than the patch of land
bounded by the Mayacama Mountains. There
were photographs of movie stars tacked to
Crystal's walls, Greta Garbo and Betty Gra-
ble, Vivien Leigh and Clark Gable. There were
photographs of Hollywood and San Francisco
and New York, and once her father had shown
her a postcard of Paris. She dreamed at times
of going to Hollywood and becoming a movie
star. She dreamed of going to mystical places,
like the ones she whispered about with her father. She knew they were only dreams, but she
loved to think about them. And she knew with
all her heart that she wanted more than a life
tied down to a man like Tom Parker. Their
father had offered him a job on the ranch, because he hadn't been able to find work else-
where. He had left high school to enlist after
Pearl Harbor. And Becky had waited patiently, writing to him every week, and waiting
months sometimes for his letters. He had
seemed so grown up when he came back, so
full of stories about the war. At twenty-one, he

was a man, or at least Becky thought so. And now, a year later, he was going to be her husband.

"Why aren't you dressed?" Becky suddenly turned on her sister, standing barefoot in the blue gingham dress their mother had told her to put on. "You should be dressed by now!" It was seven o'clock in the morning, and they weren't leaving for the church until ten-thirty.

"Mama wants me to help Grandma in the kitchen." She said it in a quiet voice, so unlike Olivia's and Becky's. It was a voice beneath which one could almost hear the husky sensuality of her singing. The songs were innocent, but the voice that sang them was filled with instinctive passion. Becky threw her own wet towel on the bed they had shared, still unmade because Crystal had fled to the fields to watch the sunrise. "How can I get dressed in here, in this mess?"

"Crystal, make the bed," Olivia said in a stern voice as she went to help Becky comb her hair. She herself had made the veil that Becky would wear, with a little crown of white satin sewn with tiny white pearls, and yards of the stiff white tulle she had bought in Santa Rosa.

Crystal smoothed the sheets, and pulled up the heavy quilt their grandmother had made for them years before. Olivia had made a new one for Becky as a wedding gift. It had already been taken to the little cottage that was going to be their home, on the ranch, and their father was going to let Becky and Tom live there until they could afford a place of their own. Olivia liked the idea of having Becky close to her, and Tom had been relieved not to have to rent a place they couldn't afford yet. To Crystal, it hardly seemed as though Becky was leaving at all. She was going to be less than a half a mile away, along the dirt track she herself often rode with her father on the tractor.

Olivia was carefully brushing out Becky's hair as the two women talked about Cliff Johnson and his French wife. He had brought her home as a war bride, and Becky had debated long and hard about inviting them to the wedding.

"She's not as bad as all that," Olivia conceded for the first time in a year, as Crystal stood silently watching. She always felt like an outsider with them. They always left her out of their conversations. She wondered if now, with Becky gone, her mother would pay more attention to her, and listen to what she had to say, or if Olivia would only spend all of her spare time at Becky's cottage. "She gave you a mighty fine piece of lace, said it was her grandmother's in France. You can do something nice

with it one day." They were the first kind
words anyone had said about Mireille since
she'd arrived the year before. She wasn't a
pretty girl, but she was friendly, and she had
tried desperately to fit in, despite the initial resistance of all of Cliff's friends and neighbors.
There were plenty of girls waiting for the boys
at home, without bringing home foreign girls
from the war. But at least she was white. Not
like the girl Boyd Webster had brought home
from Japan. That had been a disgrace his family would never live down. Never. And Becky
had fought Tom not to invite Boyd and his
wife to the wedding. She had cried, she had
wailed, she had raged and even pleaded. But
Tom had insisted that Boyd was his best
friend, they had survived four years of the war
side by side, and even if he had done a damn
stupid thing marrying that girl, he was not going to keep him away from their wedding. In
fact, he had asked Boyd to be his best man,
which had made Becky even madder. But in
the end, she had had to relent. Tom Parker
was even more stubborn than she was. It was
going to be an embarrassment having Hiroko
there, and it wasn't as though one could forget
what she was, with her slant eyes and her shining black hair. Just seeing her reminded everyone of the boys they had lost in the Pacific. It

was a disgrace, that's what it was. Tom didn't
like her either, but Boyd was his buddy, his
friend, and he was loyal to him. Boyd had paid
his own price for marrying her. No one had
given him a job when he brought her home,
and every door in town had been slammed in
their faces. Finally, old Mr. Petersen had felt
sorry for him, and had given him a job pump-
ing gas, which was too bad, because Boyd was
smarter than that. He'd been planning to go to
college before the war, but there was no hope
of that now. He had to work to support himself and Hiroko. Everyone figured that eventually they'd get discouraged and move away. At
least they hoped so. But in his own way, Boyd
was as in love with the valley as Tad Wyatt
and Crystal.

Crystal had been fascinated by Boyd's pretty
little Japanese wife when she first arrived.
Hiroko's gentle, delicate ways, her hesitant
speech, her enormous politeness and her cautious English drew Crystal like a magnet. But
Olivia wouldn't let Crystal speak to her, and
even her father had thought it best that she
stay away from them. Some things were better
left alone, and these days the Websters were
among them.

"What are you doing, standing there, staring
at your sister?" Olivia noticed Crystal watch-

ing them, and suddenly remembered that she was there. "I told you half an hour ago to go help Grandma in the kitchen."

Without a word, Crystal left the room, soundlessly on bare feet, as Becky chattered on nervously about the wedding. And when she got to the kitchen, there were already three women there, having come to help from neighboring farms and ranches. Becky's wedding was going to be the event of the year, and the first of the summer. Friends and neighbors would be coming from miles around. There were two hundred guests expected, as the women worked furiously to put the last touches on the enormous lunch they would serve after the service.

"Where've you been, girl?" Her grandmother snapped at her, and pointed rapidly at a huge ham. They slaughtered their own pigs and cured their own. Everything they would be serving was homemade and homegrown, even the wine her father would be pouring.

Crystal got to work without saying a word, and within moments she felt a sharp slap on her bottom. "Nice dress, Sis. Dad get it for you in San Francisco?" Inevitably, it was Jared, leering down at her from his enormous height. At sixteen, he was always anxious to tease and to torture. He was wearing new slacks that were already a little too short, and a white shirt his grandmother had pressed and starched until it could have stood on its own. But his feet were still bare, he was carrying his shoes, and his new jacket and tie were cast lazily over his shoulder. He had fought like cats and dogs with Becky for years, but in the past year Crystal had become the object of his attentions. He helped himself to a slice of the succulent ham as Crystal swiped at his fingers.

"I'll cut them off if you don't watch it." She waved the knife at him, more than a little teasing. He irked her constantly. He loved to tease and to play and to annoy her. More than once he had pressed her until she took a swing at him, which he always deflected easily, and then boxed her less than gently on her ear for trying. "Get away from me . . . go bother someone else, Jar." More often than not she called him Jarhead. "Why aren't you helping too?"

"I've got better things to do. I have to help Dad set out the wine."

"Yeah . . . I'll bet . . ." She growled at him, she'd seen him get drunk with his friends, but she would have died before squealing to their father. Even when they were at odds, there was still an unspoken bond between them. "Make sure you leave some for the guests."

"Make sure you remember to wear shoes." He slapped her bottom again and she dropped the knife and grabbed at his arm, but too late, as he sped down the hall toward his own bedroom, whistling. He stopped outside Becky's door for an instant, and poked his head in, as she stood in her brassiere and underpants, adjusting her garter belt, just as the door flew open. "Hi, kid . . . Wow!" He gave a long wolf whistle and Becky let out a hideous scream.

"Get him out of here!" She threw her hairbrush at him, but he slammed the door shut before it hit him. They were familiar sounds in the comfortable old ranch house, and no one in the kitchen paid much attention as Tad Wyatt came in, already dressed in his dark blue suit for the wedding. He had an air of solidity and warmth and quiet distinction about him. His family had had money once, lots of it, but they had lost most of it years before, even before the Depression. They had had to sell off thousands of acres, and he had turned the ranch around and made it successful again, by the sweat of his brow, and with Olivia beside him. But he had seen a little bit of the world before he married her. He talked to Crystal about it sometimes when they went on long walks, or sat in driving rains, or waited for a cow to give birth in the winter. He shared things with her that had been long buried and were almost forgotten. "There's a big world out there, little girl . . . with a lot of beautiful places in it . . . not many better than this . . . but they're worth seeing nonetheless. . . ." He told her about places like New Orleans and New York, and even England. And whenever Olivia heard him she scolded him for filling Crystal's head with nonsense. Olivia herself had never been farther than the Southwest, and even that seemed foreign to her. And her two oldest children shared her view of the world. The Valley was enough, and all the people in it. Only Crystal dreamed of something more, and wondered if she would ever see it. She loved the Valley too, but there was room in her heart for more than that. Like her father she loved the Valley with a passion and yet she loved to dream of faraway places.

"How's my girl?" Tad Wyatt wandered in and looked proudly down on his youngest daughter. Even there, in the kitchen filled with women, in her old blue gingham dress, the sight of Crystal tugged at his heart and her beauty took his breath away, and it was impossible for him to conceal it. He was only grateful that this wasn't her wedding day. He knew he couldn't have stood it. And he wouldn't have let her marry a man like Tom Parker. But for Becky, he was all right. Becky didn't have dreams . . . there were no stars in the secret skies of her heart . . . she had no secret visions. She wanted a husband and kids and a cottage on the ranch, and an ordinary man like Tom, with no ambition and few dreams, and that was what she was getting.

"Hi, Dad." Crystal looked straight into his eyes with a gentle smile, and without words, the love that they shared spoke volumes.

"Did Mama make you a pretty dress for today?" He had wanted her to, he always wanted her to. He smiled, remembering the stockings he had given Crystal to wear to the wedding, even if Olivia did think him foolish.

Crystal nodded, as he watched her. It was pretty enough. But not like anything you'd see in the movies. It was just a dress. A nice, white dress. The nylon stockings were going to be the best part of her outfit, invisible and sheer and exciting. But Tad knew she could have worn anything, and she would have been lovely.

"Where's your mama?" He looked around the kitchen and saw only his mother-in-law and three of his wife's friends, and Crystal.

"Helping Becky dress."

"Already? She'll be wilted before we ever get to the church." They exchanged a smile, the day was already getting warm, and the kitchen seemed to be steaming. "Where's Jared? I've been looking for him for an hour." But he looked good-natured as he said it, he wasn't easily ruffled. He had been patient with all of them ever since they were children.

"He said he was going to help you with the wine." Crystal smiled as their eyes met again, and she offered him a slice of the ham she had only moments before begrudged her brother.

"Help me drink it more like." They both laughed and he walked down the hall to Jared's bedroom. Jared's passion was cars and not ranches and his father knew it, the only one who truly loved the ranch, who understood it, who loved the land as he did, was Crystal. He walked past the bedroom where Becky was dressing with her mother's help, and knocked on his son's door. "Come and help me move the tables, Son. There's still work to do outside." They had set long tables with white linen cloths, left over from his own mother's wedding half a century before. The guests would eat shaded by the enormous trees that surrounded the ranch house.

Tad Wyatt poked his head into Jared's room

and found him lying on the bed, looking at a magazine full of pictures of women. "Can I interrupt you long enough to give me a hand, Son?" Jared jumped to his feet with a nervous grin, his tie askew, and his hair slicked back with a tonic he had bought in Napa.

"Sure, Dad. Sorry."

Tad was careful not to rumple the boy's carefully styled hair, and put a powerful arm around his shoulders. It seemed odd to him that one of them was getting married so soon. In his mind, they were still babies . . . he could remember Jared learning to walk . . . and chasing chickens . . . and falling off the tractor when he was four . . . teaching him to drive when he was seven . . . hunting with him when he was hardly taller than the rifle . . . and Becky barely older than that, and now she was getting married.

"It's a fine day for your sister's wedding." He looked up at the sky, and smiled at his son, as he directed Jared and three of the ranch hands where to put the tables. It was another hour before everything was set to his liking, and when he went back to the kitchen for a cool drink with Jared, Crystal was gone, and there was no sign of any of the women. All of them were in Becky and Crystal's room now, exclaiming over the dress, and sighing and dabbing at their eyes as they saw Becky finally in her lace and gauzy splendor. She was a beautiful bride, as most girls are, and all of them were pressed around her, offering her their good wishes, and making veiled comments about her wedding night, until she blushed hotly and turned to see Crystal quietly slipping into her own simple dress in the corner. The dress offered no excitement at all and yet in its stark simplicity, it only seemed to set off her beauty more. The treasured nylons were carefully in place, and the flat white pumps didn't add to her considerable height. And as she stood quietly in the corner, and they turned to look at her, with her sheaf of pale gold hair, and a little halo of baby's breath and white roses, she looked almost like an angel. By comparison, Becky seemed overdressed, overdone, and far less striking. Crystal seemed to be frozen in place in a rare moment between childhood and womanhood, there was no artifice to her, nothing raw, nothing sharp, only the subtle smoothness of her startling beauty.

"Well . . . Crystal looks very nice," one of the women said, as though by ordinary words one could make her less dazzling, but it couldn't be done, Crystal was who she was, and nothing could diminish that, not even the plain white dress that she wore. As one looked at her, all was forgotten except the graceful way she moved and her incredible face beneath the halo of innocent white flowers. Becky was carrying white roses, too, and the women in the room had to force themselves to turn around and exclaim over her again. But there was no denying it. It was Crystal who was the beauty.

"We'd better be going," Olivia said finally, and led the women outside to where her husband and Jared were already waiting. They were using separate cars to get to the church. The wedding itself was going to be small, their friends were invited to the lunch afterward, but very few had been invited to the church service.

Tad watched the women as they came down the porch steps, talking and laughing and giggling like young girls. It brought his own wedding day to mind. Olivia had looked lovely in her mother's wedding gown, but it seemed so long ago now. She looked so tired and so worn and so different now. Life hadn't been easy for them, the Depression had been particularly rough, but that was all over now. The ranch was doing well, their children were almost grown, they were safe and happy in their comfortable little world in their remote little valley. And then suddenly he caught his breath, as Becky stood on the porch, looking shy and proud, the veil clouding her face, her bouquet of roses held in her trembling hands. She looked lovely, and he felt tears sting his eyes as he saw her.

"Isn't she a picture, Tad?" Olivia whispered proudly, pleased at the effect their oldest daughter had visibly had on him. For years she had tried to push Becky deeper into his affections, but it was always Crystal who warmed his heart . . . Crystal . . . with her wild ways and unfettered grace as she ran at his heels. But now Becky had finally done it.

"You look lovely, sweetheart." He gently kissed his daughter, feeling the veil touch his lips with her cheek, and he pressed her hand as they both fought back tears, and then the moment was gone and they were all hurrying to the cars to get her to the church where she would become Mrs. Thomas Parker. It was a big day for all of them, and especially for Becky, and as he hurried around the car to slide behind the wheel, he suddenly stopped and felt the same pangs that had torn at his heart since the first time he saw her. Standing shyly like a doe in the plain white dress, hesitant, shy, the sun glinting on her hair, her eyes the same color as the sky, Crystal stood and watched him. There was no fighting what he felt for her, what she was to him, and always had been. She stopped for a moment, too, and they both smiled. She felt strong and alive and loved whenever she was near him. He smiled at his youngest child, as she slipped into the car Jared was driving their grandmother in, and with a wild gesture she tossed one of her white roses at him, and with a gurgle of laughter, he caught it. It was Becky's day, he didn't need Olivia to remind him of that, Crystal was who she was. And she meant everything to him. She was the rarest of the rare. She was simply . . . Crystal.

CHAPTER 2

The service was simple and sweet as the bride and groom exchanged their vows in the little white church in Jim Town. Becky looked pretty and proud in the gown her mother had made, and Tom looked nervous and very young in a new blue suit he had bought for the wedding. Boyd Webster was the best man, with his coppery hair and a face full of freckles. And as Tad watched them from the front pew, he thought of how young they all were, scarcely more than children.

Crystal was her sister's only attendant, she stood to one side, looking shyly up at Boyd,

and trying not to look with curious fascination
at his wife in the back row. Hiroko had worn a
simple green silk dress, and a string of pearls,
and black patent leather shoes. She was anxious to look as Western as she could, although
Boyd had wanted her to wear a kimono. She
had worn a ceremonial kimono at their own
wedding in Japan, and she had looked like a
doll with the traditional Kanzashi in her hair,
and the gold dagger and tiny brocade purse
filled with coins tucked into her gold obi. But
all of that was forgotten now, as Becky's close
family and friends watched her become Tom's
wife. He kissed the bride, as Jared cheered, and
Olivia dabbed at her eyes with the lace handkerchief she had carried at her own wedding.
Everything had gone off perfectly, and they
stood outside for a time, chatting with family
and friends and admiring Becky. The best man
slapped Tom on the back as he beamed, and
everyone shook hands and kissed and enjoyed
the simple celebration. Jared threw a handful
of rice at them as they got back into their cars,
and drove in convoy back to the Wyatt Ranch
for the carefully prepared luncheon that
Olivia, Minerva, and their neighbors had been
working on for days before the wedding.

As soon as they got home, Olivia flew
around the kitchen instructing ranch hands to

carry trays and platters to the waiting tables
outside. Their wives had been hired on to help
serve and clean up afterward, and the tables
laden with food seemed to stretch on forever,
turkeys and capons, roast beef and ribs and
hams, black-eyed peas and sweet potatoes, veg-
etables and salads, aspics and deviled eggs, and
cookies and sweets and fruit pies and a huge
white wedding cake set up on its own table. It
looked like enough food for an army, as Tad
helped the men to open the wine, and Tom
stood grinning at his bride, with Boyd smiling
shyly beside them. Boyd was a good-looking
boy with an open heart and kind eyes, and he
had always been fond of the Wyatts. His sister,
Ginny, had gone to school with Becky, and he
remembered Jared and Crystal when they were
babies, although he was scarcely older than
they were. But at twenty-two, with four years
of war under his belt, he felt a lifetime older.

"Well, Tom, you did it. How does it feel to
be a married man?" Boyd Webster grinned
broadly at his friend, as Tom looked around
him with unconcealed pleasure. Marrying into
the Wyatt family had been a step up in the
world for Tom Parker. He was looking forward to living on the ranch and sharing in its
comfortable profits, if not directly, at least in
life-style. Tad had been grooming him for

months, explaining to him about the corn and the cattle and the vineyards. The walnuts were the least profitable venture on the ranch, but even that was no small operation. And in walnut season, everyone on the ranch lent a hand, until their fingers were stained from picking and shelling the walnuts. For the first few months, though, Tom was going to be helping his father-in-law with the vineyards.

"Yeah, I'll bet you will," one of Tom's friends teased him over plates heaped with ham and turkey, "wine-tasting, isn't that what they call it, Tom?" The groom laughed happily, his eyes a little too bright, as Becky giggled in the center of a group of the girls she had grown up with. Most of them were married now too. With the war finally over, and the boys coming home just as the girls finished high school, there had been dozens of weddings in the valley in the past year, and some of them had already had babies. And they were already teasing Becky now about getting pregnant. "It won't be long, Becky Wyatt . . . just you wait . . . another month or two, and you'll be expecting!" The girls giggled as cars and pickup trucks continued to drive up, and their neighbors arrived, dressed in their Sunday best, reprimanding their children, admonishing them to behave, and not tear their clothes running wild with their friends around the tables. Within an hour, there were two hundred well-wishers crowded along the long tables of food, and half as many children, small ones standing close to their mothers' legs, afraid to stray too far, babes in arms, a few little boys carried about on their fathers' shoulders, and a slight distance away from the carefully laid tables, a huge crowd of children running and playing tag, with their parents' words of caution instantly forgotten. The boys were chasing each other around the trees, as several of the more adventurous ones climbed them, and the girls stood in large groups giggling and talking and laughing, some of them taking turns on the swings Tad had built years before for his own children. They joined their elders briefly from time to time, but on the whole each group was content to ignore the other, the parents assumed that the children were safe nearby, and the children were content that their parents were having too much fun to concern themselves about what their offspring were up to.

And as always, Crystal stood on the fringe of the younger groups, almost forgotten except for an occasional glance of envy or admiration. The girls always eyed her cautiously, and the boys, in recent years, had been fascinated by her, although they expressed it oddly at times, pushing and shoving, and even tugging at the long blond hair, or pretending to spar with her, or push her too hard, or doing anything they could physically to catch her attention, without actually talking to her. And the girls tried not to talk to her at all. Her looks made her much too threatening. She was set apart from them without understanding why. It was the price she paid for her beauty. She accepted the way they treated her as something that was, without yet understanding why. Sometimes, when the boys pushed her, and she was feeling brave, she shoved them right back, or hit them, or even tripped them when they annoyed her. It was her only communication with them. And the rest of the time they ignored her. She had known them all since they were born, and yet in recent years, it was as though she had become a stranger. The children were as aware as their elders were of how striking she was, how breathtakingly lovely. But no one knew how to deal with it. They were simple folk and it was as though in the past year or two, she had become someone different. It had particularly struck the boys coming home from the war, after four years away, they were shocked to see what had happened to Crystal. Always pretty as a little girl, there had been nothing about her at ten to suggest the full force of her beauty as she became a woman. But part of her appeal was that she was as yet unaware of her effect on the men around her, and she was still as patient and good-natured as she had been as a little girl. If anything, she was shyer now, because she knew her effect on those around her had altered subtly, but she didn't know why. Only her brother treated her as he always had, with rude affection. But her lack of awareness about her looks made her innocence all the more sensual, a fact of which her father was well aware, and for two years now he had told her to stop hanging around the ranch hands. He knew exactly what they were thinking and why, and he didn't want Crystal unwittingly doing something to provoke them. Her gentleness and silent way of moving among them was far more arousing than walking past them stark naked.

But Tad wasn't worried about her now, as he talked politics and sports and local gossip and grape prices with his friends. It was a happy day for all of them as their friends ate and talked and laughed, and the children played nearby, while Crystal watched them.

Hiroko stood slightly apart from all of them too, beneath the shade of a tree, silent and alone, her eyes never leaving her husband.

Boyd was talking to Tom in a circle of friends, reminiscing about the war. It was hard to believe it had ended less than a year before. It seemed lifetimes behind them now, with its terrors and its excitement, the friends they had made, and those they had lost. Only Hiroko stood there now, as a living reminder of where they had been, and what they still remembered. She was eyed with open hostility, and none of the women approached her. Even her sister-in-law, Ginny Webster, was careful to shun her. Ginny was wearing a tight pink dress, low cut over her full bosom, with a matching jacket with little white polka dots, and a peplum which accentuated her shapely bottom. She was laughing even louder than the rest, and flirting with all of Boyd's friends, just as she had years before when Boyd brought them home after school and she tried to captivate her brother's buddies. But her effect and her style were far different from Crystal's. She was overtly sexual with her bright red hair and her tight dress and her obvious makeup. She had been talked about for years, and the men loved to slip an arm around her shoulders and get a good look down her dress to her ample bosom. It brought back memories for many of them. Since she'd turned thirteen, Ginny had always been generous with her favors.

"What you got there, Ginny?" The groom sidled up to her, smelling of something stronger than the wine Tad was serving. A few of the men had been drinking whiskey in the barn, and Tom had, as always, been quick to join them. He eyed her now with obvious interest as he squeezed her close to him, and let his hand slip under her jacket. She was holding Becky's bouquet, but he wasn't referring to the flowers. He was looking straight into her cleavage. "Did you catch the bouquet? Guess you're next." He laughed raucously, displaying good teeth and the smile that had won Becky's heart years before. But Ginny knew more of him than that, which to some, was no secret.

"I told you I'd be getting married pretty soon, Tom Parker." She giggled at him, and he pulled her even closer, as Boyd blushed and looked away from his sister and his friend, catching sight of his tiny ivory bride, watching them from the distance. Boyd felt a pang as he looked at Hiroko then. It was rare that he left her side, but today, as Tom's best man, it was hard to be as attentive to her as he would have liked. But as Ginny and Tom teased and laughed, Boyd quietly slipped away, and went to find Hiroko. She smiled as he approached, and he felt his heart tug as it always did when he looked into her gentle eyes. She had brought him comfort a long way from home, and she had been devoted to him every moment since she'd arrived in the valley. It broke his heart to see how unkind people were to her. Despite his friends' warnings in Japan, he hadn't been prepared for the viciousness of their words, or the doors that had slammed in their faces. More than once, he had thought of moving away, but this was his home, and he wasn't going to run away, no matter what they said or did to him. It was only Hiroko he worried about. The women were so unkind to her, and the men were worse. They called her a gook and a Jap, even the children wouldn't talk to her, having been told not to by their parents. It was a far cry from her gentle loving family in Japan.

"You okay?" He smiled down at her, and she bent her head and nodded and then looked up at him shyly in the way that always made his heart melt.

"I'm fine, Boyd-*san*. It is very handsome party." He laughed at her choice of words and she looked embarrassed and then giggled. "No?"

"Yes." He leaned over and kissed her gently, not giving a damn who was watching. He loved her and she was his wife, and to hell with them if they couldn't understand it. His red

hair and freckles stood out in sharp contrast to
her ivory skin and jet-black hair which she
wore in a neat bun at the nape of her neck.
Everything about her was simple and neat and
nicely put together. And her family had been
just as shocked as his own when they had told
them they were getting married. Her father
had forbidden her to see Boyd again, but in the
end, in the face of Boyd's kindness and gentle
ways and obvious love for the girl, in spite of
themselves and her mother's tears, they had
relented. Hiroko had told them nothing in her
letters of the brutal reception she had met in
the Alexander Valley, she told them only about
the little shack where they lived, the beautiful
countryside, and her love for Boyd, making it
all sound simple and easy. When she first arrived she had known nothing of the internment
camps for the Japanese during the war, or the
fury and scorn she would meet in California.

"Did you eat?" He felt guilty, realizing how
long he had left her alone, and he suddenly
suspected, correctly, that she hadn't eaten. She
had been too shy to approach any of the long
tables surrounded by their neighbors.

"I am not very hungry, Boyd-*san*. It is
warm."

"I'll get you something right now." She was
slowly growing accustomed to Western food,

although most of what she cooked for them was the Japanese style he had come to love in Japan and that her mother had taught her. "I'll be right back." He kissed her again and hurried toward the tables, still laden with the food Olivia and her mother had prepared, and then as he started back toward her with a plate, he stopped, unable to believe his eyes. Still carrying Hiroko's long-delayed lunch, Boyd hurried toward the tall, dark-haired man shaking hands with Tom Parker. He stood out from the rest of the guests in a dark blue blazer and white slacks, with a bright red tie, and an aura about him that bespoke a world of ease far, far from the valley. He was only five years older than Boyd, and he looked different now, but they had been close friends in the Pacific. Spencer Hill had been his commanding officer and Tom's, he had even come to Boyd and Hiroko's wedding in Kyoto. And as Boyd approached him with a broad grin, Spencer was shaking Tom's hand and congratulating him, looking suntanned and at ease, and as comfortable there as he had been in Japan in his uniform. He was a man who seemed at ease anywhere, his deep blue eyes seemed to take in the whole scene at a glance and a moment later he was laughing at Boyd Webster.

"Well, I'll be damned . . . you again! The

freckle-faced kid! How's Hiroko?" Boyd was touched that he remembered her name, and he smiled as he waved toward the trees where she was standing.

"She's fine. Christ, it's been a long time, Captain. . . ." Their eyes met in instant memory, of the pain they had shared, and the fears, but there had been more than that, there had been a closeness that would never come again. A closeness born of sorrow and excitement and terror, and victory too. But the victory had seemed a small moment compared to the rest, and it was the years before that they all remembered. "Come and say hello to her." Spencer excused himself from the group and left Tom to his cohorts, in high spirits by then, and anxious to get back to the barn for more whiskey.

"How've you been? I wondered if you'd be here. Or if the two of you would have moved to the city by now." He had often thought that it would be easier for them to live in a place like San Francisco or Honolulu, but Boyd had been determined to go home to the valley he had so often talked of.

Hiroko's eyes filled with surprise and she bowed when she saw him. As Spencer smiled down at her, she looked as tiny and delicate as she had a year before at her own wedding. But there was something more in her eyes now, a wisdom and sadness that hadn't been there before, and Spencer easily suspected that the past year had been neither kind nor easy.

"You look beautiful, Hiroko. It's good to see you both again." He gently took her hand in his own, as she blushed, not daring to look up at him, as her husband watched them. The Captain had been so decent to both of them, he had done everything he could to discourage them from getting married, but in the end, he had stood by Boyd as he had all his men, in battle and out. He was the kind of man his men knew they could always turn to. He was strong and intelligent and kind, and relentless when they let him down, which they seldom did. There had been few men in his command who didn't want to live up to the example he set them. He worked hard, fought alongside them, and was seemingly tireless as they struggled to win the war, and now it was so strange . . . it was over, and here they were, halfway around the world, safe again, yet none of it was forgotten. "It's been a long time, hasn't it?" Spencer's eyes met Boyd's, and he saw something older and wiser there, they had both seen pain together in the war. Yet, out of uniform the handsome captain seemed much younger than he had the last time they'd met, when Boyd left Japan for San Francisco.

"I didn't know you'd be here today," Boyd said quietly, happier to see him than Spencer knew. He was the first person who had spoken kindly to Hiroko since she'd arrived in California in September. "Tom didn't tell me."

"He was probably too busy thinking about his bride." Spencer smiled a wide easy smile at them both. "I wrote and told him I'd try to come, but I wasn't sure myself until a few days ago. I was supposed to be back in New York by now. But I never seem to want to leave California." He glanced around and Boyd handed Hiroko the plate and urged her to try it, but she was more interested in their friend than the food, and she set the plate down carefully on a tree stump just behind her.

"Are you out here on vacation, sir?" Boyd's eyes were filled with the affection and respect that had marked their relationship in Japan, and Spencer shook his head and laughed openly.

"No, I'm not, and for chrissake, Webster, the name is Spencer, or have you forgotten?"

Boyd Webster blushed bright red, as he had always done, even in the heat of battle. It had won him a lot of nicknames from his C.O. and now the two men laughed again. "I figured you might court-martial me if I said it." Hiroko smiled, watching them, it reminded her of a happier time far, far from here, when she was at home, and not an unwelcome stranger.

"Believe it or not, I'm back in school again. I couldn't figure out what else to do after the war. I just finished a year of law school." He had managed to complete almost two years in one, and would be graduating from Stanford Law School the following summer.

"In the East?" Boyd figured that a man like Spencer Hill would go to a school like Yale or Harvard. He knew he had money, although he didn't know how much. Spencer never talked about that kind of thing, but he had always had an aura of education and background, and they'd all heard rumors that he was from an important family in the East, not that he ever said it. He'd gone to college, they all knew, and he was an officer, but the rest of it was a mystery, and crawling through a mine field none of it had seemed important.

But Spencer was shaking his head, looking at his young friend, thinking how far this place was from the world he knew. It seemed light years from the sophistication of San Francisco. It was a little pocket of a life he never even thought of, a world of ranches and farms, and people who worked the land. It was a hard life, and even at twenty-two, Boyd's face seemed to show it. "No, I'm at Stanford. I stopped here on the way home, and I fell in love with it. I enrolled before I went back to New York. I figured that if I waited until after that, I'd never do it. I love it out here." It seemed remarkable that Stanford was only three hours away, it might as well have been in another country. "I'll be back in the fall. I promised my folks I'd go back East this summer. I only had a few weeks with them after I got out of the service, and then I started law school. It seems a little crazy at my age, but a lot of guys seem to have gotten slowed down by the war. Some of them are even older than I am. And you, Boyd? What are you up to?" Hiroko had sat down quietly and was listening to their conversation. She wondered how much Boyd would tell him about their hardships. He never complained, not to her, anyway, and these days she knew he hardly had anyone else to talk to. It had amazed them both when Tom had asked him to be best man at his wedding. No one else ever invited them, or even talked to them, and sometimes old Mr. Petersen even had to pump the gas himself, because someone would refuse to let Boyd help them.

"Things are okay. It was hard finding work, with everyone coming home at the same time.

But we're doing fine." Hiroko watched him, her eyes giving away nothing as Spencer nodded.

"I'm glad." He had worried about them both, and had reproached himself more than once for not staying in touch. He had cared about Boyd a great deal when he was one of his men, and he had worried about his marriage to Hiroko. It was good to know that things had worked out for them. There were others, he knew, who hadn't fared as well, men who had become estranged from their families as a result of the war brides they brought home, who had turned to drink, and even suicide, abandoning the women they had brought home to an unforgiving country. But they both looked well, and they were still together, that was something. "Do you ever come to San Francisco?"

Boyd smiled and shook his head. Life was hard enough where they were, and they wouldn't have had the money for gas anyway, but he didn't tell Spencer that. He was young and proud, and he knew they were going to make it.

"You ought to come and see me sometime. I've got one more year before I'm a lawyer. Hell of a thought, isn't it?" They both laughed, but Boyd wasn't surprised. The Captain had

had an aura of success about him even then, he was well liked by everyone, enlisted men and officers. Boyd had always suspected he would be an important man one day, and being a lawyer seemed like only the first step on the ladder. Spencer looked around him, as Boyd smiled at him, and then their eyes met again. "What's Tom's bride like? She looks like a nice girl."

"She's all right. She's a friend of my sister's." And with that, they both laughed. Spencer had heard a lot about Ginny Webster. She was always sending Boyd photographs of herself in bathing suits, and asking him to find her soldiers to write to. She was just a teenager then, with the same bright red hair as her brother, and the same freckles, but a rather amazing body. "The Wyatts are good people. Tom's going to be working on the ranch with Becky's father." To Boyd, it sounded like a gift from God, but he was embarrassed suddenly, thinking that it was a lot less glamorous than studying law at Stanford. But Spencer felt only respect for them as he looked around him in open admiration. The ranch looked comfortable and clean and prosperous and the guests talking beneath the trees looked like decent, solid people. "Tad Wyatt's a fine man. Tom is pretty lucky."

"So are you." Spencer said the words very
softly, glancing at Hiroko and then at Boyd
with warmth in his eyes and a touch of envy.
There was no one he cared about, no one he
loved or who loved him as Hiroko did her husband. He almost envied them that, except that
he was in no hurry. There were plenty of
women in his life, and he was having a good
time. At twenty-seven he was in no hurry to
settle down. There were other things he
wanted to do first, like finish law school and go
back to New York afterward. His father was a
judge and had told him that the smartest thing
he could do was become a lawyer. With a law
degree, and the connections he would make at
a school like Stanford, there was a good life in
store for him. And with his looks and easy
ways, a lot of doors were going to open to
Spencer Hill. They always had, he led a
charmed life, and wherever he went, people
liked him. He had integrity and style, and he
was smart as hell. It had saved his life more
than once in the Pacific, and the lives of his
men. Whatever he lacked in experience, he
made up for with ingenuity and courage.
"Should I be mingling with the guests?"

Boyd laughed. "Sure. Come on, I'll introduce you to my sister."

"Finally," Spencer Hill teased. "Will I rec-

ognize her without a bathing suit on?" But as
they walked slowly toward the rest of the
guests, he saw instantly who she was, not only
from the bright red hair so like Boyd's, but
from the body poured into the tight pink dress
and matching jacket. The laughing girl, more
than a little tipsy on wine, and still clinging to
the wilting bouquet she'd caught from Becky,
could only be Boyd's sister, Ginny. Boyd introduced them, and Ginny blushed a bright pink
that almost matched her dress, as Spencer
shook her hand and told her how brave her
brother had been in the Pacific.

"He never told me how handsome you were,
Captain." She giggled and pressed close to
him, smelling of cheap perfume and wine, as
Boyd then introduced him to their father, but
it was obvious from the disapproving look of
the older man who shook Spencer's hand that
relations with his son were strained, and it was
easy to figure out that it was because of
Hiroko.

Spencer stood in their midst for a little
while, reminiscing with Boyd and Tom, and
then left them to help himself to a glass of the
ranch wine. He chatted with a few of the
guests, and then wandered off to stand alone
beneath the trees for a time, feeling the peace
of the countryside stir something in him that

had long been forgotten. His life was so full of urban pursuits and his studies at Stanford that he seldom had time to drive out alone to a place like this. It was like a step back in time, the old people sitting beneath the trees at the tables with the white linen cloths fluttering gently in the breeze, and the children running and shouting in the distance. If he closed his eyes, he imagined that it could be in France, or almost in another century, the families and friends talking and laughing, and the hills stretching beyond them, as he stood beneath the enormous trees, and then suddenly he sensed that someone was watching him. He turned and saw a beautiful child staring at him, she was barefoot, and taller than most of the women there, but there was no doubt in his mind that she was still a little girl. A child with the body of a woman, and huge blue eyes that seemed to pierce to his very soul as she watched him. A long, graceful hand swept a mane of white-blond hair away from a face that startled him with its beauty. He stood without moving as their eyes met, and neither of them spoke as he looked at her, unable to tear his eyes away from her. He had never seen anyone as beautiful, or as innocent, in her simple dress, her feet bare as she stood in the grass, and he longed to reach out and touch her.

"Hello." He spoke first and she seemed afraid to answer. He wanted to smile at her, but he felt paralyzed by the effect of her eyes, they were a blue he couldn't remember ever having seen before, the color of a lavender summer sky in early morning. "Are you having fun today?" It seemed a stupid thing to say, but he couldn't tell her how lovely she was and it was all he wanted to do as she watched him. And then slowly, she smiled at him, walking carefully toward him like a young doe emerging from the forest. She was curious about who he was, he could see it in her eyes, and he was afraid he'd frighten her away if he moved any closer. He would have to let her come to him, and he wanted to hold out a hand to bring her nearer.

"Are you a friend of Tom's?" Her voice was deep and smooth, and as silky as the pale blond hair that seemed to beg him to touch it. But he had to maintain some sense of normalcy. She was only a child, and he was surprised by what he was feeling. There was none of the obvious sex about her that there was about Ginny Webster in her tight pink dress, instead she was all delicate sensuality, like a fragrant flower growing wild on a mountain hilltop.

"We were in the army together in Japan."

She nodded, as though it didn't surprise her. She knew she'd never seen him before. In truth, she had never seen anyone like him. There was a polish to the man and a quiet sophistication that fascinated her. Every thing about him was immaculate and expensive, from the perfectly cut blazer to the impeccable white pants, the bright silk tie, and the elegant hands. But more than that, she was fascinated by his eyes. There was something about him that drew her to him like a magnet.

"Do you know Boyd Webster?" She cocked her head to one side in curiosity, her hair cascading freely over her shoulder. "He was in Japan with Tom too."

He nodded, riveted to her, wondering who she was, as though it mattered. "I knew them both." He didn't tell her he had been their C.O. It was unimportant. "And Hiroko too. Do you know her?"

She shook her head slowly. "No one's allowed to talk to her."

He nodded, sad for them, but not surprised. It was what he had feared for them from the first and now this startling creature had confirmed it. "That's too bad. She's a nice girl. I

was at their wedding." It was hard finding
things to say to her, because she was so young,
and because he felt everything in him constrict
with longing as he looked at her, and then he
wondered if he was crazy. She was a child, he
told himself, or a very young girl anyway. She
couldn't have been more than fourteen or fifteen, and yet everything about her made him
feel breathless.

"Are you from San Francisco?" He had to
be. People in the valley didn't look like him,
and she couldn't imagine being from anywhere
farther than San Francisco.

"I am now. Actually, I'm from New York.
But I'm going to school here." He smiled at
the words, and she laughed openly, a clear
sound like a mountain stream, as she came a
little closer. The other children were still playing in the distance, and they didn't seem to
have missed her.

"What kind of school?" Her eyes were
bright and alive, and he sensed that hidden beneath the shyness was mischief.

"Law school."

"That must be hard."

"It is. But it's interesting, and I like it. What
do you do?" It was a foolish question and he
knew it. What could she do at her age, other

than go to school and play with her friends in the valley.

"I go to school." She pulled a long blade of grass from where she stood and played with it.

"Do you like it?"

"Sometimes."

"That sounds about right." He smiled at her again and wondered what her name was. Probably Sally or Jane or Mary. People didn't have unusual names here. And then, as though it would matter to her, he introduced himself, and she nodded, still watching him with cautious fascination.

"I'm Crystal Wyatt." The name seemed perfect for her.

"Are you related to the bride?"

"She's my sister."

He wondered that Tom hadn't waited for her instead, but perhaps people here didn't realize how incredibly beautiful she was, although it was hard to imagine that they didn't.

"It's a beautiful ranch. It must be a nice place to live."

She smiled then, more openly than before, as though anxious to share a secret. "It's prettier back in the hills, there's a river you can't see from here. My dad and I ride up into the mountains together sometimes. It's beautiful back there. Do you ride?" She was curious about him, almost as curious as he was about her, as he listened to her.

"Not very well. But I like it. Maybe I'll come back some day and you and your dad can show me." She nodded, as though she liked the idea, and then someone called her. She ignored it at first, and then turned, and was sorry she had. It was her brother. Spencer felt his heart sink. They had finally missed her. "It was nice talking to you." He knew that in a moment she would leave him, and he wished he could reach out and touch her for just an instant. He was afraid he would never see her again, and he wanted to make time stand still so he would always remember that moment, beneath the trees . . . before she grew up . . . before she went away . . . before life could change her.

"Crystal!" There were several voices raised in chorus now. And there was no ignoring them. She shouted to them that she would be there in a minute.

"Will you really come back one day?" It was as though she sensed it too. As though she didn't want him to leave her, she had never seen a man as handsome as he was, except the movie stars she'd pinned up on her wall. But he was different, he was real. And he talked to her as though she weren't a baby.

"I'd like to come back. Now that I know Boyd is here, maybe I'll drive up sometime to see him." She nodded, as though in silent approval. "I'll come to see Tom too . . ." His voice drifted off, wanting to say "and you," but he knew he couldn't say that to her. She would have thought he was crazy, and he didn't want to scare her. Maybe it was the wine, he told himself, maybe she wasn't as beautiful as he thought she was, maybe it was just the mood, and the day, and the aura of the wedding. But he knew it was more than that, that she was more than that. And then, with a last look, and a shy smile, she waved and went back to the others. He stood watching her for a long time, as her brother said something to her, pulled her hair, and then suddenly she was running after him, and teasing and laughing, as if she had forgotten they had ever met, but as he started to walk away he saw her turn toward him and stand for an instant, watching him, as though she wanted to say something to him, but she didn't. She returned to watching the others as he walked back to Boyd and Hiroko.

He saw her again before he left, standing on the porch, talking to her mother and it was obvious she was being scolded for something. She carried a heavy platter into the kitchen, and she didn't come out again, and a moment later, he was driving away, still thinking of the child he had met. She was like a wild colt, beautiful and untamed and free, the child with the eyes of a woman. He laughed at himself then. It was crazy. He had a life to live in a world far from here. There was no reason for him to be attracted to a fourteen-year-old girl in the lush wilderness of the Alexander Valley. No reason except that she wasn't just any girl. Even her name told him she was different. Crystal. He said it to himself as he drove away, remembering his promise to Boyd and Hiroko to come back and see them after the summer. Maybe he would . . . maybe he really would . . . the odd thing was that suddenly he knew that he had to.

And as Crystal helped her mother clear the last of the platters away, she found herself thinking of him, the handsome stranger from San Francisco. She knew who he was now. She had heard Tom talking about him, his commanding officer in Japan. Tom had been pleased he'd come to the wedding, but he had more important things to think about. He and Becky had left in a shower of rice for their honeymoon by the ocean in Mendocino. They'd be gone for two weeks, and then they'd come home to live in the cottage on the ranch, and work with her father, and have babies. It all seemed so boring when Crystal thought of it. So expected and ordinary. There was nothing magical about their lives, nothing rare and unusual, unlike the people she dreamed about, or the movie stars she read about. She wondered if she'd be like that one day, married to one of the boys she knew, one of Jared's friends, one of the boys that she still hated. It was odd, as she thought of it, she felt pulled in two directions, toward the familiar world she knew . . . and a world far beyond it, full of mystery and handsome strangers, like the one she had met at her sister's wedding.

It was midnight by the time they'd finished the dishes and cleaned up the last of the mess left over from the wedding. Everything was put away, and Grandma had already gone to bed. The house seemed oddly quiet as Crystal said good night to her parents and her father walked her slowly to her room, and kissed her on the cheek with a tender look.

"It'll be your turn one day . . . just like Becky."

She shrugged, not anxious for it, and Jared hooted as he walked past to his own bedroom.

Her father smiled down at her again.

"Want to ride with me tomorrow? I've got some work to do you could help with." He was so proud of her, so much more than she knew, as she smiled up at him and nodded.

"I'd like that, Daddy."

"I'll wake you at five. Get some sleep now." He ruffled her hair and she closed the door softly. It was the first night she would sleep alone in the room without her sister, and it seemed so peaceful. It was her domain, finally. And she lay in bed, thinking of Spencer as she drifted off to sleep. And in his bed, in a hotel room in San Francisco, Spencer Hill was thinking of Crystal.

CHAPTER
3

Tom and Becky's first baby was born ten months to the day after their wedding. He was born in the cottage on the ranch, with Minerva and Olivia standing by, and Tom pacing the porch of the main house as he waited. He was a healthy baby boy and they named him William after Tom's father, William Henry Parker. Becky was fiercely proud of him, as was Tom. It was a bright shining moment in what had otherwise been a difficult year for the Wyatts. Their crops had been poor after torrential rains, and Tad had come down with pneumonia and never quite seemed to recover.

He was still weak when the baby was born, but he tried to pretend that he wasn't. Only Crystal knew how desperately tired he was. They went on shorter rides now, and he always seemed grateful to come home and go to bed, sometimes without even eating his supper.

But he began to improve finally by the time they christened the baby on the day that India became independent, two days before Crystal's sixteenth birthday. He was christened in the same church where Tom and Becky were married the year before, and Olivia invited sixty of their friends for lunch. It was a less elaborate party than the wedding, but it was festive anyway. Ginny Webster was godmother, and Tom asked Boyd to be his godfather, which was a sensitive subject with the Wyatts. Hiroko was still as shunned as she had been the year before. Crystal was her only friend now and even she didn't know that Hiroko was pregnant. And the local doctor had refused to take care of her. His own son had died in Japan, and he told her bluntly that he wouldn't help bring her child into the world. Boyd had had to take her to San Francisco to find a doctor, and he couldn't afford to take her there often. Dr. Yoshikawa was a gentle, kind man. He had been born in San Diego and lived in San Francisco all his life, but he had still been interned with the rest of his people after Pearl Harbor. For four years he had cared for them in the camp, giving them what little help he could with the limited supplies at hand. It had been a time of anguish and frustration for him, but he had earned the respect and devotion of the people he had cared for and lived with. Hiroko had heard about him from the only Japanese woman she knew in San Francisco, and she had gone to him trembling, after the embarrassment of being turned away by the doctor everyone thought so well of in the valley. Boyd had stood beside her as Dr. Yoshikawa examined her, and he assured them both that everything seemed to be normal. Only he knew how difficult it was for her, being in a strange land with people who hated her because of the color of her skin, the slant of her eyes, and the fact that she'd been born in Kyoto.

"You should have a nice healthy baby in March, Mr. Webster," he told Boyd, and then smiled at Hiroko. He spoke to her in Japanese, and Boyd could see her relax as the doctor spoke to her. It was as though for these few moments she had come home, and she could trust him. He told her to rest every afternoon, and to eat well, and recommended a diet of all her favorite Japanese foods, which made her giggle.

And Boyd was helping her prepare one of them when Crystal knocked on the door the day after they'd been to the doctor in San Francisco. She had dropped in from time to time, just to say hello and chat for a little while, ever since Becky's wedding. No one knew that she came, and Boyd was wise enough not to divulge the secret.

"Hi, there, anyone home?" She had left one of her father's horses tethered outside, and she walked in cautiously, her hair piled high on her head, under a cowboy hat, and she was wearing blue jeans. She was even prettier than she had been the year before, and even more womanly now, but there was still an aura of innocence about her. And she seemed totally unaware of her looks, which only helped to enhance her beauty. She was wearing one of Tad's old shirts, and as she dropped her hat on a chair and wiped her brow, her mane of platinum hair cascaded past her shoulders.

"Hello, Crystal." Boyd wiped his hands on a kitchen towel, and Hiroko smiled and offered her some of the sashimi they'd been preparing. "Have you had lunch?" It was Saturday and she was free from school. Her father was resting, and she had nothing to do that day. She had already stopped by to visit Becky and little

Willie, as they called him. He was a fat, healthy little boy, and he was already smiling.

"What is that?" Crystal looked down at the raw fish in fascination.

"Sashimi," Hiroko answered with a shy smile. She was always stunned by Crystal's fair hair and big blue eyes, and wished that if she could be born again, she could look just like her. Hiroko had dreamed more than once of having her eyes fixed "Western style," but they couldn't afford it, and Boyd would have killed her for even thinking of it. He loved her just as she was with all her delicate Japanese beauty.

Hiroko was only three years older than Crystal, but there was a seriousness to her which had deepened in the loneliness of her time in the Valley. "Would you like to try some sashimi, Crystal-*san*?" Her English had improved over the past year. She read aloud to Boyd at night, working hard on her pronunciation. Crystal had even brought her some of her books from school, and Hiroko pored over them diligently, learning quickly.

Crystal sat down in the tiny kitchen with them, and cautiously tried what they told her was raw fish. She was willing to try anything, and she had shared numerous meals with them, tasting the delicacies that Hiroko prepared with nimble fingers.

"Your father is well?" Hiroko asked quietly, and Crystal nodded with a worried frown.

"He's better. It was a hard winter for him. I stopped by to see Becky today," she smiled at her friend, "the baby's really getting cute." And then she saw an odd look pass between them. Boyd looked at his wife encouragingly, his freckles seemed to stand out more than ever in his pale face. He was so different from Crystal, whose skin bronzed to a deep tan despite her fair hair and blue eyes. But he seemed impervious to her beauty. He had eyes only for Hiroko.

"Tell her." He was smiling at his wife, and he wanted to include their only friend in the good news that seemed less of a burden now that they had found Dr. Yoshikawa. They could ill afford a child, yet it was what they had both desperately wanted. They were only surprised it had taken so long. It had taken over two years for Hiroko to get pregnant. "Go on . . ." Boyd nudged her, and Hiroko looked embarrassed, as Crystal waited. She was too young to suspect anything. But having babies wasn't something Crystal thought about much, and she looked at them with wide, expectant eyes, but Hiroko couldn't bring herself to say it. And finally Boyd had to do it for her. "We're having a baby in the spring." He looked so proud as he said it, and Hiroko turned away shyly. She still wasn't used to his American ways, and his openness in telling people things that were intensely private, and yet she was as happy about it as he was.

"That's wonderful." Crystal smiled. "When?"

"March, we think." He beamed proudly at his wife, and Hiroko helped Crystal to more sashimi.

"Seems a long way off, doesn't it?" It seemed like forever to Crystal. It had seemed endless waiting for Becky to have her baby. She had complained night and day, she was always moaning about how sick she was, and how uncomfortable. In the end, Crystal couldn't stand being around her. Even Jared got tired of her, and Tom went out alone with his friends at night. Only Olivia was sympathetic. The two women were closer than they had ever been, but Crystal didn't mind. She was her happiest spending time with her father. And her visits to Hiroko had become more and more enjoyable in the past year. They talked about nature and life and ideas, and very seldom about people. Hiroko had no friends to talk about, only her family in Japan, and she seldom talked about them now. They were so far away as to be almost lost to her.

But she confessed once that she missed her little sisters. And in exchange for the confidence, Crystal had admitted that sometimes she dreamed about being in the movies. Hiroko seemed fascinated by the idea, and thought she was pretty enough. But Hollywood was a long, long way from the Alexander Valley. It was so remote to them, it might as well have been on another planet.

Hiroko and Boyd were both there on William's christening day. He wailed lustily when the minister drenched his little head with water. And he was wearing the christening dress that had been worn by Grandma Minerva's father. Hiroko looked a little pale as they left the church, and Boyd gently took her arm, questioning her with his eyes, and she only nodded. She never complained about not feeling well, but he knew that she had started feeling poorly. She still cooked all his meals with the same attention to detail, but she hardly ate, just pushing her food around on her plate, and he had heard her getting sick on several mornings. Crystal's eyes met hers before Boyd drove her away, and the two women smiled at each other, but no one seemed to notice. Everyone was too busy admiring the baby.

At the ranch, lunch was set out as it had been on Becky's wedding day, but it was easier this time with fewer people. The women sat in small clusters talking about who was getting married and who was having babies. No one knew about Hiroko yet, and they were much more interested in whispering about Ginny Webster. She had put on weight, and there were rumors about her sleeping with Marshall Floyd. Someone had even seen them leaving a hotel in Napa.

"She's pregnant, mark my words," Olivia announced conspiratorially, and Becky added that Ginny had almost fainted the week before during a church social.

"You think he'll marry her?"

"He might," one woman offered. "But he'd better do it quick, before she gets any bigger." The women talked as the men stood apart and drank and ate, and the children played just as they had the year before. Two years after the end of the war, nothing much had changed, except that the children seemed a little older. Crystal herself no longer seemed so childlike. Her body seemed to be all curves with long graceful legs and a figure that caught the men's eyes now. Her dresses no longer concealed her as they once had, and her eyes were quieter and wiser. She had been worried about her father all winter. Jared had finished high school in June, and he was going to work full-time on the ranch with Tom and his father. His father had wanted him to go to college, but Jared didn't want to. He tinkered with the ranch cars, and went out driving with his friends. He had a girlfriend now, in Calistoga.

"He's quite a young man," one of Olivia's friends said admiringly to her, "he'll be getting married next, mark my words. I hear he's seeing the Thompson girl." His mother smiled proudly in answer, and her eyes clouded when she glanced at Crystal. She was wearing a blue dress the same color as her eyes that her father had brought back from San Francisco. "She's a fine-looking girl . . . a real beauty. . . ." The other woman had been watching Olivia glancing at Crystal. "You're going to have to lock her in the barn one of these days," the woman teased, and Olivia pretended not to notice. Her youngest child was still a stranger to her. She was so different from the other girls, and particularly from her sister. She was quiet and solitary, unlike the rest of them. She had deeper thoughts, and when she spoke of them, which was rare, it always annoyed her mother. A girl didn't need to think about deep things, or dream about the places she and Tad talked of. It was all his fault, filling her head with those things. And his fault, too, that she liked to run free in the hills, riding her father's horses and swimming naked in the streams, like some wild thing, disappearing for hours sometimes.

She wasn't like the other girls, or Becky or her mother. She never had been, and it was even more noticeable now as she grew up. She didn't even seem to notice the boys at all anymore. She seemed happiest alone, or talking for long hours with her father about the ranch or the books she read, or the places Tad had been, and she wanted to go to. Olivia had even heard them talk about Hollywood one day. And he had known that was crazy. At this rate, it wasn't going to be easy to find a husband for her, even with her looks. Looks weren't enough. She was just too different, and if anything, her looks set her apart from the rest of them, it made the women wary, and the men stare, but not in a way that flattered Olivia. It was small comfort being the mother of the prettiest girl in the valley. She was too beautiful, too free, and much, much too different. Even as the women talked, Crystal was sitting alone on the swing, soaring high, as the others played nearby. She seemed not to notice them at all, or even see them. She had grown more solitary in the past year, instead of more like them. And, busy with his own life, even Jared left her alone now. The only time anyone noticed her at all was when they heard her singing, as in church on Sunday mornings. She had the kind of voice that whether you liked her or not, you had to stop and listen. It was the only thing anyone ever said about her.

She was sailing through the air on the swing, unconcerned with what people were saying, almost unaware of the party around her, singing to herself, as she saw his car drive up, and she recognized him instantly as he stepped out. She hadn't seen him in a year, but she would have known him anywhere. She hadn't forgotten him, and only now and then had she dared ask Boyd if he'd had a letter from Spencer. But he had come to the christening, and Crystal fell silent and let the swing slow as she watched him shake her father's hand, and then go to find Boyd and Hiroko. He was as handsome as he had been a year before, perhaps even more so. She hadn't forgotten Spencer Hill for a single moment and her heart stopped now as she saw him.

He was wearing a summer suit and a straw hat. She thought he looked more dashing than he had the year before, and she saw him laughing as he said something to Hiroko. And then slowly, he looked around, past his friends, and as she sat silent on the swing, he saw her. Even from the distance, he knew that she was looking at him, and he could feel her eyes riveted to him, as he walked slowly toward her. His face was serious, and his eyes were a deep blue as he stopped very near her. And the air between them was electric with something neither of them understood. Something they had both remembered for a year could not be denied now as their eyes met. It was a kind of passion that went beyond words or simple understanding. And yet, as they both knew, they were strangers.

"Hello, Crystal. How've you been?" He could feel his hands tremble as he slipped them into his pockets and leaned against the tree from which the swing was suspended, trying to sound normal, trying not to let her see all that he was feeling. But it wasn't easy. She wasn't moving, she was only looking at him, and for an instant, it was as though everyone else at the party had vanished. There was a magnolia bush nearby, and the air was heavy with its fragrance. And it was almost as though there were a drumbeat in the distance.

"I've been all right, I guess." She tried to sound normal, wanting to ask him why he hadn't come back again, but she didn't dare. Neither of them could put their feelings into words. All she could do was look at him, impeccably put together as he had been a year before, his dark hair perfectly groomed, his face tan, and his eyes searching for something she didn't yet understand, yet she knew she couldn't bring herself to move away from him. She wanted to stand near him for a lifetime, breathing his scent, and feeling his eyes on her. The sultry afternoon suddenly seemed much hotter. He felt as though his insides had just melted, and yet he had to remind himself that she was only a child. But they both knew what he wanted to tell her was that he loved her. Except he couldn't of course. He barely knew her. It was distressing to realize that the girl he'd fought to keep out of his mind all year was even more haunting than he had remembered.

"How's school?" Her eyes seared him as she asked. She was part child, part siren, and now after only a year, she seemed to be all woman.

"I just finished my bar exams." She nodded, but her eyes asked him a thousand questions that neither of them would have been able to answer. And although he felt like molten lava inside, everything about him suggested strength, as though nothing could ever frighten him, nothing except what he felt for her, this child he barely knew. But she could see none of that on his face as he watched her hair floating in the gentle breeze of summer. "What about you?" He wanted more than anything to reach out and touch her.

"I'll be sixteen the day after tomorrow," she said quietly, and he felt his heart sink. For a moment, just a moment, he had hoped that he had remembered wrong, and she was older. And yet there had been a change in the past year. She seemed so grown up, so womanly in her blue dress. More woman, yet still child, and he wondered again at what madness drew him to her. It wasn't only to see Boyd that he had come back today. He had come to see her, too, hoping that she'd be there, wanting to see her one more time before leaving California. But there was no point torturing himself. At sixteen, she was still a baby. And yet . . . her eyes told him she felt all the same things he did. At twenty-eight, it was insane to feel this for a sixteen-year-old girl. "Will you have a birthday party?" He spoke as though to a child, and yet everything he saw told him she was a woman, as she laughed and shook her head.

"No . . ." It was impossible to explain to him that she had few friends, that the girls hated her because of her looks, although she herself didn't understand it. "My dad said he might take me to San Francisco next month." She wanted to ask him if he would be there, but she didn't. Neither of them could say any of the things they wanted. They had to pretend not to care, not to understand what they were feeling for each other, despite the gap in years, and the vast difference their lives put between them.

And as though reading her mind, he answered the question she hadn't dared to ask, about where he was going now. "I'm going back to New York in a few days. I've been offered a job by a law firm on Wall Street." He felt foolish explaining it to her. "That's part of the financial world," he smiled, and shifted his weight against the tree that seemed to be holding him up. He wasn't sure at that precise moment if his trembling knees would hold him. "It's supposed to be big stuff." He wanted to impress her, but he didn't have to work at it. She was impressed by him any way, by a lot more than just Wall Street.

"Are you excited?" She looked at him with wide-open eyes, as though wanting to see deep into his soul, and he was almost afraid she might, and he himself wasn't sure what she'd see there, probably a man frightened by what he felt for this girl . . . this girl who was no longer a child and not yet a woman, and who stirred him as no woman ever had before her. He wasn't sure whether it was just her looks, or the mystery he saw in her own eyes. He wasn't sure what it was, or why, but he knew that there was something rare and different about her. She had haunted him for the past year in spite of all his efforts to forget her. And now, standing next to her he felt his whole body go taut with the excitement of just being near her.

"I guess I'm excited. And scared." He seemed to admit it easily to her. "It's a big job, my family would be disappointed if I didn't live up to what everyone's expecting." But his family seemed unimportant now. Only Crystal mattered to him.

"Will you ever come back to California?" Her eyes looked so sad, as though he was deserting her, and they both felt the loss even before it happened.

"I'd like to come back sometime. But probably not for a while." His voice was quiet and sad, and for a moment, he was sorry he had come. It would have been easier not to have seen her again. But he wouldn't have been able not to come. He had known for weeks that he had to see her, and now she was watching him, her eyes wise and sad, the loneliness she lived with most of the time etched into the eyes that watched him. Today was a gift, one that she would always cherish. He had become a dream to her, like the dreams of the movie stars pinned up on her bedroom walls. He was just as distant and unreal, and yet she had actually met him, but he was no more accessible to her than they were. The only difference between him and them was that she knew that she loved him.

"Hiroko's having a baby in the spring." She said it to break the spell a little bit, and he sighed and looked away, as though trying to get some air, and force himself to think of someone other than Crystal.

"I'm glad for them," he smiled gently at her, wondering when she would marry and have babies. Maybe if he came back here one day she would have half a dozen children clinging to her skirts, and a husband who drank too much beer and took her to the movies on Saturday nights, if she was lucky. The thought of it almost made him feel sick. He didn't want that to happen to her. She deserved so much more than that. She wasn't like the rest of them. She was a dove, trapped in a flock of peahens, and given the opportunity, they would devour and maybe even destroy her. She didn't deserve that. But he knew that there was nothing he could do to save her. "She'll be a wonderful mother." He said it about Hiroko, but for an instant he wondered if he had meant it about Crystal.

Crystal only nodded and pushed the swing slowly with one foot. She was wearing the same white pumps she had worn to Becky's wedding the year before, but this time she had kept them on, with another precious pair of nylons.

"Maybe you'll come to New York one day." He said it to offer himself hope, but they both knew it was less than likely.

"My father went there once. He told me all about it."

Spencer smiled. His life was so far removed from hers. It made his heart ache again to know that. "I think you'd like it." He would have liked to have had the chance to show her . . . maybe if she had been older . . .

"I'd rather go to Hollywood." She looked up at the sky dreamily and for a moment she was a child again as he watched her. A child dreaming of Hollywood, and being a movie star. It was as wild a dream as his dream of loving her, although he didn't say that.

"And who would you like to meet in Hollywood?" He wanted to know who her favorite movie stars were, what she talked about, whom she dreamed of. He wanted to know all of her, perhaps in the hope of growing disenchanted. He had to forget this girl, once and for all, before he left California. She had haunted him all year, more than once he had thought of driving up to see Boyd, but when he had, he knew it was only because he wanted to see Crystal. And afraid of the fine madness she seemed to induce in him, he had purposely not come, until now . . . this last time before he left. But it was already too late. He knew now that he would never forget her.

She was thinking about his question about who she'd like to meet in Hollywood, and finally with a smile as she drifted on the swing, she answered, "Clark Gable. And maybe Gary Cooper."

"Sounds reasonable. And then what would you want to do in Hollywood?"

She laughed, playing with her own dreams, and him a little bit. "I'd like to be in a movie. Or maybe sing." He had never heard the voice that had haunted the people in the valley, even those who didn't like her.

"Maybe you will one day." They both laughed at that. Movies were for movie stars, not for real people. And life couldn't have been more real for her, no matter how beautiful she was. She knew her life would never include being in movies. "You're pretty enough to be. You're beautiful." His voice was gentle, as the swing slowly stopped moving again and she looked at him. There was something startling about the way he had said it. The force of his words surprised both of them into silence, and then she only shook her head with a sad smile. She was already mourning the thought of his leaving.

"Hiroko is beautiful, I'm not."

"Yes, she is," he agreed, "but so are you." His voice was so soft she could barely hear it.

And then suddenly, feeling brave, she asked him the question she'd wondered since she first saw him that morning.

"Why did you come today?" To see Boyd . . . Hiroko . . . Tom . . . Becky's baby . . . there were half a dozen plausible answers and only one that had brought him here. And as he looked into her eyes he knew he had to tell her. And she had to know it.

"I wanted to see you before I left." He spoke softly and she nodded. It was what she had wanted to hear, but now the words frightened her a little. This very handsome man, from another world, had actually come to see her. And she didn't quite understand what he wanted of her. Nor did Spencer himself, which made it all the more confusing.

She quietly left the swing, coming to stand next to him, looking up at him with the laven-

der-blue eyes he had never forgotten. "Thank
you." They stood together for a long moment,
and then from the corner of his eye, Spencer
saw her father approach them. He was waving
at Crystal, and for a moment, Spencer was
afraid he was angry, as though he had read the
younger man's mind and didn't like what he
saw there. In fact, he had been watching them
for a long time, and had wondered what they
were saying. There was something about the
man he liked, and he knew that he was only
passing through. And it was good for a man
like that to admire her. Tad Wyatt was only
sorry there weren't more like him in the valley.
But he had other things on his mind as he approached them with warm eyes, and a smile
that was reminiscent of Crystal's.

"You two were looking awfully serious, way
over here. Solving the problems of the world,
were you, young 'uns?" The words teased, but
the wise old eyes took Spencer in. He liked
what he saw. He had from the first, although
he also knew that he was too old for Crystal.
He saw something in her face that he had
never seen there before, except once or twice,
when she had looked up at him with open adoration. But it was something different this
time, something both happy and sad. And suddenly, Tad Wyatt realized that his baby had

become a woman. He turned to Spencer then, and spoke in his deep, quiet voice. "You've a treat in store, Captain Hill." He smiled at Crystal proudly. "That is, if Crystal will agree. The folks want to hear you sing, little one. Will you do it?"

She blushed and shook her head, the long pale mane sweeping over part of her face, the tree casting shadows on the other side, as the sunlight caught the platinum of her hair, and both men were momentarily stunned into silence by her beauty. She looked up at her father then, and the lavender eyes were filled with shy laughter. "There are too many people here . . . it's not like in church . . ."

"It won't make any difference. You'll forget them once you start." He loved to listen to her voice as they rode over the hills, her voice had the same awesome, explosive quality as a brilliant sunrise, and he never tired of her singing. "Some of the men brought their guitars. Just a song or two, to liven up the party." His eyes pleaded with her, and she could never refuse him, although it embarrassed her to think of singing in front of Spencer. He would probably think she was stupid. But he added his voice to Tad's, urging her, and when their eyes met, there was a long moment of silence between them, a moment that said everything neither of them dared to say. And for a minute, she thought that it might be her gift to him, something he could remember her by. She nodded quietly, and followed her father slowly back to the others. Spencer went back to Boyd and Hiroko then, and she glanced over her shoulder once and saw that he was watching her, and even from the distance, she could feel the love in his eyes for her. The love that neither of them understood, that had been conceived a year before, and carried for a whole year until they met again. It was a love that would not go anywhere, but at least they had that to take with them when he left her.

She took a guitar from one of the men's hands, and sat down on a bench as two others joined her and smiled at her in admiration. Olivia was watching her from the porch, annoyed as always that Tad had singled her out to make a spectacle of herself. But she also knew that people liked to hear Crystal sing. Even some of the women relented when they heard her sing in church. And when she sang "Amazing Grace," it brought tears to their eyes. But this time, she sang her father's favorite ballads, the ones they sang together when they rode out in the early mornings, and within minutes the crowd had gathered around her and no one said a word as they listened to her strong, sure voice cast its magical spell on them. Her voice was as unforgettable as her face, and Spencer closed his eyes and let himself drift in the pure, sweet beauty of it, as the sheer power of her voice held him spellbound. She sang four songs, and the last strains seemed to soar into the summer sky like angels flying toward the heavens. There was a long silence when she stopped as everyone stared at her in fresh amazement. They had heard her sing a hundred times before and yet when they heard her again, it always moved them. There was an explosion of applause, and Tad wiped his eyes, as he always did, and in a few minutes the crowd dispersed, and they went back to their conversations and their drinking, but for a moment she had made each of them fall in love with her. And Spencer couldn't bring himself to speak to anyone for a long moment after he'd heard her. He wanted to talk to her again, but she had gone off somewhere with her father, and he didn't see her again until it was time to go, and she was standing near her parents, shaking people's hands as they thanked them for lunch and gathered up their children.

Spencer thanked her parents dutifully as well, but then suddenly he had her hand in his own, and he was terrified that the moment be-

tween them was too fleeting. He might never
see her again, and he couldn't bear the thought
as he looked into her eyes and wanted to hold
on to her forever.

"You didn't tell me you could sing like
that." His voice was whisper soft as his eyes
caressed her. But she laughed, looking young
again, and embarrassed at the unexpected
compliment. She had sung the songs for him,
and she wondered if he knew that. "You might
get to Hollywood after all."

She laughed again, the sound as musical as
her singing had been. "I don't think so, Mr.
Hill . . . I don't really think so."

"I hope we meet again one day." Their eyes
grew serious and she nodded.

"So do I." But they both knew it was less
than likely.

And then, he couldn't stop himself from
saying the words. "I won't forget you, Crystal
. . . ever . . . take care of yourself." Have a
good life . . . don't marry someone who
doesn't deserve you . . . don't forget me . . .
what could he possibly say to her without
sounding like a total fool, and he could hardly
tell her that he loved her.

"You too." She was nodding solemnly. She
knew he was leaving for New York in a few
days, and their paths wouldn't cross again. A

continent, a world, a whole life would separate them forever.

And then, without saying another word, he bent and gently kissed her cheek, and a moment later he was gone, driving away from the ranch, his heart like a rock in his chest, as Crystal stood silently apart from the others, and watched him.

CHAPTER
4

On his way home, Spencer took the turnoff before the Golden Gate Bridge, and pulled the car off the road. He needed a moment to think, to compose himself, and remember. Crystal had haunted him for a year, and now she was doing it again, only hours after he had left her. The valley seemed only a dim memory now, and all he could think of was her face . . . her eyes . . . the way she looked at him . . . her voice as she sang the ballads. She was a rare bird and he knew he had lost her forever in the forest. There was no way he'd get back to her again. And it was crazy even to think of

it. She was a sixteen-year-old girl, living in a
remote California valley. She knew nothing of
the life he led. And even if she did, she
wouldn't understand it. It was too far from her
own ken. What did she know of Wall Street
and New York, and the obligations he had to
live up to. His family expected a lot of him,
and nowhere in their plans was there room for
the country girl, the merest child he had acci-
dentally fallen in love with. A girl he barely
knew, he reminded himself. His parents
wouldn't have understood that. How could
they, when he didn't understand it himself?
And like her dreams of Hollywood, and movie
stars, Spencer had had his own dreams. But
those dreams had changed when his brother
died in Guam. And now he had not only his
own life to lead, but he had to live up to his
brother's aspirations. His family expected that
of him, and at least he was going to try. And
what did Crystal know of all that? She knew
nothing, except about the valley she had grown
up in. He knew he had to forget her now. He
smiled sadly to himself as he looked out over
the bay, and at the bridge, thinking of her, and
he reminded himself that he was being foolish.
He had been dazzled by a pretty girl, which
only proved to him that he had to get on with
his life now. He needed more than law school

and hamburgers in Palo Alto with attractive co-eds to provide him amusement. There was a whole world waiting for him. A world with no place in it for Crystal Wyatt, no matter how lovely she was, or how taken he was with her at the moment. He walked back to his car, wondering what his father would say if he told him he had fallen in love with a sixteen-year-old girl in the Alexander Valley.

"Good-bye, little girl," he whispered to himself as he crossed the Golden Gate Bridge for the last time. He had a dinner party to attend that night. It was a duty he owed his father. He wasn't in the mood, but he knew he needed to get his mind off her. She was gone now. But gone or not, he knew he would never forget her.

He was staying at the Fairmont Hotel for his last few days in town, and he had taken a room with a sweeping view, just to remind himself of what he'd be missing. He was almost sorry he hadn't looked for a job in San Francisco, but that had never been his plan. He had promised his parents he would come home again, and he knew only too well what was expected of him now. His father had been a lawyer until the war, when he was appointed a judge, which was as far as his own political aspirations would take him. But he had always had far grander plans for his sons, especially for Spencer's older brother, Robert. Robert had been killed in Guam, leaving a young widow and two children. He had studied political science at Harvard and politics had been his life's ambition. He had talked of being a congressman, and Spencer had dreamed of being a doctor. But the war changed all that. With four years delay, he himself couldn't imagine spending many more years studying medicine, and law school had been the right decision. Judge Hill had assured him of it, and Spencer knew his father had secret yearnings to become an appellate justice. Be that as it may, the burden of proof rested on Spencer's shoulders now. It was he who had to follow in Robert's footsteps. The Hill family was a solid one, his mother's forebears had arrived in Boston with the Pilgrims. His father was of simpler stock, but he had worked hard to measure up, and had put himself through Harvard Law School. And now it had been important to both of them that Spencer do something "important" with his life. And to them, "important" didn't include a girl like Crystal. Robert had, of course, married well. He had always done what they wanted, while Spencer had always been free to do exactly as he pleased. And now suddenly, with his older brother gone, he felt as though he had to make it up to them, as though he had to follow in the footsteps that had never suited him before and now suddenly had to. Going to law school had been part of that. And going back to New York now. And Wall Street . . . he could hardly think of himself there, and yet he had just crammed three years of law school into two preparing for just that. But Wall Street sounded so damn stuffy. At least if he could make something useful of it, use it as a stepping-stone to a grander scheme, maybe then he would be able to stand it. He looked out the window again as he thought of it, staring into the distance, thinking of the place where he had left Crystal. He sighed then, and turned back into the room. The carpets were thick, and the furniture was new and there was a huge chandelier hanging above him. And yet, all he could think of was the ranch . . . and the hills . . . and the girl on the swing. He had two more nights left. Two nights before he had to move on to the life he had so unexpectedly inherited from Robert. Why the hell couldn't he have lived? Why couldn't he have been there for them, to do what they expected, to work on goddamn Wall Street . . . He strode out of the room and slammed the door with a vengeance. He was expected at eight o'clock at the home of

Harrison Barclay. He was a friend of Spencer's father, a federal judge and extremely well connected politically. There had even been talk that one day he might make it to the Supreme Court. And Spencer's father had insisted that he see him. Spencer had looked him up once the year before, and had called again a few weeks ago to tell him he had graduated from Stanford and was going back to New York to an illustrious law firm. Harrison Barclay had been extremely pleased for him, and had insisted that he come to dinner before leaving. It was a command performance, but Spencer knew this was only the first of many in his life, and he might as well start getting used to it. He had returned to the hotel just in time to shower and shave and change, and he hurried downstairs to the lobby, but he was in no mood to see anyone, least of all Harrison Barclay.

The Barclay home was at Divisadero and Broadway, and it was an extremely handsome brick mansion. A butler opened the door to him, and as he was led inside he could hear echoes of a party in progress, which depressed him even more. For a moment, he wasn't sure he could make the effort. He would have to talk and be charming, and sound intelligent with their friends, and it was the last thing he wanted to do tonight. All he wanted was to sit quietly somewhere, with his own thoughts, and his dreams of a girl he barely knew . . . a girl who would be sixteen the day after tomorrow.

"Spencer!" The judge's booming voice met him almost the moment he entered the room, and Spencer felt like a schoolboy who had been shoved into a roomful of teachers.

"Good evening, sir." His smile was warm and his eyes were serious as he greeted his father's friend, and shook hands with Mrs. Barclay. "It's good to see you. Good evening, Mrs. Barclay."

Judge Barclay took him instantly in tow, introducing him around the room, and explaining that he had just graduated from Stanford Law School. He mentioned who his father was, as Spencer fought not to cringe visibly. Suddenly this was the last place he wanted to be. He felt almost physically unable to make the effort.

There were twelve guests invited to dinner that night, and one of them had canceled at the last minute. Another judge's wife had turned her ankle on the way home from her golf game, but he had come anyway. He was an old friend of the Barclays', and he knew they wouldn't mind, but Priscilla Barclay was frantic as she counted out the number of guests.

There were thirteen of them, including the hosts, and she knew how superstitious at least two of the guests were. There was nothing she could do about it at this late date. Dinner was going to be served in half an hour, and the only thing she could do was ask their daughter to join them for dinner. She ran hastily upstairs and quickly knocked on her door. Elizabeth was getting ready to go to a party. She was eighteen years old, and attractive in a very restrained way. She was wearing a black cocktail dress and pearls. She was going to come out at the Cotillion that winter, but before that, in the fall, she would be attending Vassar.

"Darling, I need your help." Her mother glanced in the mirror and straightened her pearls, and then smoothed a hand over her hair as she turned to look pleadingly at her daughter. "Judge Armistead's wife twisted her ankle."

"Oh God, is she downstairs?" Elizabeth Barclay looked cool and unruffled, far more so than her agitated mother.

"No, of course not. She called to say she couldn't come. But he came anyway. And now we'll be thirteen at the table."

"Just pretend you don't know. Maybe no one will notice." She slipped into high-heeled black satin pumps that made her instantly taller than her mother. Elizabeth had two older brothers, one in government in Washington, D.C., and the other an attorney in New York. But she was the Barclays' only daughter.

"I can't do that. You know how Penny and Jane are. One of them will leave, and then I'll be two women short. Darling, can't you help me?"

"Now?" She looked annoyed. "But I'm going to the theater." She was going with a group of friends, although she had to admit she hadn't been looking forward to the evening. It was one of those rare times when she didn't have a date, they had decided to go as a group at the last minute.

"Is it important?" Her mother looked her squarely in the eye. "I really need you."

"Oh for God's sake." She glanced at her watch, and then nodded. Maybe it was just as well. She didn't want to go anyway. She'd been out until two o'clock that morning at one of the debutante balls she had gone to almost every night since graduating from Burke's the month before. She'd been having a good time, and the following week they were moving up to their house at Lake Tahoe. "All right, Mother, I'll call them." She smiled graciously, and adjusted the double strand of pearls that matched her mother's. She was, in fact, a pretty girl, but she was by far too reserved for a girl of eighteen. In many ways, she seemed considerably older. She had been conversing with adults for years, and her parents had taken great pains to include her with their friends, and in what they considered interesting conversations. Her brothers were respectively ten and twelve years older, and for years she had been treated as an adult. In addition, she had acquired the cool self-restraint that was expected of a Barclay. She was always circumspect and well behaved, and even at eighteen, she was every inch a lady. "I'll be down in a minute."

Her mother smiled gratefully at her, and Elizabeth smiled in answer. She had rich auburn hair, which she wore in a smooth pageboy, and big brown eyes. She had creamy skin, and a trim waist, and she played an excellent game of tennis. But there was very little warmth about the girl, there was only excessively good breeding, and a fine mind which had won her countless admirers among her parents' friends. Even in her own set she was both feared and respected. Elizabeth Barclay was not someone one fooled around with. She was a serious girl with an inquiring mind, a sharp tongue, and a strong set of her own opinions. There had been no doubt of her attending

college in the fall. The choice had been between Radcliffe, Wellesley, and Vassar.

She walked quietly downstairs ten minutes
later, having called her friends and apologized
profusely, explaining only that a minor crisis
had come up and she was needed at home. In
Elizabeth's life the only crisis was being a guest
short for dinner, or the absence of the right
dress to wear because it was out being altered.
There had been no real disasters in her life, no
inkling of disappointment or hardship. There
was nothing her parents wouldn't have done
for her, nothing her father wouldn't have
smoothed over, or bought her. And yet she
wasn't spoiled. She simply expected a certain
way of life, and those around her to behave
with decorum. She was unusual for a girl her
age. Her childhood seemed to have ended by
the time she was ten or eleven. From then on,
she had behaved like an adult, someone anyone would have welcomed in their opera box
or at their dinner table. But she didn't have
much fun. Fun was not important to Elizabeth
Barclay. Purpose was. And actions that had
some real meaning.

The guests were finishing their drinks when
she came downstairs, and she looked around at
the familiar faces. There was only one couple
she didn't know, and her mother introduced

them as old friends of her father's from Chicago. And then she saw another unfamiliar face, a very handsome one, conversing quietly with Judge Armistead and her father. She watched him briefly as she accepted a glass of champagne from the silver tray the butler held out to her, and she smiled as she walked across the room to her father.

"Well, well, how lucky we are tonight, Elizabeth." Her father smiled with faintly teasing eyes. "Have you made room in your busy schedule for us? How amazing!" He put an affectionate arm around her shoulders and she smiled up at him. She had always been close to him, and it was easy to see that he adored her.

"Mother was kind enough to ask me to join you."

"What good judgment. You know Judge Armistead, Elizabeth, and this is Spencer Hill, from New York. He's just graduated from Stanford Law School."

"Congratulations." She smiled coolly, and he took her in with appreciation. She was a cool number and he guessed her to be twenty-one or twenty-two. There was a polish about her that made her seem older than her years, an obvious kind of sophistication enhanced by the expensive black dress, the pearls, and the way she looked him in the eye when she shook his hand. She looked like a girl who was used to getting what she wanted. "You must be very pleased," she added with a polite smile as he watched her.

"I am. Thank you." He wondered what she did with herself, played tennis probably, and shopped with friends or her mother, but he was surprised at her father's next announcement.

"Elizabeth is going to Vassar in the fall. We tried to talk her into Stanford, to no avail. She is determined to go East and leave us here, pining for her. But I'm hoping the cold winters will convince her that she'd rather be out here. Her mother and I are going to miss her." Elizabeth smiled at his words, and Spencer was surprised by how young she was. Eighteen-year-old girls had certainly changed in the last few years. And as he looked at her, it struck him forcibly that she was everything that Crystal wasn't.

"It's a wonderful school, Miss Barclay," Spencer was friendly but cool. "My sister-in-law went there. I'm sure you're going to like it." And for some reason, from his words, she assumed that he was married. It never occurred to her that he meant his brother's wife. And for an instant, she was aware of the faintest twinge of disappointment. He was a good-looking man, and there was an intriguing magnetism about him.

The butler announced dinner then, and Priscilla Barclay shepherded her guests gently toward the dining room. It had black-and-white marble floors, wood-paneled walls, and a handsome crystal chandelier hanging over the heavy English table. There were candles lit in handsome silver candelabra, and the table shone with Limoges in white and gold, and crystal glasses that caught the light of the candles and reflected it back onto the silver. The napkins were heavy and large, embroidered with the monogram of Priscilla Barclay's mother, and the guests found their way easily to their seats with the hostess's gentle directions. There were placecards of course too, in elaborate little silver holders. And Elizabeth was pleased to find herself sitting next to Spencer. She knew instantly that her mother had done some rapid rearranging.

There was smoked salmon for the first course, and tiny Olympia oysters. And by the time the main course came, Elizabeth and Spencer were deep in conversation. He marveled again at her intelligence and how well informed she was. There was nothing she seemed not to know about, about world affairs or domestic politics, history or art. She was a remarkable girl, and he had been right, she would do very well at Vassar. In many ways, she reminded him a great deal of his brother's wife, except that Elizabeth was even a little grander. There was nothing showy or ostentatious about her. She was all fine mind and extraordinarily good manners. She even made a point of talking to the man on her right, another of her father's friends, and then eventually she turned back to Spencer.

"So, Mr. Hill, what are you going to do now, freshly graduated from Stanford?" She eyed him with interest and poise, and for a moment he felt younger than she was, and had he had a little less to drink it might actually have unnerved him.

"Go to work in New York."

"Do you have a job?" She was interested and a little blunt. She saw no point in wasting time. In an odd way, he liked that about her. He didn't need to play games, and if she could ask him questions, he could do the same with her. It was actually easier than flirting.

"Yes, I do. With Anderson, Vincent, and Sawbrook."

"I'm impressed." She took a sip of wine, and smiled up at him.

"Do you know them?"

"I've heard my father mention them. They're the biggest firm on Wall Street."

"Now I'm impressed," he teased, but in a way he meant it. "You know an awful lot for a girl of eighteen. No wonder you got into Vassar."

"Thank you. I've been hanging out at dinner tables for years. I guess once in a while it's useful." But it was more than that. She was very bright, and if he'd been in a better mood, he might even have liked her. There was no mystery to her of course, no poetry, no magic, but a very sharp mind, and an incredible directness that intrigued him. And in a cool, patrician way, she was very attractive. More so as the evening wore on and he continued to drink Harrison Barclay's wine. It was an odd way to end a day that had begun with a christening in the Alexander Valley. But he couldn't imagine Crystal here. No matter what he felt for her she wouldn't have fit in. In this setting, he couldn't imagine anyone but this girl, with the forthright brown eyes and the straightforward manner. But as he listened to her, his heart still ached for Crystal.

"When are you leaving San Francisco?"

"In two days." He said it with regret, but for reasons neither of them fully understood. He couldn't understand the dull ache he'd felt since that afternoon as he drove back to San Francisco. And she thought there was nothing more exciting than moving to New York. She could hardly wait until September.

"That's too bad. I was hoping you might come up to see us at Lake Tahoe."

"I'd have liked that. But I've got an awful lot to do. I start work in two weeks, that won't give me much time to get settled before they bury me in a sea of papers on Wall Street."

"Are you excited?" Her eyes probed his again and he decided to be honest with her.

"I'm not sure, to tell the truth. I'm still trying to figure out why I went to law school."

"What would you have done instead?"

"Medicine, if I hadn't gone into the army. The war changed things for everyone, I suppose . . . for some a lot worse than for me." He looked pensive for a moment, thinking of his brother. "I was very lucky."

"I think you're very lucky to be a lawyer."

"Do you?" He was amused again. She was an intriguing girl, and he sensed easily that there was not an ounce of weakness or indecision in Elizabeth Barclay. "Why?"

"I'd like to go to law school too. After Vassar."

He was impressed, but not entirely surprised. "Then you should. But wouldn't you

rather marry and have children?" It seemed a
more natural option to him, and it was unlikely that any man would tolerate her doing
both. In 1947, one had to opt for one, or the
other. It seemed a high price to pay to him. In
her shoes, he would far rather have had a husband and children, but Elizabeth didn't look
convinced.

"Maybe." For an instant she looked young
and unsure, then she shrugged, as the dessert
was served. And then she startled him with her
next question. "What's your wife like, Mr.
Hill?"

"Excuse me? I . . . I'm sorry . . . what
ever made you think I was married?" He
looked horrified and then he laughed. Did he
seem so old to her that it was inconceivable he
could still be single? If so, how ancient he must
have seemed earlier that day to Crystal. She
was still on his mind, even as he forced himself
to converse with Elizabeth Barclay, although
she certainly wasn't difficult to talk to. But his
mind was still far away, and a piece of his
heart that seemed to have betrayed him.

For the first time, Elizabeth looked be-
mused, and he saw that beneath the carefully
coiffed auburn hair, she was blushing. "I
thought you said . . . you mentioned your
sister-in-law earlier in the evening . . . I just

assumed . . ." He laughed as she stammered over the explanation, and he shook his head, his blue eyes alive in the light of the candles.

"I'm afraid not. I was referring to my brother's widow."

"Was he killed in the war?"

"Yes, he was."

"I'm very sorry."

He nodded and coffee was served, as the ladies withdrew, at the instigation of Priscilla Barclay. She thanked her daughter quietly as they left the room.

"Thank you, Elizabeth. We would have been in a terrible spot without you."

She smiled easily at her mother, and for an instant, put an arm around the older woman's shoulders. Priscilla Barclay was still pretty, although she was over sixty. "I had fun. I like Spencer Hill. A lot more in fact, now that he just told me he's not married."

"Elizabeth!" Her mother pretended to be shocked, but in fact she wasn't, and Elizabeth knew it. "He's much too old for you. He must be almost thirty."

"That's just right, and it might be fun to see him in New York. He's going to work for Anderson, Vincent, and Sawbrook." Her mother nodded, and moved away to chat with the other ladies, and a little while later, the gentlemen joined them. The party broke up shortly after that, and Spencer thanked the Barclays for inviting him, and made a point of saying good night to their daughter.

"Good luck at school."

"Thank you." Her eyes were warm, and for the first time he decided that he really liked her. She was nicer than Robert's wife, and actually, considerably smarter. "Good luck with the new job. You'll do famously, I'm sure."

"I'll try to remind myself of that in a month or two, when I'm pining for the easy life at Stanford. Maybe we'll meet in New York sometime." She smiled up at him encouragingly, as her mother approached them and thanked him for coming.

"You'll have to check on Elizabeth for us, when she's in New York."

He smiled, thinking it unlikely that they would meet, but he was always polite. He thought college freshmen were a little young for him . . . and then, of course, there was Crystal. . . .

"Let me know if you come to town."

"I'll do that." She smiled warmly at him, and looked younger again, and a moment later, he left them. He went back to the Fairmont, thinking of her, and her steady flow of interesting conversation. Maybe she was right, he told himself. Maybe she should go to law school. She would be wasted as someone's wife, playing bridge, and gossiping with other women. But it wasn't Elizabeth he dreamed of that night, when he finally fell asleep in the wee hours of the morning . . . it was the girl with the platinum blond hair and eyes the color of a summer sky . . . the girl who had sung as though her heart would break . . . in his dream, she sat on the swing, watching him, and he could never quite reach her. He slept fitfully that night, and for only a few hours. At daybreak he was up, watching the sun rise slowly over the bay, and a hundred miles away, Crystal walked through the fields in bare feet, thinking of him as she wandered toward the river, singing softly.

CHAPTER
5

Spencer did errands that next day, tying up loose ends, and dropping in on a few friends, to say good-bye and wish them well. And suddenly, he was desperately sorry to leave them. He regretted his decision to go back to New York, and promised himself he'd come back one day. It was a melancholy day for him, and he went to bed early that night, and took the plane to New York the next morning. It was Crystal's sixteenth birthday.

His parents were waiting for him, and he felt foolish being greeted as the conquering hero. Even Barbara, Robert's widow, was there, and her two daughters. They had a late supper at his parents' house, and Barbara had to leave to take the girls home before they fell asleep at the table.

"Well, Son?" his father said expectantly after the others had gone home, and his mother had retired to their bedroom. "How does it feel to be back home again?" He was anxious to hear an encouraging answer. Spencer had been gone for too long, six years, between the war and his two years at Stanford, and he was relieved to have him back in New York where he belonged. It was time for Spencer to settle down and become "someone," just as Robert would have done, had he lived.

"I'm not sure how I feel yet." Spencer was honest with him. "It looks the same, more or less, as the last time I was home. New York hasn't changed." He didn't add what he was really thinking . . . but I have . . .

"I hope you'll be happy here." But William Hill didn't really doubt it.

"I'm sure I will, Father, thank you." But he was less sure than he had ever been. A part of him longed to go back to California. "I saw Judge Barclay before I left, by the way. He sent you his regards."

William Hill nodded, pleased. "He'll be on the Supreme Court one day, mark my words.

It wouldn't surprise me. His sons are good men too. His oldest boy was in my courtroom the other day. He's a very fine lawyer."

"I hope someone says that about me one day." Spencer sat down on the couch in his father's study, and ran a hand through his hair with a tired sigh. It had been a long day, a long week . . . a long war . . . and suddenly the thought of what he was facing depressed him.

"You've done the right thing, Spencer. Never doubt it."

"How can you be so sure?" I'm not Robert, Dad . . . I'm me . . . but Spencer knew he couldn't say that. "What if I hate Anderson, Vincent, and Sawbrook?"

"Then you'll go to work in the legal department of a corporation. With a law degree, you can do almost anything you want. Private practice, business, law . . . politics . . ." He said the word hopefully, that was where his real hopes were, and Spencer would be perfect for it one day. Just as his brother had been before him. Robert, their shining hope so quickly extinguished. "Barbara's looking well, isn't she?"

"Yes." Spencer nodded quietly, wondering if his father knew him at all. "How's she doing?"

"It's been hard for her. But she's recovering, I think," he said, and turned away for a moment so Spencer wouldn't see the tears in his eyes, "I suppose we all are." And then he turned and smiled at Spencer. "We've rented a house on Long Island. Your mother and I thought you might like the diversion. And Barbara and the children will be there for the rest of the month of August." It was strange coming back to the bosom of his family, he was no longer sure he belonged there. He had been twenty-two when he went to war, and so much had changed since then. So much had happened to change him. And now, with Robert gone, he felt as though he had returned to lead not his own life, but Robert's.

"That was nice of you, Dad. I'm not sure how much free time I'll have once I start work."

"You'll have weekends."

Spencer nodded. They were expecting him to be a boy again, their youngest son. He felt as though he had lost his own life somewhere on the way home from California.

"We'll see. I have to find an apartment this week."

"You can stay here, until you find your feet again."

"Thank you, Dad." He looked up, and for the first time his father seemed old to him, old and cherishing hopes that had died with Spencer's brother. "I appreciate it." And then, out of curiosity, "Is Barbara seeing anyone?" It had been three years after all, and she was a pretty girl. She had been perfectly suited to Robert. Ambitious, cool, intelligent, beautifully brought up, the perfect wife for a would-be politician.

"I don't know," his father answered honestly. "We don't discuss it. You ought to take her out to dinner sometime. She's probably still pretty lonely."

Spencer nodded. He wanted to see his nieces, too, but he had too much else to think about right now. And he felt drained by the expectations suddenly being put on him.

He felt exhausted as he fell into bed that night. The impact of what had been waiting for him seemed to have fallen on him with a crushing weight, and he wanted to cry as he went to sleep. He felt like a child who had gotten lost on the way home. The one thing he knew was that he had to find his own apartment, his own life, and quickly.

CHAPTER
6

The remainder of the summer seemed to drift by, as Crystal helped on the ranch, and stopped by from time to time to play with Becky's baby. Tom was always off somewhere, checking over the vineyards with Tad or in town with his friends. And Jared spent every spare moment with his girlfriend in Calistoga. It was as though suddenly she was alone, with no one to be with, and no one to talk to. And she began riding over to visit Hiroko more and more often. Crystal would find her reading quietly, or sewing, or sketching with pen and ink, and she even taught Crystal how to write haikus. She was a gentle woman with a warm heart and the skills of a culture that fascinated Crystal. She taught her how to make little origami birds, and showed her how her own mother had taught her to arrange flowers. There was none of the obvious showiness of what she knew that went with Western ways, everything about her was quiet and discreet and very subtle. And, like Crystal, she was solitary and very lonely. She still had no friends among Boyd's relatives, she understood fully now how deeply they resented her, and she suspected that it would never be any different. She was all the more grateful for Crystal's companionship, and the two women became fast friends, as Hiroko waited for her baby.

And when school began, Crystal often went to visit her, sitting for long hours by the fire, doing her homework. She hated to go home anymore. Her mother was always with Becky anyway, and her grandmother was always scolding her. The only one who ever had a kind word for her was her father, and he had been ill again. Crystal confessed to Hiroko after Thanksgiving how worried she was about him. He looked tired and pale and he coughed all the time. It terrified her. The man who had seemed invincible to her all her life was suddenly failing. He had had pneumonia again, and he hadn't ridden out in weeks. It made Crystal want to cling to him. She knew that if she ever lost him, her life would be over. He was her cohort, her ally, her staunch defender, the others were all too quick to turn on her, to blame her for petty things, and to berate her for everything she wasn't. She didn't want to do the things Becky did. She didn't want to sit in her kitchen all day, drinking coffee and making cookies, she didn't want to gossip with the other women, or marry a man like Tom and have his babies. Tom Parker had grown fat in less than two years, and he always reeked of beer, except on the weekends, when he stank of whiskey.

Crystal knew she wasn't like the rest of them. Instinctively, she had always sensed that she was different, and she knew that her father knew it too. And Hiroko. She had long since confessed to the gentle Japanese girl that she sometimes dreamed about being in the movies. But there was no way she could leave her father now. She wouldn't have left him for anything. But one day . . . maybe one day . . . the dream of Hollywood never died in her . . . nor did her dreams of Spencer. But she never confessed her feelings about him to Hiroko and Boyd, although she told them everything else. They were her only friends, and she rode over to see them often. Hiroko was the only woman friend she'd ever had, and Crystal had long since come to love her. Hiroko offered her the encouragement and warmth she found nowhere else, except with her father.

She confessed her fears to her that she'd never escape the valley, that none of her dreams would come true. But she loved the valley too. Her feelings for it were intricately woven in with her love for her father. She loved the land, and the trees, the roll of the hills, and the mountains beyond them. She even loved the smell of it, especially in spring when everything was fresh and new, and the rains had turned everything bright emerald. Living there forever wouldn't be the worst fate imaginable, even if it meant giving up her dreams of being in the movies. She just didn't want to marry a man like Tom Parker. The mere thought of it made her shudder.

"Is he unkind to your sister?" Hiroko was curious about the others sometimes. To Hiroko, they were all strangers, even her husband's sister, who had gotten married, finally, just in time to have her baby.

"I think he's mean to her when he drinks. Not that she'd tell me. A few weeks ago, she had a black eye. She said she fell over the high

chair. I think she told Mama the truth
though." The two women still shut Crystal
out. Everyone did. She was dangerously beautiful and it threatened all the women who
knew her, except this one, who looked so different. They were an odd pair, the one tall and
thin, the other tiny, the one with shining black
hair, the other with her long mane like a palomino's. The one culture so free and so bounti-
ful in words and gestures, the other so spare
and so restrained. They had come from different worlds, to a single place, where they had
become sisters.

"Perhaps you go to Hollywood one day, and
Boyd and I will come to see you." They both
laughed as they walked down the road from
the Websters' place, talking of their dreams.
Hiroko wanted a pretty house one day, and
lots of children. Crystal wanted to sing, and
wanted to go to a place where people didn't
resent her. It was a common bond between
Hiroko and Crystal. For different reasons, they
were both outcasts.

Hiroko liked to get exercise and she didn't
like to go out alone, and Crystal always enjoyed walking with her. They would talk for
hours sometimes, as Hiroko noticed the tiniest
things as they walked along, the smallest flowers, the least plant, the most delicate butterfly,

and then later she would sketch them. They shared a common passion for nature. But Crystal was also comfortable enough with her now to tease her.

"You just see all that stuff because you're lower to the ground than I am, Hiroko." Hiroko would giggle at her and they both wished they could go into town, but they knew they couldn't be seen anywhere together. It would have created a storm almost beyond bearing. Boyd invited her to go into San Francisco with them, but she was afraid to disappear for that long, her mother would surely notice it, and her father might need her.

By Christmas, he was too weak to get out of bed, and Crystal didn't visit the Websters for several weeks, and when she came in late January, her face told its own tale. Tad Wyatt was dying. She sat in Hiroko's kitchen and cried, with the older girl's arms around her shoulders. She felt as though her heart would break seeing him slip away day by day. Everyone at the ranch was crying all the time. Her grandmother, Olivia, Becky. And Jared was never there, he couldn't stand to watch their father dying. Crystal would sit for long hours with him, encouraging him to eat, whispering softly as she put more blankets on him, and sometimes just sitting there as he slept, the tears rolling silently down her cheeks as she watched him. And it was Crystal he always wanted near him, Crystal he called for when he was delirious, Crystal he looked for when he opened his eyes again. Seldom his wife, and never Becky. They were foreign to him now, just as Crystal was to them. It was she who tended him lovingly, who even helped her mother bathe him. But the love she showed for him only made her mother resent her more. She thought the love they shared was unnatural, and if he hadn't been so sick, she would have said it. Instead she barely spoke to Crystal anymore, and Crystal didn't really care. All she cared about now was her father. Her passion for him even dimmed her memories of Spencer.

Becky was pregnant again, and Tom was attempting to run the ranch, although he was too drunk most of the time to do it. It broke Crystal's heart whenever she saw him drive up to the main house. It took every ounce of control she had not to tell him what she thought of him, but for her father's sake, Crystal remained silent. She didn't want to upset him, and she wanted everything to stay the same, but by February she knew it wouldn't.

She sat quietly by his bedside night and day, holding his hand, and never leaving him, except to bathe, or to eat something hastily in the kitchen. She was afraid that if she left him, he might die. She stopped going to school, she never even left the house, except for a few minutes to take a deep breath of air on the porch, or walk quickly to the river before it got dark. Tom followed her there once, and he stood leering at her, as she sat in a clearing, lost in thought, thinking of her father, and then of Spencer. She had never heard from him since he'd come to little Willie's christening, but she hadn't expected to. Boyd had had a letter from him at Christmas, he sounded happy in New York and he liked his job, and he told them he'd let them know if he ever came to California. But he was too far away to help her now. No one could, except God. And she prayed daily that He would let her keep her father, but in her heart of hearts, she knew that wasn't going to happen.

She took her place in the chair beside her father's bedside that night, watching him doze, and after midnight, he opened his eyes and looked around. He looked better than he had in a long time, his mind was clear, and he smiled at Crystal. Her mother was sleeping on the couch in the living room, and Crystal had been sleeping in the chair next to his bed for days, but she woke instantly when he stirred and offered him a sip of water.

"Thank you, baby." He spoke, and his voice sounded a little stronger. "You should go to bed now."

"I'm not tired yet," she whispered in the dim light, and she wanted to be there. If she left him, he might die, and as long as she sat there, maybe he'd live . . . maybe . . . "Do you want some soup? Grandma made turkey soup tonight, it's pretty good." The blond hair hung past her shoulders like a gossamer curtain, and he looked at her with the love he had felt for her for all her sixteen years. He wanted to be there forever, just to protect her. He knew how unkind the others were, how jealous, and how petty, even the girl's own mother, and all because Crystal was so lovely. Even the boys in the valley were afraid of her, she was too beautiful to be real, and yet she was, very real. He knew her well, and he was proud of who she had become. She had courage and guts and brains, as well as beauty. And for months now, he had suspected that she was visiting Hiroko, and although he himself had qualms about their friendship, he didn't try to stop her. More than once, he wanted to ask her what she was like, but he decided not to. She had a right to her own life, to a few secrets of her own. She had so few other pleasures. He declined the soup, and lay on his pillows looking at her, praying that life would be kind to her, that she would find a good man one day, and be happy.

"Don't ever give this up, little girl . . ." It was barely a whisper, and at first she didn't understand him.

"What, Daddy?" Her voice was as soft as his own, and her fingers laced with his were so much stronger.

"The ranch . . . the valley . . . you belong here . . . just like I do . . . I want you to see more of the world than . . . just this . . ." He seemed to be having difficulty breathing. ". . . but the ranch will . . . always . . . be here for you."

"I know that, Daddy." She didn't want to talk about it now. It was as though he was saying good-bye to her, and she wouldn't let him. "Try to sleep now."

He shook his head. There wasn't time. He had slept for too long, and now he wanted only to talk to his youngest child, his favorite, his baby. "Tom doesn't know how to run the ranch." She knew that much herself, but she didn't say that to her father, she only nodded. "And one day, Jar will want to do something else, he doesn't love the land . . . the way

you and I do . . . when you've seen something of the world, and mother is gone, Crystal, I want you to come back here . . . find a
good man, someone who'll be kind to my
baby," he smiled at her and her eyes filled with
tears as she squeezed his hand, ". . . and
make yourselves a good life here . . ."

"Don't talk like that, Daddy . . ." She
could hardly talk through her tears, as she
brushed his cheek with her own and carefully
kissed his brow. It was cold and damp and
clammy and she sat back to look at him again.
"You're the only man I want." But for a crazy
moment, she wanted to tell him about Spencer,
that she had seen someone she liked . . .
liked too much . . . and could have fallen in
love with. But he was only a dream, like the
movie stars on her bedroom walls. Spencer
Hill was never real in the life of Crystal Wyatt.
"Get some sleep now." It was the only thing to
say to him, just talking for a few minutes had
left him breathless and exhausted. "I love you,
Daddy." She whispered the words as his eyes
fluttered closed, and then they opened again
and he looked at her and smiled.

"I love you too, little girl. You'll always be
my . . . little girl . . . sweet, sweet Crystal . . ." And with that his eyes drifted closed
again, and he looked peaceful as he slept, and

she held his hand and watched him. She sat back in her chair, still holding his hand in her own, and a few minutes later she drifted off, exhausted by the strain of watching him day after day, and when she awoke, the sky was gray and the room was cold, and her father had died, holding her hand. His last words and his last thoughts and his last good-bye were to Crystal. Her eyes flew wide as she realized that he was gone, and she gently tucked his hand in beside him, and with a last look through eyes blinded by tears, she left the room and closed the door, and without saying a word to anyone, she ran as fast as she could to the river. She was crying openly, her body racked by sobs, and she stayed there for a long time, and when she came back, her mother was crying loudly in the kitchen, as Minerva stood silently making coffee. They had found him.

"Your father's dead." She said the words almost angrily as Crystal walked in, her face streaked with tears. It was an accusation more than a regret, as though Crystal could have stopped him. She nodded, afraid to tell them that she'd known before she left, wondering herself again if she could have done anything to keep him from dying. She remembered his words the night before . . . I want you to come back here . . . He knew how much she loved the place, it was a part of her, as it had been a part of him and always would be. She would always see her father here, in this house, but more than that, on the hills, riding his horse, or riding his tractor through the vineyards.

They sent Jared into town, and the undertaker came out to get Tad later that morning, and his friends and neighbors went to pay their final respects as his wife and mother-in-law stood by, shaking hands and crying. Olivia glanced at Tom gratefully through her tears . . . as Crystal tried to repress her own hatred of him. The thought of his running the ranch now made her shudder. But Crystal couldn't even think of that, all she could think of was the man she had loved. Her father. He was gone now, and she was left, frightened and bereft among strangers.

The funeral was the next day, and he was buried in a clearing near the river. It was a place that Crystal knew well. She went there often to sit and think, or swim, and it comforted her to think of her father nearby, keeping watch over her. She knew he would always be with her. And that afternoon, she disappeared for a while and went to visit Hiroko. Her baby was due in a few weeks and she stood up slowly as Crystal walked soundlessly into their living room. Her eyes told their own tale, and Boyd had told her that Tad Wyatt had finally died. She had longed to be able to go to Crystal, but knew there was no way she could. They wouldn't have let her in to see her. And now there she was, looking like a broken child, as she began to sob and held her arms out to Hiroko. Her heart ached as she cried. Without her father, life would never be the same again. He had left her among people whom she instinctively knew had never loved her.

Crystal stayed at the Websters' for hours, and when she went back to the ranch, it was dark, and her mother was waiting for her. She was sitting stonily on the couch, alone in the living room, and stared angrily at Crystal as she walked in, sagging with grief and exhaustion.

"Where were you?"

"I had to get away from here." It was true. She couldn't stand the oppressive atmosphere, and the people who arrived hour after hour, bringing gifts and food to give them sustenance in their grief. But she didn't want food, she wanted her daddy.

"I asked you where you were."

"Out, Mama. It doesn't matter." She had ridden over to the Websters' on horseback. It was too far to walk, and she was too tired to even attempt it after the emotions of the past few days.

"You're sleeping with some boy, aren't you?" Crystal stared at her mother in amazement. She hadn't been anywhere in weeks, she had scarcely left her father's bedside to go to the bathroom.

"Of course not. How can you say that?" Her eyes filled with tears at the unkind words that were so typical of her mother.

"I know you're up to something, Crystal Wyatt. I know what time you get out of school. You don't come home till dark most days. Do you think I'm a fool?" She was furious, one could hardly tell that she had just lost her husband. From grieving widow she had turned into a viper.

"Mama, don't . . . please . . ." They had buried her father only that morning, and already the hatred and accusations were starting.

"You'll end up like Ginny Webster. Seven months pregnant, and lucky to be married."

"That's not true." She could hardly talk she was crying so hard, all she could think of was the father she had lost, and she couldn't believe her own mother was making those accusations. She was referring, of course, to Crystal's absences when she visited Hiroko.

"Your father's not here to tell your lies to

anymore. Don't think you can fool me. If you try to run wild with me, Crystal Wyatt, you can get out of here. I'm not going to put up with your running wild around here. This is a respectable family and don't you forget it!" Crystal stared at her blindly as her mother stalked off to the room where her husband died, holding his daughter's hand. The daughter who stood alone now with no one to defend her. She stood in the living room, listening to the silence, and aching for her father. And then she walked slowly to her own room, and sank down on the bed she had once shared with her sister. She wondered why they hated her so much. It never occurred to her that it was because he loved her. And it was more than that, it was the way she looked . . . the way she moved . . . the way she saw them. She knew as she lay down on her bed in the dark, still dressed, that her life would never be the same again. He had left her alone with them, and as she began to cry in the silent room, she was frightened.

CHAPTER
7

Hiroko's baby came late. She was born not in March, but on the third of April. Crystal had gone to see Hiroko that afternoon, and she was tired and uncomfortable, but unlike Becky, she never complained about it. She was always friendly and warm and anxious to welcome Crystal. It had been six weeks since her father died, and she had come to see Hiroko almost every day. She felt at loose ends at the ranch, and her mother was always quick to criticize and to snap at her. More than ever, it made Crystal feel lonely. She suspected that there was something more bothering her mother, or maybe she was just lonely without Tad, and didn't know how else to express it. She said that to Hiroko one day and her friend thought it possible, but Boyd told her privately that Olivia had always resented Crystal, even as a child, he remembered times when she had slapped her for the slightest offense, while always visibly cosseting Rebecca. He suspected it was why Tad had made a favorite of Crystal, even the children's friends had been aware of it. It was an open secret in the valley.

Hiroko and Crystal spent a quiet afternoon, and at dusk, Crystal went home. Her mother was out, she had gone into town with Becky, and Crystal helped her grandmother put dinner on the table. She had lost weight since her father died. She was never hungry, and that night she went to bed, and at sunrise, she saddled her father's horse, and decided to ride over and see the Websters. It was Saturday and she didn't have to go to school, and she knew her friend was an early riser. But when she got there, Boyd met her at the door. He looked worried and exhausted. Hiroko had been in labor since the night before, and the baby still wasn't coming. He had called the doctor in town, but he had refused to come, saying that Mrs. Webster wasn't his patient. He was the same man who had refused to treat her eight months before, and he hadn't changed his mind since then. And Boyd knew he would have to deliver her himself. There was no way he could get her to San Francisco. Dr. Yoshikawa had given him a book to read just in case, but things weren't going as expected. Hiroko was in so much pain, and he could see the baby's head, but with each push it refused to move forward. He explained it quickly to Crystal, and she could hear Hiroko moaning in the bedroom.

"What about old Dr. Chandler?" He had retired years before and he was almost blind, but at least he was someone. There was a midwife in Calistoga, too, but she had long since refused to treat Hiroko.

"He's in Texas, visiting his daughter. I tried to call him last night from the gas station." He was thinking seriously of driving her to San Francisco, but he was afraid they might lose the baby.

"Can I see her?" She had delivered livestock before, but she had never even seen a woman in labor, and she was aware of a tremor of terror running down her spine as she followed Boyd to the bedroom. Hiroko was crouched on the bed, squatting and panting furiously, as though desperate to get the baby out of her, but she looked helplessly up at Crystal as she sank back against the pillows.

"Baby won't come . . ." Another pain ripped through her as Crystal watched, and Boyd went to hold her hands, and Crystal felt pity for her friend, struggling helplessly. She wondered if the baby would die, or worse . . . Hiroko.

Without thinking, Crystal went to wash her hands in the kitchen, and came back with a handful of clean towels. The bed was bloodstained and Hiroko's long black hair fell over her face as she crouched again, to no avail. And with a confidence she didn't feel, Crystal spoke gently to her.

"Hiroko, let us help you. . . ." She looked into her friend's eyes, willing her to live, and silently praying for their baby. She remembered the horses she had delivered, struggling silently, and prayed that her knowledge might be useful. There was no one else to turn to anyway. No one in town would come, there were only Boyd and Crystal, and the shuddering little Japanese girl. Tears were streaming down her cheeks, but no sound emerged from her, as Crystal looked and saw the baby's head. It had reddish brown hair, halfway between the color of Boyd's and Hiroko's.

"Baby won't come . . ." She sobbed in an-

guish as Boyd told her to bear down again, and
this time when she did, Crystal saw the baby's
head inch slowly forward.

"Come on, Hiroko . . . it's coming now
. . . push again . . ." But she was too weak
to try as the pain subsided, and then Crystal
realized what was wrong. The baby was facing
up instead of down. They would have to turn
it. She had done it with animals, but the
thought of doing it to her friend was terrifying
as she glanced at Boyd and quietly explained
it. She knew then that if they didn't turn the
baby, it might die, or Hiroko would. It might
already be too late for the baby now. Crystal
knew they had to hurry. Another pain ripped
into her friend, and this time she didn't tell her
to push, instead she gently pressed her own
hands into her and felt the baby in Hiroko's
womb, and barely daring to breathe herself,
she turned the baby carefully as Hiroko cried
out and Boyd held her. Another pain came
and she pushed again, as though to force Crystal from her, but as Crystal withdrew her
hands, the head moved forward again, and
suddenly Hiroko pushed as she had never
thought she could have. The pain was blinding
as the baby began to emerge and Crystal gave a
shout of victory as the head came out, and
with its body still inside the mother, it was

already crying. Tears streamed down Crystal's cheeks as she worked to free Hiroko of her baby, and there was a tense silence in the room as Hiroko pushed again, but this time she was laughing and crying all at once as she listened to her baby cry, and then suddenly with a whoosh, the baby was free of her. It was a little girl, and the three of them looked down at her in amazement. The placenta came afterward and Boyd disposed of it, as the book had described. But the book had been useless until then. It was Crystal who had saved the baby's life, and she looked down at the tiny child in awe. She looked just like her mother, and Hiroko cried with joy as she held her.

"Thank you . . . thank you . . ." She was too tired to say more, and she closed her eyes as she held the little girl, and Boyd cried watching them. He looked lovingly at his wife, and softly touched the baby's cheek before glancing back at Crystal.

"You saved her . . . both of them . . ." His tears were born of relief, and Crystal left the room quietly. The sun was high in the sky by then, and she was startled to realize how long she'd been there. The hours had flown by as she worked to save her friend, and the tiny baby.

Boyd came out to see her after a while. She

was sitting on the grass, and thinking how remarkable nature was. She had never seen anything as beautiful as their baby. Like Hiroko, she seemed to be carved out of ivory, and her eyes had the same Oriental slant as her mother's, but there was something of Boyd's look about her, too, and smiling to herself, Crystal wondered if one day she would have freckles like her father. He looked very grown up suddenly as he stared down at his wife's friend, grateful beyond anything he could tell her.

"How is she?" Crystal was still worried, and wished that they could have called a doctor. There was always the risk of infection.

"They're both asleep." He smiled, as he sat down next to Crystal. "They look so beautiful."

Crystal smiled at him. They were two children who had just grown up that morning. Life would never be quite the same again, and having seen the miracle of the baby's birth, at that moment it seemed infinitely precious to them. "What are you going to call her?"

"Jane Keiko Webster. I wanted to just call her Keiko. But Hiroko wanted her to have an American name. Maybe she's right." He looked sad as he said it, and then looked out over the valley where they had both grown up. "Keiko was her sister, she died in Hiroshima."

Crystal nodded, she knew about it from Hiroko.

"She's a beautiful little girl, Boyd. Be good to her." It was an odd thing to say to him as she looked at him. He was twenty-four years old and they had known each other since they were children. Becky had had a crush on him once, and nothing had ever come of it, and Crystal had always been sorry. He was a kind, decent man, and a lot different from Tom Parker. She looked dreamily out at the hills as she talked to him, it was a beautiful spring day and the sun was shining brightly. "My daddy was always so good to me. He was the best person I ever knew." Her eyes were filled with tears as she looked back at Boyd and wiped them with a corner of her work shirt.

"You must miss him a lot."

"I do. And . . . well, things are so different now. Mama and I have never been close. She's always favored Becky." She said it matter-of-factly with a small sigh as she lay back on the warm grass. And then she smiled, remembering again, "I guess she always thought Daddy spoiled me. He did, I guess. But I can't say I ever minded." She laughed then, and for a moment she seemed young again, but he was sorry for her.

"I guess I better go back in to them. Should

I fix her something to eat?" He wasn't sure what to do, and Crystal smiled up at him.

"When she's hungry. Mama says Becky ate like a horse afterward, but she had an easy time having Willie. Tell her to take it easy." She stood up too. "I'll come back this afternoon or tomorrow, if I can get away." Her mother was always finding chores for her. And now, with Becky expecting, she was always telling Crystal to clean her house for her, or help her with the laundry. She felt like a slave sometimes, as she scrubbed Becky's front room while she and her mother sat in the kitchen drinking coffee.

"Take care of yourself," he stood looking awkward for a moment as she went to untie her horse, and then blushing self-consciously he kissed her on the cheek. "Thank you, Crystal," his voice was hoarse with emotion, "I'll never forget this."

"Neither will I." She looked at him honestly, almost as tall as he was, as she held the reins of her old pinto. "Give Jane a kiss from me." She swung herself into the saddle then, and looked down at him again, and for an odd moment she thought of Spencer. She felt so close to Boyd after delivering the baby that she almost wanted to tell him. But tell him what? That she was in love with a man who'd almost surely forgotten her? They'd only seen each other twice after all, and yet as she rode home, smiling to herself, thinking of the baby sleeping in Hiroko's arms, she found herself dreaming of him again. It was all she had, dreams of him, and memories of her father, and pictures of movie stars tacked up in her bedroom.

CHAPTER
8

"Where've you been all day? I've been looking for you everywhere." Her mother was waiting for her in the kitchen when she got back after delivering Hiroko's baby. And for a crazy moment she felt like telling her what had happened. It had been beautiful and exciting, and very, very scary. For a girl not yet seventeen, she suddenly understood what it meant to be a woman.

"I was out riding. I didn't think you'd need me."

"Your sister's not feeling well. I wanted you to go over and help her." Crystal nodded.

Becky was never feeling well, not that she admitted to anyway. "She wants you to take care of Willie." Same old story.

"Okay."

There were dishes in the sink that Olivia had left for her, and after she did those, she walked across the fields to the cottage. Tom was listening to the radio and the room smelled of beer, as little Willie tottered around the room in an undershirt and a diaper. The room was a mess, and Becky was reading a magazine and smoking a cigarette in bed, in their bedroom. Crystal offered to make her lunch, and she nodded without ever looking up, as Crystal went back to the kitchen to make her a sandwich.

"Make me one, too, will you, hon?" Tom called out beerily. "And hand me another bottle from the fridge, will you?" She walked into the front room to give him his beer and scooped Willie up in her arms. He had been making a mudpie in the ashtray with the milk in his half-empty bottle. He cooed happily as Crystal cuddled him. He smelled foul, and Crystal knew no one had bothered to change his diapers since the morning. "Where've you been? I hear your ma was looking all over for you." He was wearing an undershirt with two half-moons of sweat under the arms, and everything about him was pungent as he eyed her. She looked mighty good to him. His own wife was fat and tired and always complaining, and the two girls didn't even look as though they were related.

"I was visiting friends," she said noncommittally, with his baby in her arms.

"Got a new boyfriend?"

"No, I don't," she snapped at him as she walked back to the kitchen. Her legs looked endless in the tight-fitting jeans, and he was admiring her rump as she went to make him his sandwich.

She didn't get back to her own house till dinnertime, after cleaning up, making their lunch, and bathing little Willie. It made her sick to see how they left him. And now they were having another child, so they could let him go filthy and wild, crying half the time because he was hungry and Becky didn't feel like making dinner. Tom went out before she left, and Crystal was relieved. She never liked the way he looked at her, and the questions he always asked about her "boyfriends." There had never been anyone. No one except her harmless dreams of Spencer. The others were all too afraid of her, and that suited her just fine. She had nothing in common with any of them. Their lives were confined to the valley. They had no idea that there was a world beyond it, and no thirst whatsoever to find it. Unlike Crystal who still hungered for more than the Alexander Valley had to offer.

Becky didn't bother to thank her before she left, and at the ranch house, her mother told her to peel the potatoes for their dinner. She did as she was told, but when she finished she went to bed, too tired even to think about eating dinner. She thought about Hiroko for a little while, before she fell asleep, promising herself to go back and see them the next morning after church. She'd have to figure out a way to get away from her mother and sister. They always seemed to have chores for her. It was all so different from when her father was alive. In two months, she had become nothing more than a ranch hand, someone to do their chores and clean up after them, someone for them to shout at and ignore, and she could see the hatred in her mother's eyes when she thought Crystal wasn't looking. She resented her, but Crystal didn't know why. She had done nothing to them, except love her father.

School let out in June, and she had only one more year until she graduated. But after that, what? Life would still be the same. She would be doing chores on the ranch, and watching Tom destroy what her father and grandfather had built, the ranch Tad had loved so dearly.

Tom was going to plow the grapes under that year, having been unable to sell them for the first time in years, and he had sold off a lot of the cattle, saying that they were too much trouble. It put money in the bank for him, but it weakened the ranch profits a lot, and they all felt it.

Becky's baby was born just after Crystal got out of school. A little girl this time, who looked exactly like her father. But it was Hiroko's baby that made Crystal's heart sing. They christened her at a church in San Francisco and asked Crystal to be her godmother. It had taken countless lies to explain to her mother where she was all day, but she had gone with them, fascinated by the sights she saw there, and she felt alive and new again as they drove back to the Alexander Valley.

It was a beautiful summer that year, Crystal turned seventeen, and she spent long hours visiting with Boyd and Hiroko and their baby. Little Jane looked as much like Hiroko as she had when she was born, and yet at the same time there was something of Boyd about her, an expression, a smile, and the reddish brown hair that was a perfect blend of both her parents'. Crystal would lie lazily on the grass for hours, under the tree in their garden, playing and holding the baby close, feeling her warmth as she gurgled. Her visits with them were the highlights of her existence. And she only went home in the late afternoons, in time to help her mother and grandmother fix dinner. Like Tom, her mother accused her of having a boyfriend from time to time, and told her she should be helping her sister with the children, but she had other things on her mind, and so did Becky. Everyone in the valley was saying that Ginny Webster was having an affair with Tom. And Crystal suspected there was some truth to it. She asked Boyd about it once, and he only shrugged and said he wouldn't believe what people said, but as he said it, he blushed almost the color of his hair. It was true then, not that Crystal was surprised, but she wondered if he would have dared to if her father were alive. It didn't matter now, Tad was gone, and Tom Parker could do whatever he wanted.

Tom and Becky christened the baby at the end of summer, just before Crystal went back to school. But this time Spencer didn't come, and her mother didn't give a big party. They invited a few friends for lunch after church, and Tom got drunk and left early, while Becky cried in the kitchen with her mother. And Crystal walked slowly to the river afterward, to sit near the spot where her father was buried. It was hard to believe that only a year before he'd been alive, and she had sat on the swing, talking to Spencer. She had still been a child then, she realized, but no longer. The past year had been too hard, the losses too great, the pain too deep. She was only seventeen, but Crystal Wyatt was a woman.

CHAPTER
9

The invitation came to his office, and as Spencer looked at it, he smiled. His father had been right. He had read it in the papers weeks before. Harrison Barclay had been appointed to the Supreme Court, and Spencer had been invited to his induction.

It had been a good year for him, full of hard work and people he liked. Anderson, Vincent, and Sawbrook was conservative, but much to his own surprise, he liked it. And he had done well. He was already an assistant to one of the partners. And his father was pleased with him. There had been some early skirmishes between the two men, particularly over Barbara. His parents had rented a house on Long Island the summer he came home, and Barbara had spent much of August there with her two daughters. And Alicia and William Hill had counted on Spencer to come too. In the end, there was no avoiding it. He had spent two weekends there, with Barbara making up to him, and his parents' eyes filled with expectation. She had waited for him, his mother said. She loves you, his father prodded. And Spencer had finally exploded. She had waited for Robert, not for him, and it wasn't his fault his brother had been killed in the Pacific. She was a nice girl, and he loved his nieces, but she was his brother's wife. It was enough for Spencer that he had become a lawyer. He didn't owe it to his parents and his late brother to marry his widow too.

Barbara had left the house in tears, and there had been an ugly scene with his parents. He left Long Island shortly after that, never to return, and he didn't see them again until well into fall. Barbara had gone back to Boston by then, with the girls, and he had heard recently from a friend that she was seeing the son of a key influential politician. It was the perfect choice for her, and he hoped she was happy. All he wanted was a chance to do well, and carve out a life for himself. He liked New York, but he still missed California. And more than once, he found himself thinking about Crystal. But less often now. She was simply too far away, and she wasn't real. She had been merely a rare and beautiful vision, like a wildflower one stops to admire in the mountains, never to be seen again, but always remembered. He had had a letter from Boyd when their daughter was born, but it had said nothing about Crystal, and he'd gotten an announcement that Tom and Becky had had another baby. But all of that seemed very remote now. It was part of the war, for him, part of another life. He was wrapped up with his work for Anderson, Vincent, and Sawbrook, and he was learning a lot about the new tax laws. His real interests were in criminal work, but none of their clients had problems in that direction. He helped to set up estates, and complicated wills, and it was interesting work he could talk about with his father.

He discovered when he had dinner with his parents that night that they had gotten the invitation too. But his father said he was too busy to attend the induction.

"Are you going?"

"I doubt it, Dad, I hardly know him." Spencer smiled at him. His father was wearing well.

STAR 149

He had just been involved in an important criminal case and Spencer was anxious to hear more about it than he had read in the papers.

"You should go. He's a good man for you to stay in touch with."

"I'll try, but I don't know if I can get away from the office." Spencer smiled, looking younger than his twenty-nine years. He was tanned from weekends at the beach, and he'd been playing a lot of tennis. "I feel foolish going, Dad. He really doesn't know me all that well. And I don't have time to go to Washington."

"You can make time. I'm sure the firm would want you to go." Always responsibilities and obligations. It chafed at him sometimes. Life here seemed so full of what was "expected." It was part of being grown up, part of being in the "real" world, but he wasn't always sure he liked it.

"I'll see." But much to his surprise, the partner he worked for echoed his father's words a few days later. Spencer mentioned the invitation over drinks at the River Club, and his mentor suggested he go to Harrison Barclay's induction.

"It's an honor to be asked."

"I hardly know him, sir." It was the same

thing he had said to his father, but the senior partner shook his head.

"No matter. He may be important to you one day. You have to keep those things in mind. In fact, I'd like to strongly recommend it." Spencer nodded, accepting the advice, but he felt foolish when he accepted the invitation. The firm even went so far as to make reservations for him, at the Shoreham, and he went to Washington on the train, the day before the induction. The room they had taken for him was airy and large, and he grinned to himself as he sat down in a comfortable leather chair and ordered a Scotch from room service. It was a pleasant way of life, and maybe it would be fun to go to see the Barclays again. He suspected that Elizabeth would be there. He had never heard from her after she went to Vassar. She probably had other fish to fry, and he had his share of attentive ladies. He'd been out with a dozen different women in the past year. He had taken them to dinner at "21," Le Pavillon, and the Waldorf. They had gone to parties, the theater, played tennis with him in Connecticut and East Hampton, but there was no one he cared about particularly. And three years after the end of the war, everyone still seemed to be in a hurry to get married. It was not a pressing need for him, there was still a lot he wanted to sort out in his own mind. Somehow just practicing law didn't seem like the end of the line to him. He liked it better than he thought he would, but secretly he admitted to himself that it lacked excitement. He was still trying to figure out how to incorporate it with something more challenging and demanding. And at twenty-nine, he figured there was still a lot of fun in store for him before he settled down with anyone for good. He had to find the right girl first, and she hadn't come along yet.

He was just beginning to find his feet again after the interruption of the war, and the shock of his brother's death. The pain of it had begun to dim by then. Robert had been gone for four years, and his parents still talked about him a great deal, but Spencer no longer felt quite as personally responsible to replace him. He was his own person now, and there were times when he felt on top of the world, and very much in control of everything he was doing. He was lonely at times, but he wasn't even sure he minded. He liked being alone. And in spite of the fact that law hadn't been what he really wanted, he had come to enjoy what he did.

The next day dawned sunny and bright, and on a cool September morning, Spencer went to the Supreme Court Building for the formal swearing in. He wore a dark pinstriped suit, and a somber tie, and with his shining dark hair and his blue eyes, he looked very handsome. Several women turned their heads to look at him, although he seemed not to notice. And afterward, he managed to shake Justice Barclay's hand briefly before the crowd swallowed him up and he was moved along. He didn't see anyone he knew, and he was sorry his father hadn't been able to come with him.

He visited the Washington Monument that afternoon, and the Lincoln Memorial, and then went back to his hotel for a bite to eat before dressing for the party he'd been invited to that evening. The Barclays were hosting a formal dinner dance at the Mayflower Hotel to celebrate his induction.

Spencer left the hotel in black tie, and hailed a cab to take him to the party, and he waited patiently on the reception line, where he was greeted warmly by Priscilla Barclay.

"How nice of you to come, Mr. Hill. Have you seen Elizabeth?"

"Thank you. No, I haven't."

"I saw her a few minutes ago. I'm sure she'll be very happy to see you." He moved on to greet her husband then, and then moved on quickly to make room for the others in the long line behind him. He went to the bar and ordered Scotch and water, and looked around at the assembled group. Most of the men were older, and the women wore expensive gowns. It was an interesting collection of the country's well-known and most important, and he felt a sudden surge of excitement at being there. He took a sip of his drink as he recognized one of the other justices on the Supreme Court, and then watched a younger woman talking to an older man, and when she turned around, he saw that the woman was Justice Barclay's daughter. She looked much older than she had a year before, and prettier somehow, and as she smiled in recognition, he remembered how poised she had been when they last met, and how attractive. She was prettier than he remembered her, and he approached her with a smile, as her warm brown eyes seemed to light up. Her auburn hair was shorter now, and she was wearing a striking white satin dress with the summer tan she had acquired at Lake Tahoe, and it struck him forcefully that she was very attractive, a lot more so than he had remembered.

"Hello, how've you been? How's Vassar?"

"Boring." She smiled up at him, her eyes locked in his as she grinned. "I think I'm too old for college." Vassar seemed so childish to her. Within three months, she had been chafing to finish and do something else, but she still had three years left. And starting her second year, she was beginning to wonder if she'd make it through. "Poughkeepsie is absolutely awful."

"After California, so is New York sometimes. The winters are a bit of a jolt, aren't they?" He laughed. He had complained bitterly himself the year before, but he was used to it again, and he liked the excitement of New York, which was a far cry from sleepy Poughkeepsie.

"It was nice of you to come. I'm sure my father was touched," she said politely, and Spencer almost laughed. In the swirling crowd around him, of hundreds of associates and friends, it was difficult to imagine Justice Barclay being "touched" by the attendance of one young, unimportant lawyer.

"It was nice of him to ask me. He must be very pleased with the appointment."

She smiled at him, sipping her own gin and tonic. "He is. And so is my mother. She loves Washington. She was born here, you know."

"I didn't. I imagine this will be fun for you too. Can you get away from school?" He was admiring the smooth sweep of her shoulders as he asked, and decided he liked her new hairdo.

"Not often enough. I hardly ever got to New

York last year. But I'm going to try and spend some time here with them, on vacations. It's a lot easier than getting back to California." They chatted on for a little while, and as the guests began to sit down, Spencer consulted one of several seating charts and discovered that he was sitting at her table. He assumed that her mother had seen to it, and had no idea that Elizabeth had requested it herself when she went over the guest list with her mother. She'd been impressed by him the year before, and was disappointed he had never tried to reach her at Vassar. "How do you like the law firm in New York?" She could no longer remember which one it was, but she remembered that it was important.

"I like it." He smiled as he helped her to her seat, and she laughed at him.

"You sound surprised."

His eyes smiled back at her as he sat down beside her. "I am. I was never all that sure that I wanted to be a lawyer."

"And now you are?"

"More or less. I keep thinking it's going to get harder, or more challenging, but it hasn't so far. It's actually very comfortable." She nodded, and then smiled proudly in her father's direction at a table nearby.

"And look what it leads to."

"Not for everyone, I'm afraid. But I'm satisfied doing what I'm doing for the moment."

"Have you ever thought of politics?" She inquired as the first course arrived. It was lobster bisque, served with white wine, and Spencer looked at her in amusement. She still had those piercing eyes that seemed to search one out, and she wasn't afraid to ask serious questions. He had liked that about her the year before, and it struck him again now. She wasn't afraid to tackle anything, and it was something that he admired. Elizabeth took the initiative herself and moved ahead. She was a woman in command, of herself, and her surroundings, and he suspected, given the opportunity, also the people around her. She was eyeing him with interest now, intensely involved in politics herself, because of her father.

"My brother had aspirations in that direction, or at least he thought so. But I'm not sure that's my cup of tea at all." The trouble was he wasn't sure yet what was.

"If I were a man, that's what I would do." She sounded so sure of herself and he envied her a little bit as he laughed. She was certainly full of spunk. He remembered that the last time he had seen her, she had told him she wanted to be a lawyer.

"What are you studying at Vassar?"

"Liberal arts. Literature. French. History. Nothing very exciting."

"What would you rather do?" She intrigued him with her sharp mind and direct approach. Elizabeth Barclay was certainly no shrinking violet.

"Give up school and do something useful. I was thinking about coming to Washington for a while, but Father had a fit when I mentioned it. He wants me to finish college first."

"That sounds sensible. You only have three more years." But it even sounded long to him as he watched her.

"Have you been back to California at all?"

"No, I haven't." He said it with regret. "I really haven't had time, and the last year has gone very quickly." She nodded, it had for her too, in some ways, and slower in others. She had gone back to San Francisco to make her debut at the Cotillion at Christmas, and for the ball her parents had given her at the Burlingame Country Club just before. And then of course she had gone to Lake Tahoe for the summer. But she was more interested in visiting New York and Washington that winter. Her parents had already invited her to Palm Beach for Christmas.

The band started up then, and Spencer invited her to dance just as they began playing

"Imagination," while they waited for their main course. And Spencer guided her gently to the dance floor. She danced beautifully, and he looked down at the shining auburn hair and the deeply suntanned shoulders. Everything about her suggested health and well-being and power. She told him that she was going to Europe with her parents the following summer, on the *Ile de France,* and asked him if he'd ever been, and he told her he hadn't. His father had promised to send him when he graduated from college, but by then the war was on, and he had enlisted right after that, and gone to the Pacific instead. She mentioned also that she was going to New York in a few weeks to visit one of her brothers. Ian Barclay worked for a law firm that was even more illustrious than the one that employed Spencer.

"Do you know them?" She looked up at him expectantly, looking very young and very pretty, and he began to feel the effects of the Scotch. He liked the feel of her skin beneath his hands, and for the first time he noticed her perfume as they went on dancing.

"No, I don't know him. My father does though." He remembered his father saying that Barclay had been in his courtroom. "You'll have to introduce me." It was the first time he had suggested anything that implied he would see her again.

"I'd like to." She looked victorious and a little regal as he led her back to the table, and they sat down to dinner and talk with her parents' friends, and by the end of the evening, he felt as though he knew her a little better. She played tennis, she liked to ski, she spoke a little French, she hated dogs, and she didn't seem particularly interested in children. What she wanted in life, she admitted to him over dessert, was to accomplish something in her life, not just play bridge and have babies. And it was obvious to him that she was crazy about her father and wanted to marry someone like him, a man who was "going somewhere," as she put it, not just someone content to sit in an easy chair and let life pass him by. She wanted to marry a man who was *important*. She was young to be that definite about it, she was not yet twenty, but she knew her own mind, and she had plenty of opportunity to meet the kind of man she wanted. And for a moment, as they left the ballroom together, he realized that she would have liked Robert a lot better than him.

"Do you want to go out for a drink somewhere?" He was surprised to hear himself say it, but he liked talking to her.

"All right. Where are you staying?" Her

brown eyes looked directly into his. She wasn't afraid of anything, and certainly not Spencer.

"The Shoreham."

"So are we. We can have a drink at the bar. I'll just go tell my mother." She did, and a few minutes later they left, most of the guests were already gone, and it was almost one o'clock, and her mother didn't object to her leaving with Spencer. He was a respectable, attractive man, and she knew she could trust him with her daughter. She waved to them as they left, but Spencer didn't want to interrupt what looked like a serious conversation with the Speaker of the House. They left quietly and caught a cab back to the hotel, and took a quiet table in a corner of the bar. He noticed several heads turn as they walked in. They made a very striking couple.

He ordered champagne, and they talked for a while longer, about New York, his job, and California. He told her how much he had loved it and that he'd like to live there someday, although he didn't see how, working for a law firm on Wall Street. And she laughed at him, all she wanted was to move to New York when she finished college, or maybe Washington now that her parents would be there for most of the year. She talked about wanting to have her own house in Georgetown.

It was obvious from the way she talked that she had never lacked for anything. It never dawned on her that she might not get what she wanted. But he had figured out that much when he met her in her home in San Francisco. Their house there was both opulent and beautiful, and it was easy to see that her life had been an easy one. Both her parents had come from families with a great deal of money.

"You have to come to Tahoe sometime. My grandfather built a wonderful house on the lake. I've loved it ever since I was a little girl." But oddly, when she mentioned it, he thought of the Alexander Valley, and he asked her if she'd ever been there. "No, but I went to Napa once, to visit friends of Dad's. There's not much there though, except vineyards and a few Victorian houses." It had seemed very dull to her, but she looked intrigued as Spencer described the valley north of it, and she saw something in his eyes that aroused her curiosity. There was a look of remembering, a look that told her there was more to it than he was telling. "Do you have friends there?"

He nodded pensively. "Two of the men who served in the army with me live there." He told her about Boyd and Hiroko then, and her eyes hardened as she listened.

"It was stupid of him to marry her. No one's

going to forget what happened in Japan." She sounded spoiled and insensitive suddenly and it annoyed him. It was exactly the kind of reaction Hiroko had been faced with constantly since coming to California.

He spoke very quietly, barely concealing his anger. "I don't suppose the Japanese will forget Hiroshima either."

"Didn't you say your brother was killed in the Pacific?" Her eyes honed in on him and he looked at her squarely.

"Yes, he was. But I don't hate them for it. We did our own share of killing there." It was a pacifist view she wasn't familiar with, and it wasn't in keeping with her father's opinions. He was an ardent conservative, and he had fully approved of the bombing of Hiroshima. "I hated everything we did there, Elizabeth. No one wins a war, except maybe governments. The people always lose, on both sides."

"I don't share your view." She looked prim and he tried to cool down by making light of it.

"I suppose you would have liked to join the army too." Along with her longing to be an attorney or a politician.

"My mother worked for the Red Cross, and I would have, too, if I'd been old enough."

He sighed. She was still so young, and so naive, and so influenced by what her parents thought. He had his own views about the war, which differed greatly from his father's. Spencer was only happy it was over, but he still remembered the friends he'd lost, the men who had served with him . . . and his brother. He looked at Elizabeth then, and he felt almost old enough to be her father, instead of only ten years older. "Life is funny, isn't it, Elizabeth? You never know which way it's going to go. If my brother hadn't been killed, I might never have gone to law school," he smiled quietly, "I might never have met you."

"That's a strange way to look at it." She was intrigued by him. He was honest and gentle and intelligent, but not as ambitious as she would have wanted. He just seemed to be enjoying life as he rolled along, waiting to see which way it would take him. "We make our own destinies, don't you think?"

"Not always." He had seen too much reality to believe that. And if he had made his, his life might have been very different. "Do you think you'll make yours?" He was as fascinated by her as she was by him. They were so very different.

"Probably." She sounded sure of it, and he admired her for her confidence and determination.

"I believe you will, given half a chance."

"Does that surprise you?" She looked so sure of herself, so unruffled, and so in control after the long evening.

"Not really. You seem like someone who's always gotten what she's wanted."

"And you?" Her voice grew softer. "Have you been disappointed, Spencer?" She wondered if he'd lost someone he truly cared about, or had had a broken engagement, but he hadn't.

He smiled before he answered her, thinking about it. "Not disappointed. Only rerouted, one might say," and then he laughed openly as he poured the last of their champagne. The bar would be closing soon, and he would have to take her back to her parents, or their suite anyway. They both knew the evening would go no further. "My parents wanted me to marry my brother's wife when I came home, his widow, I should say. That was a bit of a go-around when I got home."

"Why didn't you?" She wanted to know everything about him.

He looked at her honestly. "I didn't love her. That's important to me. She was Robert's wife, not mine. I'm not him. I'm someone very different."

"And who's that, Spencer?" Her voice was

like a caress in the dark room as she searched his eyes, "what do *you* want?"

"Someone I love . . . and respect . . . and care about. Someone to laugh with when things go wrong . . . someone who's not afraid to love me back . . . someone who needs me." He felt very vulnerable as he said it to her, and he wasn't sure why he had opened up to her. He wondered if Crystal would ever fit the bill. It wasn't likely. It was odd how the memory of her stayed with him. She was a wildly beautiful girl, from a distant place. All he knew was how lovely and gentle she was, and how he felt when he was near her. He didn't know what was inside her or what she thought, or who she would be once she was a grown-up. Nor did he know what was inside Elizabeth, but he suspected it wasn't soft. She was made of sterner stuff, and he couldn't imagine her ever needing anyone, except maybe her father. "If you had your way, what would you want, Elizabeth?"

She smiled and was as honest as he had been. "Someone important."

"That says it all, doesn't it?" He laughed, but her words had hit their mark. She was exactly what he had thought her. Tough, smart, interesting, alive, ambitious, and independent.

Spencer escorted Elizabeth to her room, and

said good night to her in the hall, and she turned as she opened the door and looked at him with a warm smile. "When are you going back to New York?"

"Tomorrow morning."

"I'm staying here for a few days. I'm going to help Mom look for a house. But I'll be back at Vassar by next week, Spencer . . ." and then so softly he could barely hear her, ". . . call me."

"How would I find you?" For the first time, he thought he might call her, although he wasn't sure why. He found her a little over-powering, and yet it might be fun to take her to dinner or the theater. She certainly wouldn't embarrass him, and she was interesting to talk to, and there was something vaguely intriguing about taking out a Supreme Court justice's daughter.

She told him what dorm she was in, and he promised to remember. And then he thanked her for the evening. "I had a great time." He seemed to hesitate, not sure what he should do next, but she looked supremely comfortable as she stood in the doorway.

"So did I. Thank you. Good night, Spencer." And then the door closed quietly, and she was gone, as he walked slowly back to the elevator, wondering if he would really call her.

CHAPTER 10

The partner Spencer worked for was pleased with him when he went back to New York with reports of the induction, and the dinner afterward. It pleased the firm to have their young attorneys rub shoulders with important people. The fact that his own father was a judge hadn't done him any harm with them either. And his father was pleased as well, when he told his parents all about it. He omitted any mention of Elizabeth though, somehow that didn't seem important and he didn't want them to get their hopes up.

And in the end, after thinking about it for a while, he decided not to call her.

But Elizabeth took matters in her own hands a month later when she came to New York to visit her brother. She looked him up in the phone book and called him. She called him on a Saturday, and he was surprised to hear her voice. He had been on his way out to play squash with friends from the office.

"Is it a bad time?" She sounded, as always, very mature, and he smiled as he looked out the window and juggled his racket.

"Not at all. How've you been?"

"Fine. Vassar is a little better this term." She didn't tell him she'd been going out with one of her professors. But boys her own age always bored her. "I was wondering if you wanted to go to the theater tonight. We have a spare ticket."

"Are you here with your parents?"

"No. I'm staying with my brother and his wife. We're going to see "Summer and Smoke" at the Music Box Theater. Have you seen it?"

"No," he smiled, "but I'd like to." What the hell, how dangerous could it be with her brother there? He didn't trust himself with her. He didn't want to get involved with someone quite so intent on her future. He still remembered her answer when he asked her what she was looking for in life, and she had answered, "someone important."

"We're having dinner at Chambord before the theater. Why don't you meet us there? Say, at six?"

"Fine. I'll meet you there. And thank you, Elizabeth." He wasn't sure if he should apologize for not calling her, but decided it was best not to say it. And she certainly made things easy for him. The best restaurant, the best show, and an introduction to her illustrious brother, Ian Barclay.

Spencer arrived at the restaurant precisely on time, and recognized her instantly, in a well-cut black evening suit and a small black velvet hat perched atop a very appealing new hairdo. She seemed to take a lot of care about how she looked, and he liked that about her. She was good-looking and chic, and she always made an impression. For a girl not yet twenty, she had a lot of style, and so did her brother Ian. Spencer found him to be an intelligent man, although a little forceful about his political ideas. But in spite of that, Spencer liked him. His wife was a very attractive English girl he had met while flying bombing raids with the RAF. She was the daughter of Lord Wingham, and Elizabeth made sure that Spencer knew it. Her life was filled with important names and illustrious people with powerful occupations. In an odd way, it made him feel powerful just being with her, as though some of it might rub off. They were all so damn sure of who they were, and where they were going, and it was easy to see why it all mattered to her so much. Ian and Sarah talked about spending Christmas at St. Moritz, and they had just been to Venice that summer. They had gone to Rome afterward, and had had a private audience with Pope Pius, because he knew her father. She had the enormous ease of the aristocracy, and seemed to expect that everyone knew the same people she did.

They enjoyed the play, and Spencer invited them to the Stork Club afterward, and they all danced and talked and laughed, and after that they went back to the Barclays' apartment on Sutton Place. They had no children yet, and Sarah was far more interested in her horses. She talked about jumpers and hunters, and they invited him to ride with them sometime. It was all very pleasant, and this time when Spencer told Elizabeth he'd call her, he meant it. He felt he owed her something after the pleasant evening he had spent, which was precisely what she had intended.

He called her two weeks afterward, and he would have called her sooner, he explained, except that he'd been buried in work at the office. But she didn't scold him for not calling. They made a date for the following weekend. She stayed at her brother's again, and Spencer took her to dinner and dancing at the Stork Club. He wasn't intent on impressing her, but Elizabeth wasn't the kind of girl one could take anywhere except the very best places. He told her about the cases he'd been working on, mostly litigation that involved business or taxes. It was interesting work, and she made intelligent comments. And that night, when he took her home, they stood outside her brother's apartment, and he kissed her.

"I had a lovely time," she said quietly, but there was something warm in her eyes just for him that didn't go unnoticed.

"So did I." And he meant it. She was good company, and she looked smashing in a silver dress her sister-in-law had brought her from Paris.

"What are you doing next weekend?"

"I have exams." She laughed. "Stupid, isn't it? It plays havoc with my social life." They both laughed and he suggested she come back to New York the following weekend.

She did, and they went out again, and this time the kisses were a little more fervent. Her brother and sister-in-law were away for the weekend that time, at a hunt in New Jersey, and she invited Spencer in for drinks at the end of the evening. They sat on the couch for a long time, kissing and talking. And afterward he felt guilty about it. She was too young for him to be toying with her, and he couldn't imagine that it would lead anywhere. Her world was more than a little beyond him. He wasn't in love with her, but he was attracted to her physically, and he knew that he liked her. He liked the sense of power that flowed so freely in her world, yet he was also aware of a certain lack of warmth. Everything was very calculated and cold. But as a tourist in that world, he had to admit that it was amusing.

Elizabeth had told him she was going home for Thanksgiving with her parents, to San Francisco. But he promised to call her when she got back. And when he did, she invited him to Palm Beach for Christmas.

"Wouldn't that be a little awkward, with your parents?" He sounded startled, but she only laughed at him.

"Don't be silly, Spencer. They like you."

"I really ought to stay here. Christmas is a little rough on my parents now." And Barbara had told them she wasn't bringing the children in from Boston. She was involved in a serious romance, and she wanted them with her. He knew his parents were going to be very lonely, and Christmas always reminded them of the son they had lost more than the one they hadn't. All of that raced through his mind, as he mulled over her unexpected invitation.

"Why don't you come down later then? I'll be there until after New Year's. You can stay at the house, we have dozens of guest rooms." A pronouncement he suspected accurately was no exaggeration.

"I'll see if I can get the time off, and I'll call you." He called her before she left for Florida, and much to his own surprise, he accepted. He still wasn't sure what he was doing with her, but whatever it was, it was not unpleasant.

Christmas passed uneventfully for him, and two days afterward, he began a week's holiday from work, and flew to Palm Beach to stay with the Barclays. They were gracious and kind, and the house seemed to be filled with guests like him, and Elizabeth's elder brother, Gregory, was there. He worked for the Treasury, and was a typically conservative banker. He was married, but his wife wasn't there, and no one seemed anxious to discuss it, and Spencer didn't pry. He was too busy with Elizabeth to care. They went to every party in town, and he decided he had never seen so many diamonds. Elizabeth herself wore a different evening gown every night, and a pretty little tiara her parents had given her the year before when she made her debut.

"Well," she asked him as they lay on the beach one day, "are you having fun?"

He laughed at the question. She was always direct with him, but he had decided he liked it. There was no playing around with her, no beating around the bush, no asking her what she really meant by that, she always told him. "Of course I am. What do you think? This is heaven. I may never go back to work, or New York."

"Good. Then I'll quit school, and we can run away to Cuba." They had flown over once for a night of dancing and gambling at the ca-sino. It had been an incredible week, and Spen-cer had to admit that he loved it. It was an easy life, filled with civilized people with inter-esting things to say and beautiful women cov-ered with diamonds. It would be too easy to get used to it, but to what purpose? It was her life, not his. But at least for a little while, it was amusing.

"Are you liking school any better now?" He rolled over on one elbow to look at her. She looked splendid in a red bathing suit, and a dark tan that set off her auburn hair and dark eyes. She was a very pretty girl, and he liked her.

"Not much. I still feel as though I'm wasting time there."

"I can see why." He glanced at the butler approaching with lemonade and rum punches on a silver tray and turned to look at her again. "It's awfully hard to go from this to school, and remember why you wanted to go there in the first place."

"To tell you the truth," she grinned happily, "I didn't."

"Well, you can't be a lawyer if you don't go to college." He smiled and helped himself to the lemonade as she sipped a rum punch and smiled at him beneath the brim of her sun hat.

"I guess I won't be a lawyer then." She sounded as though she was teasing and he laughed at her.

"Then what'll you do instead, Miss Barclay? Run for president?"

"Maybe I'll just marry one."

He looked at her half seriously. "It would suit you."

"Would you like to run for president one day, Mr. Hill?" He felt faintly uncomfortable at the gist of the conversation but he only smiled at her as he shook his head and played with the lemonade. She was a strong girl, and they were powerful people. You couldn't play with them for long. And in a way, Spencer was almost afraid to. Inside, beneath the cool air he put on for her, he was a gentle soul, and he cared about other things. Things the Barclays never even dreamed of.

"Being president has never been one of my ambitions."

"Senator, then. You'd be marvelous in public service."

"What makes you think so?"

"You like people, you work hard, you're honest and direct and you're bright." She smiled again. "And you know the right people." He wasn't sure he liked what she was saying, and he fell silent as he looked out at the ocean. He wondered if he had gone too far with her. Maybe coming to Palm Beach had been a mistake, but it was too late to change that. He was going back to New York in two days, and maybe after that he wouldn't see her for a while. She was watching him as he ran it all through his head, and she laughed. "Don't look so nervous, Spencer. I'm not going to attack you. I was just telling you what I thought."

"You have a disquieting way of doing that sometimes, Elizabeth. I get the feeling occasionally that you always get what you want. I mean *always.*" And he didn't want it to be him. At least not for the moment. Not until he felt more for her than he did just then. And he wasn't sure he ever would. They were good friends. But they were very different.

"What's wrong with getting what you want?"

"Nothing, as long as everyone agrees it's what they want too." He said it quietly and she regarded him with probing eyes.

"And is it what everyone wants?" She said the words so pointedly that he almost trembled.

"Why don't we go for a swim?" He didn't want to answer her. He wasn't ready to say what she wanted to hear, and he didn't know if he ever would be. He still cherished dreams of a woman who needed him, who was gentle and kind and warm and loving. And Elizabeth was some of those things, but not many. She was other things instead. Other things that he had not yet made his peace with.

"You didn't answer my question." She looked up at him as he stood beside her, and he knew there was no running away from her. There was nothing to do but tell her the truth. Elizabeth demanded nothing less of anyone, and certainly not of Spencer.

"I don't know yet."

She nodded, as though thinking it over, and then looked into his eyes again. "I think we'd be a good team, you and I. We have the strength and the brains to do some interesting things together." She made it sound like a business deal and it depressed him.

"Like what? Run a corporation?"

"Maybe. Or politics. Or just be like Ian and Sarah."

"With their horses and their friends, and their hunts and their clubs, and her father's castle. Elizabeth," he sat down again and looked at her, "I'm not like them. I'm different. I want other things."

"Like what?" She seemed puzzled.

"Like children. You never even think of that, do you?" But she looked startled when he said the words. Children had never been important to her.

"We could have them too," like diamonds or racehorses or investments. She made them sound like a possession to put in the back of her closet. "But there are other more important things in life."

"Like what?" he said again, amazed by the way she saw things. "What's more important than that?"

"Don't be ridiculous, Spencer. Accomplish-

ment, achievement, making a place for one-
self."

"Like your father?" It was a veiled criticism,
but she didn't hear it.

"That's right. You could be in his shoes one
day, if you wanted to."

"The trouble is," he looked at her ruefully,
"I'm not sure I want to. Can you understand
that?"

"Yes," she nodded slowly at him, "I think
you're afraid to. I think you're afraid to be
confused with your brother again. But you're
not him, Spencer, you're you, and there's a lot
waiting for you out there, if you'll just go and
get it." But he still wasn't sure that he would
ever care enough to make it worth the trouble.
But on the other hand, he couldn't imagine
working on tax cases for the rest of his life at
Anderson, Vincent, and Sawbrook. Just what
was he going to do when he grew up? He still
hadn't made his mind up about the future.

"I want to make the right decisions."

"So do I. But I think I see more than you
do."

"What makes you so sure? You're twenty
years old. You don't know a damn thing about
life yet." He was suddenly angry. In a veiled
way, she was proposing to him, and she
sounded as though she was trying to talk him

into buying a piece of property, like a house or a car or an object. And he wanted to be the one to ask her, if that was what he decided. But he hadn't, and he didn't think he ever would. He didn't love her.

"I know more about life than you think. I know where I'm going at least, which is more than you do."

"Maybe you're right." He stood up again and looked out at the ocean. "I'm going for a swim." He walked into the ocean then and was gone for half an hour, and she didn't press him again, but what she had said had shaken him. After that, he was careful not to say anything that could be misinterpreted. But before he left, she came to his room, and faced him again. And there was no avoiding her eyes this time. Spencer watched her, feeling hunted.

"I just want you to know that I love you."

"Elizabeth, don't . . . please . . ." It hurt him not to be able to tell her he loved her too. "Don't do this."

"Why not? And I meant what I said on the beach the other day. I think we could do great things together."

He laughed and ran a hand through his hair. "I'm the one who's supposed to propose, kid, and when I do, you'll know it."

"Will I?" Her eyes taunted him as he approached her.

"Count on it." He pulled her close to him then, and kissed her. She was so damn forceful that it made him want to seduce her just to show her who was boss, who was in control, and if he had any say about it, it wasn't going to be Elizabeth Barclay. But his plans went awry again. Being with her was like playing with fire, and he was never sure afterward who had seduced whom, all he knew was that they had made love, and he liked it. Her body filled him with hunger and passion, and there was an irresistible desire to control her, in bed if nowhere else. She was an interesting lover, and he also knew without discussing it with her, that she wasn't a virgin.

She drove him to the airport when he left, and he looked at her for a long time, not sure what to do. He needed time to think, and he was anxious to get back to New York now.

"I'll be back at school next week."

He kissed her softly and wanted to make love to her again, annoyed at himself for being in her power even for a moment. In more ways than he knew, she was stronger than he was.

"I'll call you."

He waved as he got on the plane, and he saw her standing there as they taxied down the runway, in her sundress and her big hat, her eyes searching him out even as they lifted into the air. He felt as though he would never get away from her now. He was no longer sure if he wanted to. Maybe she was right. Maybe she could help him find what he wanted. He wasn't sure of anything anymore, and the worst of it was that as they landed in the snows of New York, he knew that he missed her.

CHAPTER
11 ———————————

Christmas on the ranch was depressing that year. It was their first Christmas since her father had died, and all the joy seemed to have gone out of their lives. Becky spent the day with them with her children, and Tom turned up in time for dinner, reeking of booze, and openly eyeing Crystal. When he left again, Becky burst into tears and accused her of flirting with him, and Crystal was horrified. She couldn't even tell her how much she disliked him.

The family went to church together the next day, and her mother cried bitterly, thinking of the husband she had lost, and how her life had changed since then. The only joy for Crystal was the solace she always derived from singing with the congregation. They went home after that, and Crystal quietly slipped away to bring gifts to Boyd and Hiroko. Little Jane was eight months old by then and crawling all over their living room, gurgling happily and pulling herself up on Crystal's knees as they watched her. They had a tiny tree, and Crystal gave them her gifts. She had made a sweater for Hiroko, her first attempt, and a scarf for Boyd, and she had bought a doll for Jane, which she happily chewed on. For Crystal, Christmas was happier here. It was a house filled with love and warm hearts, unlike the bleak silence in her own house. Becky knew that Tom was cheating on her, and she had heard the rumors about Ginny Webster, but she seemed intent on blaming Crystal for everything, as though Crystal were to blame for it all. She insisted frequently that her sister was making eyes at her husband, and Olivia had accused her more than once of encouraging him, which brought tears to Crystal's eyes. She had done nothing to deserve their accusations, but she seemed helpless against them.

Even Jared turned on her. He had heard through one of his friends that she was visiting

Boyd and his wife, and he threatened more than once to tell their mother. It was as though they all hated her, and she barely got from day to day, except for her visits with the Websters.

"I don't know what I've done to them," she cried openly one night when she went to them, after a day of anguish at the ranch house, "why do they hate me?" She did what she was told, she worked hard, she seldom fought with them, and yet they were determined to make her unhappy.

"Because you're different," Boyd answered quietly, as Hiroko held the baby. "You don't look like them, you don't think like them. You never did." And her father was no longer there to protect her. She knew that what he said was true, but she couldn't bear the injustice of it. What had she ever done to them? Nothing. But she had been born too beautiful. She was a wild summer rose in a field of weeds, and they were determined to destroy her.

She blew her nose as she thought about it. It was unbearable living with them, but she had nowhere else to go and Boyd and Hiroko knew it, as did Crystal. The only thing she could do was leave the valley but she wanted to finish high school first. She had promised that to her father. She still thought about going to Hollywood. But it was too soon. She had to graduate first, if she survived it. But she knew she would. She wasn't going to let people like her mother and Tom Parker run her life. There was too much of her father in her for that. She would put up with it all for now. But she knew that as soon as she finished school, she was leaving. No matter where she went, she knew that she had to leave the valley. She needed money to do it, and now that her father was gone, no matter how much she loved the valley, she knew she had to leave it. The others were just too strong a force to ignore forever. She knew she had to get out before one of them hurt her. And in order to get out, she had to make enough money to do it.

In January she went to work in town as a waitress. And even that won her mother's fury. She called her a harlot and a slut and accused her of wanting to meet men, but all she did was wait on tables in the diner. Her brother-in-law came in occasionally and gave her a hard time, but whenever possible, she disappeared and went out to the kitchen to take a turn washing dishes when he was there. The people at the diner were friendly to her, and she made good money with tips, and got a fair number of propositions. She always played stupid, and turned them down bluntly when she had to, and the owner of the diner liked her, and made sure that no one went too far. She was a nice girl, and he had always liked her father. He didn't think much of Tom Parker though, and he didn't like the way he treated her. He told Crystal more than once to stay away from him when he was liquored up, and more than once he drove her home himself after dark, and watched to make sure she got home safely to the ranch house. She kept her money hidden under her bed, and she had four hundred dollars saved up by late April. It was her ticket to Hollywood, or to freedom anyway, and she guarded it with her life, counting the money late at night, in the moonlight with her bedroom door locked. She was biding her time now till she could leave. It wouldn't be long. But each day seemed like a lifetime.

Little Jane was a year old by then, and Crystal rode her old pinto over to see her on a bright Sunday morning. She spent the day with them, and it was late when she went home, but she knew the road well. And in the end, she decided to take a shortcut, riding over the fields, and smelling the air, as she sang her favorite old ballads softly. For the first time in a long time, she felt good again. Her father had been gone for more than a year, and the bitter ache of it was a little dimmer. She felt strong and young and alive, and all she could think of now was her future.

But as she tied her horse into his stall in the barn, and took off his saddle, as she hummed to herself, she heard a noise just behind her, and turned around, startled. It was Tom, sitting on a bag of feed and drinking.

"Have a nice day, Sis?" There was an ugly look in his eyes and she looked away, pretending not to notice, but her hands trembled as she put the bridle away, and she heard his step right behind her. "Where do you go on that old horse? Got a boyfriend in town?"

"No." She turned to face him, and she didn't like what she saw. His eyes were red, and she could see that the bottle he held was half empty. "I was visiting friends."

"That Jap again?" He had heard the rumors, too, and he had told Becky, who had reported it to their mother.

"No," she lied to him, "friends from school."

"Yeah? Like who?" His voice was rough from drinking and hers was cool, but she was trembling inside.

"It's not important." She started to leave the barn, and he grabbed her roughly by the arm. He caught her unaware and she flew backward and tripped over his foot, stumbling to keep her balance.

"What's your hurry?"

"I have to get home to Mama." She tried to look him in the eye, but she was afraid to. Even as tall as she was, she was no match for Tom Parker. He liked to tell his friends he was as strong as a bull, and even bigger where it counted.

"Mama . . . isn't that sweet," he mocked her, "home to *Mama*. She don't care. She's with Becky anyway. The dumb bitch is knocked up again. Christ, you'd think she'd have learned by now. We hardly ever do it, and when we do, she gets pregnant."

Crystal nodded sympathetically, trying to pull away from him, but he had her arms in a viselike grip and it was obvious he had no intention of letting her go anywhere, at least not for the moment.

"I told you to stick around, didn't I?" She nodded, mute with terror. At seventeen, she had never been manhandled before, and it was small consolation to realize that if her father were alive, he'd have killed him. "Want a drink?"

"No, thanks." Her face was white with fear as she shook her head.

"Sure you do." He held both of her arms

with one hand, and forced the bottle to her
mouth with the other. He tipped it up, spilling
it all over her shirt, but getting a fair dose of
the bitter liquid through her clenched lips in
spite of her efforts to resist him.

"Stop! Leave me alone . . . let me go!"

He laughed, watching her discomfort as
tears filled her eyes, and then suddenly he
threw her down into a pile of hay they kept
there for the horses.

"Take your clothes off."

"Tom . . . please . . ." She started to get
up and back away from him, but he grabbed
her legs, and pulled her back to the floor where
he was kneeling, the bottle cast aside, filling
the barn with the smell of cheap whiskey.
"Please . . . don't . . ." She didn't tell him
she was a virgin. She didn't know what to say
to him. She was crying as he tore her blouse
off.

"You give it away anyway, don't you, Sis?
Come on, be a good girl for your brother."

"You're not my brother . . . *stop it!*" And
then, with a clenched fist, fighting for her life,
she hit him. She hit him squarely in the eye,
and he groaned, but he grabbed her and
slapped her hard. So hard he left her breathless.

"Bitch! I told you to take your clothes off!"

He was pulling at her jeans with one hand, and pinning her to the ground with the other, his full weight pressed down on her, and she thought he would break her arms. But she didn't care. He'd have to kill her before she'd let him take her. She fought like a wild animal, but she was no match for him, again and again he threw her to the ground, cursing and calling her names, and then suddenly with a dull ripping sound, he tore her jeans off, and her pale thighs were exposed to him as she trembled.

"No, don't . . . Tom . . . *please* . . ." She was sobbing as he tore her underwear, still holding her prisoner with one powerful hand, her arms high above her head, his knees straddling her, as he grabbed her with his free hand, and then as she sobbed and begged, he pulled his pants down, just far enough to let her see him lunging toward her. There was no hesitation as he found his mark, and pressed his way inside her, smashing her to the ground with each thrust as she screamed and groaned in anguish. He slapped her again, and this time drew blood. There was blood dripping from her mouth, and she was lying in a sea of it as he raped her. Her back was torn to shreds by the straw and the floor, and she lay gasping with pain and terror as he came, and then slapped her hard again. But there was no fight left in her now. There was no point. She lay crumpled and beaten, as he stood up and pulled up his pants. He picked up his bottle and took a gulp and then laughed as he looked down at Crystal.

"You better wash up before you go home, Sis." He laughed again and slammed the barn door as he went back to his wife, and left Crystal lying on the barn floor, bleeding and broken and wanting to die. She lay there and sobbed until there were no tears left. There was nothing. She wanted to die as she lay there. It was a long time before she crawled to her knees, and staggered to the hose they used to fill the horse trough. She let the water run as she retched and poured the cold water over her, washing her face and her arms, and then she looked down at her torn jeans and the shreds of her underwear and the blood he had smeared over her as he took her. She sank to her knees again, whimpering softly. She couldn't go home again. She couldn't explain it to them. She couldn't tell anyone. Somehow they would blame it on her. And with trembling legs she stumbled into the horse stall, and clutching the old pinto by his mane, she led him from his stall and swung herself onto his back in the cool night air, and riding slowly across the fields, she went back to the Websters'. She had left them only two hours before, and she saw their lights come into view as she began to sob again. Her whole body ached and she was caked with blood and half naked. The pinto stopped in their garden, and she slid from his back as Boyd saw her from the window and hurried out to her, with Hiroko just behind him.

"Crys . . . oh, my God . . . *oh, my God* . . ." He thought someone had tried to kill her and she collapsed mercifully at their feet in a pool of blood, unconscious.

CHAPTER
12

Boyd carried Crystal inside, and they laid her on their bed. Boyd took the baby, and Hiroko sat beside her and bathed her with warm towels. She touched her bruises gently, and when she saw her back she cried. Her back and her legs, and the bruise on her lips. It was a wonder he hadn't killed her. Crystal lay there and cried in the bed where she had helped to deliver their baby, and the next morning she sat in their kitchen, staring at them emptily. She couldn't have faced anyone but them. They had become her family, and she cried again as Boyd handed her a cup of coffee.

"I'll take you home in the truck. You can tell your Mama where you've been. And then we're going to see the sheriff."

She shook her head miserably. Every inch of her body ached, and she hadn't slept all night. And she could hardly see through the shiner he'd given her. Except for the pale hair, it was hard to believe it was Crystal. But she knew she couldn't go to the sheriff. If she did, Tom would kill her. "I can't do that."

"Don't be a fool," Boyd growled at her. He wanted to kill Tom himself.

"I can't do that to Becky and my mother."

"Are you crazy? The man raped you." Crystal started to cry again, and Hiroko reached out and took her hand.

"He must be punished. Boyd is right."

But Crystal stood watching them through her tears in silence. It was her shame now too. And she was confused by all that she felt, she felt angry and frightened and broken, and for some odd reason, guilty. Was it her fault? Had she led him on over the years, without knowing it? Or was it another punishment for the way she looked? She wasn't sure, but it didn't matter anymore. It had happened. And it was just one more reason to get the hell out of the valley she had once loved, and now hated. She had nothing to leave there anyway except loss and pain and sorrow, and the Websters.

"You can't let him get away with this, Crystal." Boyd spoke quietly this time. But inside he was still trembling with rage. "I'll take you home." They hadn't called her mother the night before. They hadn't done anything except take care of Crystal. She left her horse there and got in the truck with Boyd and she was silent on the ride home, thinking of what she would do now. Hiroko held her tight before she left, and stayed home with Jane, but Crystal couldn't even speak to her before they left. She was speechless with grief and shame and terror.

Boyd followed her inside, and her grandmother was in the kitchen. She took one look at Crystal standing in the living room in a pair of jeans Boyd had given her, with her face bruised and her hair still matted from the night before, and ran to get her daughter. Crystal was clean now, but still disheveled. And a moment later, her mother ran into the room, pulling her bathrobe around her.

"Where the hell have you been? Oh my God . . ." And then, looking at Boyd, "What are you doing here?" He had been unwelcome in her house since marrying Hiroko, except for the christening and the wedding. But he hadn't been invited back since then.

"I brought her home. She stayed with us last night." But he didn't like the look in Olivia Wyatt's eyes, there was no compassion, only accusation. She made no move toward Crystal as the girl stood staring blindly at her, and Boyd helped her into a chair as her mother watched them.

"What did you do for something like this to happen?"

Boyd turned to face Olivia Wyatt again and with eyes filled with rage he told her what Crystal couldn't bring herself to say. "Your son-in-law raped her."

"That's a lie!" She flew at them both, and then turned on Boyd. "Get out of here. I'll take care of this." And then to Crystal, "How dare you tell him that about your sister's husband?"

She looked up at her mother in mute amazement. No matter what happened to her, her mother didn't care. And Crystal couldn't hide from it anymore. The woman hated her. Maybe she always had. But it didn't matter now. For Crystal, it was all over. In a single night she had grown up, and her last tie to her family had been severed.

But Boyd was staring at Olivia in open fury.

"Look at her! She should be in the hospital, but she was afraid to go last night." And he had been afraid to force her.

"She's a tramp. Who were you with yesterday? You never came home last night."

"I did come home . . . Tom was in the barn . . . he wouldn't let me go. He was drinking." Her voice was dead, as were her eyes. Something in her had died the night before. Something in her that, in spite of everything, had once loved her mother, but never would again. They had betrayed her.

"I should throw you out of here. Go to your room!"

Boyd couldn't believe what he was hearing and he turned to Crystal and looked down at her with fresh compassion.

"Come home with me, Crystal. Don't stay here."

But Crystal only shook her head. She had to finish it here now, and she wasn't going till she did that. Whatever that meant, whatever it took. But she was staying until she left for good. And somehow she suspected her mother knew it and was glad. She didn't know why, but she sensed that her mother wanted her to leave the ranch. And she would. In time. When she was ready.

Boyd was looking at her. "Crystal, please

. . . don't stay here." But Crystal didn't move. She stared at him with unseeing eyes, thinking only of what she had to do, and her mother strode to the door and threw it open.

"I told you to get out of here, Boyd Webster, or didn't you hear me?"

He stood with his legs braced as though to fight her. "I'm not going."

"Do I have to call the sheriff?"

"I wish you would, Mrs. Wyatt."

"It's okay, Boyd . . ." Crystal spoke up finally. "I'll be all right. Go on home . . ." He didn't want to leave her. But her eyes told him that he had to. "I'll be okay . . . just go on home. . . ." She sounded quiet and strong, and her eyes were old and sad as he hesitated for a long moment and then walked slowly to the door, with a look over his shoulder at Crystal.

"I'll come back later." He slammed the door and a moment later, his truck roared away as her mother approached her filled with accusation, but she wasn't prepared for what Crystal did next. As her mother turned on her with fresh venom, her arm raised to slap the battered girl, Crystal grabbed her arm, and held it so hard the older woman winced, and suddenly shrank from her in terror.

"You stay away from me, you hear? I've

taken all I'm going to take from you, Ma . . .
you and Tom and everyone else around here!"
Her voice was shaking and her eyes were suddenly blazing. She hated all of them, hated
them for what they had done to her, for the
love they had never offered her, and the pain
they had repeatedly inflicted. Tom's horrific
deeds of the night before were the culmination
of all of it. And for an instant she wondered if
her mother had treated her differently since
her father died, whether Tom would even have
dared lay a hand on her. But he knew no one
gave a damn . . . what difference would it
make? But it was going to make a lot of difference to him now. She moved past her mother,
and went to the cupboard where her father had
kept his guns. They were all still there, except
the ones Jared used, and she was taking one, as
her mother began to scream, and her brother
walked in the door, and looked at the hysteri-
cal scene with total confusion.

"What the hell . . . Crys . . . for chrissake, Sis, what are you doing?" He saw the
look in her eyes and thought she was going
after their mother, as Olivia screamed incoherently, and their grandmother stared in mute
horror.

"Stay out of this, Jar!" She pointed the gun
briefly at him, and when he saw her looking at

him, he thought for a minute that she had gone crazy.

"Give me that!" He reached for the gun, and she butted him with it, just hard enough to let him know she meant business.

"She's going to kill Tom!" Her mother screamed, and Crystal turned on her with the rage none of them had ever seen before, the rage that had been building for months, born of helplessness and despair, and the sorrow of losing her father, and the total frustration of watching Tom destroy everything he had worked so hard to build. But none of them understood that.

"You're damn right I am!" She looked Jared straight in the eye, and all vestiges of childhood had fallen from her. She looked almost beautiful as she stood there in the white heat of her anger, in spite of her uncombed hair and the ugly hue of her bruises. "And if you want to know why, go look in the barn."

"What the hell's he done now?" Jared looked worried, he'd probably gotten drunk again, and shot one of the horses. But he was more worried about what his sister was about to do in retaliation.

"Why don't you ask him?" Her lavender eyes were like icicles as she looked from her mother to her brother.

But Olivia was screaming again. "Don't believe her! She's lying!"

"What makes you think so, Mama?" Crystal's voice was strangely quiet, and with the gun pointed at them, she seemed to have regained her composure. She wasn't his victim anymore, she was going to kill him for what he'd done, and the thought of it made her feel a whole lot better. "Why do you think he wouldn't do it? Why am *I* always wrong?" She started to cry then, but they were tears of rage mixed with tears of sadness. It was so damn painful to admit once and for all that her own mother didn't love her. "Remember . . ." Her hands were trembling as she held her father's rifle, but she kept it pointed alternately at Jared and her mother, and no matter what they did, she wasn't going to let them stop her. "Remember . . . when I was a little girl, Ma . . . you loved me then, didn't you? . . . you said I never told you lies, like Jar or Becky . . . and I didn't . . . I never did . . . I loved you then too . . ." For an instant, she almost faltered. "Why do you hate me so much now? Ever since Daddy died, you act like I did something to you . . . but I never did . . . I never did . . . did I?" She was asking the room at large, and at first there was no answer. But all the hatred she suspected was in her mother's voice as she growled her answer.

"You know what you've done. Sweet-talked your father, didn't you . . . singing to him all the time . . . riding around with him like a little tramp . . . and at the end . . . you must have talked him up real sweet. . . ." She looked bitterly at Crystal, who still understood none of her mother's anger and resentment.

What Olivia was saying didn't make any sense. "What are you talking about?"

"You know what I'm talking about, you little conniving tramp. You got what you wanted, didn't you? But you're not going to get anything from me, not as long as I'm alive anyway," and then suddenly, terror filled her eyes as she stared at her daughter. It was obvious that she thought Crystal was going to kill her, as Crystal nervously fingered the rifle. But Crystal bolted for the door, as Jared stared at their mother in confusion, and as he saw Crystal fly past, he ran after her, but she was too quick for him, she had always been faster than he was. He ran after her through the fields, but she was still brandishing the rifle, and she fired in the air, and shouted a warning to stay away from her. He knew something had happened, but he still didn't know what. All he knew was that he had to stop her, before she did some-

thing crazy to Tom, or even Becky and the
children. She wasn't making sense, and he still
didn't understand what had driven her crazy.

Tom heard them coming long before they
got to the house, and seeing her flying across
the fields with a gun, he pulled his own shotgun from the rack near the door, and he was
waiting for her when she got there. She had
already fired two shots in the air, and she had
four left as Becky came screaming out behind
Tom, hysterically grabbing at him. She didn't
know what was going on, but she sensed instantly that something terrible was about to
happen.

"What are you doing?" Becky was shaking
and terrified as he shoved her roughly behind
him and told her to get back in the house and
stay with the children. She did as he said, and
she was cowering in the living room as Crystal
confronted him and aimed the rifle at him with
trembling hands, and Jared came up breathless
behind her.

"Put it down, Sis." He spoke quietly, afraid
of what she'd do, but Tom only grinned. He
looked drunk, as usual, but his hands looked
terrifyingly steady as he pointed the shotgun at
Crystal.

"Nice to see you again, Crystal. Is this a
social call or are you just out hunting with

Jared?" He looked unperturbed, as Jared stood helplessly beside her.

"Tom, put the gun down. Both of you, stop it." Jared looked terrified. They had both obviously gone crazy, and suddenly as he looked at his sister, he knew what had happened to her, and for an instant he wanted to take the gun from her himself and kill his brother-in-law, but there was no wresting the rifle from her hands, as she aimed it at Tom's head, and then lowered it to his crotch with satisfaction.

"I came to thank you for last night." Her voice shook as they each held their guns trained on each other. "You're not going to do that to anyone again, are you, Tom?" She wanted him to be afraid, to cry, to plead, to beg, as she had done the night before, but he only leered at her, the taste of her still fresh on his lips, like the ugly grin he wore. And then, with no warning, she took a shot between his legs, but it missed him. And without waiting to see if he'd been hit, he let both shots fly at her. One whistled past her ear, and as she turned in startled horror at the sound, she saw Jared fall beside her. He had been shot clean through the head, and he fell dead instantly, the blood splattering everywhere, as Crystal knelt beside him. There was a distant scream from somewhere, and all she could remember later was

Tom leering over her, and Becky screaming, as Crystal lay cradling Jared in her lap, sobbing and holding him, but he was gone. And it was her fault. She might as well have shot him herself . . . he was dead . . . dead . . . as Tom quietly walked up and took her father's rifle away from her, and walked back inside to call the sheriff.

CHAPTER 13

The sheriff came half an hour later, and Jared was still lying in the field in Crystal's arms. They led her away, and their questions were all a blur afterward. She remembered the ambulance coming for Jar and her mother screaming hysterically as Becky sobbed and held her. She remembered the children staring at her, and the sheriff telling her she had done a terrible thing, and then trying to explain to him that she hadn't shot Jared. But they knew. And then it all came out, what Tom had done, and they'd gone to the barn to look, and her blood was still there on the barn floor. They had taken her to the hospital then and Boyd and Hiroko had come with her. They signed statements about the condition she'd been in the night before, and photographs were taken of all her bruises. The sheriff let her stay with the Websters instead of putting her in jail, and they went to the inquest with her. She was to be charged with attempted murder, but Tom wanted them to drop the charges against her, because it meant being charged with rape and manslaughter himself. The judge called it an accident then, and Tom was accused of statutory rape, and in the end all charges were dropped, and Jared's death was declared to be of accidental causes. They all left the courthouse together, and Crystal didn't see Tom or her mother again until Jared's funeral. She sat in the back of the church with Boyd and Hiroko, and by then it was all over the local papers.

All of Jar's friends were there, and the girl he'd been seeing in Calistoga. Everyone cried, including Tom, who looked accusingly at Crystal as he left the church. He was a pallbearer for his brother-in-law, which made Crystal's stomach turn, but Olivia had wanted it that way. In her mind, his death wasn't Tom's fault, but Crystal's, and he was laid to rest in a simple grave beside his father. It was a day Crystal would never forget, and she stood staring blindly at the sky, thinking of them both, and how different life had once been. It was all over now. For all of them. There was nothing left but anger and guilt and lies, and the sorrow of losing her father and her brother. And as Boyd led her away, she stopped for a moment to look at her mother.

"Don't come back to the ranch again, Crystal. Your father's not here to defend you now, and I know what you are. We all do. You're a murderess and a tramp and you don't belong here, no matter what you made your Pa believe before he died." Her venom was limitless for her youngest daughter, but Crystal only shook her head, her own rage spent. She would have to live for a lifetime, knowing that her anger had cost her brother's life. And she would have done anything now to change that, even if it meant letting Tom go unpunished. There was no taking back what he'd done anyway, no changing it, no restoring her to what she had been, or bringing Jared back to life. His life was over, and hers was marred forever.

"You won't have to fight me, Ma." She spoke quietly. "I don't want to come back. I don't ever want to see the place again. It's all yours. I'm going."

"How about putting that in writing for me and your Mama?" Tom spoke from just behind her, and the smell of him almost made her retch as she fought to ignore him.

"You don't need it in writing. I'm leaving here tomorrow." But there was nothing for her to leave anyway, except a piece of land she had once loved. The people she cared about were gone, the only ones left might as well have been strangers.

"See that you don't come back." Tom's voice was a low rumble, as Boyd stepped forward and took her arm.

"Come on, Crystal. Let's go now." He held her arm firmly and led her away, and as they drove away, tears slid silently down her cheeks and Hiroko gently patted her hand, as she looked out the window. There was nothing anyone could say. The course of life had been irreversibly altered, and Jared's had been ended. He'd been barely more than a boy, and he was gone. Crystal didn't say a word all the way back to the Websters', and when they got there, she left them and went for a long walk alone. She walked through the tall weeds behind their house, and for miles, following the creek, singing softly to herself . . . the songs her father and brother had once loved, and as she sang "Amazing Grace," their memories seemed to engulf her. There was no one to hear her now, no one to care, and worse still, no one to love her. And as she walked back to Boyd and Hiroko's house, she knew a loneliness she had never felt before, a loneliness so powerful she wondered for a moment if she would even survive it. But she knew she had to go on. She had to do what she had promised her father and herself years before. She had to go on now, to other worlds, other places. Alone. But with their memories always close beside her. And with the memory of Jar was the guilt she knew she would carry for a lifetime. If she hadn't gone after Tom with her father's rifle, he would never have died. In a way, it was as though she had killed him herself, and she knew now that she would have to live with that knowledge forever. Nothing would ever change it, or make the hurt any better. Nothing would ever make her less guilty of it, no matter what happened in her life, in her mind she had killed her brother, as though she had squeezed the trigger herself.

And as she wandered back slowly through the tall grass, she sang the songs they had sung together as children, as the tears coursed down her cheeks, and she looked up at the sky in lonely sorrow.

"Good-bye, Jar . . ." She whispered the words she hadn't said to him in so long. ". . . I love you. . . ."

CHAPTER
14

Crystal stayed with Boyd and Hiroko for a few days. She had meant to leave the day after the funeral, but she was so overwhelmed with guilt and grief that she couldn't. She needed a few days just to catch her breath. She played with Jane, and went for long walks alone, and Hiroko let her be. She knew exactly what she needed.

Crystal had gone home briefly before the funeral to collect her things, and she had retrieved her small cache of money from the mattress. Boyd and Hiroko had tried to talk her into staying long enough to finish school, but she knew that she couldn't. She couldn't have faced anyone there, overnight she had outgrown them. She was due to graduate in six weeks, but it no longer seemed to matter. She had to leave now and she knew it.

"But where will you go?" Hiroko looked deeply worried as they finished dinner two days after she got there.

"San Francisco." She had already made her mind up. She had five hundred dollars. It would get her a room, and she was determined to get a job somewhere as a waitress. For long enough to make some more money, and then she was going to Hollywood. She had nothing to lose now and she knew she had to try it.

"You're too young to move to the city alone." Boyd looked at her worriedly and there were tears in Hiroko's eyes too, but Crystal knew that she could handle anything, the child in her had been killed, as surely as Tom's bullet had killed Jared.

"How old were you when you were drafted?"

"Eighteen."

She smiled sadly at him. "That must have been a lot rougher than moving to San Francisco."

"That's not the point. I had no choice."

"Neither do I." She said it quietly. Her hair

was pulled back from her face in a long braid, and he could already see that the bruises were starting to heal, although she still had a hell of a shiner. But even with her bruises, she was beautiful. And there was a quiet strength about her now that there was no denying. It was time for her to move on, and she knew it better than anyone. Her days in the valley were over forever.

Boyd drove her to the bus depot the day she left, and they waited for the bus together. She promised to let him know where she was and to write, and for a long moment they both had to fight back tears as he hugged her. She had said good-bye to Hiroko at the house and that had been even harder.

"Take care of yourself, kid," Boyd said. She was like a sister to him, and he and Hiroko were all she had left now. They were the only family she cared about, the only family she had anywhere, and it was agonizing to leave them, but there was a whole world waiting for her, a world full of new hope and promise. And she was young enough to make a new life for herself somewhere, a life without people like Tom Parker.

She waved good-bye to Boyd as she boarded the bus, and blew him a kiss, as the men on the bus watched with envy. And then, in silence, she watched the valley slip away, and in spite of the painful memories she carried with her, she felt a stirring of excitement.

The world was full of exciting places she wanted to see, and San Francisco was only the first stop, and after that, who knew where the winds of fortune would take her.

CHAPTER
15

The bus stopped at Third and Townsend and she got out and looked around. Everything looked busy, and exciting, and dirty. She had only been to San Francisco twice, once with her father when she was a child, and once with Hiroko and Boyd when they christened the baby. But this was a different part of town, and it was seedy and ugly. There were drunks lying on the street, cars rushing by, there was a smell of beer and wine and unwashed bodies, but still she felt a sense of adventure. She bought a map at the bus station, and a newspaper and sat down to study them, as passersby glanced at her. She was simply dressed, with her old suitcase in her hand, but she was still very striking. And she knew she had to find a room before nightfall. The question was where, and she had absolutely no idea where to start looking. There were several rooms advertised, and boarding rooms in Chinatown, but she wasn't sure where to start. She just had to take a chance and start somewhere. She picked out two addresses and went outside to hail a cab, and she asked the driver which of the two neighborhoods was safer. He recognized instantly that she was from out of town, and he stared at her in her blue dress, her hair pulled back in a ponytail. She looked young, but he had never seen anyone as pretty as she was. He wondered what she was doing in San Francisco all alone, he had a granddaughter her age, and he wouldn't have liked her hanging out at Third and Townsend.

He looked at the paper for her, and suggested a listing Crystal hadn't even noticed. It was in an Italian district near Telegraph Hill, somewhere in North Beach.

"Let's try this one first. It sounds better than the other two, and it shouldn't be too expensive." She didn't notice that he never threw the flag. He could afford to give a little gift to a kid like her. He wasn't going to charge her a dime, she was so young and pretty he wanted to help her. "You here to visit friends?" He suddenly wondered if she was a runaway, but she didn't look as though she was hiding from anyone. She just looked like a young kid in the big city for the first time, as he glanced at her again in the mirror. She told him she wasn't visiting anyone, with a cautious look in his direction, and she tried to look confident as they chatted. She didn't want him to know how green she was. "Where you from?"

"The Alexander Valley. North of Napa." She felt sad as she said the words. It seemed days instead of hours since she'd left it.

"Just visiting?"

"No," she said quietly, looking out the window. "I'm going to live here." For a while. And then who knew? The world was waiting to open its doors to her, just as her father had promised. And yet the pain of leaving the old world was still fresh as they drove toward North Beach.

They crossed Market Street and looked east. He drove her past the piers on the Embarcadero, and then back up through Chinatown, and beyond it to North Beach, where the address was. It was a small, simple house with clean curtains in the windows, and two old women were sitting on the stoop, talking animatedly, their hair pulled tightly back in buns, wearing aprons over their black dresses. They reminded her for an instant of Grandma Minerva, and then she forced the thought from her mind. Her days in the valley, and all its memories and people were behind her. She thanked the driver, and asked him how much she owed him.

"Nothing . . . it's all right. . . ." He sounded gruff and he looked embarrassed, but he wouldn't let her pay him. She was just a kid after all, and so pretty and so young, it had been nice just looking at her. She thanked him and he watched as she approached the two old ladies, carrying her suitcase. And then he drove away, whistling to himself, hoping she'd be okay. She was young, but she was a real beauty, and she looked like she could take care of herself. The two old women noticed it too as she asked them about the room for rent. They stared at her for a minute before answering her, and said something to each other in Italian.

"Excuse me?" She looked suddenly even younger as she set her suitcase down, and a halo of pale hair seemed to frame her face. The two women were staring at her and she wondered what they were thinking. "The room? . . . do you know anything about it?"

"How come you not in school?" The older of the two eyed her suspiciously, fingering her apron. She had big black eyes, and a face covered with wrinkles.

"I graduated last year," she lied, and the women continued to look her over. "Could I see the room?" She wasn't going to let them intimidate her.

"Maybe. You got a job?" She sat back against the steps and Crystal smiled, trying to show a confidence she didn't quite feel yet. What if she needed a job to get a room, what would she do then? She was beginning to panic, but decided to tell the truth, at least part of it. She had to.

"Not yet. I just got here this afternoon. I'm going to start looking for a job as soon as I find a room."

"Where you from?"

"A few hours north of here."

"Your mama and papa know you're here?" Like the cabdriver, she wondered if Crystal had run away from them, but Crystal shook her head with eyes that told the old woman nothing.

"My parents are dead." She said it with such quiet strength that for a moment the woman didn't speak. And then slowly she stood up, still staring at her. She had never seen a girl who looked quite like her, the pale hair, the long legs, the delicately carved face. She looks like a movie star, she had said to her friend in Sicilian.

"I'll show you the room. You see if you gonna like it."

"Thank you." Crystal looked quiet and self-possessed as she picked up her suitcase.

It was a tiny airless room. There were four of them on one floor in what had once been the woman's home. Now there was a total of six rooms that the old woman was renting, and all of them shared a single bathroom. The woman herself had the only room with its own bath. It was on the main floor, next to the kitchen, which, for another five dollars a month, the tenants were allowed to use. The room itself was forty-five dollars a month, and it was bare and looked out on the building behind it. But to Crystal, it was worth it. She didn't know where else to go. And it was clean enough. There was a heavy lock on the door, and she sensed that she would be safe here, with the old woman watching the comings and goings of her boarders.

"You pay me one month in advance, cash. And you wanna move out, you give me two weeks notice." Not that they ever did. They came and they went, but she kept the place clean, and she only tolerated decent people. No drunks, no prostitutes, no men who dragged women in. She only wanted clean, quiet types, like Crystal. There were two elderly men, and a young girl living on the third floor, and on the same floor as Crystal's room there were three girls, and a young man who sold insurance. "You don't get a job, you can't keep the room, unless you got enough money without one."

"I'll find work as soon as I can." Crystal looked her squarely in the eye. She peeled four tens and five singles out of her billfold. It was the money she had earned working at the diner, and she was grateful she had saved it. The other girls her age spent it on nylons and movies and sodas, but Crystal had saved almost every penny she earned, and had hidden it from her mother. "Are there any restaurants near here looking for help?"

The old woman laughed. There were plenty of them, but she knew none of them would hire Crystal. "You speak Italian?"

Crystal shook her head with a smile. "No, I don't."

"Then you gotta look somewhere else. They don't hire girls like you around here." She was too pretty and too young, and they only hired Italian men to be waiters in the restaurants in

North Beach. "Maybe downtown." But when Crystal began looking the next afternoon, none of the places she tried wanted to hire her, even though she told them that she'd had experience in a diner. They just laughed, and most of them wouldn't even let her leave the number of the pay phone at Mrs. Castagna's. She was discouraged as she bought a sandwich and took it back to her room, and Mrs. Castagna was sitting on the steps as usual, watching her tenants come and go, and chattering with the people she knew on the street, in her own dialect.

"You find a job?" She eyed Crystal as she walked slowly up the stairs. Her feet hurt in her uncomfortable shoes, and the blue dress looked as wilted as she did. And she shivered in the chill air as the fog rolled in. It was May, but it was a lot colder than it had been in the valley, and she wasn't used to it yet. She lit the little gas stove in her room with a nickel. Mrs. Castagna saw to it that her tenants got nothing for free. She wasn't going to support anyone. She had raised ten children in that house, and they were grown and gone now. She was making good use of their rooms, and the house brought her a decent income. Unlike Crystal, who counted her dwindling funds with nervous fingers as she sat in the room's only chair, and looked at the crucifix over the bed. The only other decoration was a colored drawing of the Virgin Mary, painted by one of Mrs. Castagna's daughters, who, Crystal later learned, was in a convent. The others were married and had kids, and visited home frequently on Sundays.

Crystal pounded the streets for two weeks, and was beginning to panic at not having found a job yet. She had started to wonder if she ever would, as she walked home late one night. She had tried to find a job in Chinatown, as a cashier, or even a dishwasher, but they only laughed at her, as they had two days before in North Beach. She was always the wrong color, the wrong sex, and spoke the wrong language. But that night, she walked home through the famous Barbary Coast. There were nightclubs and restaurants, and couples walking down the street arm in arm, laughing and talking. Unlike North Beach, it seemed bright and alive, and a great deal flashier. She was wearing a blue skirt and a white blouse, and the white pumps she'd had for years, and a sweater she had borrowed from Mrs. Castagna. It was black, like everything else she owned, and ten sizes too big, but the old woman felt sorry for her, shivering in the cold at night. The only other thing she had that was warm was an old sheepskin jacket she used to wear riding in the early mornings with her father. Her wardrobe was a far cry from what she saw women wearing in stylish San Francisco. But she didn't care anymore. All she wanted was a job, doing anything, scrubbing floors if she had to. It was a far cry from her dreams of Hollywood, but she had to eat and pay Mrs. Castagna. She had to earn a living somehow. She had decided to try the hotels the following week but thought she'd give the restaurants one last try, as she stood outside an elaborate facade with a sign that said simply HARRY'S. Everything was garish here, and there was a smaller sign that promised a floor show.

Crystal wandered hesitantly inside, oblivious to the stares of the couples who were leaving. They were well dressed and a number of the women wore low-cut dresses. She stood for a long time watching a man on the stage with two musicians accompanying him as he sang Cole Porter's "Too Darn Hot." And then the headwaiter hurried over to her, and asked her brusquely what she wanted.

"You can't come in here unless you're joining a party." They didn't want hookers at Harry's, or rubberneckers who stood in the doorway catching the show for nothing, but it was obvious, even to him, that Crystal was no hooker. In her outsized sweater and worn-out clothes, she looked more like an orphan. "What do you want?"

She looked him straight in the eye, and tried to pretend her knees weren't shaking. "A job. I'll do anything. Wash dishes, wait on tables, anything . . . I need a job very badly." He started to say something to her, and then looked at her more closely. She was so pretty it made your heart ache just to look at her, and her eyes seemed to reach out and touch you. He had been about to turn her away, and then suddenly he wondered if Harry would like her. He glanced at his watch and wondered if the boss would still be upstairs, but it was too late, and he knew that he wasn't.

"You ever work in a restaurant before?" He straightened his bow tie and kept an eye on the tables, but his eyes kept coming back to her. She had a face that made you want to stop and stare at her for a lifetime. But she seemed totally unaware of the effect she had had on him. There was an openness about her and a certain gutsiness, despite her obvious nervousness, and he instantly liked her. "Ever been a waitress?"

"Yes." For fear that he'd turn her away, she didn't tell him it had been in a diner.

And then he looked at her more closely. "How old are you?"

"Eighteen." She told the lie as though she wouldn't know how to tell one.

He started to shake his head at her, glancing at the door through which she had entered. "You gotta be twenty-one to work here. It's the law."

"Then I'm twenty-one . . . please . . ." Her voice was gentle and her incredible blue eyes smiled as part of him melted. "Please . . . no one will ever know."

"Christ," he almost groaned, "the boss will kill me." But she sensed that he was relenting.

"I'll work hard. I swear I will. Just try me for a few days . . . a week . . . anything . . ." Her eyes reached out to him and he knew he couldn't turn her down. She was just too pretty, so vulnerable and so young, and something told him she needed the job and would work hard. What the hell, he could tell Harry he didn't know. And they could can her if she was no good. He glanced back at her, and saw her watching him with earnest concentration.

"All right, all right. Come back tomorrow afternoon. One of the girls will give you a uniform. And put some makeup on. You look like a kid like that. And for chrissake," he growled, "get rid of that sweater."

"Yes, sir." She grinned, looking like a kid

again and she smiled up at him as he stared at
her. He had never seen anyone as beautiful as
this girl . . . and she was eighteen . . . He
just prayed Harry wouldn't find out, or he'd
kill him.

"Be here at four o'clock. Sharp."

"Yes, sir. Thank you." Her voice was husky
as she thanked him. It was a wonder no one
else had snapped her up. With those looks they
could have made her a dancer, or even a strip-
per. But she was too innocent for that. There
was a lot more to Crystal Wyatt than he
thought, as she hurried out the door before he
could change his mind, and almost ran all the
way back to Mrs. Castagna's.

The first thing she did was return Mrs. Castagna's sweater with her thanks, telling her
that she was now working. She said it with
pride and confidence, as though she'd been
made president of General Motors.

"You got a decent job?" Mrs. Castagna eyed
her suspiciously. The girl was too pretty for
her own good. Already the man who sold insurance was hanging out in the halls, hoping to
run into Crystal on the way to the bathroom.
But Crystal seemed not to notice him. She was
quiet and she handled herself well. She didn't
run around flirting with men or acting cheap.
She was decent and polite. She stayed in her

room and never even used the kitchen. And for reasons Mrs. Castagna couldn't yet explain, she liked her.

"I'm working in a restaurant," Crystal told her proudly, and the old woman smiled at her. She was a sweet girl and she reminded her of one of her granddaughters.

"Doing what?"

"Waiting on tables."

"Good." The old woman pretended to growl at her, but it was no secret that she liked her. She was a good girl, and she hadn't given her any trouble. "Make sure they pay you. The rent is due in ten days. And it's too late this month to give me notice." She put the fear of God into all of them. It kept them in line. But it only made Crystal smile. She could see through her, and she liked her too.

"I know, Mrs. Castagna. But I'm not moving out."

"That's good, that's good." She waved and went back to her kitchen as Crystal left.

The next afternoon she walked the dozen blocks to Harry's on the Barbary Coast, excited and thinking about work, wondering if it would be very different from the diner.

She appeared at exactly four o'clock, with her hair pulled back tightly in a tidy knot, and wearing the lipstick she had bought that morning in Woolworth's. It was red and a lot too bright for her creamy face, but when she'd looked in the mirror, she had decided she looked a lot older.

The maître d' who'd hired her the night before introduced himself as Charlie and put her in the care of an older but very attractive waitress named Pearl. She laughed and said that it was really Phyllis, but no one had called her that since she was a kid. She said she'd worked there for years, and she had been a dancer long before that. She helped Harry out now and then by hoofing for him when one of the performers didn't show up, or singing if they wanted her to. She had known Harry for years, and she didn't tell Crystal that long ago, she had been his mistress. She looked Crystal over carefully, found her a clean uniform, and showed her around the kitchen.

"Things get pretty busy round about eight. But it slacks off a little by ten, and then they come in again for the last show at midnight." It was as much a restaurant as a nightclub, Crystal realized fully now, and she was excited as she looked around her. She hoped that they would keep her. Pearl invited her to dine with them, and the rest of the help, before they opened. And as she listened to the comfortable chatter around her she knew that she loved it.

There were waiters and waitresses, and bus-
boys, and cooks and dishwashers in the
kitchen. It was a bigger place than she'd realized, and she decided it was just as well she
hadn't known or she would never have dared
to go in and ask for work. And then, with a
smile, she realized she didn't even know how
much they would pay her. Pearl told her she
could keep her tips, and if anyone got drunk
and gave her a rough time, all she had to do
was tell Charlie, the maître d', or one of the
bartenders.

"It's a nice place to work," Pearl explained,
"they don't make us take much shit here. Harry's a great guy." The warmth of memory
touched her eyes as Crystal watched her. And
then, much to Crystal's horror, "You a virgin?" Crystal stared at her in silence and suddenly Pearl laughed. "No, not like that, hell,
who is?" although Crystal looked as though
she might have been. "I meant you ever
worked in a place like this before?"

Crystal laughed, relieved at having the question explained. She lowered her voice and explained conspiratorially, "Actually, I worked
in a diner back home."

Pearl grinned and patted one of Crystal's
slender hands. "Then you got a lot to learn,
sweetheart. Stay close to me and I'll teach

you." Crystal thanked her lucky stars for Pearl, particularly later when they got busy. It was hard waiting on tables, with Charlie keeping an eye on her, and people expecting her to remember what they wanted, but she fought to keep it all straight and when she served her last dinner, she knew she'd done well and Pearl confirmed it. And she had made twenty-one dollars in tips. It was almost exactly half a month's rent. She wanted to run home and tell Mrs. Castagna.

"You want a ride?" Pearl had an old car, and they left together that night, as Crystal accepted gratefully. Her feet were killing her as she thought of buying new shoes before the next evening.

"Thanks for the ride." She smiled winningly at her new friend as they pulled up in front of Mrs. Castagna's on Green Street.

"Any time. This where you live?" Pearl looked up at the house curiously. "You live with your folks?"

"No," Crystal shook her head quietly, "I rent a room here."

Pearl nodded, thinking that eventually she could do better. She was the kind of girl men would tip heavily, just for the pleasure of talking to her, and hoping to win her favor.

"Good night," she called, and waved, as she

opened the door with her key, and Pearl drove away in the old Chevy. And for the first time in weeks, Crystal slept peacefully that night, she was exhausted. But she was working, and she had made an absolute fortune. And as she drifted off to sleep, she decided she loved San Francisco. It was a long way from home, but that was exactly what she wanted.

CHAPTER
16

Crystal met Harry two weeks after she'd started working in his restaurant. The job was hard, but the pay was fair, and the tips she got every night were terrific. The people who worked there were friendly to her, and many of them, sensing how young she was, took her under their wing and treated her almost like a daughter. For the first time since her father's death, people were kind to her, and she felt welcome. And suddenly, she seemed to blossom. There was no one shouting at her, no one resenting her for who and what she was. She hummed to herself all the time, and the minute she got to work, she looked happy. Harry had heard a lot about her, and he was curious about the girl everyone said was a knockout. He was sure they were exaggerating, but the moment he laid eyes on her, he knew they weren't. He was watching her from across the room, and later Crystal saw him conferring with Pearl but she didn't have time to wonder what they were saying. A little while later, Pearl signaled her, and Crystal felt suddenly nervous as she approached them. She wondered if he knew she was not yet eighteen, and if she was going to get fired, as she approached the table where they were talking.

"This is Harry, Crystal. The Boss." She shook his hand, feeling scared, but her smile showed none of her fears as Harry stared at her in fascination. She was even prettier than they'd said. She was stunning.

"Hello, Harry." Her voice was deep and gentle as he watched her. Looking at her was like finding diamonds in your bathtub.

"I hear you've been doing a good job." He'd heard a lot more than that but he didn't tell her. "You like it here?"

"Yes. A lot." She smiled shyly at Pearl, who looked back at her proudly. She'd taken an interest in her, and at times it was almost like having a daughter.

"Pearl tells me you can sing a little bit." He was understating the case, but he wanted to move on her with caution. "Ever think about singing on a stage?" Crystal shook her head with a look of amusement. "You might like it." Crystal seemed to hesitate as he glanced at Pearl. "Pearl could teach you a thing or two, and with a face like yours, we could put you on the stage one night and see how you like it." He was trying to sound casual so as not to scare her off, but he already had a plan in mind, and he'd been talking to Pearl about it for the last half hour. With her looks it was crazy just having her run in and out of the kitchen with dinners.

"Want to give it a try?" He looked encouraging and for a minute, Crystal felt a rush of excitement. She loved to sing, and the idea of doing it for an audience in a restaurant made her tingle. She wanted to hug him for giving her the chance, but she tried to look cool as she nodded.

"I'd like that." And then she laughed her soft, husky laugh. "What if they throw rotten eggs?"

"Then we take you off quick." He grinned. He was a nice man, and Crystal liked him. "You wanna see if Pearl here can teach you a few things? She sings pretty good and she's a

damn fine dancer, was anyway, before she hurt
her ankle." He had met her years before, when
she was working at the Fox Theater, and
they'd been lovers for years, although they
weren't any longer. He had only given her the
job years later, when she couldn't dance anymore, and all she could do was wait on tables,
but he still had a soft spot for her. It showed in
the way he looked at her and talked about her
dancing. "Let Pearl show you a thing or two,
okay, kid?"

"Okay." She said the word breathlessly,
smiling at Pearl, as he walked away. She wondered what would happen if she couldn't do it.
She waited until he was out of earshot and
then looked at Pearl. "Think I can do it?" She
wanted to very badly as Pearl nodded thought-
fully, wondering for a moment if Harry might
fall for Crystal. She was so beautiful but she
hadn't done anything to encourage him. She
didn't have to.

"Don't worry. You'll do fine. And when
they hear that voice of yours, they're gonna go
crazy. I'll teach you a few tricks and a few
dance steps. They're gonna love you. Come in
tomorrow at two, and we'll fool around for a
while with the piano." She looked at the girl,
envying her her youth, and yet she liked her
too much to resent her.

"You don't mind doing it?" Crystal looked at her gratefully, and Pearl laughed.

"Hell, no. It's fun for me." She shrugged then with a nostalgic smile. "I don't mind doing it for Harry."

Crystal met her there the following afternoon, and Pearl showed her a few simple steps. And Crystal was impressed at how limber she was, and how graceful.

"You're good." Her eyes were bright with admiration and Pearl was touched as she shook her head almost shyly.

"Not anymore. I used to be. But it's been a hell of a long time since I broke my ankle. They never fixed it right and that was the end of it for me. But even before that, I was just an ordinary hoofer."

They played around for an hour on the stage. Pearl showed her how to move, how to hold the mike, how to dance just enough to keep her body moving to the music and then she told her to sit in a chair near the piano. "Now let's hear you sing. You don't need me to teach you how to do that. Just let it go. Sing something you like and go with it." They settled on a song Crystal knew her father had loved to hear her sing and Pearl played it by ear, as Crystal let herself drift into the music. She sang softly at first, hesitating and feeling self-conscious. And then suddenly, the memories of her father and her early years began to engulf her, and her voice grew along with the pain and the tenderness she felt. Her eyes were closed and there were tears rolling down her cheeks when she finished. And Pearl sat staring at her in silence, awestruck. She was a lot better than even Pearl had suspected. Crystal's voice had a purity and a power that would have her audience breathless. "Jesus Christ. I didn't know you could sing like that. You ought to go to L.A. and make a record."

Crystal shrugged and wiped the tears from her cheeks, as the other waitresses began to arrive for work. "Maybe one day." But she still doubted that it would ever happen. Pearl made her promise to come back and rehearse again the next day, but they both felt buoyant. It was as though they were sharing an important secret. And that night Pearl told Harry the kind of news he liked to hear. "You got yourself a winner. She doesn't know it yet, and I don't want to scare her, but she's fantastic. She's got a voice that'll knock you dead. With a little training, she could be real big one day. Wait till you hear her." Harry looked pleased and the next afternoon he snuck down from his office to listen. There were tears on his cheeks too this time, and he grinned to himself all the way back upstairs to his office.

Pearl rehearsed with her through all of May and part of June, and on a slow Thursday night, Pearl and Crystal knew she was ready. She'd rehearsed over twenty songs, and her performances for Pearl had been smooth and disarming. Harry knew she was going to sing that night and he was standing quietly off to one side, watching in nervous anticipation. Finding a girl like her was something that happened once in a lifetime.

"Good luck," he whispered, more to himself, as she got up on the stage in a pale blue satin evening gown Pearl had lent her.

She got up on the stage cautiously, with a look of sudden terror in Pearl's direction, wondering if it was a mistake to even try it, and her mentor gave her the victory sign, as the others stood in the corners of the room and waited. And then suddenly, as the spotlight hit her and the music came up, Crystal forgot that any of them were there, and began singing her heart out. She sang Billie Holiday's song "God Bless the Child," and as everyone listened, her friends stared. She was everything Pearl had said she was, and Harry had hoped for. She was extraordinary. Her voice overwhelmed everyone in the room with its unexpected power and poignancy. She brought tears to their eyes and they applauded for what seemed like hours. And as they did, Crystal knew she was where she belonged now. She had dreamed of a moment like this, and now it had come. She didn't even need Hollywood now, all she needed were these people, this place, this moment.

Afterward Harry bought her a bottle of champagne, and invited her and Pearl to sit with him, as he beamed at Crystal.

"You ever think you'd be a singer when you grew up, kid?"

"No, sir." She'd dreamed of being a movie star, but never a singer.

He patted her hand, poured her another glass of the sparkling wine, and winked at Pearl before smiling at Crystal again. "Just call me Harry."

And as she sat there, she felt her whole body tingle. She had loved it. It was a dream come true, and suddenly all the agonies of the past months were forgotten. And when she went home that night, she felt like Cinderella. She wasn't just a waitress anymore. She was someone. She was a singer. She was still grinning to herself as she walked up the stairs, and a lower door creaked loudly open. A familiar face peered up at her as Mrs. Castagna scowled.

She loved pretending to terrorize everyone, but she had developed a secret soft spot for Crystal.

"What you looking so happy about? You got a boyfriend?" Her voice resounded on the stairs, and Crystal bent over the banister to smile at her.

"Better than that . . ." She wasn't quite sure how to explain it. "I started doing something different tonight." She grinned with joy at the memory of singing at Harry's, and the endless applause that had come after.

But the scowl on Mrs. Castagna's face had deepened. "You ain't doing something bad, are you?" In the short time Crystal had lived with her, she had become her self-appointed mother, but Crystal only shook her head and smiled at the old woman.

"Of course not."

"Then what you do?"

"They let me sing tonight." She beamed as she said it, and the old woman in black looked suddenly surprised. She'd never thought of Crystal as having talent. She was just pretty and young, and she waited on tables somewhere. She paid her rent on time, and once in a while she brought Mrs. Castagna flowers when she got her paycheck.

"What kind of singing?" The old woman continued to look suspicious.

"You know, like in a nightclub."

"I don't know. I don't go to places like that." It was clear that this new development was cause for disapproval. "You come down here and tell me about this." Crystal was tired, but she didn't have the heart to refuse her. She walked slowly down the stairs, her pale hair cascading over her shoulders. She had changed back into her own clothes again, and Pearl's blue gown was carefully hung in her locker at Harry's.

Mrs. Castagna was waiting for her at the foot of the stairs, and Crystal looked down at her like a girl coming home from her first prom. Her eyes still looked dreamy and happy.

"You look like you been up to no good, Miss Crystal Wyatt. What they make you do in that place?"

"They don't make me do anything. They let me sing, on a stage, in a beautiful blue satin dress they let me wear."

"You sing good?" Mrs. Castagna narrowed her eyes, as though expecting to see something different, but all she saw was that Crystal looked happy.

"Okay, I guess. The audience seemed to like it."

Mrs. Castagna nodded, as though deciding if it was true, and then she looked back up at Crystal. "You come in and show me." She turned on her heel and walked back to the door of her own small apartment, as Crystal followed her, grinning in amusement. She sat down in her favorite chair then, and looked expectantly up at Crystal. "You sing for me. I'll tell you if I like it." Crystal started to laugh then, and sat down on a straight-backed chair.

"I can't just sing like that. It's not the same here."

"Why not?" The old woman looked non-plussed. "I got ears too. Sing."

Crystal smiled again, suddenly reminded of her own grandmother when she was a child. Minerva had liked to hear her sing too, but she had liked to hear her sing hymns. "Amazing Grace" had always been her favorite. "What would you like to hear? My grandmother used to like 'Amazing Grace.' I could sing that." It was an amazing negotiation, in the small room, with her landlady staring expectantly at her. But her taste was more eclectic than Minerva's.

"Is that what you sang tonight?"

"No . . . I sang other things . . ."

"Good. Then you sing the same for me. I'm waiting."

Crystal closed her eyes for a minute, wondering if she could do it. And then she forced herself to remember how she had felt on stage that night . . . the excitement . . . the rush . . . the headiness of the music . . . and then slowly, she began to sing one of her favorite ballads. It had been her closing song, and it had held everyone's attention. She sang it now, without the spotlight, or the piano, or the blue gown, but somehow it didn't seem to matter. All that mattered was the song again, and the words she had loved since her childhood. Mrs. Castagna seemed to fade away, and she could feel her father sitting there with her as she sang the song from beginning to end, and when it was over, the magic of her voice seemed to drift away carrying both of them with it. And when she looked at Mrs. Castagna again, she saw tears on her cheeks, and it touched her. For a moment, neither of them spoke, and then the old woman nodded.

"You sing good . . . very good . . . you never told me you could do that."

"You never asked me." Crystal smiled gently at her, tired again now, more tired than she had been before. The excitement of the night was turning to bittersweet nostalgia. She was thinking of her father, and the ranch, and the times she had sung for him. And as Mrs. Castagna looked at her it was almost as though she knew that. She got up then, without a word, and walked stiffly to an ancient credenza. She stood bent over it for a moment, and when she returned, she was carrying a bottle and two glasses.

"We're gonna drink some wine. To celebrate. One day you gonna be very famous."

Crystal laughed, and watched her open the bottle. It was half empty, and she saved it for special occasions. Crystal noticed that it was sherry.

"You got a beautiful voice. That's a gift from God. You got to treat it good, what you got is very precious."

"Thank you." For a moment, she wanted to cry as she accepted the glass of the sweet liquid, and Mrs. Castagna held her glass up to her briefly with a look of enormous importance.

"You're a very lucky girl that you can sing like that. Brava, Crystal . . . Brava!"

"Thank you." They clinked their glasses together briefly and Mrs. Castagna took the first sip with a look of contented pleasure, and then when they had both had some of the sherry, she set her glass down.

"How much they pay you for that?"

"Nothing. I mean nothing different than I was making before. It's just fun to do, that's all . . . I loved it." She was embarrassed thinking about it now. She didn't want to get paid for doing what she loved, but it sounded stupid to say it.

"You gonna make them rich. People are gonna come from everywhere to hear you."

"They come to Harry's anyway." Crystal was embarrassed by her enthusiasm, but the old woman looked shrewd as she picked up her glass again and took another sip of the sherry.

"You tell them you want more money. You got a voice like an angel." That sounded like an exaggeration to Crystal, but the audience had certainly liked her. "You hear me? You tell them you want a lot more money now. Big money, not just garbage. You gonna be famous one day. And when you are, you remember that I said it." She watched Crystal finish her sherry with a smile, and she talked to her as she would have to one of her own granddaughters, not that any of them had a talent like Crystal's. And then she looked at the young girl very gently. "You sing for me again sometime?"

"Anytime you want me to, Mrs. Castagna."

"Good." She stood up with a satisfied look. "Then you go to bed now. I'm tired."

"Thank you for the wine." She spoke softly and had a sudden urge to kiss her. It had been so long since she had kissed anyone, or anyone had taken her in their arms to hug her . . . not since her father died . . . or since she had left the Websters in the valley. But the old woman looked at her solemnly and didn't seem to invite it. "Good night . . . and thank you again."

"Go to bed . . . !" She brandished her cane at her. "Take care of your voice . . . you gotta rest now!" Crystal laughed again as she bid her good night and closed the door softly behind her.

She walked slowly up the stairs, and was thinking of her as she undressed. She was a kind old soul behind the pretense of toughness, and Crystal liked her. She thought of Pearl then too, and how kind she had been to her, but as she turned off the light and lay in her bed, her thoughts drifted back to the valley. She felt far, far from home, and after the excitement of the night, she felt suddenly homesick. And as she closed her eyes, she thought of a day long since . . . of sitting on the swing . . . and talking to Spencer. It had been two years since she'd seen him. She wondered where he was now and if he remembered her. It seemed unlikely that he would, and yet as she drifted off to sleep, she knew she would never forget him.

CHAPTER 17

The partners' dinner at Anderson, Vincent, and Sawbrook was a stupid affair they organized every year at the club, but it was a command performance for the junior members of the firm, and after some consideration, Spencer decided to invite Elizabeth Barclay. He had seen her only half a dozen times since Palm Beach. She was busy at school, and she only came to New York about once a month, allegedly to visit her brother. But she always called Spencer when she was in town, and more often than not, he took her out to dinner. It wasn't that Spencer didn't enjoy her company. He did, more than he wanted to in fact, but somehow they always wound up in bed, and she always managed to make him feel pressured. He knew she wanted more than he had to give, and he didn't want to get seriously involved, and he didn't want to disappoint her. He still had his own ideas about the kind of girl he was looking for, and Elizabeth wasn't it, although he wasn't always sure of that when he was with her, especially after he'd made love to her. There was a fierce sensuality beneath her cool exterior that drove him wild, but he wanted more than that. He wanted just what he had told her from the first, a woman who needed him, who loved him as he was, who was gentle and kind and compassionate, a woman he was head over heels in love with. He didn't want someone who was going to reshape him into the image she had in mind, and in Elizabeth's case, he suspected that that image was a portrait of her father.

But he took her to the partners' dinner nonetheless, and dancing afterward, and as usual they made love after that as he tried to convince himself that just sleeping with her wasn't going to involve him in a deeper commitment. She had said as much herself after Palm Beach, but he was never entirely sure she meant it.

It was late June, and she had finished her second year at Vassar. She was going back to San Francisco the following week, and from there to Lake Tahoe for the summer.

"Why don't you come?" she asked him innocently.

"I can't get away."

"Of course you can, Spencer, don't be silly." She was a woman who never took no for an answer. She was twenty-one now, and more sophisticated than ever. And she teased him frequently about why he had never introduced her to his parents. But he knew that if he did, he'd never get them off his back again, particularly his father. She was exactly the kind of girl they hoped he would settle down with someday, but at thirty he still knew he wasn't ready.

"Not everyone can take the summer off, my dear," he teased as they lay in bed. He knew they'd have to get up in a while, so he could take her back to her brother's apartment, although Spencer was sure he knew about their affair, and he wasn't even so sure that Elizabeth hadn't told him. "I'm a working stiff."

"So's my father, and he's taking two months off." She lay in bed and looked happily up at Spencer. She enjoyed sex, and she was careful about using birth control. She had no intention of getting pregnant. And even that annoyed him sometimes. She always thought of herself, she never took risks unless she wanted to, and it might have meant more to him if she had been afraid that she might get pregnant. But there was nothing vulnerable about Elizabeth Barclay.

"I'm not exactly in your father's shoes," he grinned, "or hadn't you noticed?" She was still pressing him about politics, but he only laughed at her. He was busy enough at the firm, and she had been impressed that night by how obviously respected he was by the senior partners.

"Wait a few years, Mr. Hill. Your star is yet to rise."

"Perhaps . . . but I sense other possibilities on the horizon." He turned over and made love to her again, and as always, it was satisfying, physically if not otherwise, and sometimes that made him feel guilty. He felt like a bastard sleeping with her, and not being in love with her. Something told him he should have been, but he just wasn't. He was in lust with her, he told himself, and maybe that was good enough, for the moment.

"Now, what about Tahoe?" she reminded him again as she lit a cigarette. "Come out for a week, two if you can manage it. My father will be thrilled to see you."

"I'm not sure he'd be so thrilled if he could see us now."

"No," she smiled as she blew smoke in his direction, "you're right. But Daddy is very old-fashioned."

"How quaint of him." Spencer grinned. She was amazing.

"And so are you."

"Am I? Old-fashioned?" He seemed surprised. "What makes you say that?"

"I always get the feeling you're waiting for bolts of lightning to come down from the sky before you decide it's right. As far as I'm concerned, Mr. Hill, this is good enough. That's all you get in this world, you know, companionship, a good screw, good friends, a job you like. You don't have to wait for violins and harps and voices of angels. That's not what life is all about." But the trouble was he still believed it was, and she didn't.

"Maybe you're right." He ran a gentle hand along the inside of her thigh, but he still wasn't convinced. He still believed in harps and violins and thunder and lightning. She knew him well, and that was comforting. But from time to time he was still haunted by the child he had last seen two years before, sitting on a swing in a blue dress, looking at him as though she was imprinting him on her heart forever.

He still remembered the color of her eyes, the feel of her skin when he touched her hand. But he also knew that was crazy.

Elizabeth was looking carefully at him, and he nervously wondered if she could read his mind. "Spencer, my darling, you're terrific in bed, but you're also a dreamer."

"Should I thank you for the first, and apologize for the latter?" It still bothered him sometimes that she was so blunt. With Elizabeth there was no poetry, no magic, only hard facts. Maybe she should have been a lawyer.

"Don't apologize, just come to Lake Tahoe."

"If I do, your parents will think we're getting engaged." That worried him too. Elizabeth Barclay wasn't the kind of girl one played around with.

"I'll handle that."

"What'll you tell them?"

"That you had business in San Francisco and I invited you to the lake. How does that sound to you?"

"Passable, except your father is smarter than that, isn't he?"

"Yes, but so am I. I won't give anything away. I promise."

He didn't want to compromise her, but more than that, he didn't want to compromise himself. But as he thought about it while they dressed, he realized that if he went, he could stop off at the Alexander Valley and visit the Websters. And maybe see Crystal again. The thought crossed his mind, and just as quickly he repressed it.

"I'll think about it," he told her as he watched her dry herself off after a shower.

"Good. I'll tell Mother you're coming. How about August?"

"Elizabeth! I told you I'd think about it!" But she only smiled, and he laughed. She was incredible. She had the subtlety of a cement mixer, but he had to admit she had great legs, as he watched her put her stockings on, and lost control of himself again. It was four o'clock that morning before he took her back to her brother's apartment. And he was exhausted when he kissed her good night and promised to call her.

CHAPTER 18

Spencer sat on the plane staring out the window, on the trip to California. He had agreed to go, finally, after several phone calls from Elizabeth in San Francisco. She insisted that it would be fun, and both her brothers and several of their friends would be there. And it wasn't that Spencer didn't want to go, it was more that he was afraid of what he'd do when he got there. For several months he had felt her subtly swaying him, convincing him subliminally of what she'd said in Palm Beach after Christmas, that they made a good team, and life didn't have much more than that to offer. He still wasn't totally convinced, but he had to admit they had a great time in bed, and there were damn few women as bright as she was. He had made a point of going out with everyone he could, as though to prove to himself that there was no one better out there. And he never heard the music and poetry that he dreamed of. The thunder and lightning, as she called it. But all he found were women who bored him to death, didn't know what he was talking about half the time and thought that Napoleon was only a dessert. He was sick of all of them, none of them had her fire, and there was something flattering about a girl who wanted him as badly as she did. After almost a year of dating her, he had to admit that she never bored him. But he had promised himself not to do anything crazy in California. He had only been able to get away for a week, and he still wanted to go to Booneville to see Boyd and Hiroko . . . and maybe . . . just maybe . . . he'd run into Crystal. He knew she was eighteen by now, and he wondered how much she had changed in two years, if she was still as beautiful as she had been, as magical and rare. He still remembered the way she had looked at him, and it made his stomach flutter a little each time he thought of her. He knew that Elizabeth would have laughed at him if he'd told her. And compared to Elizabeth, Crystal had been a child and still was undoubtedly. But by now, she would be more grown up. And he wished he could see her again, although in some ways it was hard to imagine.

When the plane landed in San Francisco, he planned to rent a car and drive straight to the lake. She had told him it was a six-hour drive, but he didn't want to waste any time staying in the city. With only six days, he wanted to get there as quickly as he could. And as he walked into the airport, he hurried toward the car rental desk, and started when he heard a familiar voice just behind him.

"Want to hitch a ride?" He turned, and she was smiling at him. She was wearing white slacks and a red sweater with the string of pearls she always wore, her shining auburn hair perfectly groomed beneath a little straw hat, and she was wearing the tiny diamond earrings that had been a gift from her mother. Elizabeth had come to meet him at the airport, and he was touched. She had style, and he liked that about her too. But then, suddenly, he was annoyed at himself. He was always taking stock, as though checking her liabilities against her assets. It was all so rational, which was so unlike him. All his life he had been a romantic. But with Elizabeth, there was never room for that. It just wasn't what mattered.

"What are you doing here?" he asked awkwardly, but it was obvious as he kissed her.

"I came to pick you up. I figured you'd be too tired to drive. How was the flight?" Not "I missed you . . . I love you" . . . but she was there at least, and that meant something.

"Thank you for coming, Elizabeth." He looked down at her with gentle eyes, the deep blue of the Pacific Ocean. "That's a long ride for you, isn't it?"

"I stayed in the city last night." She was always practical and well organized, it was one of the things about her that he admired most.

They walked briskly to the baggage claim hand in hand, and she teased him for bringing a briefcase.

"It gave me something to do on the flight."

"Too bad you didn't fly out with me, I could have found something for you to do." He liked that about her, too, she was, in the vernacular, a hot little number. "Did you bring your golf clubs, by the way?"

"No. Just my tennis racket." He had stashed it in the suitcase with his clothes.

"That's okay. My brothers can lend you theirs." In truth, he hated golf, but he didn't want to hurt her feelings. All the men in her family played golf. "We've planned a pack trip too, and my mother is absolutely insisting on a barn dance and a hayride."

"Sounds like fun. Kind of like going to summer camp. Do I get a T-shirt with my name tag sewed on, a Boy Scout knife and a mess kit?"

"Oh shut up." She kissed him on the neck, and with his bag in hand, he followed her to the car she had left outside. It was a brand-new Chevrolet station wagon with wooden sides, which they were going to keep at the lake for their summer vacations. She gave him all the news of her family, and reported that Ian and Sarah had arrived the day before. They were in high spirits, and after two weeks at the lake, they were going to Europe to visit Sarah's parents at their castle in Scotland. It was their summer home, and Elizabeth made it sound almost cozy. It was a very grand life, and Spencer offered to drive, as he swung his suitcase into the car.

"You're sure you're not too tired?" She looked as though she cared, and he smiled at her, suddenly glad he had come, in spite of all his misgivings.

But he was in no way prepared for the grandeur of their summer home. It was a huge stone mansion, with impeccably kept grounds,

and half a dozen "cabins" for guests. The so-
called cabins were bigger than most people's
houses. They arrived after midnight, but the
butler had waited up for them with hot choco-
late and sandwiches which Spencer devoured,
and a little while later Ian and Sarah walked
in, with Elizabeth's older brother, Greg. They
were all in high spirits after a midnight swim
in the lake, which Sarah assured him was absolutely freezing. They were going to go fishing
the next day, and they invited Spencer to join
them.

It was an easy, happy life, filled with laughter and interesting people. Guests arrived from
San Francisco, and there were sumptuous dinners every night, as the whole group converged
on the enormous dining room and sat together
at the long table. Elizabeth looked beautiful in
the candlelight, and Spencer enjoyed several
long talks with her father. He even played golf
with him, and apologized profusely for how
bad his game was. But Justice Barclay didn't
seem to mind, he enjoyed talking to him, and
thought his daughter had made a wise choice.
He made it obvious to everyone how much he
liked Spencer.

And Spencer was actually disappointed
when the week came to an end. He had meant
to leave a day earlier, but he didn't want to go

anywhere. He didn't even want to go back to New York and the law firm.

"Why don't you ask them for another week off?" Elizabeth suggested as they lay in their boat, basking in the warm sunshine. But Spencer laughed as he looked at her. For all her intelligence, she seemed to think that everyone was as important as her father.

"I don't think they'd be too pleased."

"I hate to see you leave." She said it quietly, and for an odd moment, she looked at him sadly. "It's going to be lonely without you."

"Surrounded by your family and ten thousand friends? Don't be silly, Liz." But he had to admit he was going to miss her too. He had even given up his plan to visit the Websters in the Alexander Valley. There just wasn't time, and it was so pleasant being with all of them. So pleasant that he was beginning to think that he loved her. "When are you coming back to New York?" They had been sneaking into each other's rooms in the main house, and suddenly the thought of another month without her depressed him.

"After Labor Day. And then I have to go back to goddamn school." She rolled over on her stomach and looked at him mournfully. They were in one of the Barclays' two speedboats.

"You make it sound like jail." He laughed softly and she smiled, and touched his lips with gentle fingers.

"Isn't it? Without you it feels like it sometimes." He suddenly wished she would be in New York. He now knew that he wanted to be with her. He looked at her strangely then, and wondered if the lightning had finally struck. He sat listening to his own inner voices, wondered if there was going to be thunder too. "What were you thinking just then?" Her eyes narrowed as she looked at him, worried at what was on his mind. He was always so elusive.

"I was thinking how much I'm going to miss you." Lake Tahoe had finally done it to him, it was the most beautiful place he'd ever seen, with the tall pines, and the vast lakes, and the beautiful mountains beyond. Everything was so easy here, so healthy and natural and happy. He loved places like that, and he wished the week would never end as she looked at him with new tenderness. She liked the look in his eyes, and what he was saying.

"I'm going to miss you too, Spence." He smiled at the silly name, but it was no sillier than "Liz," which didn't really suit her.

And then, without a word, he pulled her into his arms and kissed her. He looked startled when he finally pulled away and told her what she'd waited to hear since the first time they'd met. "I think I'm in love with you."

She smiled happily. "It certainly took you long enough."

He laughed. "That's a hell of a thing to say. I finally realize I'm in love with you, and you complain that I should have done it sooner."

"I was beginning to think I was going to be an old maid."

"At twenty-one, I don't think I'd really worry." And then he realized what she had just said, and knew with certainty that he was going to have to do something about what he felt. He couldn't keep her hanging on forever. It had been long enough, and he felt closer to her than he ever had before. It was the real thing, he told himself, she was a great girl, and just as she had said, they could do great things together. "Will you marry me, Elizabeth?"

"Is this a formal proposal?" She looked thrilled and he rolled over and got up on one knee as he smiled at her.

"Now it is. Will you?"

"Hell, yes!" She gave a whoop of joy and threw her arms around his neck, almost overturning the boat as she did.

"Wait a minute! Don't drown us for chrissake! This is not supposed to be a tragic story."

"It won't be, my love. I promise you that. It's going to have a very happy ending." And he was sure of it too as he kissed her again, and they finally started the boat and went back to shore, to tell her family. But as they docked he felt a little foolish. It was difficult sharing your most private moments with an entire family. There was nothing private about living with the Barclays.

They found her father in the living room, talking to Washington. But he turned to them with a smile as he put down the phone. Spencer knew from the look on his face that he suspected something. Elizabeth looked as though she had swallowed an entire flock of canaries.

"Yes, Elizabeth?" He smiled at them both. She already knew he was crazy about Spencer.

She didn't wait for her fiancé to speak. She wanted to tell him first. "Spencer just asked me to marry him." She beamed and turned to her future husband as though for confirmation.

"I should have done it a lot sooner than this, sir. May we have your blessing?"

Harrison Barclay got quickly to his feet and shook Spencer's hand, looking benevolently on both of them, and particularly his own daughter. "You've had that for a long time. I wish you both much happiness." He hugged her then and looked at them both seriously. "When were you planning to do it?"

"I'm afraid we haven't gotten that far yet. We'll have to talk it over."

"If I had my way, I'd like to see Elizabeth finish school, but I suppose two years is too much to ask of you young lovebirds. How about one? You could be married, say . . . in June, and Elizabeth could transfer to Columbia for her last year, that is if you're planning to stay in New York."

"As far as I know we are. June sounds fine." Spencer looked pleased and Elizabeth looked mildly disappointed.

"Why do I have to stay in school?" she whined, almost like a child, but her father answered her firmly.

"Because you're too smart not to, and Vassar is a great school. June is only ten months from now. We'll give you an engagement party in the fall and announce it formally, and you'll be busy after that, planning the wedding with your mother." And as though on cue, his wife walked into the room, smiling brightly. "Priscilla, we have great news for you." He looked from his daughter to Spencer as she waited. "The children just got engaged."

"Oh darling . . ." Priscilla Barclay was quick to embrace her daughter, and then she kissed her future son-in-law, as he stood there feeling as though he'd been swept up by a wave and carried out to sea. In a matter of minutes he'd gotten engaged, and was getting married in June. But it was what he had wanted.

They all chattered excitedly and announced it to the others over lunch. Ian was delighted, and Sarah was ecstatic. And Spencer had called his parents. And it was agreed that the engagement party would be in San Francisco, the day after Thanksgiving. Spencer assured them that he'd ask his parents to fly out. And Elizabeth announced that she wanted to be married in Grace Cathedral. She was still annoyed that she had to spend another year away at school, but Spencer mollified her by reminding her that she could come to New York every weekend.

It was an exhausting day for him, and when he went to bed that night, and waited for her, he felt overwhelmed by his own emotions. He hardly had the strength to make love to her, and he almost fell asleep in her arms, he had to force himself to stay awake long enough to remind her to get back to her own room, and the next thing he knew it was morning.

Elizabeth drove back to the city with him, and took him to the airport. She said she had some shopping to do, and wanted to spend a few days in the city. But he still felt as though he was in a daze when he kissed her good-bye, and got on the plane. He sat and watched San Francisco shrink beneath him as he headed toward New York, as it finally dawned on him. He was actually going to marry Elizabeth Barclay.

CHAPTER
19

Predictably, Spencer's parents were pleased with the news. In truth, they were both ecstatic, and they promised to go to San Francisco over Thanksgiving for his engagement. By the time Spencer had left, plans for the party were well under way, and it sounded as though the Barclays were going to invite at least five hundred people.

"She must be a lovely girl, darling," his mother said. "When are we going to meet her?" She was a little hurt that they had never met before, but Spencer promised to introduce them when Elizabeth got back from San Francisco.

And the next weeks seemed to fly by. It seemed only moments later when he was picking Elizabeth up at Idlewild, and he drove her to Poughkeepsie. He had bought the ring at Tiffany's. It was all he could afford, but it was a handsome diamond set with sapphires on either side, and she squealed with delight when she saw it. The stones weren't large but they were very good and the ring was pretty.

"Spencer, it's exactly what I wanted!" He slipped it on her finger in the car, and they decided to go back to his apartment for a few hours, before going up to Vassar. Elizabeth giggled as they lay in his bed, and she flashed her ring at him. She suddenly seemed very young and very happy. "God, I missed you so much. The rest of the summer was awful."

"It was lonely here too." And he felt better now that he saw her. He had actually had second thoughts, and had spent several nights in absolute terror, wondering what he had done, and why, but one of his closest friends had assured him it was normal. And now that he saw her again, he knew he had done the right thing. They made love for hours, and he was lonely for her all the way back from Poughkeepsie the next morning. She was going to come to New York the following weekend, and meet his parents.

And when she met them, they loved her. She was exactly the kind of girl his father had hoped he would find, and he was extremely impressed by her connections. She talked blithely about people they only read about, and even his mother was impressed by how well dressed she was, how intelligent, how ladylike. It was a match they both applauded. His father had already bragged to everyone that Spencer was marrying Justice Barclay's daughter.

Elizabeth came to New York almost every weekend after that, and in November, they all flew out to California together. The Barclays gave a beautiful Thanksgiving dinner for the family, making the newcomers feel welcome. The two sets of elders enjoyed each other's company, and the two mothers got along extremely well. It was clearly a match that had been meant to happen. Ian and Sarah had flown out for Thanksgiving and the engagement party too, although Gregory was too busy in Washington, and Elizabeth was only mildly disappointed. She and Greg weren't really close. He seemed to lead his own life, divorced from most family events and vacations.

And by then, everyone knew that Greg was involved in a messy divorce.

The party the next day was spectacular. There were four hundred guests for cocktails and a buffet supper, and the Barclay home was filled with San Francisco's most important socialites, even the mayor came, and there was dancing late into the night. Spencer thought Elizabeth had never looked lovelier, in a black velvet gown, and he held her close as they danced, and he beamed at her.

"Happy, my love?"

"Never more so." She loved introducing him to her friends. He was so incredibly handsome. All the girls she knew envied her, and he chatted with them, and Elizabeth knew they were all wildly envious of her.

The young people went for a drive the next day, and stopped for lunch in Sausalito. It was Saturday, and everyone was in a good mood, although tired after the late night the night before. They were all going out for dinner later that evening, and maybe a little dancing afterward, while their parents went to the Bohemian Club for a quiet evening. And on Monday they would all be leaving again, the young people and the elder Hills to New York, and Justice and Mrs. Barclay back to Washington.

They only had two more days and nights, and they wanted to enjoy them.

"Hell of a party last night, wasn't it?" Ian asked his future brother-in-law, as they stood looking at the bay from Sausalito.

"It was fabulous." Spencer still felt as though he were dreaming. It all seemed so unreal to him, the people, the place. And for a moment, he thought again of visiting his friends in the Alexander Valley. But once again, there was no time. This was truly a whirlwind visit.

"Wait until you see the wedding Mother puts on." Sarah was going to be Elizabeth's matron of honor.

They all went back to the house to rest for a while late that afternoon, and they were in high spirits when they went out that evening. Sarah was wearing a spectacular pink satin dress, and Elizabeth was wearing a dark blue chiffon cocktail dress she had bought at I. Magnin. She said it set off her engagement ring, and Spencer smiled as he kissed her.

Their dinner that night was excellent, and afterward they went up to the Top of the Mark for drinks, to admire the view, and Spencer looked out into the sparkling night and squeezed Elizabeth's hand. It was a beautiful sight and she was a beautiful girl, and he loved

her. They stayed there until eleven o'clock,
and when they left, Ian said he had heard
about a terrific little place to go dancing. It
was fairly close by and they even had a floor
show. The group declared in unison that it was
a great idea, and they piled back into the car
and went to the address Ian gave them. It
looked like a cozy little nightclub, and although it was crowded when they arrived,
with a hefty tip from Spencer, the maître d'
gave them a table. There was a small band
playing "Some Enchanted Evening" and Spencer led Elizabeth out on the floor to dance,
holding her close to him. He loved feeling her
next to him, and when they sat down again he
took her hand as the room darkened, and a girl
came out with a microphone in her hand. She
was wearing a pale blue satin dress and her
blond hair almost concealed her face, as the
spotlight found her and grew. Spencer caught
his breath and stared at her. As she began to
sing, he felt as though he was going to faint as
a vise clutched his heart. It was Crystal.

She was even more beautiful than he remembered her, and he could barely think as he listened to her sing. She looked ten years older
than she had before, and the body molded into
the blue satin dress showed him curves he had
never suspected. But it wasn't her body he was

staring at, it was the face that had haunted him, the eyes he remembered so clearly, the color of an August sky. And her voice tore through his soul, with a sadness and pain that he felt viscerally as he listened to her. He could hardly breathe as he stared, not noticing Elizabeth watching him. He wanted the moment never to end, but eventually she disappeared and the lights came up, as the band began playing music they could dance to again. But Spencer couldn't speak to any of them. All he wanted was to reach out and touch Crystal. And when Elizabeth looked at him she saw that his face was pale. He had pulled his hand away long since, without realizing it, as he looked raptly at Crystal.

"Do you know that girl?" She was frowning at him, disturbed by the way he had watched the girl who'd been singing. And she had watched the girl carefully, but there had been no sign of recognition. She hadn't been able to see across the lights, and she didn't know that Spencer was there as she sang about a lost love and a broken life with heartrending conviction.

"No . . . no . . . I . . . she was very good, wasn't she?" He took a long swig of Scotch, as Ian chatted with Sarah.

"She's very pretty, if that's what you mean." Elizabeth looked annoyed and wondered if he was drunk, but she didn't think he was. But whatever had come over him, he had been mesmerized, and now he looked stricken. He asked her to dance again, but he was strangely quiet afterward, and a short time later they left. It was one-thirty, and when Ian said he was tired, they all agreed it was time to leave.

Spencer made idle conversation with them in the car, but Elizabeth sensed that he was distracted. She waited until they got to the house before she asked him again, looking deep into his eyes, "Spencer, the singer at the restaurant Ian took us to . . . did you know her?"

"No." He spoke quietly, he knew he had to lie. It wouldn't make sense to her, it didn't even make sense to him. It never had. But the feeling was still there. Even more so. "She just looked like someone I used to know."

"You never look at me like that." It was the first time she had been really angry at him, and he didn't know what to say to her.

"Don't be silly." He tried to brush it off, and he kissed her good night. But she didn't come to his room that night, which was just as well. He stood for almost an hour, staring out at the bay, and thinking of Crystal. She was so much more beautiful than he had remembered her, and there was something crying out in her. It had only been a song, he knew, and yet he sensed what was behind it, the anguish and the pain, and the loneliness . . . he could still hear it now . . . along with the thunder and lightning. He smiled to himself, imagining angels' voices, and violins and harps. It was crazy and he knew it. But as he closed his eyes that night, all he could see was Crystal.

CHAPTER 20

On Sunday morning, Spencer came down to breakfast early, and chatted easily with Justice Barclay and Ian over scrambled eggs, crisp bacon, and coffee. Like her mother, Elizabeth ate breakfast in her room, and she didn't see her future husband until midmorning. Nothing was said about the night before, and she didn't ask him about Crystal again, but he sensed a strain between them until that evening.

It was their last dinner with her family, and everyone was flying back to New York the next day. And with a sense of panic, Spencer knew there would be no chance for him to go back

and see Crystal. He had thought about it all
day, and later that afternoon he had made a
phone call. And they had told him Harry's
would be open that night. He made a quiet
decision then, and he felt terrible lying to Elizabeth, but knew he had to. When he came out
of the little room where they kept the phone,
he smiled easily and told her he had called a
friend from law school.

"Do you want to invite him over for a
drink?" She had relaxed again by then. Spencer had been sweet to her all day, and she decided she'd been foolish the night before. She
had nothing to worry about, he'd probably had
a little too much to drink, and just thought the
girl was pretty.

But Spencer shook his head. "I told him I'd
drop by after dinner." But he didn't invite her
to come. She had to pack anyway, and she
wanted to talk to her mother about the wedding. They had a lot of plans to make before
Elizabeth went back to Vassar.

They had an early dinner, and Spencer's father toasted her. It was a warm, pleasant time
together after a wonderful weekend. But the
wedding seemed aeons away. She hated the
thought of having to finish the year at school,
even though Spencer insisted that it would go
quickly.

Spencer left the house at nine o'clock, and took a cab to the restaurant. He sat silently, staring out the window as they drove, feeling desperately guilty. He had just gotten engaged, and now he was running off to see another girl. It was the kind of thing he couldn't even imagine doing to her, and yet he knew he had to see Crystal before he left, or at least try to. Maybe she had changed even more than he thought, maybe she was just a very lovely bumpkin, or maybe she had become a harlot. He wanted her to be, he wanted her to be cheap and boring and stupid. He wanted her to be none of the things he had dreamed she was. And he wanted finally to be able to forget her. But before he could, he had to see her again, just once, he told himself as he paid the fare and walked quickly into Harry's.

He ordered a Scotch, and waited for her to come on again. He had decided not to approach her until after she sang. He wanted to hear her sing one more time. And when she came out, she took his breath away again. She sang to his soul as he sat and watched her. And when she left the stage, he asked the headwaiter to take her a note. In it he reminded her of their meetings in the Alexander Valley, at her sister's wedding and then the christening of their baby. It was odd realizing suddenly that she might not even remember him. But she came into the restaurant, and stood looking at him for an instant, looking as though she had seen a ghost, and as he stood up, he knew instantly that she had carried the memory for years, just as he had. She was wearing a plain white silk dress, and with her long pale hair spread over her shoulders, she looked like an angel. She stood looking at him for a long time before she spoke. Her voice was deeper than he remembered it, and she was tall and graceful, but he had never seen eyes quite like hers, eyes so full of love and pain, the eyes of a doe, he remembered now, emerging slowly from the forest. He held out a hand to her, and as she took it in her own, he thought he would melt at her touch. He had to force himself to let her go. All he wanted was to reach out and hold her. It was the same feeling she'd evoked in him before, but she had been barely more than a child then.

"Hello, Crystal." He could feel his voice shake as he spoke, and he wondered if she heard it. "It's been a long time."

"Yes, it has." She smiled at him shyly. "I . . . I didn't think you remembered me." He had thought the same, and he didn't tell her he had never forgotten.

"Of course I remember you." He tried to

treat her as a child, but it didn't work anymore. There was nothing childish about Crystal now in the close-fitting dress Pearl had helped her pick out with the money Harry had given them for "costumes." And it had paid off. People were starting to come to the restaurant, just to see Crystal. "Can you sit down for a little while?"

"Sure." She took a seat next to his, she didn't have to go on again until midnight.

"When did you come to San Francisco?" He was trying to remember how old she was, but figured that she couldn't be much more than eighteen, although now she looked a great deal older. And he knew instinctively that life hadn't been kind to her. He could hear it in the way she sang, and now he saw it in her eyes as she answered. There was something hidden there, something terrible and painful, and he felt it without her saying anything, as though he knew, and had always known everything about her. It was as though she were a part of him. And just as he had two years before, he felt irresistibly drawn to her. It was exactly what he had been afraid of.

"I came here last spring," she answered. "I was waiting on tables then, but I've been singing all summer."

"You're even better than I remembered."

"Thank you." She felt shy with him. All she wanted was to just sit there and feel him near her. "It's easy. I guess because I like it." But their words seemed to be nothing. They kept looking at each other, each wondering what the other was thinking. He couldn't stop himself then, he had to know how she was, and why he felt that something had happened to her.

"Are you all right?" His voice was gentle, and she was touched by his question. No one ever asked her that, not the way he had. No one had in a long, long time, and it brought tears to her eyes as she nodded.

"I'm okay."

And then, sensing that there was more, "What made you move to San Francisco?"

She hesitated for a long moment, and then sighed, tossing her hair back over her shoulder, and for an instant she looked like a child again, the same girl who had talked to him from the swing in another place, another lifetime. "My father died. It changed a lot of things for me."

"Did your mom sell the ranch?"

She shook her head, and almost choked on the next words. "No, Tom runs it now."

"And your brother?" Spencer still remembered him, a shaggy-haired boy with long legs,

who liked to tease his sister. He remembered
him pulling Crystal's hair, and her slugging
him, but all in good fun. They had both
seemed like children then, but no longer.

"Jared died last spring." She could hardly
say the words as Spencer stared at her. Things
had been hard, but she didn't tell him just how
much harder. Or how Jared had died. Or why.
That it had been her fault. She still felt that
way about it.

"I'm sorry . . . was it an accident?" He
couldn't have been sick. He was too young.
Spencer's heart went out to her as she hesitated again, and then nodded. She was looking
at her hands so as not to look at him, and then
slowly she raised her eyes and he almost fell
backward from the strength of what he saw
there. It was anger and hatred and fear, and
lost dreams. It was powerful stuff, and he quietly took her hand in his own and held it.

"Tom shot him." Her eyes bored into him
like streaks of lightning.

"My God . . . were they hunting together?
What happened?"

"No." She shook her head slowly, she
couldn't tell him everything. She couldn't tell
him Tom had raped her. She had never told
anyone except Boyd and Hiroko, and she knew
she never would again. She would have to live

with the shame of it for a lifetime. "It was my fault." She spoke quietly. The guilt was too strong even to let her cry. "Something happened between me and Tom, and I went a little crazy." She took a breath, as though fighting for air, and Spencer held her hand even more tightly. "I went after him with my father's rifle. Tom took a shot at me, and it hit Jared."

"Oh, my God . . ." He looked at her in horror, barely daring to imagine what might have driven her to go after her brother-in-law with her father's gun. And then understanding instantly the guilt she still carried with her.

"The sheriff said Jared died of accidental causes. And I left a few days after he was buried." She said it so simply, except that the course of her life had been changed forever. While he was going to parties in Washington, and Lake Tahoe and Palm Beach, Crystal had lost her father and her brother. It was horrifying to think about it, and he was impressed that she had survived it at all, and grateful that he had found her in San Francisco.

"My Mom and I were on bad terms anyway after my father died. And now I guess she thinks I killed Jared. In a way, I did. It was my fault. I shouldn't have gone after Tom but . . ." Her eyes suddenly filled with tears. She knew she couldn't explain it to him. But as he listened, he longed to kiss and hold her. "My mother and I never got along. I think she hated me for being so close to my father."

"Have you heard from her since you left?"

"No." She shook her head. "That's all over." She smiled bravely. "I'm here now. This is my life. That's the past. I have to think about what I'm doing here. I can't look back. I left all that. It's all gone now."

She looked quietly up at Spencer. And then she wondered if he'd seen the Websters. "Have you seen Boyd and Hiroko?"

He shook his head guiltily, this was twice now he hadn't managed to get to the valley. "No, I haven't. I meant to, but I was only here for a few days. Are they all right, or do you know?"

She smiled sadly at him, and he felt his insides turn to mush again. She had been an incredible child, and she had become an incredible woman. There was a sensuality about her that shrieked at him, a gentleness and femininity that made him want to stay beside her always and protect her, and yet an amazing strength too. It was her strength that had helped her survive. "I had a letter from Hiroko last week. She's expecting another baby. I guess they want a boy this time, but Jane is so sweet." She told him a few stories about their

child, and then she had to go on again, and he
promised to wait for her. He could have talked
to her for hours. He didn't want to leave her.
Ever again. He sensed that she needed him.
And he wanted to be there for her.

She seemed to be singing just for him this
time, her voice reaching into him like wanton
fingers. There was a sexiness about her mixed
with innocence that made men want to reach
out and touch her. It was almost one o'clock
when she came off the stage, and they talked
for another hour until the place closed, and he
offered to take her home. He waited while she
changed, and it was like a glimpse into the past
again when she came out in a wool skirt and a
white blouse and a plaid jacket she had found
in a thrift shop. She looked like a little girl
again, but the eyes that looked into his were
those of a woman. The woman he had
dreamed about for three years and had never
forgotten. The woman who had dreamed of
him, always knowing how much she loved
him.

He walked her slowly back to the place
where she still rented a room from Mrs. Castagna, and they stood outside for a long time,
talking about his life in New York, his friends,
anything in order to keep her there, and then,
as though it was what they both had been wait-

ing for all night, he reached out and pulled her close and kissed her.

"Spencer . . ." Her voice was a whisper in the cold night air as he held her close as much to keep her warm as to feel her near him, "I've dreamed about you all these years . . . sometimes I would pretend to myself that if you'd been there, everything would have been different." But she had survived it, even without him. He respected that about her. And she was making something of herself. He wondered if she still dreamed of going to Hollywood, but he didn't ask her.

"I wish I had been there." He turned her face up to his with a gentle finger under her chin, "I never forgot you. I've thought about you lots of times . . . I just never thought you'd remember me either. I figured you'd be different, or maybe even married by now," that had been his last fantasy. He had never thought he would find her alone, singing in a nightclub in San Francisco, and he marveled at the hand of fate, which had led him to her. He might have gone back to New York without ever knowing she was there, without seeing her. But now that he had, he had no idea what to do about it. He had come to San Francisco to get engaged to Elizabeth Barclay. And now he was standing outside a house on Green Street, falling in love with Crystal Wyatt.

"I love you, Spencer." She whispered the words, as though she was afraid she would never have the chance again, and he felt his heart melt. How could he tell her about the girl he was going to marry?

He folded her into his arms and kept her close to him. He wanted to keep her there forever. "I love you too . . . oh God, Crystal . . . I love you. . . ." How could he say that to her? He couldn't promise her anything, all he could do was hold on to her for one brief moment, and then go back to New York with Elizabeth the next morning. Or did he have to do that at all? Why couldn't he have Crystal instead? There was nothing wrong with that. For one bright shining moment, he knew with total certainty that he had always loved her. And no matter what it cost him now, he had to tell her. "I've loved you since the first time I met you." It felt good just saying the words to her, as though he had waited three years to find her and tell her. Nothing else mattered now. Nothing, and no one.

She pulled away to look at him then, and she was smiling up at him. The child he had once met on the swing had grown into a woman, and as he held her, he knew how desperately he loved her. Beyond words, beyond reason. Beyond anything. She was everything he wanted.

"I used to think about you all the time . . . you were so handsome that time when you came to the ranch in those white pants and that red tie." He didn't even remember what he'd worn, but she did, just as he remembered the white dress he'd seen her in the first time, and the blue one after. And then, as though she could read his mind, and sense despair, she looked up and asked him, "When are you going back to New York?"

"Tomorrow morning." It sounded crazy now. All he wanted to do was stay here with her. Forever. But he had his whole life to sort out now. And Elizabeth to contend with. But that didn't matter now. Nothing did. Except Crystal. She was what he had been waiting for, when he had held back for so long. And now he knew why. This was what he wanted. It wouldn't make sense to anyone. But it did to him. It made perfect sense as he held her.

"Will you come back to California again?" Her heart was pounding as she asked him.

"Yes." Their eyes met and held for a long time. He knew he was coming back now. He was going to have a lot of explaining to do. But he would have walked over hot coals to be with her.

"I'll come back as soon as I can. I have some sorting out to do in New York first. But I'll call you." He made her write down her phone number for him and he kissed her again, feeling the sweetness of her lips and tasting the promise of his future. It was a future he looked forward to, not one he feared. He had no doubts now, in the heat of the moment.

He hastily scribbled the name of the law firm where he worked, and the number, and wrote down her address, then he pulled her into his arms for a last time. He didn't want to leave her. But he felt as though in a few short hours, his entire future had been settled, and this time it was a future he wanted.

"I don't want to go . . ." he whispered into her hair as he held her tight, and she closed her eyes, remembering how good it felt to be held by someone she loved. It made her feel safe and happy just being with him, but she hardly dared believe everything she was hearing. It was like a dream come true, and it was so good it frightened her. What if he didn't come back? If he disappeared? But she knew he wouldn't do that. She pulled herself away from him and it was almost a physical pain for both of them as she looked at him, as though trying to engrave him on her mind to keep him close to her forever. Or for as long as it took for him to come back to her. She would barely live waiting for that moment.

"I love you, Spencer."

"Don't look so sad then."

"I'm scared." She was honest with him. She instinctively knew that she could be.

"Scared of what?"

"What if you don't come back?"

"I will. I promise." And with all his heart he meant it. Every ounce of his being was alive and filled with hope. She was everything he wanted. "I love you, Crystal." He walked her to the door, and kissed her again. She clung to him and a moment later she was gone, tiptoeing past Mrs. Castagna's apartment. He could hear her footsteps as she ran upstairs, and as he watched from the street he saw her put her light on. She came to the window, and waved to him, and then, like a man who had found his dream, he set off on foot for the house on Broadway. For a mad moment, he thought of walking into Elizabeth's room and telling her everything. But he knew he had to think things out and speak to her in the clear light of day so she wouldn't think he was drunk or crazy. He wasn't crazy though. He knew he was saner than he'd ever been and he knew exactly what he wanted. All he had to figure out now was how to get it.

CHAPTER
21

They were all at the breakfast table the next morning when he came downstairs. His parents, Elizabeth, and all the Barclays. It would have been the perfect moment to tell them what he had to say. But as he walked into the room looking clean-shaven and pale after two hours sleep, he could hardly break into their animated conversation.

"You must have come in awfully late last night," Elizabeth mentioned under her breath as she carried on a conversation between his father and her mother. They were all ready to catch their plane, and the Hills were sharing a final meal with the Barclays. Everyone was talking about wedding plans and he had an overwhelming urge to scream at all of them, but he controlled it. And suddenly it no longer seemed like the time or place to tell them about Crystal. Spencer realized suddenly that he owed it to Elizabeth to tell her first, and in private.

He poured himself a cup of tea from the silver teapot, and let them go on talking as he sat in silence. Ian was quick to notice it and laughed at him, unable to resist the opportunity to tease him.

"Is my future brother-in-law hung over? I know how law school buddies are. Every time I see them, I get so drunk, Sarah threatens to divorce me."

"I do not!" Sarah blurted out as she looked at him with a warm smile. "I only did that one time when you got arrested." The assembled company laughed easily, all except Spencer who looked inexplicably unhappy.

"Cheer up, Son. You'll feel better and you can have a drink on the plane." But it wasn't a drink he wanted, it was Crystal.

They said good-bye to the Barclays shortly after that. They were flying back to Washington directly. It was remarkable that Justice Barclay had been able to get away at all. Even one day away from the Supreme Court was rare for him, but this had been important. He would have flown to the moon for the engagement of his baby.

Elizabeth hardly spoke to him until they were on the plane, and then she looked at him seriously. She sensed that something was wrong with him, she had never seen him so quiet or so unhappy.

"Is something wrong?" It was the perfect opening but he didn't dare take it. His parents were sitting across the aisle and Ian and Sarah just behind them, and he wanted to spare Elizabeth the pain of hearing his news in their presence.

He shook his head unconvincingly, and Elizabeth turned to stare out the window. She was annoyed at him, but she didn't ask him anything again. And a little while later, she fell asleep as he watched her. It made him feel guilty just looking at her. But not guilty enough to want to go ahead with the wedding. He didn't love her. He knew that now. He was much too in love with Crystal.

He could still feel the satin of her hair on his cheek, her lips on his . . . the touch of her hand . . . he thought he'd go crazy before they landed. He had promised to drive Elizabeth to Poughkeepsie that night. And he

dreaded being alone with her. He knew he had
to tell her the truth, but he hated hurting her.
But he knew he had to. The thought of how
stunned his parents would be, and how furious
the Barclays would be at his betrayal depressed
him. But it all had to be faced. And he was
willing to face it.

His parents and Ian and Sarah shared a cab
into New York when they arrived, and he
picked up the car he had left at the airport. He
put Elizabeth's bags in the trunk with his own,
and they drove in silence for the first few miles,
and finally Elizabeth couldn't stand it any
longer.

"Spencer, what's wrong? What happened
last night? You were fine when you went out."
And he wasn't fine now. That was clear to
both of them, but only he knew why. And he
knew he had to tell her.

For one mad moment Elizabeth remembered the girl they'd seen singing at Harry's on
Saturday night, and she remembered the look
on his face, and wondered if that had anything
to do with it. But it couldn't. Or could it? He
had looked as though he was going to pass out
in his seat when he saw her. "Is there something I should know about?" She looked at
him and he stared straight ahead for a long
time before speaking and without saying a

word he pulled off the road, stopped the car and turned to face her. He looked anguished and pale, and he felt more than a little crazy. But she was strangely calm as she waited.

"I can't marry you." He couldn't believe he was saying the words. But he had. And even more unbelievable was the way Elizabeth looked. She looked interested, but suddenly not even worried.

"Would you like to tell me why?"

"I'm not sure I can." He didn't want to tell her he didn't love her. That was too cruel a blow, and it wasn't fair. It wasn't her fault she wasn't Crystal. It wasn't her fault he hadn't heard thunder and lightning when he'd first met her. She had everything to offer him. She was intelligent and attractive, she came from a good family, she kept him entertained, and he liked her. But he just didn't love her. "I just know I can't. We'd never be happy."

She looked at him, and for an instant he thought she looked amused. "That's the dumbest thing I've ever heard. The one thing I never thought you were was a coward."

"What does that have to do with it?" He looked even more miserable than before, and she lit a cigarette and watched him.

"It has everything to do with it. You've got cold feet, Spencer Hill, and you're too damn scared to face it and ride it out. You're ready to call off everything and run like a rabbit. Everyone gets scared . . . so what? So be gutsy for chrissake. Be a man. Go get drunk somewhere, go cry with your friends, and face it. Don't you think every man feels the way you do?" But every man wasn't in love with Crystal. And Elizabeth was frighteningly cool as she watched him. "Why don't you take a week off, catch your breath, and we'll talk about it when I come down for the weekend."

"Elizabeth . . . it isn't that simple." He was still holding back. He didn't want to tell her about seeing Crystal again . . . about falling in love with her when she was fourteen. It would have made him sound like a lunatic. And at the moment, in truth, he felt like one, as he tried to explain it to the woman he was engaged to.

"It's just that simple, if you want it to be." She smiled at him as she stubbed out her cigarette. "Why don't we just pretend we never had this conversation?"

He sighed miserably and sat back against the seat, staring blindly out the window. "I think you're even crazier than I am."

"Good. Then we'll make a good match, Spencer, won't we?"

"No, we won't, dammit!" He turned to look

at her again. "I am not what you want, and I never will be. I don't want the same things you do. I don't want fame and fortune, and 'importance.' I will never be the man you want me to be. I don't want that."

"And what about me, as long as we're talking about all that? Where is it that I fall short, which is what you're really talking about anyway, isn't it? We're talking about what I'm not, not what you're not." She was always painfully honest, and smart enough to know what she was seeing, even if she didn't know the reasons for it.

"You don't need me." It sounded like such a lame reason for breaking their engagement that even Spencer felt foolish after he said it.

"Of course I do. But I don't have to whine about it, do I, or is that what you're expecting? And I happen to love you, if that makes any difference to you. But no, I'm never going to wander around pretending that I believe in rainbows and miracles and visions of angels playing harps to tell me I love you. I like you. I think you're smart and fun and you could go far, if you'd just give yourself half a chance, and once you get there we'll have a hell of a good time. And that's about all I want. Is that so awful?"

"It's not awful. Nothing's awful. And you're

not awful. And I like you a hell of a lot too
. . . but we need more than that." His voice
was too loud in the small space of the car, but
she didn't seem to notice. He was pleading for
his life and she didn't appear to understand
that. "I need violins and harps and rainbows. I
believe in them. Maybe I'm just a hopeless romantic, but if we settle for less than that now,
ten years from now . . . five . . . two . . .
we'll bitterly regret it."

"We also happen to have a damn good sex
life. Don't forget that."

He smiled at how bluntly she put it. And she
was right. It was crazier still that he was
madly in love with a girl he had never even
slept with. And suddenly, as he listened to
Elizabeth, and himself, he wondered if all his
dreams of Crystal were pure illusion. With her,
it was all harps and violins and dreams and
memories and visions. With Elizabeth, he had
substance. But he needed both. At least he
thought so.

"Or doesn't sex matter to you, Spencer? I
wouldn't have said so from what I've noticed."
She was laughing at him and he couldn't help
but smile in answer.

"I'd say it does."

"At least you're honest. Not very brave, but
honest, at least." And then she leaned over and

kissed his neck, and ran a hand up his thigh. "Why don't we stop at a motel somewhere and discuss this?"

"For chrissake, Elizabeth, I'm serious. I've just told you that I don't want to marry you, and you want to go to a motel. Didn't you hear me? Aren't you listening? Don't you care?" He was feeling frantic.

"Of course I care. But I'm not about to start waving my hankie. I think you're behaving like a ten-year-old and I'm not going to indulge you. I think something happened last night to scare the pants off you, and I'm not even sure how I know that. And in some spirit of religious zeal, or something similarly foolish, you want to head for the hills. Well, I don't want to hear it. So drive me back to school and go home and sober up, and call me in the morning." She was a cool one, there was no denying it. In a way, he respected her for it, and in another way it scared the hell out of him. And it was precisely why he did not want to marry her, but Crystal. Elizabeth was eyeing him again as he started the car with a look of desperation. "Do you feel a need to confess about last night? Is that what this is all about? Why don't you find a priest then and let him give you absolution? And then we can get on with our lives like normal people."

"That has nothing to do with it."

"I think it does, and I think you know it too. And you know what, Spencer?" She lit another cigarette and looked calmly out the window. "I don't want to hear about it. Go have your *crise de conscience,* as the French call it, privately, without destroying our lives in the process."

"Getting married would destroy our lives. Believe me, I know what I'm saying." He sounded serious, but she wasn't convinced yet.

"Infidelity per se is not an adequate reason for divorce, no matter what the law says. So if that's what this is all about, if you happen to have gone bonkers with your friends last night, don't burden me with your sordid stories. Just go sober up like every other normal, decent, self-respecting man, tell me a lie, buy me a nice piece of jewelry and stop whining." Spencer turned to look at her in total amazement.

"Are you serious?"

"Not entirely. But for the most part. We're not married yet. If you go crazy occasionally, I might make allowances for it. Once we're married, however, I might be considerably less good-natured."

"I'll make a note of that." She was an extraordinary girl, and suddenly here he was acting as though he was still going to marry her, instead of Crystal. "You certainly are open-minded."

"That is what this is all about, isn't it?"

"Not necessarily." He still absolutely refused to tell her about Crystal. It was none of her business. And yet she demeaned it by treating it like a one-night stand and being willing to put up with it. It made talking to her even harder. "I think it has to do with a disparity of our views about what we want out of life. In some ways, I want more than you do, and in other ways you want more than I'll ever want. And that, my friend, does not constitute a marriage made in heaven."

"There is no such thing." They were back on the highway again, and she had moved closer to him.

"That's where I don't agree with you. I think there is."

"I think you're crazy." She put a hand on his crotch as she said it, and he swerved on the road with a look approaching terror.

"Elizabeth, stop that!"

"Why? You've always liked it before." She was amused by him. She was laughing at him. And she refused to take what he was saying seriously.

"Have you heard anything I've said to you?"

"All of it. And frankly, my love, I think it's bullshit." She kissed him on the neck again, and in spite of himself he felt an uncontrollable stirring. He had a mad impulse to make love to her just to convince her. But convince her of what? That it was over? Why did she refuse to believe him? What did she know that he didn't? She was unbelievably willful and stubborn.

"It is *not* bullshit. I mean it."

"Right now maybe you do. But by tomorrow you'll be embarrassed. I'm going to spare you that embarrassment by not believing a word you've said. How's that for good sportsmanship?"

He pulled off the road again to look at her, but he had to laugh at himself. Here he had been afraid she would do something desperate, and instead she was completely unmoved by his announcement and his speeches. She was totally unflappable. And the worst thing was that part of him liked that.

"You're *much* crazier than I am."

"Thank you." And with that, she leaned over and kissed him hard on the mouth, forcing her tongue between his lips, and at the same time slowly undoing his zipper. He was trying to pull away from her, but a part of him didn't want to.

"Elizabeth, don't . . ." But she was kissing him and fondling him all at the same time, and the impulses she created were too difficult to resist even under the awkward circumstances. He couldn't believe what was happening, but a moment later, they were lying on the seat together, struggling frantically beneath each other's coats, with her skirt hiked up around her waist, and her underwear pushed down around one ankle. And the steam on the windows of the car was ample testimony to their passion. It was brief and ardent and Spencer felt totally out of control, and afterward, as they sorted themselves out again, the episode depressed him. But Elizabeth was in better spirits than ever.

"That was ridiculous." He was behaving more than ever like a madman, he chided himself. Maybe he was having a nervous breakdown.

"I thought it was very nice myself. Don't be such a stuffed shirt." And she proceeded to laugh at him all the way to Poughkeepsie. She kissed him fondly on the mouth when they arrived at Vassar, despite all his protestations, and promised to have a serious talk with him in New York the following weekend. And instead of relieved or guilty or sorry or miserable, all the way back to New York, Spencer felt desperately foolish. And it was only that night, as he lay in bed thinking about Crystal again, that he realized the full measure of his problem with Elizabeth. Having gotten him to propose to her, she was now not going to take no for an answer. And all he wanted was to go to California to run off with another woman. It had shades of a comic opera, except that it was so damn serious. He was even tempted to call his father to discuss it, except that he was convinced his father would think he was crazy. And for the moment he himself wasn't sure he wasn't.

The next morning he thought about calling Crystal at Mrs. Castagna's, but he couldn't tell her anything yet. She didn't even know he was engaged. But he suddenly felt that he owed it to her not to call until he had settled the problem with Elizabeth. And he was even more furious with himself for making love to her in the car on the way to Poughkeepsie. All he needed now, to complete the picture of utter confusion, was for Elizabeth to get pregnant. But he knew from the past that she only took chances when she knew that couldn't happen. But even without that complication, Spencer was in the midst of an intolerable dilemma. And for the next week he couldn't eat, he couldn't sleep, he couldn't concentrate on his work. All he could think of was Crystal, and his thus far unsuccessfully broken engagement. And from time to time he wondered if Elizabeth was right and there was no such thing as a marriage made in heaven. They had a good time after all, in bed and out, she was smart, and they got along . . . but Crystal was so much more than that . . . at least he thought she was . . . although in truth he had to admit, he barely knew her. And by the end of the week, he could hardly think straight. He had weighed it all so much and so often and with such care that none of it made any sense whatsoever. It never had. All he knew was that for years now he had been haunted by the romantic visions he had of Crystal, which were in sharp contrast to the realities of the woman he was still engaged to.

He looked like hell all week, and one of his friends at the office even commented on it, trying to be playful.

"Must have been a rough weekend, Hill." Spencer smiled, but the next day when they played squash he was so distracted, he lost both games, and afterward he looked mournful when they stopped for drinks, and he knew he had to talk to someone. George Montgomery had just recently come to the firm. He was Spencer's age, and he had a bright future. He was the nephew of the senior partner of the firm, Brewster Vincent.

He looked up suddenly, desperate to talk to him, as the other man sensed he was deeply troubled. "What's eating you?"

"I think I'm crazy."

"I suspect you're right, but who isn't?" George smiled at him and ordered another beer for both of them. "Any special reason why you've just noticed?"

He didn't know what to say to him. How could he even begin to tell him about Crystal? "I ran into an old friend in San Francisco this weekend."

George suspected instantly, from the look on his face. "A woman?"

Spencer nodded miserably. "I haven't seen her in years, and I thought I'd forgotten her . . . but suddenly . . . Christ, I don't even know how to explain it."

"You wound up in bed with her," George suggested with a grin. Something similar had happened to him two days before he got married. "Don't worry, it's just cold feet. You'll get over it."

"And if I don't? Then what? Besides, just for the record, I didn't sleep with her." He said it to preserve her reputation more than his own, as though it mattered. George didn't even know her.

"My sympathies then. Don't worry, Spencer. You'll forget her. Elizabeth is a great girl. You could do a lot worse than be related to Justice Barclay." Was that all anyone thought of then? The importance of the connection with her father?

Spencer looked up at him, and suddenly George knew it was serious. "I told Elizabeth I wanted to break the engagement."

George whistled as he set his glass down. "You're right. You are crazy. What did she say?"

Spencer only shook his head. "She doesn't want to hear it. She thinks it's an ordinary case of cold feet and told me to stop whining." It would have been funny, except that to Spencer, it wasn't.

"She's a good sport at least. Does she know about the other girl?"

Spencer shook his head unhappily. "I didn't tell her. But I think she suspects it. She doesn't realize how serious it is though."

George looked firm as he looked at him. "It isn't."

"Yes it is. I'm in love with her . . . the other one, I mean."

"It's too late for that. Think of it. Think of

the stink it will make if you break the engagement."

"And if I don't? I spend the rest of my life thinking about someone else?"

"No, you won't. You'll forget her." He sounded sure of it, but Spencer wasn't. "You have to."

"Other people break engagements." Spencer looked agitated, and to make matters worse, he hadn't slept in days, which had depressed him even more.

"They don't break engagements to Justice Barclay's daughter." George looked positive, and his attitude annoyed Spencer. Everyone was so damn impressed by who she was, and Spencer had never been sure that was important. He had proposed to her because he liked her, because she was intelligent and full of life, and he thought they might have an interesting life, and in the end, because he had told himself that he loved her. But he had never felt this way about her. He had known that from the first. It was why he had not asked her to marry him for an entire year. And then suddenly he had decided it would be all right. But he'd been wrong, and now what? He still didn't have the answers.

"Why is all that so important, George?

What difference does it make who her father is?"

"Are you kidding? You're not just marrying a girl, you're marrying a life-style, a name, an important family. You don't just walk in and out of a life like hers. They'll make you pay for it somehow, and even if they don't, your name will be mud from here to California." But as he said the words, Spencer thought of his parents, and how disappointed they would be. But he couldn't marry her just to please them.

"I can live with that, if I have to." But could he? And what if Crystal wasn't right for him? What if it was all juvenile infatuation? After all, he hardly knew her. "The point is, do I love Elizabeth or not? And the truth is, George, I don't know. How could I love her if I'm head over heels in love with someone else?"

"I think you just need to put it out of your mind, and come to your senses. Come on, I'll buy you dinner. Have a few drinks, go to bed, and don't say anything more to her for chrissake. You'll feel better in a few days. It's probably just what she said. Cold feet. Everyone gets them." But Spencer wasn't so sure. At least he slept peacefully that night, and in the morning, he saw the announcement of his engagement in *The New York Times*, with a very pretty photograph of Elizabeth taken in Washington at her father's induction. It made it all seem real again, and as he walked to work, he wondered if George was right, if he just had to put Crystal out of his head. But what in God's name was he going to tell her? That he'd made a mistake? That he didn't love her after all? That he had to marry someone else? And what about Crystal? She needed him, or at least she needed someone. It wasn't fair to her, and the thought of giving her up made his soul ache. But he didn't have to tell her anything.

In San Francisco that day, Crystal saw the announcement in the papers. He hadn't even thought about that as he struggled with his dilemma. She was eating dinner at Harry's with the rest of the staff, when Pearl suddenly handed her the *Chronicle* with a look of interest. But she wasn't as surprised as Crystal was when she saw Spencer's face smiling up at her from the paper.

"Weren't they here the other night? I think I waited on them." Pearl was pensive. She was always fascinated by the socialites she read about in the papers. "Saturday, I think it was. She was kind of full of herself, but I remember he was very nice. He was crazy about you. You should have seen his face when you were singing."

Crystal felt her hands turn to ice, and her fingers trembled as she handed back the paper. She had read enough. It said that Spencer Hill, of New York, was going to marry Justice Barclay's daughter, Elizabeth, and both families had flown into town for Thanksgiving to celebrate and give a party for four hundred friends at the Broadway mansion. Hedda Hopper said that the party had been incredible, with caviar, champagne, and a buffet that made the one at the White House look sick, and Artie Shaw and his band had played for the young couple till the wee hours of the morning. The date of the wedding was in June, and Miss Barclay's gown was going to be made by Priscilla in Boston. Crystal stared into her plate in disbelief. He hadn't said a thing to her about getting engaged. All he had told her was that he loved her. And that he would come back to California. He had lied to her. And as she remembered all that he'd said, she felt her heart ache. She had believed him.

"You ever hear of him before?" Pearl inquired, chewing her food carefully. She was getting heavier lately, but she was still a terrific dancer.

"No," Crystal shook her head, and went to empty her plate. It was still full, but she was no longer hungry. She sang her heart out that night, trying not to think of him, but it was hopeless. He was all she could think of, and two days later, when he called her, she almost didn't take the call, but Mrs. Castagna had insisted. "It's *long-distance!*" She had shouted, impressed, and Crystal's hands had been shaking when she finally took the receiver.

"Yes?"

"Crystal?" It was his voice and she closed her eyes as she listened. She didn't answer for a long moment, and he said her name again, sounding worried and unhappy.

"Yes?"

"It's Spencer."

"Congratulations." His heart stopped as she said the word and then instantly he knew. The Barclays would have put the announcement in the local papers. He had wanted to tell her himself, but now it was too late. She knew already.

"I came back to New York to break it off. I swear. The night I came back I even told her."

"I guess you both decided you didn't mean it."

"It wasn't that . . . it . . . I don't know how to explain it."

"You don't have to." She wanted to be angry at him, and she was, and yet now, listening to him, all she felt was enormous sadness. She had lost so many people she cared about, and now he was just one more. He was gone. Out of her life now forever. Like the others. But this time could have been so different. "You don't owe me anything, Spencer."

"That's not the point . . . Crystal, I love you . . ." It was a terrible thing to say to her in the face of the announcement of his engagement. "I don't mean to make things more difficult. I just want you to know that. Maybe our lives were just too far apart. We never had a chance to get to know each other. . . ." It was a poor excuse. Instinctively he knew how well they would get along, how perfectly suited they would be. But he had opted for cool reality instead of gentle illusion. "It all got so complicated once I got back here." She had seemed so unreal to him then, but talking to her on the phone made him ache to hold her again and feel her near him.

And at her end, as she listened to him, she was silently crying. She wanted to hate him, but she didn't. "She must be a very special person."

He hesitated for a moment, wanting to tell her the truth, how much more special she was to him than Elizabeth, and yet that wasn't real. It couldn't be. He couldn't let it. "It's very different from what you and I have felt. It doesn't have the same kind of magic."

"Then why are you doing it?" She didn't understand anymore. It was all too confusing.

"To be honest with you, I'm not sure. Maybe because it was too complicated not to."

"That's not much of a reason to get married." He knew it too, and there was very little he could say in answer.

"I know that. I know this sounds crazy, but I'll write to you . . . just to see how you are . . . or can I call you?" He couldn't stand the thought of losing sight of her again. Not again. He needed to know that she was all right, and be there if she needed him, but she didn't want that.

The tears rolled slowly down her cheeks again, and she shook her head. "Don't . . . you're going to be married. We never had anything anyway. Just a dream. I don't want to hear from you. It would just remind me of what we never had." What she said was true, but it depressed him even more to know that she wanted no contact with him.

"Will you call me if you need anything?"

"Like what?" She smiled through her tears. "How about a movie contract in Hollywood? You got one of those?"

"Sure . . ." He smiled through his own

tears. "For you, anything." Anything except what they both wanted more than life itself. And he was screwing it up, because he had decided Elizabeth was the "right thing." Talking to Crystal again he was no longer sure. Maybe she was right not to let him call her. He wanted to get on the next plane now just to be with her, but he couldn't do that to either of them, he had to try and do things right with Elizabeth. He owed her that much. And he wouldn't have done that to Crystal. "I guess I'm going to be seeing your name up in lights one of these days . . . or I'll be buying your records." And he meant it.

"Maybe one day." But she wasn't thinking about that now. She was only thinking of him, and how much she would miss him. "I'm glad I saw you again . . . even with all this . . . it was worth it." Even for a few days of dreams. At least she had seen him. And held him. And touched him. And he had told her he loved her.

"I don't know how you can say that now. I feel like a real shit . . . especially with your seeing it first in the papers."

She shrugged. Maybe it didn't matter now. Maybe nothing did. He had never been part of her life. He had only been a dream, from beginning to end . . . but a nice dream. And then, wishing she was stronger than that, she started to cry again, but it hurt so much to say good-bye to him, knowing it was forever. "I hope you'll be happy."

"So do I." But he sounded less than sure of it. "Promise you'll call me if you need me. I'm serious, Crystal." He knew she had no one else now, except the Websters, and they couldn't have done much to help her.

"I'll be okay." She smiled and fought back the tears again. "I'm tough, you know."

"Yeah . . . I know that . . . I just wish you didn't have to be. You deserve to have someone terrific to take care of you." He wanted to add "and I wish I were that person," but it would have been too cruel, and too pointless for both of them. And then, knowing there was nothing left to say, "Good-bye, Crystal, I love you." There were tears in his eyes and he could barely hear her whispered answer.

"I love you too, Spencer . . ." And the phone went dead in his hand, and she was gone. Forever.

He wrote to her once, just to tell her how sorry he was, and how much she had meant to him, as hard as it had been to put it into words, but the letter came back unopened, unanswered. He wasn't sure if she had moved,

but he didn't really think so. She was just wise
enough not to start something neither of them
could finish. And she knew that now she had
to put it behind her. It wasn't easy. It was the
hardest thing she had ever done, except leaving
the ranch and the valley, but she forced herself
to try and forget him. She didn't even want to
sing the songs anymore that she had sung that
night when he had come back to see her. Everything reminded her of him, every morning,
every day, every night, every song, every sunset. Every waking moment was spent thinking
of him. In years past, all she had had were her
dreams, but now she had enough more to
make it infinitely more painful. She knew the
exact color of his eyes, the smell of his hair, the
feel of his lips, the touch of his hands, the
sound of his voice when he spoke in a whisper.
And now all of it had to be forgotten. She had
her whole life ahead of her, and no one to love,
but she had her gifts from God, Mrs. Castagna
reminded her frequently, and she had Pearl to
remind her that Hollywood was still waiting.
But now, without Spencer, none of it seemed
quite so important.

CHAPTER 22

And for Spencer, things settled down again eventually. He thought of Crystal a lot, but he was determined to make an honest commitment. He went to Palm Beach for Christmas with Elizabeth, and he began to find his footing again. He thought constantly about writing to Crystal, but he never did again. He knew Crystal wanted to be left alone, and he felt much too guilty. And Elizabeth overlooked all of it, like a social faux pas she was too gracious to mention.

They had a nice Christmas in spite of it and returned from Florida relaxed and tanned, and there were only six months left until the wedding.

Elizabeth usually kept him busy with parties in New York, and trips to Washington to visit her parents. He scarcely had time to think of anything that spring, but still more often than not, there were gnawing thoughts of Crystal and he did his best to fight them. There was no point driving himself crazy over her. He was doing the right thing, he told himself, almost daily.

Mrs. Barclay went to San Francisco in early May, to oversee the last details. They were to be married in Grace Cathedral, just as Elizabeth wanted, and the reception was going to be at the St. Francis Hotel. She had wanted it at home, but she also wanted to invite over seven hundred people, and they had no choice but to do it at a hotel. There were going to be fourteen ushers, and a dozen bridesmaids. It was the kind of wedding he had read about, but never even been to. And he flew out to San Francisco with Elizabeth in June, the day after she finished school. It was the end of her third year, and she was transferring to Columbia in the fall, so she could graduate after they were married. It was the only condition her father had set on them before he agreed to the marriage. He wanted Elizabeth to graduate, and he was only very sorry that she wouldn't be graduating from Vassar. But all Elizabeth wanted was to be with her husband. They were in high spirits on the plane, and Spencer knew that there was going to be a constant round of parties when they got to California. The wedding was still a week away, on the seventeenth of June, and they were going to Hawaii for their honeymoon. She could hardly wait, and the week before she had announced airily that she was putting Spencer "on restriction" before the wedding. He was teasing her mercilessly about it on the plane, and telling her he could no longer be held responsible for his actions. But their opportunities were going to be more limited than before. Her father had taken a room for him at the Bohemian Club, as well as for all the ushers coming from out of town, among them George from Spencer's office. He still remembered how sure George had been that he was doing the right thing and he believed it too. Until he set foot back in San Francisco.

He suddenly found himself thinking of Crystal night and day. He was so close now, and he desperately wanted to see her. But drinking a great deal more than usual, and keeping his own counsel this time, he forced himself not to. It would have been a cruel thing to do to her anyway, and he plunged himself heart and soul into their wedding plans, and the elaborate parties being given for them daily.

There were parties in Atherton, Woodside, and several in San Francisco, and the Barclays gave a huge reception dinner for the wedding party at the Pacific Union Club the night before the wedding. Spencer had had his bachelor dinner the night before, and Ian had organized it for him. It included several strippers, and a flood of champagne, and Spencer had successfully resisted the urge to go to Harry's on the way home and tell Crystal he still loved her. He tried to explain it to Ian incoherently, but then remembered he wasn't supposed to.

"That's right, son," Ian had grinned, "we always drink champagne in crystal glasses." They had put him to bed in his room at the club, and Spencer was greatly subdued the next day at the rehearsal dinner. They all were. And Elizabeth looked radiant in a pink satin evening gown. She had never been more beautiful than she was these days. Her mother had bought her some exquisite dresses in Washington and New York, and she was wearing her hair longer now, in a French twist, which showed off the incredible diamond earrings her parents had given her for her wedding. They had given Spencer a Patek Philippe watch, and

a platinum cigarette case embedded with sapphires and diamonds. His own gift to them was
a gold box, engraved with a line from a poem
he knew meant a great deal to Justice Barclay.
And he gave Elizabeth a ruby necklace and
matching earrings that were going to take him
several years to pay for. But he knew how
much she liked rubies, and she was used to
only the best. And as he smiled at her that
night, at the Pacific Union Club, he knew she
deserved it.

The wedding was at noon the next day, and
the ushers left the Bohemian Club in a convoy
of limousines. The bride was coming to the
church in her late grandfather's 1937 Rolls,
which was still in perfect condition. The Barclays only used it on state occasions, and Elizabeth looked radiant as two maids and the butler settled her with the fourteen-foot train
carefully draped inside the car, her father staring at her in mute admiration. She wore a
crown of lace, encrusted with tiny pearls, and
set into it, carefully designed, was her elegant
little tiara. The thin French veiling cascaded
around her like mist, and the high-necked lace
gown showed off the slenderness of her figure.
It was an incredible dress, an incredible day,
an unforgettable moment, as the chauffeur
drove them to Grace Cathedral and children

on the street pointed at the bride. She looked beautiful, and her father had to fight back tears as they walked solemnly up the aisle to the strains of *Lohengrin,* and children's voices sang like angels with the chorus.

Spencer watched her approach, and he could feel his heart pound. This was the moment they had waited for. It had finally come. It was done. And as she smiled at him through her veil, he knew he had done the right thing. She looked lovely. And in moments, she would be his wife. For always.

They walked back down the aisle, followed by the bridesmaids and ushers, smiling at their friends, and the reception line took forever. It was one o'clock before they left the church, and one-thirty when they arrived at the St. Francis. The newspapers were waiting for them there. It was the biggest wedding San Francisco had seen in years, and there were crowds of people in the street, watching as the limousines arrived. It was obvious that she was somebody very important. They hurried into the hotel, and they danced and ate and drank all afternoon. And it occurred to Spencer more than once that it was a little like a political reception. People had arrived from Washington and New York. Several other Supreme Court justices were there, and all the most important Democrats in California. And they had gotten a telegram from President Truman himself.

And finally, at six o'clock, she went upstairs to change, and took off the gown she'd never wear again. She looked at it sadly for a moment, thinking of the endless hours of fittings, the attention to detail, and now she would have to put it away, to save for her own daughters to wear. She wore a white silk suit when she came downstairs, and a beautiful hat by Chanel, and the guests threw rose petals as they left. They were driven in the old Rolls to the airport. Their flight to Hawaii wasn't until eight o'clock, and as they stopped for a drink in the restaurant, Elizabeth looked at her husband and smiled victoriously.

"Well, kid, we did it."

"It was beautiful, darling." He leaned over and kissed her. "I'll never forget you in that dress."

"I hated to put it away. It seemed so strange, after all that care and excitement over it, that I'd never wear it again." She was feeling tender and nostalgic, and she slept with her head on his shoulder on the plane that night, and he smiled happily, certain that he loved her. They were going to Hawaii, and then they were going to join her parents for a week at

Lake Tahoe before Justice Barclay went back
to Washington, and they went back to New
York to look for an apartment. She was moving in with him until they found what they
wanted. She wanted to live on Park Avenue,
which was too expensive on his salary, but she
insisted she wanted to contribute too. She had
gotten a trust fund when she turned twenty-
one, but he was uncomfortable about her helping him. They hadn't worked it out yet, which
was why it seemed simpler for her to move in
with him until things were settled. And she
hadn't had time to look for a place anyway,
while she was at Vassar.

But he knew everything was going to go
smoothly, as she slept and they flew steadily on
toward Honolulu. They stayed at the Haleku-
lani on Waikiki, and the days drifted by like
moments, as they lay on the beach, and went
back to their room several times a day to make
love. Her father had arranged a visiting mem-
bership at the Outrigger Canoe Club, and he
called once to see how they were, in spite of his
wife's protests. She thought they should leave
them alone, but he wanted to know how they
were, and he was anxious to see them at Lake
Tahoe.

They flew back on the twenty-third of June,
and were happy and brown when they arrived.

Justice Barclay had a car waiting for them, and Spencer drove to the lake, on the same day that Pearl showed Crystal the pictures of their wedding in the papers. She had meant to show them to her long before. The article talked about Elizabeth's incredible wedding gown, and the fourteen-foot train. Crystal felt a knot in her chest as she read the details, and stared for a long time at a picture of Spencer, holding Elizabeth's hand and smiling.

"They're a good-looking pair, aren't they?" Pearl still remembered that they had come to the club the previous winter. She had a good memory for faces and names, and she still remembered reading about their engagement in the paper, around Thanksgiving.

Crystal didn't answer her. She only folded the newspaper and handed it back to her, trying to forget that she still loved him. It was a bleak day, and she went home early that night. She looked sick, and she told Harry she had a terrible headache. They had enough entertainers that night anyway, and a lot of their customers were away. Harry's had become a very popular club, in great part due to her, and her growing reputation as a singer.

But as she lay in bed that night, trying to forget the pictures she'd seen in the papers, Elizabeth and Spencer were sitting quietly near

the lake and talking. Her parents had already
gone to bed, and it was late, but there was always a lot to say. And they were talking about
some things her father had said about Mc-
Carthy's witch-hunts. Spencer had disagreed
with him violently. He thought many of the
accusations being made were unfair, and Elizabeth was teasing him now, telling him that he
was a dreamer.

"That's bullshit, Elizabeth. The House
Committee is running around accusing innocent people of being Communists. That's dis-
graceful!"

"What makes you so sure they're innocent?"
She smiled. She was in full agreement with her
father.

"The whole country can't be red, for chrissake. And besides, it's no one's business."

"With the unrest in the Far East, how can
you say that? Communism is the biggest threat
to our world today. Do you want another
war?"

"No. But we're not talking about a war.
We're talking about attitudes in our own country. What happened to freedom of choice?
What about the Constitution?" He hated talking politics with her. He liked her better when
they were making love, or holding hands, or
just sitting in the moonlight. "Anyway, I just

happen to disagree with your father." They'd been discussing it for hours, and after the long flight from Hawaii, and the drive to the lake, he was exhausted. "Let's go to bed."

"I still won't agree with you," she laughed.

"Maybe not, but at least you'll have something else to think about, other than politics." She smiled and followed him back to the house, but he was too tired to make love to her that night and it had unsettled him to go back to San Francisco. Just being there always reminded him of Crystal.

But she was far from his mind the next day, as they water-skiied on the lake, and had dinner with friends of the Barclays. And the day after that, everyone was shocked at the news from Korea. It was called a police action by the government, but it sounded more like a war to Spencer. Young men were being drafted instantly and the reserves were being called up. And when he heard the news, he suddenly realized what it meant for him, as he turned to his wife, and she was horrified when he told her.

"You did *what*?" Her brown eyes were huge in her face and it was obvious that she was on the verge of tears.

"I thought it wouldn't make any difference, and I wanted to keep my commission." He had stayed in the reserves, and now the reserves were being called up. In moments, he could be on his way to Korea.

"Can you give up your commission now?"

"It's too late for that." And it was later than he knew. The telegram calling him back into the armed forces was already waiting for him at his office. George Montgomery called him that afternoon, and Spencer told Elizabeth with somber eyes. He wasn't afraid to go. In an odd way, he wanted to, but he was desperately sorry for her. They had only been married for two weeks, and he was leaving for Korea. He had been told to report to Fort Ord in Monterey, and he had two days to get there. Elizabeth was in shock, and Justice Barclay was serious when he heard the news.

"Do you want me to try and get you out of it, Son?"

"No, sir. Thank you. I served in the Pacific before. It wouldn't be right to shirk my duty." He had strong feelings about that kind of thing, but Elizabeth fought him tooth and nail that night. They had just gotten married and she didn't want to lose him. But Spencer was firm. "I'm sure it will be over soon, sweetheart. It's not a war, it's a police action."

"That's the same thing!" She wailed. "Why won't you let Daddy fix it for you?" She was

furious with him, and she had implored her
father to help her, but he wouldn't do it unless
Spencer asked him to. And in truth, he admired him for what he was doing. He was only
sorry for his daughter. She was barely out of
her wedding dress, and he was going off to
war. It seemed damn unfair, even to him, but
the only good that might come of it, in his
mind, was that as long as Spencer would be
away anyway, he wanted her to go back to
Vassar. She only had one year left, and it
would keep her busy while Spencer was in Korea. He made the necessary phone calls to Vassar himself the next day and she was even
more upset when he told her it was all arranged for her. Elizabeth sobbed in her room
at the cruelty of the fates. In a matter of days
everything she wanted had slipped through her
fingers. She had married him, and now he was
going off to war, and she was going back to
school, as though nothing had happened, as
though their wedding had never taken place at
all. Her father wouldn't even let her live in
New York and stay in Spencer's apartment.

"Spencer, I don't want you to go."

"Darling, I have to." He made love to her
tenderly, and wished secretly that she weren't
always so careful. He would have liked to leave
her with a baby. It would give her something

to think about and look forward to, and it would give him something even more meaningful to come home to. But she always used her diaphragm, and at the crucial time of month, forced him to use precautions too. She never took risks, but he didn't argue with her now. They had enough on their minds. He had to report to Fort Ord, and she was going back to Washington with her parents in a few days.

"Can't I at least stay with you in Monterey?"

"They won't even let me see you. There's no point. Go back with your mom and dad, and relax a little before you go back to school, and before you know it, I'll be home. And you can always go to New York and stay at the apartment on week-ends." It was like a nightmare for her, and he was desperately sorry in a way, and in another way he was anxious to go. He had enjoyed the camaraderie of war in some ways, and the past year at his desk on Wall Street had been secretly boring. Not that he would have admitted it to anyone, and not to her, but the thought of going to Korea was exciting to him.

She drove to Monterey with him, and after a long tearful good-bye, she went back to the lake to be with her parents. She was flying back to Washington in two days. And by then,

Spencer was up to his neck in a refresher course in combat training. He didn't even have a chance to call her before she left, and as Elizabeth sat between her parents on the trip east, she cried bitter tears for her husband. Her mother patted her hand sympathetically and handed her a fresh supply of hankies, as her father slept most of the way. He was tired and he had a lot of work waiting for him when he got back. For all of them, it was going to be a very long summer. Elizabeth only hoped that Korea wasn't going to be a long war. She wanted to start her life with her husband.

CHAPTER
23

Spencer was at Ford Ord for seven weeks, going over obstacles and being trained in mock maneuvers. It seemed amazing to him that in five years he had forgotten so much, but as the weeks dragged on, he felt taut and healthy again and his body seemed to remember more than his mind did. He fell into his bunk exhausted every night, too tired to move or talk or eat, or even call his wife. He had to make an effort to call her every few days just so she wouldn't be too worried. But Elizabeth complained more than she was worried. She was angry about him being away, when he could have been at home, going to parties. This wasn't how she'd envisioned spending the early days of their marriage. But who could have known that the war in Korea would come along to change everything. In an odd way, it was a reprieve for him, but a reprieve that he hadn't thought he wanted. He was sure when he married her, and yet now sometimes, when he called, he felt as though he were talking to a stranger. She told him about parties she went to with her parents' friends, and she had been to dinner at the White House with the Trumans. It was an odd time for Elizabeth, she was married, and yet it seemed like she wasn't. She had gone to Virginia to stay with friends, and the following week her mother was going to take her back to Vassar.

"I miss you so much, sweetheart." She sounded younger than she had before, and he smiled.

"I miss you too. I'll be home soon." But neither of them knew when. It could be months or years, and just thinking of it depressed her. She didn't want to go back to Vassar again, didn't want him to go away, and more than once she reproached him for staying in the reserves, but it was too late now. The damage was done, he was back in the army.

They gave him two weeks leave before ship-

ping out, but they told him he had to stay
within two hundred miles, in case they decided
to ship him out sooner. He almost hated to tell
Elizabeth about it, because she'd want to come
out, and he didn't think it was worth it. By
then, she had to be back at school within a few
days, and it would just upset them both saying
their good-byes again, and if they called him
back early, she would be bitterly disappointed.
He told her about his leave finally, and she
agreed with him, it seemed pointless to come
out, with the risk that he might have to leave
her at any moment. She suggested that he stay
at the house in San Francisco instead, and with
a thoughtful look he nodded.

"Are you sure your parents wouldn't
mind?" He didn't want to impose even if the
house was unoccupied. He didn't want them to
think he was taking advantage.

"Don't be stupid, you're family now. I'll ask
Mother if you like, but I know she'll think it's
fine." And when Elizabeth did ask her, Priscilla Barclay was quick to come to the phone
herself and urge Spencer to stay there. There
was a caretaker, and an old Chinese woman
who had worked for them for years, occupying
the house in the Barclays' absence.

"Just make yourself at home." She felt terrible that he was being sent away, and even

more so for her daughter's sake. Elizabeth had been miserable since leaving Spencer in California. It would be a relief to send her back to school. At least there she'd have something to do while she waited for her husband to come home from Korea.

Spencer drove to the city in a rented car, and moved into one of the elegant guest rooms. He had two weeks to himself and nothing much to do, but it was a relief to get away from the men he'd been living with, and the world of combat boots and dog tags. He was concerned about what he'd heard of the action in Korea. It sounded like an ugly little war, and he wasn't looking forward to going back to the Pacific. He was nine years older than he'd been the first time, and at thirty-one, he was a lot less anxious to be daring and brave. He had too much to live for now, and a hero's death in a strange land held little appeal for him, yet there were times when it was exciting to be free again. He had called the law firm where he worked when he got the news, and all of the senior partners had been very kind, and wished him well, and told him they'd be waiting for him, and so would his job, when it was over. But he would have to rethink all that one day too. Having a breather from it now, he was no longer quite as sure that he wanted to

go back to Wall Street. He was still a lot more
interested in criminal work, and there was certainly no hope of it there. But he'd have to talk
to Elizabeth about it anyway, before he did
anything drastic. And he suspected she would
want him to go back to the same firm on Wall
Street.

Spencer took a long walk around town, on
his first afternoon in San Francisco. It was a
warm August afternoon, and Crystal turned
nineteen that day. She was sharing a small
birthday cake at the restaurant with her
friends, and Harry gave her the night off, and
she bought a bottle of champagne to share
with Mrs. Castagna. She had moved into one
of the better rooms recently, when the man
who sold insurance got drafted and was sent to
Korea. It was a little larger and there was a
window that looked over a tiny corner of
someone's garden. But otherwise, nothing
much had changed. She was doing well singing
at Harry's restaurant, and she'd gotten several
favorable write-ups in the papers. She'd even
sung at several very fancy parties.

Boyd and Hiroko had come to see her twice,
with little Jane, when Hiroko came to see Dr.
Yoshikawa. And their new baby had been born
a month before, but this time there had been
no one to help her. The baby had been breech,

and he had died before Boyd could get anyone
to help her. He had had to go all the way to a
midwife in Calistoga, and left Hiroko alone
with Jane. It was lucky the midwife had agreed
to come, he hadn't told her his wife was Japanese, and she had saved her life. But she was
still in bed a month later, and Crystal had
promised her she would come to visit, but she
dreaded going back to the valley, even to see
her friend. It was just too painful for her. She
knew that Tom was still carrying on with
Boyd's sister, but Hiroko's last letter said that
he had reenlisted to go to Korea. Boyd had
been called back, too, but he had been suffering
from asthma for the past few years, and this
time they had refused to take him, which was
just as well. It would have been too hard on
Hiroko if he'd left her alone among still hostile
neighbors. Five years after the war, things
were still the same. Their hatred of her hadn't
dimmed. Their memories were long and their
hearts cold, especially now, with the hostilities
in Korea. To them it was all the same thing,
Korean, Japanese, most of them didn't know
the difference.

Crystal was lying on her bed, after she left
Mrs. Castagna, and feeling happy after two
glasses of champagne as she thought about her
life. She wondered where Spencer was, if he

had reenlisted too. Not that it mattered. He was gone from her life. He no longer existed. Except in her heart where he had always lived. And she couldn't help wondering if he was happily married. She tried not to let herself think of him now, but it was never easy, and with the champagne, he crept back into her mind and she let herself think of him, like a kind of birthday present.

It was hot in her room that night, and she decided to go for a walk in North Beach. There were people sitting in restaurants, and standing around the sidewalks talking in Italian. There were children scurrying past, chasing each other, and fleeing their mothers in the warm night air, and for a moment she was reminded of her own childhood, and being teased by Jared. She was wearing jeans and an old shirt, and her cowboy boots, and her long hair hung down her back in a single braid as she walked to the corner store to buy an ice-cream cone.

"Happy birthday," she muttered to herself, and then walked slowly back toward Mrs. Castagna's. The ice cream was dripping messily as she fought not to lose what was left, and looked like a child herself, leaning into the street as it dripped on her cowboy boots and she grinned at a little girl watching her. But what she didn't see was the tall, dark-haired soldier watching her from the distance. He had been lonely in the empty house and he had walked for miles that night, thinking of her and his wife, and tempted for the first time in a long time to go back and see Crystal. But he had satisfied himself with walking past the house where he knew she had once lived, when he had seen her just after Thanksgiving. He had assumed she'd be at work, and she should have been, and his heart raced the moment he saw her. It was like seeing a dream again, the girl in the blue jeans and the cowboy boots, standing over the gutter, and eating an ice cream, and for a moment he wasn't sure if he should approach her. She looked like a little girl as he stared at her, and then, as though she sensed him watching her, she turned, and froze as the ice cream fell from her hand. She straightened up and stared at him and then hurried back to Mrs. Castagna's, but he reached the front steps before she did.

"Crystal, wait . . ." He didn't know what he was going to say to her, but it was too late now. He knew he had to see her.

"Spencer, don't . . ." She turned to look at him with all the longing she had felt and he knew with absolute certainty how wrong he had been to leave her. Without saying a word, he reached out and touched her hand, and Crystal wanted to resist him but she couldn't. "Crystal . . . please . . ." He was begging her. He only knew that he had to talk to her, even for a minute, just to see her, and hold her, and be near her. She looked at him, and they both knew that it was all still there, just exactly where they had left it, only more so. He said not a word to her but pulled her into his arms and held her, and this time, she didn't fight him.

He knew what a fool he had been, to listen to Elizabeth, and to George, and himself. He had been wrong to marry her when all he wanted was Crystal. He had tried to do the right thing, and in spite of everything, he hadn't. All he wanted now was this girl, with the platinum hair and the lavender eyes. The girl he had loved for four years now.

"What are we going to do, Spencer?" she whispered as he held her.

"I don't know. Take what we can, I guess, for as long as we can have it." It was like an addiction that picked up just where they had left it. Elizabeth was all but forgotten as he looked at Crystal.

"Why did you come back here?" She meant to the place where she lived, not just San Francisco.

"Because I had to. I wanted to see you again, or at least the place where I last saw you."

"And then what?" She looked up at him sadly, all her strength and resistance seeping away from her, leaving only the love she had felt since she'd first met him. "You're married now." She had read about the wedding in the papers. "Where is . . . your wife?" She hated the word, and she had to force herself to say it. It was easy to think now of how different things might have been if he hadn't gone ahead with his engagement. They both thought of it as he looked at her, and he held her hand in his own as he ached to kiss her.

"She's in New York." He didn't even want to say her name, not now, not in the presence of Crystal. "I'm shipping out to Korea in a few days, and I had some time to spare . . . I . . . Christ, Crystal, I don't know what to tell you . . . I feel like such a bastard. I've made a mistake. I know that now. That's a hell of a thing to say right after getting married. I thought I was doing the right thing. I told myself that. I wanted to believe it was, but when I see you, my head spins . . . my whole life turns upside down. I should have run off with you last November and to hell with doing the 'right thing' and being noble. We had just got-

ten engaged . . . I thought . . . oh Christ
. . . what do I know?" He looked anguished.

But for a moment, her eyes sparked fire at
him, and the deep lavender eyes were angry.
Her voice came at him like a growl, and he
didn't blame her. "And where does that leave
me, Spencer? Playing games with you when
you're on leave? . . . when you have a weekend off? . . . when you can get away? What
about me? What about *my* life, after you leave
me?" She had promised herself she wouldn't
see him again, even if she had the chance,
which she had doubted. There was no point to
it. He had made a choice, and she was going to
live by it, even if he wasn't. That was why she
had returned his letter unopened. "What exactly did you have in mind?" She was clearly
angry now, and it only made her more appealing to Spencer. "A little fun before you leave?
Well, forget it. Go to hell . . . or back to her
. . . that's what you'll do anyway, just like
you did last time."

He looked at her unhappily, he couldn't
deny what she said, even though he wanted to.
He wanted to promise her he wouldn't go back
to Elizabeth, but they were married now, and
he didn't know what to do about it. He
couldn't tell her the marriage was over before
it even started. But that was what he thought

and what he wanted. He wanted to stay with Crystal forever. "I can't make you any promises. I can't give you anything right now, except what I am, right now minute by minute. And maybe that's not much . . . but it's all I have to give, that and the fact that I love you."

"What does that mean?" Her eyes filled with tears as she looked at him and her voice was deep and husky. "I love you too. But so what? What does that get us six months from now?"

"For the moment . . ." He smiled sadly at her, he didn't want to hurt her, and he wondered if he'd been wrong to come, but he just couldn't help it. "For right now, it'll get you a bunch of letters from Korea . . . if you'll read them this time." She turned away so he wouldn't see her cry. He was so handsome and she had loved him for so long, and when she looked up at him again, she realized that deep in her heart she didn't care that he was married. He was hers, right then, for as long as they had, and maybe, just maybe that was worth grabbing and holding, until he left for Korea.

Crystal bowed her head, thinking of what he had said, and then slowly she turned again and looked up at him. "I wish I had the courage to tell you to go . . ." But she didn't finish the sentence.

"I will if you want me to. I'll do whatever you want." . . . and dream about you for the rest of my life . . . "Is that what you want, Crystal?" He looked down at her and touched her cheek with long, gentle fingers as he spoke softly. He loved her. He would have done anything for her. It was exactly the kind of love he had talked to Elizabeth about before. The kind they had never had, and never would, he knew now.

But she only shook her head, her eyes boring into him with silent adoration. "No, it isn't what I want." She was honest with him, she always had been, and he could barely hear her speak, but his heart trembled as she said it. "Maybe all we have a right to is this . . . a few days . . . a few borrowed moments . . ." It didn't seem like much, but it was all they had, and to both of them, it was worth it.

"Maybe there'll be more than that one day . . . but I can't promise you that yet. I can't promise you anything. I don't know what's going to happen." He looked upset but he wanted to be honest. She smiled strangely at him then and took his hand in hers, and began to walk slowly up the steps at Mrs. Castagna's.

"I do."

He felt like a very young boy again, as he

followed her into the house, still holding her hand and watching the mane of shining hair, and her long, lean body mounting the stairs just ahead of him. She turned only once to put a finger to her lips and signal to him to stay silent. She took her key out of a pocket of her jeans and let him into the room. She didn't want Mrs. Castagna to hear them. She would have been sure to cause a scene. She didn't like girls taking men to their rooms, or her male boarders to bring in women. It happened from time to time, but when she found out, as she often did, lying in wait for them just inside her front door, she registered strong disapproval.

"Take your shoes off," Crystal whispered, slipping off her cowboy boots, and revealing a pair of red socks that had once been her brother's. She smiled at Spencer then and sat down on the edge of her bed, looking like a little girl again. There were moments when he remembered easily the child she had been, and then just as suddenly she returned to being a very desirable young woman.

He was whispering as he sat down next to her, and she smiled shyly as he touched her hair, and then kissed her. It was a gentle kiss, a kiss filled with longing, and gratitude for her willingness to accept the little he could give her. "I love you so much . . ." he whispered slowly into her hair, "you're so beautiful . . . so good . . ." He ached with desire for her, and it took all his strength to resist the urge to tear her clothes off. But when he reached nimble fingers into her shirt, he saw her flinch for just an instant. He pulled away, wondering what he'd done, but she kissed him fervently then, and forced herself to let him explore her. He watched her cautiously, afraid to frighten her, sure that she was a virgin. "Are you afraid?" She shook her head and her eyes were closed as he laid her gently on the bed and slowly undressed her. He stopped only long enough to pull the shades, and when she lay naked and splendid on her narrow bed, he took off his own clothes, and helped her to slip under the covers. He remembered how shy she had been as a young girl and he didn't want to embarrass her, or scare her, or hurt her. He wanted everything to be perfect for her, and he wanted it to be a moment they would both treasure forever. She was even lovelier than he'd dreamed, and as he entered her at last, they both moaned softly. She writhed in his arms, and he kissed her endlessly, holding her and whispering his love for her softly. They lay together for a long time, and when it was over, he clutched her close to him, as though they could become one body and one soul if he held her for long enough, and nothing could ever part them.

She lay dreamily in his arms, and he frowned when he saw a single tear roll down her cheek. "Crystal . . . are you okay?" And then, feeling a terrible pang of guilt, "Are you sorry?" He had so little to offer her, he had no right . . . and yet he knew how much he loved her.

But she shook her head and smiled at him through her tears, as she whispered, "I'm not sorry . . . I love you."

"Then what's wrong?"

"Nothing." She shook her head again, but for a moment the memory of Tom had enveloped her, even though this was so different.

"Tell me." He pulled her even closer to him, and her tears fell on his naked shoulder. She wiped them away, but they only came faster. He encircled her tightly with his arms, worried about her. She needed him so badly, she was so vulnerable and so young and she had no one to take care of her, except him. It wasn't fair, and soon he would have to leave her. "I won't let you go till you tell me what you're thinking."

"I was thinking how happy I am." She smiled through her tears, but he didn't believe her.

"You could have fooled me. I could have

sworn you were crying." He loved being with her, loved the sweet smell of her flesh, and the clean silk of her hair. He loved everything about her. "Something happened to you, didn't it?" His voice was so gentle, it only made her cry more. He had suspected but he hadn't dared ask her, and the story of her going after Tom Parker with her father's gun hadn't been forgotten.

And now, as she looked at him with sad eyes, she nodded.

"Do you want to talk about it?"

She shook her head, looking childlike again. "I can't . . . it was too awful. . . ."

"It must have been. But it doesn't matter now, little love. Whatever it was, it's all gone now. And maybe if you talk about it, it'll be less of a burden."

She looked at him hesitantly for a long time, wondering what he would think of her if she told him Tom had raped her. And then, slowly, knowing that she could trust him, she told him the awful tale. He lay very still, holding her, letting her tell him all of it as she clung to him and sobbed. Spencer's eyes blazed, listening to her, but his voice was gentle and kind and she felt safe lying in his arms.

"You should have killed him. It's a damn shame you didn't. I think I would have if I'd

been there." And he meant it, but she shook
her head vehemently. She knew better now.
But it was too late for Jared.

"I was wrong . . . if I hadn't . . .
if . . ." She couldn't bear to say it again, even
to Spencer. "If I hadn't done that, he wouldn't
have killed Jared. . . . Oh, Spencer . . . it
was all my fault . . . I killed him." She
sobbed endlessly in his arms, as he kissed her
and held her.

"It's not your fault. None of it was . . .
that part was an accident, and it was Tom's
fault, not yours. He shot him, Crystal, you
didn't. He raped you, and that wasn't your
fault either." His soul burned just thinking
about it, and his hands clenched involuntarily
at the images she had painted . . . the barn
floor . . . and the leering face over her . . .
his brutality . . . and his killing her brother.

As all the while, Crystal was looking miserably up at Spencer. "I wanted to kill him. I
wanted to hurt him as badly as he hurt me
. . . that was wrong . . . and Jared died because of it." He'd paid the price, and so had
she, she had lost her brother, her home, her
family. It was a hell of a price to pay for Tom
Parker's sins, and for a minute, Spencer knew
that if he had been in her shoes, he would have

pulled the trigger, and he was a much better shot than she was.

"You have to put it out of your mind now. You can't change any of it. All you can do is decide not to carry it with you."

"I can't ever do that. What I did killed my brother."

"That's not true." He sat up, and she cuddled up next to him as he put an arm around her shoulders. "You didn't do anything, Crystal. Do you understand that?" She shook her head again and he knew instinctively that he would never convince her. She would carry it with her all her life, and secretly believe that it was her fault Tom had raped her, for some reason she couldn't quite explain, and for very obvious reasons she felt as though she had killed her brother. Believing that had changed her life, and Spencer didn't want it to mark her any further. "You have to look ahead of you now, and think of all the good things in store for you. You've got your singing, and you may have a big career one day." Then with a smile, "And you've got me now." For a minute . . . or a day . . . or perhaps a lifetime.

She smiled up at him, and kissed him gently on the cheek, and he returned the kiss to her lips with fresh passion. And as they kissed, they were both wondering what would happen, what the future held for them, if anything. But it was too soon to think about that yet. Everything was brand-new between them. After a long while she calmed down and stopped crying, as she nestled beside him.

"Do you really think I might have a big career one day?" It seemed hard to believe, but she liked the sound of it, and he seemed convinced, which pleased her.

"Yes, I do. And I mean that. You have an incredible voice. One day you're going to be a big star, Crystal. I really believe that."

"I don't see how." It seemed like light years from Hollywood to San Francisco, but she still had her dreams, and she liked what she was doing.

"Give yourself time. You just started. Life is just beginning for you. When you're my age, people will be lined up in the streets begging to hear you." She laughed at the thought, and teased him as her long blond hair brushed his shoulder.

"Thanks, Grampa . . ."

"A little respect for your elders." But his hand touching her thigh demanded her full attention, and a moment later she lay in his arms again, and all else was put aside as she gave herself to him with her whole heart. All she wanted was what they had, even Hollywood seemed to dim in comparison to what she had with Spencer.

She slept in his arms that night, breathing quietly, her face like a child's, her head on his shoulder, and he had never been happier in his life. He knew that this was what he had lived for.

And in the morning, they went for a long walk and went out to breakfast. She talked animatedly about Harry's restaurant and how much she loved singing there. It was as though they had always been together as Spencer grinned at her and listened. The shy little girl was gone, and he was left with the woman he had always dreamed of.

They looked like newlyweds and no one would ever have guessed that he was married to another woman. Crystal was chattering happily and he laughed and bent over and kissed her. He was fascinated by everything she said. It wasn't politics for a change, or the kind of things he and Elizabeth argued about. It was just real life, and the things that mattered to both Spencer and Crystal.

They went back to her room afterward, and made love again, and that afternoon when he took her to work, he was stunned to realize how much he missed her. Every hour away from her was painful to him, and he went back to the Barclays' house to pick up some things so he could move in with her while he stayed in San Francisco. He thought of Elizabeth briefly as he packed his things. But she didn't seem important now. Nothing did. Except Crystal.

Feeling dutiful, he called Elizabeth that night after he dropped Crystal off at work, and woke her up, although it was only ten-thirty. She said she was bored, and she sounded plaintive as she asked him when he was leaving for Korea.

"No news yet. I'll call you when I know." And then he told her he was staying with friends, he said he was too lonely at the Barclays'. She smiled as she talked to him then, and he promised to call again in a few days. And if she needed to, she could leave a message for him at the Barclays'. He'd call in for messages from time to time. But his voice was cool, although she didn't seem to notice.

And half an hour later, he left the house again. And Elizabeth left his mind, as completely as she seemed to have left his life. It was almost as if they had never been married. But he refused to let himself think about it, as he watched Crystal sing that night, and knew her songs were just for him. And after work, they walked back to the house on Green

Street. He had never been happier in his life, and she looked pretty in a flowered dress. She left her satin evening gowns at work. They were only for when she sang, and she looked young again, with her hair loose, and her face free of makeup as she turned to him with a peaceful smile. All her sorrows seemed to have left her since he'd walked back into her life. And their whole world was limited to each other.

"Spencer," her voice was soft as she looked at him, "will you write to me when you're gone?"

"Of course, I will." But they both knew that when he came back, he would have to face the issue of his marriage. And Spencer didn't know yet what he was going to do. He was living day by day, and Crystal asked nothing more of him. He made no promises he couldn't keep this time, kept no secrets from her. All they knew was what they had, and for two brief weeks, it was perfect.

CHAPTER 24

Spencer went back to Monterey on September third, and two days later he was due to fly to Taegu by way of Tokyo, and before he left, he went to San Francisco for one more night with Crystal. Harry had given her the night off, and they walked for hours, talking and holding hands. They wanted the night never to end, and they wanted to remember each moment they had shared. Neither of them regretted anything. It had been perfection.

"You're not sorry, are you?" He was always worried about her, but in a matter of hours there would be so little he could do for her.

She was going to have to be strong while he was gone, and perhaps forever after that. But strength wasn't something she lacked. What he regretted was that there was no one to watch over her, as he would have liked to.

"No, I'm not sorry. I love you too much to regret anything." She smiled at him. She looked peaceful and she seemed to have grown up even more in the two weeks she'd spent with him. She was comfortable with him, and their nights together had been filled with loving. "I'm going to miss you so much though." And then, with worried eyes, "Keep safe, Spencer . . . don't let anything happen to you."

"Nothing will, silly. I'll be fine. I'll be back before you know it." But neither of them knew what would happen when he did come back from Korea. There still didn't seem to be any easy answers, and maybe there never would be. But he wondered if perhaps, away from both of them, it would all come clearer to him. He knew he had to do something eventually. They couldn't go on like this forever. But he had made Crystal no promises about the future yet and she asked him for none now. She wanted nothing from him except what he'd given her in the two weeks since he'd found her on the street eating her ice cream on her birthday.

They went back to her room again, and made love for a last time, and there were tears in her eyes when he dressed. It hurt just seeing him in his uniform, and she walked stealthily downstairs when he left to drive back to Monterey, and stood outside on the front steps in bare feet and her nightgown.

"Go back inside. I'll call you when I get there." He was whispering again. For two weeks they had successfully managed to elude Mrs. Castagna.

"I love you." She choked on her tears as she said the words, and he held her close, wanting to imprint her on his mind and body forever—he wanted her to remember him and the two weeks they had shared, in case he never came back at all. He was going to war after all, and God only knew what would happen.

"I love you, Crystal." It was all he could say to her, as he hurried down the stairs and around the corner to the car he'd parked there. And a moment later, he waved as he drove away, and she walked silently upstairs to the room that was so empty without him. He was gone and she knew she might never see him again, and yet she knew that she would never forget him. He was too precious to her, too embedded in her heart ever to leave her now, no matter what happened.

He called her when he reached Monterey. And the final hour had come. He was leaving that morning at ten-thirty. He called Elizabeth after that, and had to content himself with leaving a message for her. She was in classes, but it was a relief for him. He had been avoiding her for days, and only calling her when he knew he had to. It was difficult to play the game, and she knew him too well. She picked up every inflection, every mood, dissected every sentence. But so far, although he knew he should feel terrible about it, he had managed to fool her. It wasn't what he had planned, but all his plans had gone awry the moment he had seen Crystal. He had had to be with her, as long as she was willing to let him stay with her. And every moment with her had been precious.

And as the flight to Hickam Field in Hawaii left Monterey, Spencer looked out the window and saw the last of the West Coast, and all he could think of was Crystal. The girl of his dreams, the woman he loved beyond reason.

And at the same moment, she stood looking up at the sky, knowing that far south of there, he was leaving and heading for the war. She prayed for his safety, and closed her eyes, and then fighting back tears, she went back into the house, and went silently to the room she had shared for two weeks with Spencer. It suddenly seemed as though it had been only moments. There had been so much left unsaid, so many things they wanted to do and didn't have time for. He had wanted to drive up to the valley too, but Crystal had been reluctant. As much as she wanted to see Boyd and Hiroko and Jane, she didn't want to run into her mother or her sister or Tom. She didn't want to go back there again, and two weeks later when Boyd called from the gas station to tell her that her grandmother had died, she didn't want to go back then either.

They were going to bury Grandma Minerva on the ranch, near her father and Jared. She had died in her sleep, and Boyd said he heard her mom was real upset, but Crystal hardened her heart and thanked him for letting her know, but said she wasn't coming.

"Thanks for telling me though." Another chapter closed. Another one gone. The only family she had left were Becky and her mother, and they were dead to her now. "How's Hiroko?"

"She's back on her feet again. But . . . it's been kind of rough on her . . . You know . . ." She had been mourning the baby she had lost, and for two months now, nothing had consoled her. And this time the doctor had told her there could be no more children. There would be only Jane . . . little Jane Keiko . . . the baby Crystal had delivered with Boyd. Her godchild.

"Why don't you come down to see me here?" She didn't tell him she had seen Spencer. It was their secret.

"We might sometime." And then, hesitantly, "You know Tom is gone, don't you? He left for Korea two weeks ago. I think your sister's real upset. At least that's what my sister tells me. I think she's damn lucky to be rid of the bastard." He couldn't restrain himself and Crystal's eyes were cold as she listened. She hated all of them now, all of them except Boyd and Hiroko and Jane. Her life had gone far past them.

"Who's running the ranch?"

"Your mom and Becky, I guess. They've got enough ranch hands to manage okay, unless they all get drafted." It was going to be like the war again, or so it seemed. It seemed so cruel after only five years respite. But at least Boyd wasn't going anywhere. She was glad for Hiroko that they had refused him. "You okay, Crystal?"

"I'm fine. Just hanging around down here, singing my heart out." There had been a lot more than that, but she didn't want to tell anyone, not even the Websters. "Why don't you think about coming down?"

"We'll try. And Crystal . . . I'm really sorry about your grandma." She had almost forgotten that that was why he had called her, and so had he, but old man Petersen was signaling to him to get back to work, and he had to get off the phone quickly.

"Thanks, Boyd. Give Hiroko and Jane my love. And let me know if you're coming down to San Francisco."

"We will." He hung up and she sat staring into space in Mrs. Castagna's hallway.

"Something wrong?" She appeared like a ghost whenever she heard what she thought was an interesting phone call.

Crystal turned to her with a sigh. "My grandmother died."

"That's too bad. Was she very old?" Mrs. Castagna looked sorry for her. She was so alone, and so young and pretty and decent.

"Almost eighty, I think." But she had looked a hundred, and she had never seen her granddaughter again, but Crystal wouldn't let herself think of it now. It was too late for that. Grandma Minerva was gone. And she had enough to worry about, with Spencer in Korea.

"You goin' home to the funeral?" She was curious about everything.

Crystal shook her head. "I don't think so."

"You on bad terms with your family, ain't you?" There was never a phone call, never a letter, except from some people called Webster, and she never went anywhere either, except in the last few weeks with the boy she'd hidden in her bedroom. But Mrs. Castagna had pretended not to know it because she liked her.

"I told you, my parents are dead." Mrs. Castagna nodded, she had never quite believed her. But Crystal's eyes gave away nothing as the old woman looked at her. She was even older than Minerva had been, but she was full of life, and had no intention of dying for a long time.

"How's your friend?" For an instant, Crystal didn't answer. She knew she had to mean Spencer, and she looked noncommittal as she started back up the stairs to her bedroom.

"He's fine."

"He go somewhere?"

She stood at the top of the stairs and looked down at her with a look of sorrow in her eyes that said it all. "Yes. To Korea."

The old woman nodded, and went back to the kitchen, to look out her window. She had wondered about him. She knew he was staying upstairs, but Crystal had been alone for so long that she'd let them be, which was very unusual for her. Crystal hadn't given her any trouble in over a year, and he looked like a nice man. It was just too bad she was sleeping with him, but a girl like that, with no parents, no one to look after her, it wasn't surprising. And he was the only man she'd ever seen Crystal with. He looked like a good man, a decent person. It was too bad he'd gone to the war. She hoped, as Crystal did, that he'd survive it. And upstairs, in her room, Crystal lay down on the narrow bed she'd shared with him, and cried, praying that she'd see him again, that he'd live, and come home to her, maybe this time forever.

CHAPTER
25 ————————————————

The next six months seemed endless to them all, Crystal as she sang in the restaurant night after night, Elizabeth at school, and Spencer in Korea. He wrote to them both as often as he could, but sometimes he felt crazy when he mailed the letters. What if he'd made a mistake, if he'd gotten the two letters confused, if he'd used Elizabeth's address and Crystal's name, and his wife still got the letter? He was so tired sometimes that it was entirely possible, but in point of fact, he made no mistakes. He just worried about it a lot. And he tortured himself constantly about making a decision.

He told Crystal how he felt, how he longed
for her, and how much he loved her. But he
made no promises about after the war. He
hadn't figured out yet what to do about Elizabeth, or whether or not he really wanted to
divorce her. He knew how much he loved
Crystal and he also knew he had to give one of
them up, he couldn't go on like this forever.
But he owed Elizabeth something too. He had
started something with her, and it wasn't her
fault he didn't love her. It wasn't anyone's
fault. But it certainly complicated things, and
for the moment, he was too busy just surviving
the war to make a real decision. He knew it
had to wait till he got home, and in the meantime, he wrote to Elizabeth about what he saw,
the costumes, the monuments, the customs,
the people. He knew she'd be fascinated by it,
along with the political implications. And it
wasn't that Crystal was less aware of things, it
was only that their sphere of interests was different, and his need for Crystal's heart was far
greater. Elizabeth wrote to him about how
tired of school she was, an old song he'd heard
before, and about her parents' dinner parties
during vacations. She'd been to stay with Ian
and Sarah several times in New York, but they
were helping to start a new hunt in Connecticut, and now they were spending all their

weekends in Kentucky, buying Sarah new horses. And more than once, Elizabeth mentioned how glad she was that she hadn't gotten pregnant. It was just the opposite of what Crystal had hoped, but with the situation so confused, Spencer was relieved that neither of them was pregnant.

The letters from Elizabeth were more like newsletters from back home. The ones from Crystal fed his soul and kept him going.

Elizabeth graduated in June, and her parents were there of course. She had invited Spencer's parents too, and she sounded immensely pleased with herself that it was all over. He got the letter when he was in Pusan, feeling as though he would die from the humidity and the heat, helping his men to negotiate their way through the narrow pathways between rice paddies. It was a bitter fight, and more than once, he felt they didn't belong there. He knew he and Elizabeth would have some real battles over it once he got home, if they were still married. It was an odd thought as he wrote to her, particularly since she didn't know what he was thinking, or what had happened with Crystal before he left San Francisco.

And that summer, when Elizabeth went to the lake, as she always did, Crystal finally decided to go back to the valley. She had thought about it for a long time, and with Tom Parker gone, she decided to brave it. All she had to face now were her own painful memories of her father and Jared. And it was odd being there and not going to the ranch, but she had no desire to see her mother or Becky.

She stayed with the Websters for a few days and it felt good being back, as she lazed in the sun and inhaled the perfume of the valley. She even forced herself to drive past the ranch, and it looked overgrown and deserted. All the ranch hands had finally been drafted, and she'd heard from Boyd that her mother was using Mexicans to come in daily and tend the vineyards and the corn. She and Becky had finally sold off the last of the cattle. And it was Spencer who wrote to her later on and told her that Tom had been killed trying to recapture Seoul, and as Crystal read it, she felt a pang of guilt to realize she was glad. She would never forgive him for killing her brother. She wondered how Becky had taken the news, and if she would stay on the ranch with her three children and her mother. It had occurred to her too that they might even sell it. She hated the thought but there was nothing she could do about it anymore. It was someone else's life

now, not hers. Sometimes it was hard to believe she had ever lived there.

At Christmas, Boyd and Hiroko came down
finally to hear her sing. They looked happy
and well. They had left Jane at home with old
Mr. Petersen's wife, who was eager to have
her. She was three and a half years old, and
looked more than ever like Hiroko, from the
pictures they showed her. But above all, they
were impressed by how well Crystal looked.
She had grown even slimmer, which accented
her remarkable figure. And she had been learning new tricks from going to movies. Her fa-
vorites were *An American in Paris* and *Born
Yesterday*, and Pearl was still coaching her
from time to time in voice and dance. But by
then she had far surpassed her friend's knowledge.

Boyd and Hiroko were amazed by the power
of her voice when they heard her. Crystal had
turned Harry's nightclub into a gold mine. He
was even bragging about her to friends, and it
came as no surprise to him when two agents
from L.A. came to the restaurant and gave
Crystal their card and asked her to call them.
They invited her to look them up if she ever
came to Hollywood, and suggested that she
should come down sometime for a screen test.
It was late February by then, and Crystal was

beside herself with excitement as she showed
Pearl the card, but she still didn't feel ready for
Hollywood yet. And secretly, she wanted to
wait for Spencer where he'd left her. She wrote
to him about the agents in her next letter,
which he got a month later, in March, as he sat
near the 38th Parallel.

He wondered if she would go to Hollywood
to look them up. Part of him wanted her to,
and another part of him wanted her to wait to
begin her life until he got back from Korea. He
knew it wasn't fair, but now that he was so far
away, he was afraid to lose her. She was young
and beautiful and she had a right to a full life.
But he was desperately afraid now that she'd
find a life without him. But there was less danger of that than he knew. All she cared about
was Spencer, as she waited.

She heard from him less frequently now, but
she knew from him that conditions had grown
worse, and the constant attempts at a truce
were failing, with new deaths and countless
disappointments every time. Spencer sounded
depressed when he wrote to tell her about it.
Like everyone else, he wanted the war to end,
but it seemed to go on forever. And Crystal
was startled too when he told her that Elizabeth had met him in Tokyo for R and R. He
almost made her sound like a casual acquain-

tance, but Crystal was passionately jealous just thinking of it. Why couldn't she go to Tokyo too? He had been gone for so long, as she waited devotedly for him, living at Mrs. Castagna's and singing at Harry's. There was no other man in her life. She didn't want anyone. Only Spencer. And no man she ever met ever measured up to him. She was twenty-one and beautiful beyond words, and she loved him more than anything. His only flaw was that he was married. Her friend Pearl tried to encourage her to find someone else, to no avail. Crystal wasn't interested, and she had plenty of offers. The men who came to Harry's to hear her sing went wild over her, and she was constantly being invited out, but she never went. She was faithful to Spencer.

She seemed to get more beautiful each year, and by that summer, Harry thought she had never looked better. There was a luminous quality about her as she sang that made the whole room go quiet. And there was a gentleness and a sweetness about her that made her more beautiful still. Harry was curious, too, about why there was no man in her life, and he wondered sometimes if there was someone she was seeing quietly, but Crystal never talked about her love life, and Harry never asked her.

In Washington, Elizabeth had gone to work, assisting with the House Committee on Un-American Activities investigations. She was deeply committed to her work, and she had a prestigious job. They were single-handedly changing the course of several lives in Hollywood, and in May, Elizabeth was particularly enraged by the testimony of the well-known playwright Lillian Hellman. She refused to testify on the grounds that although she might not be a Communist herself, her testimony might affect the lives of the people she worked with and liked. Elizabeth had long talks with her father about it at night, and she wrote about all of it in letters to Spencer, explaining to him about what she was doing, and how she felt about McCarthy. He stayed off the subject when he answered her, and inquired about her health and her parents, but not her job. He hated everything she was doing. She knew he disapproved of it, but she had to do what she believed in, and she liked the job. And she wouldn't have given it up for anything, except if Spencer came home and went back to work on Wall Street. But she was intending to talk him into moving to Washington anyway. And in the fall of 1952, she decided to give up his apartment for good. She bought a house on N Street in Georgetown from the money from

her trust fund, and put most of Spencer's belongings in brown boxes. It was a pretty brick
house, and it suited her perfectly. It was near
Wisconsin Avenue's better shops, and she
bought antiques with her mother when she had
time, and that winter there were photographs
of the house in *Look* magazine, which she sent
to Spencer. And as he looked at the article, it
struck him that none of the photographs included anything of his. He wondered what she
had done with all his belongings. And suddenly he felt as if he had no home to go to
when the war was over. He didn't even know
where they lived, he couldn't visualize it, except for the photographs in the magazine. And
it all looked so sterile and perfect. He couldn't
even imagine making love to her in the fussy
little bedroom where she'd posed. And seeing
it only made him lonelier for Crystal, and her
room at Mrs. Castagna's, which only made
him feel crazy again about what he was going
to do when the war was over. Did he have an
obligation to Liz? Or to himself, to do what he
really wanted?

Elizabeth spent Christmas in Palm Beach
with her parents, as usual, that year, and after
that she flew to Tokyo again to see Spencer for
R and R. He had dreaded seeing her this time,
and he had reminded himself that she was his

wife, after all, but as they lay in bed side by side, he could hardly bring himself to touch her. All she did was talk about her job and Joe McCarthy.

"Why don't we talk about something else," he said politely. He looked tired and thin and he didn't want to hear about the war she was waging on imagined Communists in Mc-Carthy's name. All she had was an investigative job, but listening to her one would have thought she was McCarthy's avenging angel, and hearing her depressed him even more. He knew who the real Communists were and he was tired of fighting them. He had been in Korea for more than two years and he wanted to go home, but the current truce had been violated again, and he was beginning to feel he would never get out of Korea. And all he wanted from her was a little warmth and comfort. But she was the wrong woman for that, as he was beginning to see very clearly. She hardly seemed to notice him, all she thought about was her work and her friends and her parents. It didn't even seem like a marriage to him, and yet she was his wife and not Crystal.

And when he tried to talk to her about the war and his disillusionment, she brushed him off, and made it seem unimportant.

"You'll be back on Wall Street before you

know it." He didn't answer her at first, but later he told her what he had been thinking, just to test the waters.

"I don't think I'll go back." She nodded, pleased. That fitted in well with her plans. She wanted to move to Washington permanently anyway. She had come to love it.

"There are plenty of good law firms in Washington. You're going to love it, Spencer."

"I want to rethink my life when I get home." He eyed her seriously, tempted for a moment to tell her about Crystal. The charade had gone on too long, and it was exhausting. But now was not the time. Instead he suggested they go out and wander the streets of Tokyo and enjoy the luxuries of the Imperial Hotel.

Most of the men on R and R stayed on Lake Biwa but her father had made their reservations. He wanted them to go first class. Elizabeth loved to talk about her father's generosity. She was constantly telling him about the antiques her father had bought them for the new house, the little French chandelier, the Persian carpet. Spencer was sick of hearing about it. And he felt like a fraud as he listened, pretending to be interested or pleased or grateful. He had signed on for a lifetime of gratitude, he realized now, and he knew that wasn't what he wanted. It diminished him and made him feel unimportant because he didn't have as much money and power as they did. That was all that mattered to them, Elizabeth and her parents. And he had no desire to compete with them. He wanted a life of his own in a world where he was respected. But he couldn't begin to tell her that, not in a few days before he went back to the war in Korea. Everything she talked about seemed so unimportant now. He had seen women and children die, he had cried over dead babies he had found by the roadside and buried. He had lived with shattered ideals and distant dreams for too long now. And when he tried to say that to her, she didn't even want to listen, or hear him. She was totally self-centered and totally unaware of the agonies he'd endured in the past two years. And in the end he was sorry he'd gone to meet her. He vowed to himself not to do it again if the war went on. He would wait and resolve their differences when he got back to the States. Here, it was too unreal, too strange, and in an odd way too painful.

He went back to the war even more depressed this time. He felt alienated from everyone, and he had developed a passionate hatred of Korea, and the miseries he had to endure there. He tried to write to Crystal about it at first, but when he reread the letters, he always decided not to send them. They sounded whining and cowardly, and unmanly. So what she got instead were long silences interrupted occasionally by a brief letter that told her only that he was still alive, and said tersely at the end that he still loved her. He was unable to communicate with anyone anymore, even Crystal. He couldn't describe how brutally tired he was, how sick with dysentery, how demoralized by the constant killing, how angry at the death of his friends. And eventually it all boiled up inside him, until finally he was silent.

When that happened, Justice Barclay had military connections check on him, and they said he was fine, just busy winning the war. But Crystal had no connections to turn to. All she knew was that he had stopped writing to her, and at first she thought he'd been killed— but when she checked, his name appeared on none of the casualty lists of those wounded or killed or missing in action. He was alive somewhere, and he was no longer writing to her. It took months for it to sink in, that he wasn't dead, the letters weren't getting lost, he simply wasn't writing. And she assumed that it meant their love affair was over. It was hard to believe at first, after all they'd said and shared, but there was no hiding from it after several

months, it was over. After years of her waiting
for him, he had simply decided to stop writing.
He had probably seen his wife again, and decided to stay married. But he could have told
her at least, he could have said something, instead of simply disappearing into silence. It
hurt terribly at first, and left alone with her
own confusions, she mourned him. She
mourned him almost as she would have if he'd
died, and it felt like it for a while. She even
took two weeks off and went by herself to
Mendocino. She did a lot of thinking there and
when she came back, she knew she had to
move on, with or without him.

She called the agents then, the ones who had
approached her months before, and after a
brief conversation, she agreed to go to Hollywood for an audition.

She told Harry the night she went back to
work, and he was surprised at first, but he had
always known it was only a matter of time before someone found her and gave her the
chance she'd waited for all her life and deserved. She had nothing else to wait for now.
The moment had come and she knew she had
to grab it.

"Who are these guys?" Harry was suspicious of everyone, and for years now he had
protected her like a father, keeping drunks

away, and the men who constantly tried to harass her. "Do you know anything about them?"

"Just that they're agents in L.A.," she said honestly. There was still an aura of innocence about her.

"Then I want you to take Pearl with you, she can stay as long as you need her. And if it doesn't work out, you come right back here with her. Another chance will come along one of these days. I want you to wait for the right offer."

"Yes, sir." She grinned at him, looking like a kid again, and thrilled that Pearl was going to go with her. The prospect of Hollywood still scared her, but she knew more than ever that it was what she wanted. People had been telling her for years that she'd be a star one day, Boyd, Harry, Spencer, Pearl, and now she wanted to try it.

Harry gave her a farewell party before she left, and he gave them money to stay at a decent hotel, and she spent most of her savings on a new wardrobe. It was hard leaving Harry. It was a little bit like leaving home. She had made friends and found safety there, and now she was going out in the world to find fame and fortune. It would have terrified her if she hadn't wanted it so badly.

It was hard leaving Mrs. Castagna too. She left a bag there, but she gave up her room. And the old woman had cried and offered her one last glass of sherry. It tore at Crystal's heart-strings to leave her, but she promised to write from Hollywood and tell her about the stars she met there.

"You see Clark Gable, you give him my love!" she admonished over the last glass of sherry. "And you take care of yourself! You hear me!" Crystal had kissed her when she left, and she had cried openly when she left Harry.

"If you need money, kid, you call me!" But he'd been too good to her already. She wouldn't have dared ask him for more, and she was determined not to. Besides, if her screen test went well, maybe she'd get a part soon. She had high hopes as she and Pearl left on a Thursday afternoon, by train because it was cheaper. They had already reserved a hotel room in L.A., and Crystal had an appointment with the agents the following morning.

She walked into their office with trembling knees, wearing a plain white dress and white shoes, with her hair pulled back off her face and very little makeup. She looked clean and pure, and incredibly beautiful. At twenty-one, she was even better-looking than they remembered. And as they stared at her, they were overwhelmed by their good fortune.

But what Crystal didn't know, and Pearl smelled, was that they were ranked among Hollywood's least successful agents. Still, they were able to arrange a screen test for her the next day, and set up an appointment with someone they wanted her to meet. He was someone who could be extremely useful if he chose to.

The last twelve girls they had sent him had been rejects. But even Ernesto Salvatore would agree, this one was a beauty.

The screen test almost frightened her to death, but it was exciting, and after she started to relax, she did well. She and Pearl spent the rest of the day visiting the sights. They took the tour of the movie stars' homes, and went to Grauman's Chinese Theatre. They walked up and down Sunset, and stood at Hollywood and Vine as Crystal laughed and let Pearl take her picture. And she and Pearl giggled as they noticed passersby staring at her, wondering if she was a starlet. She was suddenly noticeable here, and two little girls asked for her autograph, convinced that she was "someone," and Crystal loved it.

They went back to the agents' building. At the end of the day they had asked her to return to their office, but they hadn't explained further. She wore a black dress Pearl had picked out for her, shiny black patent high heels, and she wore a stiff petticoat that made the dress stand out. The dress was strapless and it revealed the creamy pink satin of her shoulders. There wasn't an inch of spare flesh on her. Everything was smooth and silky and perfect. And Pearl had insisted she wear a big picture hat, and showed her how to tuck all her hair in with one graceful twist. And she had instructed her exactly how to take her hat off.

When Pearl and Crystal arrived at her agents' office again, the man the agent had talked about was already waiting for her. He was tall and dark, and good-looking. He wore a dark, well-cut suit, a white shirt, and a narrow tie. And everything about him suggested that he was someone important. Crystal guessed him to be about forty-five, and the moment he looked at her, he knew he'd found a gold mine.

He had already seen her screen test early that morning. She was unpolished certainly, and unsophisticated in terms of the business, but her voice was good, and with her looks she could have been a deaf mute for all he cared. The agents were right for once. This one was a beauty.

He liked her smile, and the way she moved, and as the stiff black skirt swirled, he admired a glimpse of the legs that were going to make her famous. And then as she glanced at him, Crystal took the hat off, exactly the way Pearl had taught her. With a graceful gesture, her blond mane tumbled down, and the three men almost gasped as it fell like angels' wings over her shoulders. The man in the dark suit smiled, and rose to introduce himself. This girl was worthy of Ernesto Salvatore. He walked slowly toward Crystal, and she saw something intriguing in his eyes, as though he could look through her and deep into her and see her innermost secrets. But she had nothing to hide from him. Nothing and no one.

"Hello, Crystal," he said quietly, "My name is Ernesto Salvatore. But you can call me Ernie." He shook her hand, and glanced at Pearl, wondering if the aging redhead was her mother. She had good legs, too, he noticed as she crossed them carefully, but they weren't half as good as Crystal's. Hers were long, and she reminded him of a long-stemmed rose. And he liked the innocent look she had. All she needed was more makeup and some training. A voice coach, someone to show her how to move, some acting lessons for a while, and then "Zoom! To the top!" But he said nothing to her or the agents. Crystal was watching him nervously, wondering just exactly who he was, and why he had wanted to see her.

"Could you be in my office Monday afternoon?" She paused for a moment, wondering if she trusted him, and then she nodded.

"I think so." Pearl smiled at how cool she was, and she noticed the look of approval in Salvatore's eyes as he watched her. He told her where the office was, and handed Crystal his card, with a nod of satisfaction at the agents. This time they had finally done it. After dozens of losers, and several recent truly bad ones, they had finally come up with a real diamond.

Salvatore was a well-known personal manager, some very big stars had started with him, although not many. And there had been a few very unsavory scandals. Two much publicized suicides of women he'd handled and had affairs with. And other incidents he chose not to remember. But more importantly, Ernie Salvatore was the tip of an iceberg that frightened some, but he had some very important connections. And just looking at him, one sensed that. But not Crystal. She was too naive to sense anything odd about Ernie Salvatore.

"Can you move to L.A.?" He looked into Crystal's eyes. He was wondering just exactly who she was and where she had come from.

She seemed so young and innocent, and he wondered who she had to protect her, other than the aging redhead who had come to the meeting. But he didn't really care where she was from. He was going to make her over. He was going to turn her into what she had always wanted to be. A star. And a big one.

If she would let him.

"Yes, I can move to L. A." All her life she had dreamed of coming to Hollywood, and now she was going to do whatever she had to. Within reason. She had no one to answer to now, except herself . . . not even Spencer.

Salvatore had a deep, sultry voice, and an aura of command, and she watched in fascination as he approached her for a closer inspection. But he loved what he saw. She was flawless. "How old are you?"

"Twenty-one," she answered calmly. "I'll be twenty-two in August." She wasn't even a minor. It was perfect.

She was innocent, she was pure, and she was exactly what he'd been looking for, for ages. And he was going to play it for everything it was worth. He even knew of the right picture for her. All he had to do was call the director and have the star kicked off the picture, but for Ernesto, it was a small feat, and he had every intention of making the call the following morning.

He told her what he wanted her to do. He wanted her to go shopping, buy some clothes, a lot of them, he said as he peeled off a roll of bills. And come to his office on Monday morning. He was going to have the director there, he could see for himself, and by that afternoon she'd be working on a picture. He just prayed she could remember lines, but the acting coach would teach her some tricks to help her. He wondered if the other woman would stick around, too, and he turned and asked Pearl finally if she was Crystal's mother.

She smiled, flattered that he had asked, but she shook her head. "No, I'm just a friend."

"And your mother?" He turned to Crystal. "Where is she?" Girls like her always had ferocious mothers who were a pain in the ass for him. It was a lot easier when there was no one. Especially if there was any trouble later.

"Dead," Crystal said quietly in her silky voice.

"And your father?"

"He's dead too." Her eyes looked sad and he knew it was the truth as she said it. It was even better than he thought. He could do exactly what he wanted with her. He even liked her name. It had a good ring to it for Hollywood.

Crystal Wyatt. She was going to go places. He
thanked them all then, left, and a few minutes
later Pearl and Crystal left too. Crystal looked
dazed, and she stared at Pearl in amazement.
"What does all that mean?"

"I think," she said dabbing at her eyes with
emotion, "it means that you've made it. Wait
till I tell Harry!" But for a minute, Crystal was
almost disappointed. It was everything she
wanted and yet she knew that she wouldn't be
going back to the safe comfortable world of
Harry's. She was out in the real world now,
and she was suddenly a little frightened of
what she would find there. Ernie Salvatore did
not seem anything like Harry.

"What exactly does a personal manager
do?" Crystal asked Pearl, thinking of him
again.

"I'm not sure. I think it's kind of like an
agent."

"He looks scary, doesn't he?" Crystal had
never met anyone like him before, and she still
wasn't sure if she liked him.

"Don't be silly." Pearl brushed it off. "I
think he's very handsome." But Pearl's standards were a lot different from Crystal's. And
she was still haunted by memories of Spencer.

They spent the weekend exploring Beverly
Hills with a car and driver who had mysteri-

ously appeared at the hotel, sent by Ernie Salvatore. And they went to two movies, and the La Brea Tar Pits. And on Monday, Crystal reappeared in one of the dresses she'd bought with Ernie's money. He had called it an advance when he gave it to her. But it still made her feel a little nervous. He had given her five hundred dollars, and although the prospect of shopping with his money excited her, it also scared her. Why was he doing all this? What did he want from her? She remembered hideous tales she'd heard of agents and managers in Hollywood, but she tried to tell herself this was a dream come true, wasn't it? If she couldn't have the man she loved, then at least she could have her dream of stardom, and Ernie was going to help her get it.

She had bought four dresses, a handbag, two pairs of shoes, and three hats, and there was still almost two hundred dollars left over. The outfits played on her virginal looks, yet all of them had a vague suggestion of sex. A slit here, a glimpse there, a bit of veil, an open button. The heels were very high, and the skirts full, and just short enough to show the legs that Salvatore had almost applauded. And the promised director who was waiting for her in Ernie's office was as impressed as Salvatore expected. He owed Ernie some favors anyway, so the outcome had been certain. He promised to fire his star, as long as Crystal could at least talk and remember her lines. But the part wasn't a complicated one, nor was the story.

"You got it, babe." The director smiled. "We start shooting next week on Monday. That gives you a week to study the script and get ready."

She stared at him in amazement. The dream was coming true after all. And all thanks to Ernie. And suddenly everything around her seemed unreal and she felt as though she were moving underwater.

The director left shortly afterward, after promising to send her the script, and a few minutes after he left, Ernie handed her a contract.

"What do I do with this?" She looked blankly at him. Things were moving much too quickly. She wanted to talk this over with someone, but there was no one to talk to. Pearl looked as starstruck as she felt herself, and even Harry would have been out of his league with Ernie Salvatore. The agents had already told her that he was one of the best managers in town, and they had turned her over to him without a qualm. In no uncertain terms, they had released her. But something told her that she shouldn't trust him. She wished she could

talk to Spencer about it all, but he was in another world, and through his silence she had
finally understood that he had left her. But after almost three years, she still longed for him.
She had been barely more than a child when he
left three years before, but even he had told her
that she should go to Hollywood. Maybe he'd
be impressed with her if she finally did it.
Maybe he'd see her name up in lights one day
. . . maybe he'd come back to her when she
was a star . . . but even that sounded crazy.
He was gone, back to Elizabeth. For all she
knew, he was back in the States by then, and
he had never called her. Her days with Spencer
were over now, and she had her long-awaited
career to think of. At last. It felt almost like
Christmas.

Salvatore handed her a pen with a knowing
smile, and patted her hand very gently. "Don't
be afraid, my dear. You're going to be a very
big star. This is only the beginning."

"Is the contract for this movie?" She was
still confused, and she was wondering how he
had gotten it so quickly. How had he known
she would get the job? Or had the director
brought it with him?

"This is an arrangement between the two of
us. This way I can handle all the contracts for
whatever movies you make. It's much simpler

this way. One contract between the two of us, and I handle all the rest of the nonsense for you."

"What kind of nonsense?" She was looking straight at him, and he was slightly less amused than he had been. She was a bright one. But she was also hungry for what he had to offer, and he knew it. She had bought the clothes, ridden around all weekend in the limousine, and like all the rest of them, she was dying to be in a movie. All the lures were in place. All she had to do now was sign the contract. And she would. He was sure of it. They all did.

"You don't want me to bore you with all of that, do you, Crystal?" And then he laughed, as though she was being incredibly childish. "You trust me, don't you, my dear?" How could she not? The agents had said he was one of the biggest. She glanced at Pearl, who almost imperceptibly nodded. And with that, Crystal took the pen, glanced at the contract she didn't understand, and signed it. "Perfect." He took the pen away from her, and then took her hand in his own and kissed it, and then slowly his eyes moved up into hers and she felt a chill run up her spine. The way he looked at her was disturbing. But as he moved away from her again, she told herself that she was

being stupid. He knew what he was doing, and
he was obviously good at it. He had gotten her
a job in a movie, hadn't he? But he had also
gotten someone else fired to do it. She didn't
let herself think of that as he told her that he
was moving her to another hotel, a better one
than the place Harry had reserved for her.
This one was in Westwood.

"Can I afford that now?" She didn't even
know what she was going to make on the picture, but Ernie laughed at her worries.

"Of course you can." And then he glanced
at Pearl. "And will you be staying too?" But
something subtle in his eyes said that she
wasn't welcome and she felt it.

"I . . . well . . ." She looked at Crystal
nervously. It was almost as though in the last
few minutes, she had become useless. "I suppose I should get back to San Francisco." She
looked apologetically at both of them, and
Crystal looked disappointed. Salvatore saw it,
too, and smiled at them both as he put away
the contract. He locked it in a drawer where,
he assured Crystal, he kept his most valuable
possessions.

"Why don't you stay until next week when
Crystal starts work? She'll be awfully busy
then anyway. And I'm afraid she'll have to do
a little work this week too." He turned to her

with a fatherly air and explained that he wanted her to get to work with a voice coach. She would have to go to acting classes of course, but she would also learn a lot right on the set, if she paid attention.

Pearl agreed to stay until the following weekend, and Ernie assured them both that he would have them moved to the new hotel before nightfall. He suggested they go back and pack their things, and the driver would take them to the hotel. And with their permission, he would join them later that afternoon, for cocktails. And five minutes later they were back in the car again, and Crystal was strangely quiet. She was thinking of everything that had just happened to her, and she was still too overwhelmed to believe it. Pearl chatted on endlessly, about how handsome he was, how debonair, what a great opportunity this was for her, and what a big star she would be before she knew it. And Crystal didn't know why, but she still didn't trust him. She didn't say anything until they got to the hotel, and then she turned to Pearl as they were folding their clothes back into their valises.

"Do you really think he's okay? . . . I mean . . . oh, I don't know . . ." She sat down on a chair, and kicked off the high heels, wishing she could wear blue jeans for their evening out. But he had already told her that from now on she had to think of her image. She had to wear beautiful, sexy clothes, makeup, well-groomed hair, and she had to be seen all over town at every party where she was invited. And he was going to see to it that she was invited to all of them. It sounded exciting, but suddenly she couldn't help wondering why he was so anxious to do so much for her. She shared her fears with Pearl, who told her she was crazy.

"Of course he's okay. Are you kidding? Did you look around that office? It must have cost a million bucks just to decorate it, or something like that. You think he'd have an office like that if he weren't someone important? Baby, you fell right onto the gravy train and you don't even know it. And he's doing all this because he knows you're going to be a big star one day. The only one who doesn't know it is you, you dummy." She grinned at her young friend, and Crystal laughed. Listening to Pearl she suddenly felt better, and after they called Harry before they left the hotel, she felt terrific. He told her how proud of her he was, and what a big break she was getting. It was why she had come after all. And she had gotten exactly what she wanted. And they were right. She was crazy to worry about all of it. She had

nothing to worry about at all. All she had to
do now was sit back and enjoy it.

The suite in the new hotel looked like something in a movie set, as did the red velvet and
white marble lobby. It was a small hotel in a
good neighborhood, and it was undeniably
very showy. But Pearl told her it would be a
great place for her to be seen, and suggested
she change clothes several times a day and
walk around the lobby. Crystal laughed at the
idea, but that afternoon she decided to try it,
and the two women laughed uncontrollably as
Crystal changed clothes three times and kept
going back down to the lobby, ostensibly to
mail a letter, get another key for her friend,
and ask if someone had dropped off a package.

"Did anyone see you?" Pearl asked excitedly. She had insisted Crystal go alone, and
Crystal was still laughing when she came back
to relax and change into her blue jeans. She
had brought them with her just in case, along
with her cowboy boots and Jared's red socks,
which were still among her most treasured
possessions.

"Yeah." Crystal was still laughing as she
hung up her dress and peeled off her nylons.
"The desk clerk saw me. He probably thinks
I'm a hooker."

"Wait until he starts going to your movies,

then he'll know who you are!" She said it so
proudly that Crystal turned slowly to face her,
and walked across the room to give her a hug.
She had been such a good friend for the last
four years. It was going to be strange when
Pearl left, being without her.

"Thank you." Crystal said it very softly.

"What for?" Pearl sounded gruff but it
barely concealed how much she loved her.
Crystal had become the daughter she'd never
had, and it was going to kill her to leave on
Sunday and go back to San Francisco.

"Thank you for believing in me. I'd never be
here if it weren't for you and Harry."

"That's the dumbest thing I ever heard. The
agents found you at the restaurant. We had
nothing to do with that."

"You had everything to do with that. Harry
hired me, you trained me. You taught me everything I know about singing on the stage.
You've believed in me for all these years and
now you've brought me down here. That's a
hell of a lot, if you ask me."

"Don't be silly. Just be happy here." She
turned to smile at her as she walked to the
huge red Formica and gold bar, and helped
herself to a beer in the fridge, and then sat
down on a tall black velvet stool and toasted
Crystal with the bottle. "To you, kid . . ."

And then grandly, waving at the suite he had reserved for them, "And to Ernie."

"To Ernie!" Crystal agreed, helping herself to a Coke, and feeling a lot better about him than she had that morning. She wasn't sure anymore why she had been worried, but she knew she had been. And obviously, without reason.

He arrived at six o'clock for drinks, as promised, and found Pearl more than a little sloshed, and Crystal in blue jeans. And Crystal felt as though she'd been caught cheating on her homework. She knew she was supposed to look glamorous, and behave herself, he had told her about the morals clauses in studio movie contracts. And here she was in blue jeans only hours after signing the contract. But he laughed at her, and even seemed amused at Pearl, and Crystal decided that he was much nicer than she had originally thought him. And when she looked at him more closely as he opened the champagne he had brought, she decided cautiously that he was actually fairly handsome. But his looks were very different from Spencer's. Spencer was all distinction and handsome young warrior. This man looked as though he had been making his way through drawing rooms in Europe. At least once she had had several glasses of champagne, that was how Pearl described it. She called him suave and debonair, and after a few minutes, Ernie ignored her, and concentrated on Crystal. He spoke to her in a gentle voice, and told her how happy he was about the contract. He also put a thick envelope in her hand. It was a gray envelope, with his name and the address of his office engraved on very expensive paper.

"I forgot to give you that this morning. I'm awfully sorry, Crystal. I don't usually make mistakes like that." He smiled, and he looked as though he was accustomed to being forgiven. He was accustomed to a lot of things, things Crystal had never even dreamed of.

"What is it?" She opened the envelope cautiously and was surprised to see a check, and when she took it out of the envelope, she saw that he had signed it. Why was he giving her more money, he had already given her five hundred dollars for clothes, as an "advance," but an advance on what, she wondered, and as she looked up, she saw that he was smiling.

"It's the money I owe you for signing the contract. You don't expect to seal a major business deal with just a kiss, do you? Although I must say, if that's the case, I'd rather like it." Crystal looked at him in embarrassment. She didn't understand anything about their business arrangements.

"You owe me that?" She looked amused, and suddenly delighted. She hadn't even started the picture yet and she was already making money. And living like a queen in the hotel where he'd set her up. Who ever said Hollywood was tough? They must have been crazy . . . but then again they didn't know Ernie Salvatore. She'd rolled in right at the top, just as Pearl had told her.

"Actually, my dear, I owe you twenty-five hundred. But the five hundred for clothes was an 'advance' from me, as I mentioned, so I subtracted it from your check." He didn't want her feeling as though she owed him too much, not yet anyway, or it would scare her off. And that was not what he wanted. She had to feel as though she was earning the money from him, and she was. He had made a fat fee on her that afternoon, for her very first picture. And from that, he would pay her a small salary, and pocket the rest, which was the agreement she had signed in his office that morning. "I'll set you up at my bank, Crystal. You can open an account tomorrow morning." She had never had a bank account before, and the idea excited her, as she took another sip of the champagne he had poured, and then in a little while he stood up, and told them to have a good evening. He smiled down at Crystal as she walked him to the door, and he kissed her cheek before he left, but this time there seemed nothing strange about him, and she was even beginning to like him. Who wouldn't have, as Pearl said. He was so good to them. The fancy hotel, the suite, the champagne, and Crystal was grinning as she waved her first check after he left them.

"I'm not sure if I should spend it or frame it." But the next morning, she decided easily on the former. After Ernie's secretary called her that morning with the information, she went to his bank and then to a jewelry store across the street, and bought Pearl the charm bracelet she had been staring at earlier. She had been fascinated by it, because all the charms were related to the movies. Dark glasses, a megaphone, tiny klieg lights with a diamond in them, a gold director's chair, and a little chalkboard that actually snapped open and shut like the ones they were going to use on the set of Crystal's first movie. Pearl cried as Crystal put it on her, and they spent the rest of the afternoon laughing and talking and acting like tourists. Ernie had offered them the limousine again, and it never dawned on them that he had done it to keep track of exactly what Crystal was doing. It just seemed like an enormous kindness to them, and the driver was very pleasant.

The voice coach came to meet her that afternoon, and when she sang for him at the piano in the suite, he was surprised by how good she was. It was just too bad she wasn't going to have a singing part in the movie. He was also doubling as drama coach for her, and he gave her several pointers about the script and told her not to worry. And before they knew it, the week had flown by and Pearl had left, with tears and hugs and promises to call her. And suddenly Crystal was alone in Hollywood. Her dreams had come true, she was starting work on a movie the next day, and as she went for a long walk in the cool night air, she suddenly found herself thinking of Spencer. She wondered where he was and what he was doing and who he was with. If he was in Korea, or back home, and if he ever missed her. But no matter how hard she tried, she found she could never erase him from her mind, or forget the two magical weeks they had spent together. And no matter what else happened in her life, she knew she would always love him. He was still as vivid in her mind as he had been the day he left, and the days before . . . and as when she was fourteen and fell in love with him at first sight, at her sister's wedding.

"My, my, that's a serious face. You ought to remember that for a dramatic part." The voice spoke just behind her, and she wheeled around in surprise, to find herself looking up at Ernie. She was only a few blocks from the hotel, but she had been miles away in her own mind and she hadn't heard him approach. "I thought you might be lonely without your friend, so I dropped by to see how you are. And they told me at the desk you had gone out for a walk. Mind if I join you?"

"Of course not." He had been so kind to her, how could she object to anything he did? And in truth, she had been feeling very lonely. And thinking of Spencer never helped. It was always a blow to remember how he had simply faded away into silence. It had happened between them before . . . between Becky's wedding and the christening of their baby . . . and then until they'd met again in San Francisco the Thanksgiving he'd gotten engaged, and then again just before he left for Korea. But this time had been different. She hadn't slept with him before. She hadn't loved him as she did now. But there was no point thinking about it anymore. There was nothing she could do about it. He had given her up, he had stopped writing to her, or even answering her letters, and she knew he had lost interest long before that. From letters filled with love and telling her how much he missed her they had drifted down to barely more than postcards and then nothing.

"Are you excited about tomorrow?" Ernie smiled down at her benevolently and reminded her about her movie.

"Very much so." She was honest with him, and he liked her aura of fresh excitement. It was a nice change after the jaded starlets he usually went out with.

"You're going to be very good. Maybe next time we'll get you a singing part and really show them your stuff." He had heard her sing on the screen test, and he knew just how good she was. But he had wanted to launch the face before he worried about the rest, and he knew exactly what he was doing.

"I'd like that a lot." She missed singing, even in the few days since she had left San Francisco.

"Your voice coach says you're terrific."

"Thank you." She smiled at him, and he could almost feel his body tremble as he watched her. And then suddenly he had a thought, as long as he was going to play father confessor to her, or benevolent tutor, he might as well take her to dinner.

"Have you ever been to the Brown Derby?"

He asked innocently, but he already knew from his driver that she hadn't. He got reports of her activities daily. He wanted to be sure that she wasn't a little whore, sleeping around, damaging his and her own reputation. But so far she'd kept her nose clean, maybe because her friend from San Francisco was there. But he suspected she would anyway. He had even wondered once or twice if she was still a virgin. She was that kind of girl, and he liked that. It would make it that much easier to groom her.

"No, I haven't." She smiled at him, all innocence, and all startling beauty. In any light, in any outfit, dressed, combed, or in blue jeans, the girl was a knockout.

"Would you like to go there for dinner tonight? But I warn you, if we go, I'm going to bring you home very early. You have to get a good night's sleep before you start work tomorrow."

"Yes, sir." But her eyes had lit up like Christmas. "I'd really like that." Her ingenuousness amused him. She was going to be a good one.

He glanced at his watch, calculated quickly, and offered to walk her back to the hotel and pick her up again in an hour. He was wearing gray flannel slacks and a light tweed jacket, and he wanted to change into a suit before he took her to dinner. "I'll be back at eight o'clock. And I plan to have you back home and in bed by ten, come hell or high water." And unfortunately, without him. But Ernie was much too smart to move on her too quickly. "Sound okay to you?"

"It sounds terrific!" She leaned over to kiss his cheek, as she would have a grandfather's, and he was ashamed as he dropped her off and slid into his Mercedes. He had a number of cars, and he had left one of his limousines at her disposal for the entire week. He preferred the Mercedes anyway, and he wanted to be alone with her tonight in any case. And he was glad he was when he picked her up and saw the beautifully cut tight white silk dress she was wearing, with a little matching jacket. She looked absolutely stunning, and he was extremely pleased he had tendered the invitation. And so was most of the dinner crowd at the Brown Derby.

She walked in, chatting easily with him about her life in the valley as a child and then stood rooted to the spot, aware suddenly that everyone was staring at her. And they stared harder and longer when they saw who she was with. He certainly had a knack for finding the prettiest girls in town. No one could deny that, and this one was the best yet. He seemed to know everyone in the place, and Crystal almost fainted when she saw a man who looked like Frank Sinatra walk past her. Ernie walked her slowly toward their table, greeting everyone and introducing her to names she had only dreamed of.

"Don't look so scared." He spoke to her very gently, and smiled. He was delighted with everyone's reactions, and she had done well. The white dress made people stop and stare, particularly once he made her take off her jacket, which offered a generous view of cleavage. It wasn't something she usually played on, in fact she usually went to great lengths to hide it, but Pearl had insisted she buy the dress, and she had decided to wear it to dinner at the Brown Derby. And she was glad she had. Ernie said that he loved it. And as dinner progressed, he surprised her. She felt very much at ease with him.

He was pleasant and kind, and he had very good manners. There was nothing insinuating about the way he talked to her. He wasn't a white slaver after all, he was only a manager, as he called himself. She confessed to him then that she'd wanted to be a movie star all her life. It was a story he'd heard before, but he smiled as though this was the first time. Cary Grant was at the bar, and Rock Hudson came in to meet someone briefly and stayed for quite a while, as Crystal looked around in amazement. It was all so much more than she'd ever dared to hope for. She felt tears sting her eyes as she looked at him, and he looked suddenly worried.

"Is something wrong?"

"I can't believe this is happening to me." He smiled. He liked them like that. Fresh, and young. He would have liked to keep her out later that night, to get to know her better, but he wanted her rested the next day for the movie. That was more important. She was more than just a girl to him. She was an investment.

They dawdled over coffee and he told her he wanted her seen around town on the arms of the right men, and he discreetly mentioned to her a list of those who were going to call her. She recognized some of them, and for a moment she thought that maybe he was kidding, but as she looked into his eyes, she knew he wasn't. "Why are you doing all this for me?" She still didn't understand him. Why her? But he knew exactly what he was doing.

"You're going to make us both rich one day." He smiled as though he had found a diamond in his coffee. "You're going to be very famous."

"How do you know that?" Why was she different from the rest? She had no sense of how spectacular she was, particularly now with the dresses he had urged her to buy and the careful makeup. It was a long way from work shirts and cowboy boots, but for the moment she didn't miss them.

"I've never been wrong yet," he boasted quietly and patted her hand as he asked for the check, and then as they waited he asked her the question he'd been wondering about since he'd met her.

"How encumbered are you romantically?" She looked pensive and he smiled. "In other words, do you have a boyfriend?" She had understood him, but she'd been thinking it over.

"No, I don't." Her voice was quiet and her face was sad as she thought of Spencer.

"Are you sure of that?"

"Yes."

"Good. But you did?" She nodded. "And where is he now?" He wanted to be sure she was free and there wouldn't be any trouble. He could handle it of course, but he didn't like to.

"I'm not sure where he is," Crystal went on. "In Korea, or back in New York. Either way, it's no longer important." But she had to fight back tears as she said it.

And then she sat back and watched Ernie

greet his friends as they drifted past them. He was attractive and gracious and he had a certain style about him that was beginning to grow on Crystal. She had never known anyone like him. She noticed too that he wore a single ring, a heavy gold piece with a good-sized diamond. His suit was expensively made, and the white shirt he wore was made by a costume maker in Las Vegas, but it looked as though it had been made by a tailor in London. There was something stylish about the man, and it was obvious that he cared about the way he looked, and there was a raw sensuality that Crystal was aware of, but there was something else too, a forcefulness that still frightened her a little bit. He concealed it well but one sensed that Ernesto Salvatore was a man who always got what he wanted. But there was no sign of that, as he turned to her with a friendly smile.

"Ready to go?" He asked amiably as he got up and led her past at least a dozen famous faces. Some of them acknowledged him but this time he didn't stop. He just walked her to the door pretending not to notice the people staring at her, and a few minutes later he dropped her off at her hotel. She thanked him, and he left, and she went upstairs to get a good night's sleep before starting work the next morning.

But once she was in bed, she found she couldn't sleep, and for once she wasn't thinking of Spencer. She was thinking about her new manager, and although she had to admit he was charming, just as Pearl had said, Crystal didn't know why, but he scared her.

CHAPTER
26 ─────────────

Crystal began to work on the movie and as her coach had promised, it was easier than she thought. The hours were long and rigorous, but everyone seemed anxious to help her. She studied her lines every day, and had intended to go to bed early every night, but she was amazed by the number of men who called her. Ernie had mentioned all of them, so she knew they had called her on command, but they were always polite and pleasant, and charming. They arrived in dinner jackets, driving expensive cars, actors and singers and well-known dancers. She had even seen some of

them in movies. And they escorted her everywhere. To Chasen's, and the Cocoanut Grove
and the Mocambo. It was all like a fairy tale,
and words failed her each time she tried to
describe it to Pearl when she wrote her. She
told her about the parties she was going to,
and the people she had met there, and for a
moment she wondered if she'd even believe
her. It was the kind of story one read in movie
magazines, but it was true. All of it. And she
told her about the picture.

And halfway through the picture, Ernie
called her himself. "Having fun?"

"I'm out every night." She laughed breathlessly and he laughed in answer.

"Then how come you're home now?"

"I was so tired, I canceled tonight. I didn't
think I could get dressed one more time."
There was a comment he was tempted to
make, but he didn't think she was ready for it.
Instead he chose to answer her innocently and
not scare her.

"Not even once? Just for me?"

"Oh, Mr. Salvatore . . ." Her voice drifted
off. She was exhausted. She had to get up at
four every day, and be on the set by five-thirty
in the morning for makeup and costumes.

"What happened to 'Ernie'? Have I done
something wrong?"

"No, I'm sorry." He sounded so nice and she owed so much to him, she knew she couldn't turn him down. She just wished he hadn't called her. She was truly exhausted.

"Don't be sorry, just remember next time. How about a quiet dinner somewhere? You don't even have to dress to be seen."

She sighed in relief, and it was nice of him to call. She smiled as she glanced out her window. "Could I wear jeans?"

"I'd be honored. And bring a bathing suit, if you have one."

"Where are we going?" She sounded intrigued and was only faintly worried.

"To Malibu. To a quiet place I know. You can relax, and I'll get you home early."

"I'd love it." She dressed hastily, brushing her hair back into a tight knot, and slipping on her jeans and one of the old shirts she'd brought from home, and the cowboy boots she'd had for years. As she looked in the mirror, she suddenly recognized herself again, and it felt so good not to be dressed up and wearing makeup.

He picked her up in his Rolls ten minutes later, and she saw that he was wearing jeans too. He laughed with pleasure at how she looked. "People are so dumb. I'd love to put you in a picture just like that, Crystal, but no

one would ever understand it." He saw that
the boots were the real thing, and the jeans
were, too, and he remembered her tales of the
valley when they'd had dinner at the Brown
Derby.

She was more comfortable with him than
she had been before. The absence of expensive
clothes, and not being in a fancy restaurant
where she was stared at helped, and it never
dawned on her to ask where they were going.
They chatted on easily for a while, talking
about her childhood, and his in New York, and
then suddenly she saw that they had stopped
in a driveway outside a house perched just
above the ocean. "Where are we?"

"My place in Malibu. Did you bring a bathing suit? I have an indoor pool. The ocean is
too cold here." She felt a tremor of fear run up
her spine, and yet he had given her no indica-
tion that she needed to worry. But the emo-
tional scars left by Tom had never entirely
faded, and she suddenly wondered what Spencer would think of her being here with Ernie.
But it didn't matter anymore. And he was
married anyway. And this was her life and no
one else's. She forced Spencer from her mind,
and followed Ernie to the front door, which he
opened with a single key. There was no one
there, and Crystal looked frightened. "Don't

be afraid, little one." He smiled gently at her. "I won't hurt you. I just thought you needed a night off." He was right, she did, but she wasn't sure she was safe here. Her instincts told her not to go inside, but she felt foolish making a fuss, he was being so pleasant, and he had already been so kind to her.

She followed him through the door and saw that they were in a beautiful house, with glass walls and high ceilings, there were thick white rugs, and long white leather couches, and the room looked even larger with the clever use of mirrors. And outside the huge picture windows, the sun was setting slowly over the Pacific. It was beautiful, and it made everything seem more real as she watched it. It reminded her of sunsets on the ranch that she had watched in happier times with her father.

"Would you like a drink?" He walked to the bar and opened a refrigerator hidden behind a mirrored door, but she shook her head. She had every intention of staying sober.

"No, thanks."

"A soda perhaps?" She asked for a Coke, and he smiled. She was really just a kid, hidden in that magnificent body. He had never seen a girl as beautiful, and he was still marveling to himself at how he had found her. "You don't drink, or you don't trust me?"

She hesitated and then laughed. "Both, I guess."

"Smart girl." He poured himself a vodka and tonic and invited her to sit on the couch. She was still trying to figure out where the pool was, but now that they were inside, the house looked much larger. It had seemed deceptively small before they entered.

"I ordered dinner for us. I'm sure it's well hidden somewhere. I have a man who comes in every day. But I don't use this place very often. I live in the Hills." And he knew she was still living at the hotel. "You can use this place whenever you want, Crystal. Just come here to relax. After a hard day on a picture you'll need it." She was touched by how kind he was. He had done so much for her. It was hard to understand why he did it. To make money, of course, but there was more to it than that. He did all the little things too, the flowers, the small gifts, the selection of her escorts, and now this, an evening at the beach in jeans. It was just exactly what she would have wanted. But he was good at that. It was what he did best. He had remarkable instincts for people.

She let her head fall back against the couch, as the sun set behind him, and she sighed happily. "I think this is the best day I've had here."

"Good. Would you like to swim before dinner, or would you rather wait? A walk on the beach perhaps?"

She smiled peacefully. "I'd love that." He set down his drink and threw open the door to the terrace as a cool breeze swept in and he followed her down the stairs to the sand, as she began to run, feeling the wind on her face and in her hair, and for the first time in a long time, she was truly happy. She looked like a child again as she walked and ran, and took off her boots to put her toes in the ocean. It was growing dark, but he followed her quietly, watching her with pleasure, like a proud parent. And she returned to him finally, her face bright from the cool air and the wind on her cheeks.

"Are you cold?"

"I'm all right." But he could see that she was, and he took off his jacket and put it over her shoulders. It smelled of the cologne he wore, she hadn't noticed it before, and she realized suddenly that she liked it. She wondered if he'd ever been married, or if he had children, who he was behind the facade, but he offered nothing of himself. He seemed to be there only to please her and eventually they walked back to the house and he went to look for their dinner. He found fresh lobster waiting for them, with a delicate mayonnaise, and a big spinach salad. There was a bottle of champagne left in a silver ice bucket, and hard-boiled eggs filled with caviar.

"Have you ever had caviar before?" She shook her head, she had only heard of it, and he smiled paternally at her. "You might not like it at first. Some things are like that." But she tried it to please him, and decided that it wasn't bad. But as they sat at a low table on comfortable chairs, she liked the lobster and champagne a lot better. She drank sparingly, and he didn't press her to drink more than that. He had time, lots of it, and he didn't want her till she wanted him. And he knew that she would in time. She was too indebted to him by then not to.

They talked about where she had lived, about her father when he was alive, about all the things that mattered to her, and he listened as though the world depended on what she said. And half an hour after dinner, he offered her a swim again, smiling warmly. "It might relax you."

She laughed at his choice of words. "If I were any more relaxed I might go to sleep on the floor." It had been a long, hard day, and it took its toll on her. And the fresh sea air had made her sleepy. "A swim might feel good, if I don't drown from all that lobster."

"Don't worry, I'll save you."

She smiled up at him gratefully, unaware of the picture she made just sitting there easily in her blue jeans and her boots and her old shirt and her pale gold hair. "I think you already have."

"I hope so." Her benefactor smiled benignly at her and told her where to change, while he went to turn the lights on in the pool. And a moment later she emerged again in a white bathing suit that took his breath away. She had no idea how devastating she was, which was just as well. He liked that about her. And the audience would too. He never forgot that.

"I hope it's warm enough." He watched her slip into the water, and then went to change as she floated happily. The pool was enormous and warm and she thought she had never been as comfortable in her life. She looked up at him happily when he returned, wrapped in a luxurious white towel. It was tied tightly around his waist, and as she watched, he untied it, and she gasped. He was naked. She discreetly turned away, afraid to embarrass him, and she heard him laugh. "Don't worry, Crystal. I won't rape you. I've never been accused of that." But he had been accused of other things, of which she knew nothing. He slipped easily into the pool, and she began to swim quietly, afraid she might see something that she shouldn't. And as he passed her, he smiled at her. "Why don't you take your suit off too? It's so warm it's like being in a bathtub." He seemed to have no ulterior motive, he was just at ease with himself, and with her, and he made no attempt to touch her as she smiled and tried to look unconcerned, but knowing that he was naked made her nervous.

"No, I'll be all right. Thanks."

"As you like, my dear." He was very smooth, and very smart, and he never rushed the current object of his attentions. They all came to him in time, for one reason or another. And a moment later, he stepped out easily, standing casually beside the pool, and without wanting to, she had noticed that he had a beautiful body. He was long and lean and trim, and he swam every day. He had the body of a much younger man as he offered her more champagne, but she didn't dare look at him, and suddenly he wondered again if she was a virgin. It would have been inconvenient certainly, but no obstacle was insuperable. He would have been willing to make the sacrifice for her, but as he looked at her, he had to smile. She was flapping around like a fish, trying desperately not to look nervous. "If I turn down the lights a little bit, will you feel better?

I'm afraid it's a terrible idiosyncrasy of mine. I hate bathing suits. You'll have to forgive me."

"Not at all." She tried to seem grown up and behave the way she thought a movie star would, but he was making her extremely nervous. And before she could answer, he turned the lights in the room down low. There were only dim lights in the pool, and lights near the ceiling that looked like candles.

"Better?"

"Much." She lied.

He took a sip of champagne and slipped back into the water again, and this time he swam directly at her, and took her waist firmly in his hands under the water. She froze suddenly, looking into his eyes as he held her.

"What are you going to do to me?" She was terrified.

"Make you a movie star." He whispered softly, but suddenly she wondered what he wanted in exchange for that. Maybe the stories about Hollywood were true, but she prayed silently that this time they wouldn't be . . . please God . . . not this time . . . "I won't hurt you, Crystal. Trust me." She nodded, unable to speak as he held her, and slowly, ever so slowly he moved closer to her and kissed her. "You're very beautiful . . . the most beautiful woman I've ever seen probably." He kissed her again and she started to cry.

"Please . . . don't . . . please . . ." She was shaking so violently that it touched him.

"I'm sorry, little girl. I didn't mean to frighten you. I only want you to be happy." And then, as she stared at him, he swam to the edge, got out, and wrapped himself in the towel again, and she was openmouthed with amazement. He liked her, he admired her, he wasn't going to rape her. She felt desperately foolish suddenly, and went to sit next to him at the edge as he sipped his champagne.

"I'm so sorry . . ." She knew she had to explain her behavior. "I was raped four years ago . . . I'm afraid I . . . I thought . . ." She started to cry and he gently put his arms around her, as he whispered, "I'm so sorry. Don't be afraid of me. If you're honest with me, I'll never hurt you." There was a veiled threat in that, but Crystal was too relieved to notice. She sank against him gratefully and let him hold the champagne glass while she sipped it.

"This is all so new to me. And everything has happened so suddenly. I don't know what to think half the time. I'm sorry if I behaved like a jerk."

"It's all right." He smiled benevolently.

"You're a cute jerk, and I like you." It sounded like something Spencer might have said and his understanding touched her. "Do you want to go back now, Crystal? I know you have to get up early. Or do you want to swim for a little while?"

She needed to relax again, after her terrible stupidity, and she looked at him with open eyes, the deep blue taking him by surprise, she was so lovely. "Actually, I'd like to swim for a while. Is that all right? Are you in a hurry?"

He laughed and shook his head. "Of course not."

She let her guard down this time, and it seemed less ominous when he slipped the towel off again and got back into the water. She swam laps for a while, and then floated on her back, and then suddenly she looked over and he was beside her. He turned on his stomach so as not to embarrass her, and then gently leaned forward and kissed her again, and this time she didn't fight him. She felt she owed him that much for making such a fool of herself before, but as he kissed her, he gently caressed her breasts, and she was startled to discover that she liked it. She started to swim away from him, but he followed her, not with any violence, but only swimming gracefully along with her, his hands touching her, and then slipping into her bathing suit as he kissed her again. She wanted him to stop, and yet for a moment of sheer madness, she knew she didn't. She swam to the steps and tried to catch her breath, and then she felt him behind her, slowly peeling her wet suit from her elegant body. She started to turn to look at him, but he pressed himself against her back, his hands making music as he worked them expertly. She threw her head back in sudden anguish and moaned softly.

"Ernie, don't . . ." There was no conviction in the words this time, as he touched her again and again, his fingers agonizingly gentle. He was a master, and she was only a novice. She had walked into his trap with him, and for the moment, she didn't even know it. "Oh God . . . don't . . . please . . ." He stopped just as suddenly, as though at her command, and her whole body shuddered as she turned to him, waiting expectantly, and without saying a word, he pressed forward and entered her just beneath the water. Her eyes grew wide in astonishment but within seconds, the pleasure of him overtook her. He made love to her like a symphony and when the crescendo rose, it was Crystal who pressed him close to her, wishing he would never stop. And afterward, as he smiled at her, she was embarrassed. She couldn't blame him for what he'd done, she had wanted it. It wasn't that she wanted him, but what he'd done to her was like nothing else she had ever known. Not even with Spencer.

"Are you angry at me?" He looked worried and she frowned at him, angry not at him, but at herself.

"No," she whispered hoarsely, "I don't know what happened to me . . . I . . ."

"I'm flattered." He kissed her lightly and touched her nipples again, and within moments she was aching for him. He spent hours in the pool with her, making love to her, and at midnight, he carried her slowly upstairs. The bedroom was all white velvet and thick furs, foxes, bears, and a white mink bedspread he laid her on, dripping wet, as he dried her carefully with a towel, and attended to all the right places first with the towel that had been wrapped around his waist, then with gentle fingers, and finally with his lips and a tongue that darted in and out of her like fireflies. She was screaming for him when he finally gave in to her, and they indulged their passion all night long. She had never done anything like it before. It had been different with Spencer before he left. This was anguished, frightening, and no matter how often he took her, Crystal found she wanted more. It was almost like a drug, she thought to herself, but it wasn't. It was an extraordinary power he had, an expertise, and a desire to teach her new things. But she was frightened when at last they stopped.

"What are you doing to me?" She was exhausted, and she had to leave for work in half an hour. She had never experienced anything like it.

"All my favorite things, my pretty girl." And then he smiled at her almost wickedly. "Once more?"

"No . . . no . . ." She shook her head. She couldn't explain it to herself, and she knew she had to get away from him, or she was afraid she might want him to do it all again. She took a hot shower, and then a cold, but he left her alone. There were steaming coffee and hot rolls waiting for her when she came out dressed again, and she stared at him. "Why are you doing all this for me?"

He laughed, and touched her cheek with a single finger then, smiling happily. "Because you're mine. As long as you want to be anyway. How does that sound to you?" It sounded frightening, and it sounded wrong. And yet he had given her the career she had always wanted. he had given her escorts to take her out, he had even given her new clothes. And now he had given her a night like no other she had ever known. Was that so wrong? But secretly she knew it was. And she felt desperately guilty. And the thought of Spencer almost broke her heart. The memory of what they'd shared seemed sullied now somehow. That had been all innocence and love. But this was different. She felt like a harlot. She didn't love this man, but he had been good to her, and if he wanted her for a time, what harm was there in it? Was it really so wrong? There were people who would have told her she was playing with fire, and there were others who would have told her he was a kind man. Both were true. He was many things. But for the moment, he wished her no harm. He kissed her again gently then, and when she left for work, he told her to take the Rolls.

"How will you get back?"

"I'll have my driver come out and pick me up. Don't worry, little girl. I'll be fine." He kissed her gently again, and the merest touch of him reminded her of what he'd done to her the night before. It was a far cry from what Tom Parker had done to her on the barn floor . . . and it was farther still from what she and Spencer had shared . . . there was no love in this, but Ernie was here now, he was good to her . . . and what did it matter anyway? . . . Spencer was gone. Forever.

CHAPTER
27

That afternoon when Crystal went back to the hotel, there was a package waiting for her. She took it upstairs and opened it carefully, and her eyes grew wide with embarrassment and amazement. It was a diamond bracelet from Ernie. She didn't know what to do with it, she was afraid to put it on. She just sat holding it and shaking. She was still horrified at what she'd done the night before. She'd never done anything like it, and she never wanted to see him again, except that night when he called, he was gentle and kind, and he seemed to sense what she felt without having to say it.

"Did you like the bracelet?" He sounded like a child who had brought flowers to his mother.

"I . . . yes . . . Ernie . . . it's incredible. But I can't keep it." It made her feel like a paid whore. There was no love between them at all, just the amazing things he had done to her body.

"Why not? Pretty girls deserve pretty things." At least he didn't tell her she'd earned it. "Can I come by in a little while?"

"No . . . I . . ." She started to cry silently, still afraid of him, and her own reactions. She didn't know what had happened to her the night before. And all day on the set she'd been consumed with guilt as she tried not to think of Spencer.

"Baby, I won't hurt you." He sounded sad and she felt sorry for him. It wasn't his fault she'd behaved so badly. At least she didn't think so. He hadn't forced her. He had lured her, with his caresses and his nimble fingers. "I just want to talk to you for a little while."

"I'll meet you in the lobby."

"That's fine. I'll be there in half an hour." He was wearing slacks and a clean white shirt, with a cashmere sweater thrown over his shoulders when he arrived, and he strode in and kissed her lightly on the cheek, as heads turned. He was a well-known figure in Hollywood, and she was a very beautiful woman.

He ordered drinks for them at the bar, and she sat looking awkward and embarrassed as he gently took her hand in his own, and he seemed to know just what she was thinking. "Don't feel bad about what happened last night. It was natural, and beautiful. We can be friends, you and I." But friends didn't make love in the swimming pool all night, and Crystal eyed him with tear-filled eyes.

"I don't know what happened." She wanted to tell him how much she loved Spencer, how long she had waited for him. But she didn't. How much he had meant to her before he left her. It wasn't important anymore. She had a right to her own life, but not with a man like Ernie. He was too rich for her blood, too experienced, too powerful, and she knew it. "I think I just went a little crazy." It was a poor excuse, but it was all she could say to him as he sipped his drink and smiled, struck again by her wondrous beauty. She had the kind of face that made people stop and stare at her, and made men want to reach out and touch her. He had seen the rushes of her film the day before, and it was obvious that the camera loved her.

"I went a little crazy too. There's no harm

in it, Crystal. And you're such a pretty girl, I just lost control of myself. Will you forgive me?" He knew just how to handle her as she watched him cautiously. "That's why I sent you the bracelet. To apologize for last night." He knew just how guilty she felt, and he wanted her to think of it as an apology, and not a payment. He knew to her that would be important. She was a lot different from most of the starlets he took out, who were only too happy to offer their bodies in exchange for his favors. But this one was a different breed entirely. She was decent and warm, and way out of her league. But he liked that. "I'm sorry, Crystal . . ." His eyes seemed so sincere, and she began to feel a little better. Maybe they had both just gone a little mad, she tried to tell herself she was as responsible for it as he was, but she didn't know Ernie Salvatore. "One day you'll look at it as a souvenir of your early days in Hollywood. You can show it to your children." She had hesitated, but he had looked so hurt when she tried to give the bracelet back, that in the end he'd convinced her to keep it. "Can we start over again?"

She nodded slowly, not sure she wanted to, but she felt beholden to him again as he told her how beautiful she had looked in the rushes. It was all thanks to him after all, and they sat for a long time, talking about the film. And he had already lined up another picture for her.

"So soon?" She looked amazed, and very grateful. "When does it start?" She was hesitant and still shy, and she was desperately trying to forget how he had looked at the side of the pool without his towel.

"About a week after you wrap this one up. I figured early April." He told her who was in it, and she stared at him. She knew all the names and some of them were important.

"Do you mean it?"

"Of course." And he didn't tell her what it had cost him to get her in the picture. "It's a smaller part this time, but I think they might let you sing. And the cast is pretty hot stuff. Just being in the same movie with them will do you a lot of good." He seemed to know everything about getting her career off the ground, and he worked hard for her. And the next morning she saw her name in the papers. It talked about the next film she was going to be in. It was true. He had really done it.

He took her out to dinner that night, after the article in the paper about her new picture, and there was a photograph of them in the newspaper the day afterward, and the caption read, "Personal Manager Ernie Salvatore and his new friend, Crystal Wyatt." It was like reading about someone else and she stared at it in silent wonder. She sent a copy of it to Harry and Pearl and she still called them every few days. She missed them terribly, but not half as much as she missed Spencer. She still wondered if she'd ever hear from him again, but in her heart of hearts, she knew she wouldn't. And as she thought of it, she felt desperately lonely without him. And the only friend she had now was Ernie.

He sent her flowers, brought her gifts, and embarrassed her more than once by sending the Rolls and his driver to pick her up on the set after work. But he made no further attempt to seduce her. He was waiting for her to come to him, and he knew that eventually she would, in one way or another. And two weeks after her first visit, he invited her to Malibu again. She hesitated but by then she was more comfortable with him, and she thought nothing would happen. They didn't swim in the pool this time, and she walked along the beach with him. She was starting the new picture in a few weeks, and they had a lot to talk about. And then suddenly he turned to her, and smiled. There was something fatherly about him, she thought now. He had taken her under his wing, and made all her decisions for her. After four years of fending for herself, it was a new experience for her, but she had to admit that she liked it.

"I've been wanting to ask you something, Crystal." He hesitated as they watched the sunset again, and gently took her hand. "How would you like to stay with me for a while?"

"Here?" She thought he meant for the weekend, and all she could think of was the night he had made love to her, and she blushed again at the memory of it.

He smiled again, she was still so innocent and so young. At nearly twenty-two, she was still a child, by Hollywood standards at least. "Not just here, silly girl. In Beverly Hills too. I thought it might help you a little with your career, and it would be a lot more pleasant than staying at the hotel, and less expensive." He tried to make it sound practical, instead of what it was. A proposition.

"I don't know . . . I . . ." She turned her lavender-blue eyes to him and even the hard core of Ernie Salvatore melted a little. "Ernie, what do you mean? You've already been so kind to me. I shouldn't . . . I wouldn't want to take advantage." She still didn't understand, as he put his arms around her.

"I mean I want you to come and live with me. I want to be near you." There was a long silence as she looked at him and then stared sadly out at the sunset. Where was Spencer? Where had he gone? Why wasn't he offering this to her instead of Ernie? "Hollywood is a tough place. I want to offer you my protection." What more could she ask? And yet, she knew she didn't love him.

She slowly shook her head. "I can't."

"Why not?"

She looked at him honestly, putting her career on the line, but she couldn't lie to him. He had already done too much for her, for her to want to be dishonest with him. "I don't love you."

He didn't tell her that meant nothing to him. It wasn't her love that he wanted. It was the rest of her, her body to warm his nights, her face to sell to the movies. He made a healthy profit from what she did, for himself and the far more important people who backed him. He was the front man for an interesting group, but for all anyone knew, he was the man who counted. And she would be good for him. He had known that from the very first moment he saw her.

"Maybe love will come in time. We're friends, aren't we?"

She nodded, still looking out at the sunset. He had been good to her, better than anyone, but what he wanted was more than she wanted to give him. But everything he did for her was on such a grand scale, the clothes, the cars, the movies, the diamond bracelet. "Can I think about it for a while?" There were others who would have shuddered at the thought of putting off Ernie Salvatore, but he looked patient and kind as they walked back to the house. He poured her a glass of wine, and she sipped it as they listened to music. It was peaceful being with him. He never pressured her, he was just there, and in some ways he understood what she wanted. She wanted to be a movie star. It was still a childish dream, and yet she knew he could make it happen. But she didn't want to sacrifice her integrity for that, to live with a man she didn't love. But what else did she have? In truth, she had nothing. Only a dream. And the memory of a man who had left three years before, and was never coming back, no matter how much she still loved him.

"Do you want to go home now?" He was always ready to do what she wanted, and as she smiled at him, he leaned over and kissed her. It was the first time he had done that since the night they'd made love two weeks before. For two weeks now, he had put an ever proper distance between them and demanded nothing of her. And he demanded nothing now. But he offered her his heart and his home, and to

Crystal that seemed enormous. He kissed her again, tenderly, and his hands touched her gently. She started to pull back, but he pulled her closer to him, and there was surprising strength in his hands as he did it. "Don't go," he whispered, "please . . ." She almost felt sorry for him. He gave so much, and he asked so little of her. She let him kiss her, and within moments, her body responded to his, and this time it was Crystal who peeled his clothes off, and they made love on the huge white leather couch with the mirrors overhead and the vast sunset behind them.

There was no remorse this time, no surprise. She knew what she'd done, and why. She felt she owed it to him, for all that he had done. She knew she didn't love him, but there was nothing else, and no one. This was her life now. Hollywood, with its flash and its glamor, and he was an integral part of it. She couldn't fight it anymore. She already owed him too much, and he had too much to offer. Life had always been too hard for her, and she was tired of it. With Ernie, the hardships were over.

They stayed at Malibu that night. She had no one to answer to except herself, no reason to go back to the hotel. No one would care what she did or even know. Not Harry. Not Pearl. Not even poor old Mrs. Castagna. And when she went back to the hotel three days later to pick up her mail she found the letter from Spencer that Pearl had mailed her. After all this time he had finally written to her, trying to explain his long silence. He told her how much he hated the war, and how he had given up hope for a while but that he still loved her. But it was too late now. She had already agreed to move in with Ernie. And Spencer's letter told her nothing she didn't already know. He was still in Korea, and he didn't know when he was coming home, and he was still married. She had been right to go to Hollywood. Maybe nothing would ever change with Spencer. But loving him was a luxury she could no longer afford. She had sold her soul to Ernesto Salvatore. And she never answered Spencer's letter.

Ernie helped her move her things into his home in Beverly Hills, and overnight her life changed. There was a cook, and two maids, and she had a pink satin dressing room that looked like a movie set for Joan Crawford. And when she went to hang up her clothes, she found that the closets were already full of clothes he had bought for her, and spread out luxuriously on a chair was a new white mink coat. She slipped it on over her jeans and giggled like a little girl as she twirled and looked at herself in the mirror. She called Pearl and told her about it too, and that she had moved in with Ernie. Pearl didn't sound surprised or shocked. If anything, she sounded a little jealous.

They went everywhere together, to all the best restaurants, all the biggest parties, to premieres and openings, and the Academy Awards just before she started her new picture.

"That'll be you one day," he whispered to her as Shirley Booth rushed up to the stage to pick up her Oscar for best actress for *Come Back Little Sheba.* Gary Cooper won the award for best actor for *High Noon.* And *Singin' in the Rain* with Gene Kelly was the favored picture. It was all like a dream to her, the dream she had had since her childhood in the valley.

"Happy?" He asked as he smiled at her one night after they made love, and she nodded peacefully. She was happy, strangely enough even though she didn't love him. He took care of her, he pampered her, he saw that everyone was kind to her, and when she started her new movie, they treated her like a queen. She was important now. She was Ernie Salvatore's girl. She wanted more than that eventually. She wanted to be a good actress, and singer, although she seldom sang now. It was part of another life. And she was concentrating mostly on her acting. But what she had with Ernie was very pleasant. She worked hard with her voice coach and the acting teachers who came to the house now to teach her some of the fine points of acting. She had a good memory, and good timing when she delivered her lines. She was always on time, and never made a fuss. People liked her on the set because she worked hard and was well prepared. Little by little, the acting community was coming to know and respect her. And most of them also knew about Ernie. The Rolls picked her up at night, and sometimes Ernie was waiting in the back-seat with a bottle of champagne in a silver bucket filled with ice, and two Baccarat glasses. It was a way of life she had only read about, and now it was hers. All of it. The dream had come true. She had become what she always wanted, and for the moment she didn't care about how much she had sacrificed to get it.

She finished the second film in late May, and Ernie took her to Mexico for a few days. He said he had some business to do there, and she enjoyed seeing something so new and different. There were sweet little children wandering the street in bare feet with bright happy faces and big eyes, there were bright costumes, interesting sights. She loved it, although she knew very little of Ernie. And when they got back to L.A., he handed her a script with a smile, as he bent to kiss her when he came home from his office. He was looking as trim and elegant as usual, and there were moments when it was almost like being married. She was used to him by then, it was comfortable being with him, and he never pressed her to say what she didn't feel. It wasn't important to him.

"What's that?" She grinned. They were going to the Cocoanut Grove that night for dinner and dancing.

"Your Academy Award. Looks like you've made it, kid." It was a script, but for another studio with a role made for her, and he had gotten it for her. Word was getting around. She was in the papers constantly, he was paying his press people a fortune to spark everyone's interest in Crystal. And when he took her anywhere, people stared at her in disbelief. People just didn't look like that. Not even in Hollywood. She still had the wary look of a doe emerging from the woods, and with it a body that caught everyone's attention. He taught her how to dress, how to walk, how to enter a room so that everyone would stop what they were doing. And he had to admit, she was a natural. She was going to be a big star one day.

A very big one. He had no doubt now, especially with the offer that had just come across his desk, and soon there would be others. And she belonged to him anyway. And one day, if he had to, he would tell her.

The script was for a movie that would begin in July, and the woman they'd signed for the supporting role had picked a fight with the star, so they had to fire her. They were desperately searching for someone else, and Crystal fit the bill perfectly. Besides, she already had a reputation for being easy to work with, and in Hollywood that was rarer than diamonds. She was going to make it big, and quickly.

There were times when Ernie even wondered if he loved her, not that it mattered to him. He was past all that. At forty-five, he'd been divorced five times, and he had two kids, somewhere in Pittsburgh, both of them were older than Crystal, and he hadn't seen them since they were babies.

She spent hours reading the script and making notes. It was a good part and she was amazed they would even consider her for it. She had more lines than she'd had in the other two, and this one was going to be a great deal harder, it required a lot of emotion, and she knew she'd have to work hard with all her coaches, but she loved it. "Ernie, it's wonderful," she told him when she found him at the pool. He had a phone out there, and he was always making deals and calls and signing papers. Even in the Polo Lounge they never left him alone. Sometimes he spent the night there in a bungalow with business associates until a deal was settled.

"It's a good picture, Crystal. It's going to do you a lot of good."

But for a moment she looked worried as she sat down and looked up at him. "Do you think I can do it?"

He laughed at her, and kissed a handful of the soft blond hair. It took the hairdressers on the set forever to put it up, but she had flatly refused to cut it. And she was the only girl he knew in Hollywood who would have cared if she could do justice to the picture. Most of them only wanted to get parts for what they would do for them, without a second thought for the quality of their work, but not Crystal. It was what set her apart from the rest, that and her looks. He had picked himself a winner. "You'll do a great job."

"I'll have to work like a dog to remember all those lines."

"You'll be fine." They went out to celebrate that night, and she worked night and day on the script before her first day on the set.

They started on July ninth, and for the first two weeks she hardly slept. She worked with her coaches until after midnight. And at four o'clock every morning she got up. And at five the chauffeur drove her to the studio. William Holden and Henry Fonda were in the movie with her, and she was awestruck when she first met them. They were friendly to her and everyone treated her with respect, but she never had time to make friends. She worked too hard to talk to anyone or hang around after work. And her coaches even came to her dressing room on the set during her lunch break.

She even saw Clark Gable on the set once, visiting a friend, and she thought she'd never seen a better-looking man. She told Ernie about it that night in excited tones, and he laughed.

"Wait a couple of months. He'll be telling his friends he saw Crystal Wyatt!" She laughed at him. Ernie always made her feel so important. But she hardly saw him these days. She was too busy on the set, and she had no time to go out. She felt like a recluse, and she was barricaded in her dressing room, studying as usual, when someone pounded on the door four days later. She heard excited shouts and opened the door to see what had happened.

"It's over! It's over!"

"The picture?" She looked shocked, wondering what had gone wrong. They had barely started, and this one was scheduled to be longer than the others. They had told her to plan on working through September.

"The war!" One of the stagehands was standing in front of her with tears of joy rolling down his face. He had two brothers over there, and suddenly Crystal gasped as she understood. "The war in Korea is over!" He threw his arms around her and they embraced as tears filled her eyes too. For months now, she had tried to forget him. And she had never answered the letter he'd written to her in April. But he would be coming home now, like the others. Spencer . . . the man she'd betrayed when she moved in with Ernie . . . and now he'd be coming home. But to whom? He was still married to Elizabeth. And she was living with Ernie. And unless Pearl told him, he wouldn't even know where to find her. And for an odd moment, as she watched the others laughing and talking and crying, she wondered what she would do now.

CHAPTER
28 ─────────────

Elizabeth stood behind the gate, trying to see
his face, pushed on all sides by the crowds that
had come to greet them. It had taken him
three weeks to muster out, and she had wanted
to meet him in Japan and fly to Honolulu for a
few days. But the army had insisted he fly back
to San Francisco, and he would be free the moment he set foot on terra firma. Her parents
were there, and his, and there were hundreds
of women talking anxiously. They were the
lucky ones. There were countless others who
stayed home and mourned. No one was coming home to them. But Spencer had survived it.

He had been wounded once, but it had only been a flesh wound and he had been back in combat a week later. It had been an ugly war, a "police action" that had cost lives, the second war he had served in in twelve years.

She had taken a month off from work, and they were going to go to the lake with her parents. The Barclays had invited his parents to come too, although he didn't know it yet. And there was a huge surprise party planned at the house in San Francisco.

As Elizabeth watched him hurrying out of the plane, she straightened her hat, and stood nervously waiting. It had been a long time since she'd seen him, and now everything would be very different. Their stays at the Imperial Hotel had become awkward eventually because he was under so much strain and now this was real life again, which might take even more adjustment. They had never really lived together before the war, and he'd been gone for three years now. And at twenty-four she had become very independent and she was up to her ears in politics. She had entrée everywhere, and she had met some very interesting people in Washington during his absence. But the last thing on her mind was politics as she finally saw him. He seemed very tall and thin as he looked over the crowd, and then walked slowly toward them, conversing with a few of his men. He still hadn't seen her. She saw him shake hands with them and then they hurried off to find their wives, and he continued through the crowd as she pressed toward him. His mother was crying, having just seen her son for the first time in three years, but he still didn't know that they were there. His eyes were sad as he scanned the crowd, and there was gray in his hair that hadn't been there before. At thirty-four he looked even more handsome than he had the day Elizabeth met him at her parents' dinner. And then suddenly, with a look of surprise, he saw her face beneath the big straw hat, and he hesitated for a moment and then dropped his duffel bag and ran toward her, pulling her into his arms and off her feet as he swung her around, and his parents hurried toward him. Even Justice Barclay had a tear in his eye as he shook Spencer's hand heartily, and Priscilla was crying openly as she hugged him.

"It's so good to have you back safe and sound."

"Thank you." He hugged and kissed them all and his mother saw something different in his eyes, something that hadn't been there before, and that worried her. It was the kind of grief she had known when her oldest son died.

He looked as though he had lost something in the war, a faith, a belief, a sureness he had had before. It had never been a war he believed in.

They crowded into the waiting limousine and drove to the house on Broadway chatting and talking and laughing and crying. The two older women looked at each other several times in sympathy, with tender smiles. They were the mothers of sons, and sometimes that wasn't easy. Only Elizabeth was in high spirits as she held her husband's hand, and he had an arm comfortably around her shoulders. But they had seen each other in Japan several times, unlike their parents who hadn't seen him since the war had started three years before. It had been a long, long time, for all of them, and Spencer showed it most of all. He leaned his head back and closed his eyes, speaking to all and none, as Elizabeth chatted animatedly with her mother.

"I can't believe I'm home." He wasn't yet, but this was close enough. He was back on American soil, with his wife at his side. But that was something he still had to deal with. He had been torturing himself about it ever since he'd left San Francisco.

"Welcome home, Son." His father patted his arm and tears choked him as Spencer reached over and squeezed his hand hard.

"I love you, Dad. Christ, I hope this country stays out of trouble for a while. I've had it."

"I hope this time you didn't stay in the reserves," Elizabeth chided him with a smile, and he laughed.

"Not on your life. They're going to have to call on another boy next time. I'm staying home to get fat and sit on my ass while my wife has babies." He said it half jokingly and also to test the waters. There were a lot of things he wanted to discuss with her and that one was important to him. Elizabeth made no comment and only smiled, but nothing had changed when they closed the bedroom door shortly after they got to the house on Broadway. He threw his uniform on the floor and longed to see it burn, and after a shower he approached Elizabeth with caution. He had resolved a lot in his mind while he was gone, but not everything. Elizabeth was more real to him now because he hadn't heard from Crystal in so long, and she had begun retreating into his dreams again. Although he missed her, he hadn't decided what to do about Elizabeth and their marriage. She had changed a lot in three years and there were a lot of things he wanted to know about her, especially whether or not she wanted children. But he had decided long since that he wasn't going to play games with her anymore. He wanted to know exactly who she was and what she wanted, and if it wasn't right for him, they weren't going to stay married. He had to give her a chance, but he had a right to what he wanted, too, and he wasn't sure it was Elizabeth Barclay. He had seen too many men die, seen too much pain, to waste his life now with the wrong woman. Life was too short, and at thirty-four, his was already half over. The meaning of life had become too dear to him to waste even a moment with a woman he didn't want to be with. And he brought the subject up as she sat in the bathtub that afternoon as they dressed for dinner. She was luxuriating in a froth of scented bubbles.

He sat down gingerly on the edge of the tub, freshly showered with a towel around his waist, feeling a little awkward with her. He looked handsomer than ever. His body was as firm as a boy's. It had been a hard life for all of them in Korea.

"How do you feel about having kids these days?" She looked up at him in surprise, and smiled at the question.

"Generally, or my own?" Her brother and Sarah had finally announced openly that they didn't want any, and she hadn't been shocked by their decision.

"Ours actually." He didn't smile as he

waited for her to answer. That was another thing he was no longer willing to wait for.

"I hadn't given it much thought lately. It wasn't exactly foremost in my mind with you away." She smiled and moved her legs gracefully in the bubble-covered water. "Why? Is that something we have to resolve today?" She looked annoyed, and it was odd having him stare at her in the bathtub.

"Maybe. I think the fact that we even have to 'resolve' it says something, don't you?"

"No, I don't. It's not something anyone should rush into."

"Like your brother and Sarah?" He realized he was looking for a fight with her. He wanted to make a decision, and soon. Having two women on his mind for the past three years had almost driven him crazy.

"They have nothing to do with this, Spencer. I mean us. I'm twenty-four years old, I'm not over the hill yet, thank you very much, and I have an important job in Washington. I'm not going to jeopardize that for a baby." He had his answer. But he was still angry at the way she said it.

"I think your priorities are all wrong."

"You see it differently. For you, it's just something cute to come home to. For me, it's a major sacrifice. That makes a big difference."

"Yes, it does." He stood up, and tightened the towel around his waist, and she smiled, thinking how silly he looked in the pink towel. "It shouldn't be a sacrifice, Elizabeth. It should be something we both want."

"Well, 'we' don't. You do, and maybe one day I will, but not now, this isn't the time. My job is just too important." He was already tired of hearing about it, and she knew how much he hated McCarthy.

"Is the job really that important to you?" But he knew it was. It was all she had talked about in Tokyo when he met her on leave there.

"Yes." She looked him in the eye. She wasn't afraid to be honest with him, she never had been. "The job is very important to me, Spencer."

"Why?"

"Because it makes me feel independent." It was something he didn't want in a wife, and yet . . . there was something about her . . . it wasn't even that he was used to her yet. They had only been married for two weeks before he left. But there was something challenging about her, it made him want to conquer her, and in his heart of hearts, he knew that Elizabeth would never be conquered. "I took a leave of absence to come out here to meet you, but I'm going back to work when we get home, Spencer, I hope you know that."

"I do now, don't I?" He lit a cigarette as she watched. The war had been hard on him, and on a lot of others. And he had come through it all right finally after the rough period when he had stopped writing to Crystal. But there were times he would never forget, like the men who had died in his arms, needlessly, all for a fight that wasn't theirs anyway. It had eaten at his heart, and it was hard to come home now and put it behind him. "And where is home, by the way? I gather we've given up New York. Where does that leave me? Unemployed, I expect."

"You didn't like your job there anyway." She sounded unimpressed. She was a tough opponent. "You told me that in Tokyo."

"Possibly. But it might be nice to earn a living. I'm not quite as 'independent,' shall we call it, as you are. I need a job, Elizabeth."

"I'm sure my father will be happy to introduce you to anyone you want. And I had some ideas on that subject myself, like something in government. It would suit you to perfection."

"I'm a Democrat. That's not the fashion these days."

"So is my father, so am I. There's room for everyone in Washington. That's what it's all about. This is a democracy, not a dictatorship, for God's sake." It was ridiculous, he had been home for four hours, and they were fighting over politics and her job, when all he wanted was to feel comfortable again and settle down with a woman he loved, and who loved him. But there was nothing comfortable about being there. He had no home, no job, and he felt suddenly lost without the army. And even that confused him, all he had wanted was to come home, and now that he had, he was unhappy.

He dressed and went downstairs, and two hours later he was stunned. Two hundred people he didn't know had been invited to dinner. It was a surprise party for him, and his father sensed quietly that he wasn't ready for it. From Seoul to San Francisco in one speedy leap was too big an adjustment. Spencer had trouble sleeping that night, and he let himself out of the house and walked for miles, listening to the foghorns and winding up in North Beach. But every time he heard a sound somewhere on the way, he jumped, fearing a sniper.

He was standing outside Mrs. Castagna's house, looking up at her windows, and his heart was beating wildly. This was the moment he had dreamed of coming home for. The windows were all dark, and he wanted to run in and surprise her. But as he stood there, he wondered again why she hadn't answered his letters.

He tried the front door with a trembling hand, but it was locked, and he rang the bell. No one answered for a long time, and then a woman came, looking sleepy, and wrapped in a bathrobe.

"Yes? What do you want?" She spoke through the door, and he could see her through the glass panes. She was middle-aged and not very attractive.

"I'm here to see Miss Wyatt." He was wearing his uniform and it was obvious that he was a soldier.

The woman looked pensive for a minute and then shook her head. She thought she knew everyone by then, and then she remembered. "She don't live here."

"Yes, she does." He nodded insistently, and then suddenly realized she might have moved. It frightened him to realize that he didn't know where she was now. "She lived in the corner room upstairs." He pointed. But that had been three years before. Maybe that was why she hadn't answered his letters.

"She moved away before my mother died." His heart almost stopped. Mrs. Castagna was gone too. Everything had changed. He had waited for this moment for so long and now she was gone, and everything familiar with her.

"Do you know where she moved to?" They were still talking through the door, but the woman wouldn't open it. It was too late and she didn't know who he was. For all she knew he was drunk, or a maniac, and she wasn't going to let him in. She was one of Mrs. Castagna's unmarried daughters, and she ran the place now, with austerity and great caution. She had raised the rents, and she was thinking of selling the place. She and her sisters and brothers had decided that they'd rather have the money.

"I don't know where she went, mister. I never even met her."

"Did she leave a forwarding address?" The woman shook her head and then waved at him, wanting him to go away so she could go back to her apartment.

He started down the steps and then looked up at the darkened windows again. She was gone, and he had no idea where to find her.

He went to Harry's after that, sure that he'd find her there, and they were closing as he got there. The maître d' had taken his jacket off, there were two men scrubbing floors, and all of the chairs were on the tables.

"Sorry, sir, we're closed." He looked annoyed as Spencer walked in. The doors were supposed to be locked, but someone had obviously forgotten, and left them open.

"I know . . . I'm sorry . . . is Crystal here?" He felt suddenly frightened as he asked. What if she wasn't? What if something had happened to her? In all that time he'd been involved with himself and the miseries of his own existence. He had let her down. And now God only knew what had happened to her.

But the headwaiter shook his head, anxious for Spencer to leave. "She moved to L.A. But we've got a great little gal to replace her. Come back tomorrow night." But the only other "gal" he wanted was the one he loved, the one whose memory had kept him going in Korea.

"I'm an old friend. I just got back from Seoul . . . do you know where she is in L.A.?" Maybe she'd gone to Hollywood after all. The thought of it excited him, but he was anxious now to find her. They had a lot to talk about, a lot to say, and he owed her an explanation for his long silence. But the man only shook his head, looking uninterested and unsympathetic. Returning soldiers from Korea weren't his problem.

"No. Harry would know. He's away on vacation for two weeks. Call when he gets back."

"What about . . ." He groped for the name

and then remembered it with a surge of relief. It had been a miserable evening. "Pearl . . . is she here?"

"She'll be here tomorrow at four. You can call her then. And listen, pal, I've got to close up. Why don't you just call back tomorrow." And then, gratuitously, "I hear she's making movies now. Crystal, I mean. It's too bad she's not singing. She was the best." He smiled briefly, trying to be friendly as he walked Spencer firmly toward the door, and he nodded. And a moment later, Spencer was standing outside, with no more idea where Crystal was than he had had when he'd gone there. She was gone. To Hollywood. Just as she'd always dreamed. And he had to face Elizabeth alone, and decide what the hell to do about his marriage. Maybe it was better that way. Maybe it would be better to make the decision once and for all before he saw Crystal, and then he could go to her with a clean slate. The thought of it weighed heavy on him as he walked slowly back to the house on Broadway. And when he went to their room, Elizabeth was sound asleep. She had no idea that he'd been gone. She looked peaceful as she lay there, and he looked down at her in the soft light from the open bathroom doorway. He wondered what she was dreaming about, if anything . . .

if she even had dreams. She was so matter-of-fact and businesslike. Even his return was treated like a social event, something to be organized and planned. There was no tenderness, no gentle touching or holding hands. He hadn't made love to her since he got back, and the truth was he didn't want to.

He slipped into bed beside her after he turned off the light again, and lay listening to the rhythm of her breathing. And then he rolled over and looked at her in the dark, gently stroking her hair, and thinking that she deserved more than he had to give her. She opened an eye then, sensing him there, but she was half asleep as she stirred.

"You awake?" She lifted her head, trying to see the clock, but she was too sleepy to focus. "What time is it?" she murmured sleepily.

"It's late . . . go back to sleep . . ." he whispered, and she turned over, with her back to him, nodding.

"Good night, Elizabeth." He wanted to tell her that he loved her, but he couldn't bring himself to say the words, and all he could think as he lay there was that Crystal was in Hollywood, and he still didn't know where to find her. He was going to call Pearl the next day, at the restaurant, and he prayed that she would know. But he had made up his mind not

to contact Crystal until his own life was settled. It wouldn't take long, and it was fairer to
her. But he ached with the longing to see her.
It had been a lonely homecoming for him, a
day long awaited that had finally come. But
now that he was home again, all he knew was
that he felt like a stranger.

It was dawn before he slept, and when he
finally did, he dreamed of guns going off in the
distance . . . and there was someone talking
to him through it all . . . someone whispering, saying something he couldn't hear because
the guns were too loud . . . but as he listened
desperately, crying in his sleep . . . he was
sure that the voice was Crystal's.

CHAPTER
29

All of his plans had been made for him, he discovered the next day. They were going to Tahoe for three weeks, his parents would be there for the first two, and the Barclays had planned several dinners to entertain them.

"You'd better buy some clothes before you go up to the lake," Elizabeth told him. All he had with him were his uniforms, his fatigues, his combat boots, and his dog tags, hardly suitable for their life-style at Lake Tahoe. She went with him and he felt like a child again as she helped him pick things out and insisted on charging everything to her father. He made a note of the amount, and assured Justice Barclay that the moment he got home and set up his checking account again, he would send him a check. He had let Elizabeth close his bank account in New York when she gave up his apartment and moved to Georgetown.

"Don't worry about it, Son," Harrison Barclay laughed, "I know where to find you."

Everything was so easy and so prearranged. They drove to Lake Tahoe in convoy, Elizabeth in the station wagon with Spencer, and the two older couples in the limousine. They stopped in Sacramento for lunch and then drove up to the lake, where everything was organized to perfection. There were luncheon parties for him almost every day, a dinner party for fifty, they went swimming in the afternoon, and it was ten days before he had a chance to go fishing with his father. He sat in the speedboat staring at the water and William Hill looked at him sadly.

"You're having a hard time readjusting, aren't you, Son?"

Spencer sighed. It was a relief to be alone. There was constant tension with Elizabeth, and in spite of their enormous kindness to him, he was sick to death of the Barclays. "Yes, I am." He looked honestly at his father and nodded. "I didn't think it would be like this when I came back."

"What did you think would be different?" He was a wise man with a kind heart and he wanted to help him. He hated seeing him so unhappy.

"I don't know, Dad . . . I have no place to call my own. I've been in somebody else's country for three years, and now I'm in somebody else's house, with somebody else's friends, doing what somebody else wants . . . I'm too old for that. I want to go home, and I don't even have one."

"Sure you do. You have a beautiful home, your mother and I visited it last Christmas."

"Good for you. I live in a house I've never seen, with furniture I didn't buy, in a town I hardly know." He painted such a bleak picture and he was so sorry for himself that his father had to laugh with gentle humor.

"It's not as rough as you think. Give yourself a chance. You haven't even been home two weeks yet."

Spencer ran a hand through his hair, and his father smiled at the familiar gesture. It was so good to have him back, healthy and alive, he wasn't worried about his son's reactions, and in his opinion, they were normal. He and Alicia had spoken about it the night before, and she had suggested he try to have a talk with Spencer.

"I don't know, Dad." He thought about telling him about the affair with Crystal before he left, but he didn't really want to. She was his, and what he felt for her was intensely private. At least he knew where she was now. Pearl had given him her phone number in L.A., and he clung to the slip of paper as if it were a lifeline. A dozen times in the last two weeks he had picked up the phone, but he had forced himself not to call her. It was too soon. He hadn't settled anything yet, and he knew he had to. But Elizabeth was acting as though everything was fine and that made it even harder.

And as though sensing that there was more, William Hill decided to ask his son a delicate question. "You're still in love with Elizabeth, aren't you?" It was such a good match, he would have hated to see it fall apart at their feet, only because Spencer was nervous and impatient. But for a long time his son didn't answer.

"I'm not sure of anything anymore. I'm not even sure I know her."

"You've been gone a long time, Son. At your age, even at mine, three years seems like forever."

"I want kids. She doesn't. That's pretty basic, Dad."

"She's still very young. Give her a chance too. Go home, settle down, get used to each other again, then try to work things out. She'll come around. She's had to be on her own for the last three years, it's a big change for her having you around again too."

But Spencer looked disgusted. "She's never on her own. She's always got her father. He'd pay for my underwear if I let him." He was referring to their recent purchases in town and his father laughed.

"There are bigger problems than that in life. They're good people, Spencer, and they want you both to be happy."

"I know . . . I'm sorry . . . I must sound ungrateful. I'm just so damn confused." He stared out at the lake again and then back at his father. He spoke in a softer voice this time, and there was something distant and sad in his eyes that had troubled his father ever since he got home. "There was someone else before I left, Dad . . . someone I'd known for a long time." He didn't tell him she'd been fourteen when he first met her.

William Hill looked unhappy as he looked at his son. "Was it serious?"

"Yes." Spencer didn't hesitate as he said it.

"Very. They're very different . . . as different as two women could be . . ."

"Have you seen her since you got back?"

Spencer shook his head, but he was planning to. It was all he lived for.

"Don't. You'll only complicate things for yourself. You're married to a lovely girl, make a go of it. Stick by what you started."

"Is that what life's all about?" The gray in his hair glinted in the sun, and William Hill was surprised again when he saw it.

"Sometimes. Sometimes marriage is just sticking things out, whether you want to or not."

"It doesn't sound like much fun."

"Sometimes it isn't." He reached out and touched his hand. "Take some advice from an old man, Spencer, don't turn your life upside down. It would be a terrible mistake. Stick with Elizabeth. She's a fine girl, and you married her. You owe her something after she's waited for you all this time." He knew he did too. It was why he had come back to her at all, after three years of dreaming of Crystal.

His father got a fish on the line then and they were distracted for a while, and afterward his father looked at him seriously again, touched that Spencer had confided in him. He only hoped that he had swayed him in the right direction.

"Give it a lot of thought, and be patient for a while. Everything will work out. You'd never forgive yourself if you let her down now. Think of that too. You don't owe the other girl anything. You married Elizabeth. And now you have to stand by that." It all made sense, but it depressed him immeasurably as he started the motor and they went back to the dock as he nodded.

"Thank you, Father." He looked at him for a long moment before they went back to the house, and for the first time he had felt that his father loved him for who he was, and not just as a stand-in for Robert.

"Catch anything?" Elizabeth was in high spirits when they returned. She loved the lake and seeing all her old friends again, and the fuss being made over Spencer.

"A pair of old shoes." He grinned, he was looking better than he had in days. Talking to his father had taken some of the pressure off. "Three fish . . ." he leaned over her and she pretended to hold her nose . . . "and a kiss for my wife." But at least she let him kiss her. They went inside after that, and Elizabeth filed her nails while he showered. She told him about the party they were going to that night and he looked at her pensively. "Let's stay home tonight."

"Darling, we can't. They're expecting us. And they're friends of my father's."

"Tell them you have a headache, or my war wounds are acting up." He grinned boyishly at her, he wanted a night alone with her. They hadn't had a moment alone since he got back, but she didn't seem to mind it.

"Tomorrow. I promise." But the next night, her brother arrived and she insisted it would be rude not to go out with them. And the day after that they went to a black-tie party. He felt as though he were in jail, being fed on champagne instead of water. But it was lonely being with her and surrounded by people all the time. He tried to explain that to her as they lay on the beach, but she insisted that he was being silly. "How can you be lonely with all these nice people around?"

"Because I'm not ready for that yet. I want to be alone with you, just to talk and get to know each other again." But she refused to understand that. And then, in an instant, he knew what he had to do. He decided to go to L.A. on the weekend. He finally knew what he was going to tell Crystal. He had made up his mind. And when he came back he was going to tell Elizabeth he wanted to divorce her. He wanted to tell her when they left the lake. He didn't want a huge ugly scene with all their parents.

"But my parents are having people over for you." She was furious. They had had people over for him almost every night.

"I'm sorry. I can't help it. I have some business to take care of in Los Angeles." His voice was suddenly cool. He knew what he was going to do now.

"What is it?" She looked at him suspiciously. He didn't even have a job at the moment.

"Some investments I made when I finished law school."

"Can't it wait?"

"No, it can't. Not for another minute. This is important, Elizabeth. I have to." He didn't call Crystal before he left. He was going to call her from down there and surprise her.

Elizabeth was still sulking when he left and she was at a luncheon with her parents as he drove back to San Francisco and left the car at the house, and then he took a cab to the airport. It was a two-hour flight, and when he got there it was a sultry afternoon in late August. He took a taxi into town, and checked into the Beverly Hills Hotel with money that he had borrowed from his father. And the moment he got to his room, he dialed the number they'd given him at Harry's. A maid answered and said something about "Salvatore," which made him smile. She always seemed to rent rooms from Italians. He asked for Crystal Wyatt and was told she was working. Pearl had told him she was working on another movie. He was excited for her, and he felt like a new man as he asked where he could find her. He felt suddenly as though his whole life had come into focus. He felt at peace again, and in control of his fate. At last, he knew he had made the right decision.

"At MGM," the woman answered, and told him the lot number in all innocence. He jotted it down and then hurried out of the hotel, and gave a cabdriver the address he had looked up in the phone book. It was a long drive from the hotel, and he could feel his heart pound as he thought of seeing her again. He had never felt that way about anyone but Crystal. He knew he had explanations to make, and apologies for acting crazy. He knew he owed her a lot of things but they had a lifetime now for him to make it all up to her. And he smiled to himself in the back of the cab, thinking of her and their future.

The entrance to MGM was impressive, and he stared around him like a tourist as they

drove onto the lot after being stopped by a se-
curity guard. He told them he wanted to see
Crystal Wyatt, and what movie she was in.
And the guard told him it was a closed lot and
he needed a pass to get in. But when he told
him where he'd been and for how long, the
guard hesitated and glanced over his shoulder.
His own son had died over there, and he would
have done anything for a soldier. "Don't tell
anyone I let you in," he said as he waved them
in and Spencer thanked him. The cabdriver
headed toward the lot the guard had sent them
to, as dozens of actors walked by in spectacular costumes. There were cowboys and Indi-
ans, and chain gangs, and beautiful girls in
bathing suits and slinky dresses. It was a whole
other world from Harry's in San Francisco.
And when he paid the driver, he stopped for a
minute and looked around, and then walked
cautiously into the sound stage. It was an enormous building almost like an airplane hangar,
and in the distance he could see people clus-
tered under bright lights, there was a man
shouting at them, and everything else was silence. He stood very still and when they took a
break ten minutes later, he went a little closer.
And then, as though in a dream he saw her
standing with her back to him, but even at that
distance he knew instantly it was Crystal. He

wanted to run up and throw his arms around her as his heart raced, but he approached cautiously, not wanting to disturb anyone, and then as though she sensed him nearby, she turned, and they both froze. She was still the same, only more beautiful than she had been three years before. The child was gone at last, and she had left behind her this very rare woman. Her hair was swept back in a graceful knot, and she was wearing a strapless white dress and white satin shoes, all of it covered with tiny brilliant sparkles. She looked like someone in a fairy tale as tears filled his eyes and blurred his vision, as slowly she walked toward him. She didn't speak, she only stood staring at him, like a woman in a dream, and then she was in his arms and she was kissing him, and he thought his heart would break. He had never loved her more than at that moment. He had survived the war just to come back to her, to hold her again. It was everything he had looked for in San Francisco and hadn't found. But he had found it here, just as he knew he would, with Crystal.

"Oh God . . . you'll never know how I missed you. . . ." All the anguish he had felt, all the loneliness, all the misery ripped through him again as he held her, and tears rolled down their faces. She knew what she had done and it was breaking her heart. She had told herself he wouldn't come, but he had. He was back again. And she was living with Ernie Salvatore. But she couldn't think of Ernie now. She couldn't think of anyone. Only Spencer, holding her close to him and kissing her, as she touched his face with hungry lips and gentle fingers. "Oh darling, I only love you . . ." He pulled away from her then and smiled. "You look so beautiful." He smiled tenderly at her like a proud father. "Are you a movie star now?"

She looked embarrassed as she kissed him again. "Not yet, but I'm getting there. This is a terrific picture." She told him who was in it and he was impressed. She had actually done it while he was gone. She had gone to Hollywood, and now she was in the movies. But then she touched a finger to her lips and whispered to him, "They're getting ready to roll again. Come to my dressing room." He followed her on tiptoe to the room where she dressed and ate and studied for hours. It was small and clean and tidy, and a woman was putting out her costume for the next scene, as Crystal smiled and told her she could go, and then she turned to Spencer again. "I'm free for another hour." Her eyes searched his face, wanting to know why he had come, where he had been, when he'd come home, and if he was still married.

"Is this really happening? Is this you?" She looked at him in awe, and remembered the endless months of his silence. And as they sat, holding hands, he tried to explain it all to her, the loneliness, the pain, and his confusion, his despair over being there, the feeling that nothing mattered anymore except the constant misery and destruction he was seeing.

"It was as though nothing here was real anymore . . . not even you for a while, I guess. I felt as though I would never get back here. I couldn't even talk to anyone. And everyone's letters just made it worse. They tried to make everything sound normal and happy here, which made the contrast between their lives and mine even more brutal. I think some of the other men felt like that too. We talked about it a lot on the plane coming home. Until then, no one ever really wanted to say it. No one ever wanted to admit how bad it was, if we had maybe we wouldn't have been able to stand it." He had never been so cold in his life, or so hopeless or unhappy. "It's all over now, I guess . . . except it's hard to forget it." He was looking at her sadly as he said it.

"I thought you had decided to end it between us." Her voice was low and sad, her thinking that had changed her life. It had brought her to Hollywood, and pushed her into living with Ernie. She figured she had nothing to lose, and he'd been so good to her. He'd done so much for her, she felt as though she owed him so much. And he made everything so easy.

Spencer looked grief-stricken as she said it. "I wouldn't have done that without saying anything to you. I didn't know what to do then . . . I kept getting letters from Elizabeth that made me feel so damn guilty. She expected me to come back to her, to go on like before, but I knew I couldn't. We met in Tokyo a couple of times, and even that made things worse when I went back. It was like spending a weekend with a stranger. It's like that now. I've been back for two weeks, and I'm going crazy." He looked at her with earnest eyes, and Crystal looked away. She was the one who felt guilty now. She was the one who owed a debt to Ernie.

"I tried to find you the night I came back," he went on, "I went to Mrs. Castagna's, but the woman there said you'd gone, and then I went to Harry's, but they were closed . . ." He looked as desperate as he had felt as he told her. And she wasn't surprised that there was someone different at Mrs. Castagna's house.

Her last letter to her, months before, had been answered by a postcard from her son telling her that his mother had died, and Crystal had been sorry to hear it. She had liked her. "Finally Pearl gave me your number, and I called this morning when I got here. Your landlady told me where you were, and now here we are." He smiled, looking like a boy on Christmas, and Crystal didn't tell him that it wasn't her landlady but her maid, or more precisely, Ernie's.

"What are you going to do about Elizabeth?" Her heart pounded as she asked, and part of her prayed that he had decided not to divorce her. It would make things easier for her, for a while at least. She couldn't just walk out on Ernie, not after he had put her into pictures, and everything else he had done for her. But like Spencer with Elizabeth, she didn't love him.

But Spencer looked calm as he answered her. He had worked it out in his head on the plane coming down. He was going to tell her as soon as they got back to Washington. He was going to pack up his things then, what was left of them, and take the first plane back to California. He didn't have a job now anyway. He could look for one in Los Angeles just as easily as he could have in Washington or New

York. A lawyer could get a job anywhere. And then, as soon as he found one, and was divorced, he was going to marry Crystal, if she'd have him. It was all incredibly simple.

He smiled at her then. He was too happy even to feel guilty. "I'm going to divorce Elizabeth. I guess I should have told her a long time ago. I think I knew when I left three years ago, but it seemed like such a rotten thing to do to her. We had just gotten married. I don't know. I was a damn fool not to do it then, though. I just can't carry on the charade any longer. It's a stinking thing to do after she waited all this time," he remembered what his father had said to him at the lake, "but I'm not even sure she cares. All she cares about is her work and her goddamn parties." There was more to it than that, but not much, from what he'd seen since returning from Korea. "She's at the lake now, and we're flying back to Washington in a few days." He looked Crystal straight in the eye. "It's almost over. I could be back here in a week or two, and as soon as I find a job, I'll file for divorce, and after that we can get married . . ." He was sure Elizabeth would be reasonable and agree to divorce him. And then suddenly he looked worried. What if things had changed for Crystal? Although after the way she'd kissed him, he didn't think so. But he added cautiously, ". . . if you'll still have me." And if Elizabeth would divorce him. But he was sure she would once he told her how he felt about continuing their marriage.

Crystal looked at him for a long time, then her eyes filled with tears, saying nothing. This was what she had wanted years before, what she'd dreamed of while he'd been gone, and what she'd lost hope of ever hearing. She had thought he had opted for Elizabeth, and hadn't even bothered to tell her.

"Well? . . ." He asked, watching the tears roll down her cheeks, and he wasn't sure if they were tears of joy or disappointment. He took her in his arms and held her close as she cried, and he smiled, looking over her shoulder. "Don't cry, sweetheart. It won't be that bad. I promise. I'll take care of you . . . I swear I will." It was all that he had ever wanted. He pulled gently away from her then, and she looked at him as she shook her head. There was a lot she still had to tell him.

"Maybe now you won't want me." She had to tell him about Ernie.

"I can't think why not. Unless you got married while I was gone," he grinned, sure that wasn't the case, "but even that can be taken care of. We can go to Reno together for six weeks, and get married there, if you are." He was teasing, but she was looking at him as though her heart was breaking. This was worse than that. He was finally getting free, and she was tied to Ernie. But if he'd written to her . . . if he'd stayed in touch . . . if he'd explained . . . and then she remembered the letters she hadn't answered. She had thought it was too late and she hadn't wanted to torment herself, or play games with him any longer. It had gone on for so long, and she had thought when he talked about Elizabeth meeting him in Tokyo for R and R that he had decided to continue their marriage.

"Spencer . . ." She struggled to find the words to explain it to him, but she knew it wasn't going to be easy. "I'm living with someone. My manager actually . . . it's a long story . . . and I don't know what to tell you." He sat staring at her, unhappily, waiting to hear, but this wasn't what he had expected. He hadn't known what he would find. He knew he might find her angry perhaps, or indifferent, or changed. But he hadn't expected to find her still in love with him and living with someone else. And he didn't like the arrangement. "When I came to Hollywood, I was introduced to him by two agents. They said he was the best in town, and in no time at all, he got me a job in a picture. In fact, I started work a week after I got here. He did everything for me, bought me clothes, found a hotel for me, he even paid for it. . . ." She didn't tell him about Malibu or the diamond bracelet. "I signed a contract with him, and he does everything for me, Spencer. I owe him so much . . . I can't just walk out on him . . . it wouldn't be fair . . ." It sounded like slavery to him and he couldn't believe what he was hearing.

"Are you in love with him?"

She shook her head miserably. "No, I'm not. And I told him about you in the beginning. But I told him it was over. I thought it was then. I hadn't heard from you in months, and I thought you were wrapped up in Elizabeth . . ." Her voice faltered as she started to cry again and Spencer began to pace the room with a look of fury.

"I was wrapped up in surviving, if that's of any interest to you." He looked down at her in utter frustration. All the while he'd been floundering, and aching with frostbite, living in ditches in the Korean countryside, she had thought he didn't love her.

"I'm sorry . . . you were gone for so long . . . and . . . everything was so different here. I wanted to make it in Hollywood so badly." It was honest of her, but it didn't make

it any easier for Spencer to hear, and he didn't
like any of what he was hearing.

"Badly enough to sell your body along with
the rest of you?"

"Look, God damn it," she stood up, suddenly as angry as he was, "when you left the
States, you were married, or don't you remember that little detail? I waited almost three goddamn years for you, Spencer Hill, and half the
time you didn't even bother to write me. And
in the end, you'd write ten words on a sheet of
paper that could have been to anyone. You
didn't say anything about us, or the future, or
what you were going to do. You just expected
me to sit there and wait, and I did, for a hell of
a long time too. But I wanted a life too. I had a
right to more than just sitting at Mrs. Castagna's for the rest of my life, waiting for the
Messiah." He didn't answer her, because what
she was saying was true. He couldn't deny it.
"So I came down here, and Ernie took me under his wing. He's a powerful man, Spencer.
He could make me a big star one day. And I'm
not going to stay with him forever, but I'm not
going to just walk out on him from one day to
the next because you say so. I owe him more
than that, and I don't want to make an enemy
of a friend. He's been good to me, and I owe

him something. Besides, if I do something like that, one day he could hurt me."

"You mean physically?" Spencer looked horrified, but Crystal was quick to shake her head.

"Of course not. I mean professionally. For all I know, he might tear up my contract."

"Don't be so sure. He's no fool. He's in business, he knows what he's got on his hands. What kind of contract did you sign with him anyway?" He was worried about that, too, but that was the least of their problems.

"A standard one." She tried to sound confident, but in truth, she knew very little about the contract. Ernie always told her it wasn't important.

"What does that mean?"

"He acts as a buffer between me and the studios. They go to him, and he irons everything out for me." It was a good party line, and she had bought it.

"Who pays you? Does he, or do the studios pay you directly?" Spencer was very suspicious. He had heard about contracts like that before, with managers devouring entire fortunes of big stars, and the actors themselves ending up with nothing.

"Ernie writes the checks. That way he can take out my taxes."

"Have you ever seen the studio contracts, or the checks from them for your earnings?"

"Of course not." Crystal looked annoyed. "He handles everything for me. That's his job." That was exactly what Spencer had been afraid of.

"Then you can be damn sure he's making a fortune off you, and you, my love, are getting peanuts compared to what they're paying."

"That's not true!" She was quick to defend him, but she knew also that her contract with Ernie wasn't the issue. "Anyway," she seemed to deflate as she sat down again, looking sadly up at Spencer. "I can't just walk out on him. I could eventually. But he's not going to understand it if I just move out tomorrow, and it wouldn't be fair to him. Any more than it would have been if you'd dumped Elizabeth two weeks after the wedding." She was playing on a nerve, and she knew it. But she felt she had an obligation to Ernie, even if Spencer didn't understand it. He'd been too decent to her for her to turn her back on him at the drop of a hat because of Spencer.

"So what are you saying, Crystal? That it's over? That you want to stay with him?" His voice trembled as he asked her, not in anger but in terror.

But her eyes filled with tears as she answered. She wanted to walk out of her dressing room, holding Spencer's hand, and walk straight to the nearest church and get married. But she also knew she couldn't do that. Not yet anyway. Not for a while. She wanted to handle the situation with Ernie very gently. And she had made a good point before, he could have been a powerful enemy if he was angry. And he would have had a right to be if she just dumped him after all his kindness.

"I need time. I need time to talk to him, to finish this picture, and then tell him I need to live alone or something like that. But I can't just do it in a week, Spencer. It took you three years with Elizabeth. Give me a month, or two at least. I want to do this very gently. And I'm in the middle of a movie."

"Why so long? Because you're afraid he'll damage your career or because you love him?" He still wasn't sure what she felt for the man or why she felt so indebted to him. He didn't understand the intricacies of the way Ernie worked, or how he played on her sense of obligation, her fears, and her conscience.

"Because I think I owe him that. As a courtesy, if nothing else. You don't just walk out on a man who does that much for you. And I still want him to be my manager after I leave him."

"That might not even be smart, Crystal. And for chrissake, there are plenty of others."

"Not as good as Ernie." He had convinced her of that too, and it made Spencer angry again, listening to her. It sounded as though they were going to be stuck with the guy forever.

"You sound like Elizabeth when she talks about McCarthy. Christ, I come home from the war and all I want to do is settle down and have a normal life, and everyone is up to their eyebrows in their goddamn careers. Except me. Cute, isn't it?" He was feeling sorry for himself, but Crystal wasn't sure she blamed him. She was only grateful he still wanted her after hearing about Ernie. Some men would have walked out when she told them.

"You'll find a job here. The studios might even hire you. They all have battalions of lawyers." She wanted to suggest that Ernie find something for him, but she didn't dare, and it would be a while before she could ask Ernie to do that.

"What do you want me to do while I wait for you, Crystal?" He didn't understand what the rules were, and she gently reached a hand out to him as she answered.

"Just be patient. I'm sorry about all this." She looked embarrassed as she lowered her

eyes, and he leaned over and kissed her silky
hair, and then tilted her chin up to him so that
he could see her.

"Don't worry about it. I deserved it. It
could have been a lot worse. You could have
told me to go screw myself. I'm damn lucky
you'll still have me."

"I love you . . ." She whispered the words
as he held her, and then there was a soft knock
on the door, to tell her that she was in another
scene in ten minutes. She looked up at Spencer
unhappily, not wanting him to go but she had
to go back to work again, and then she had to
think of a way to tell Ernie. "What are you
going to do now?"

"Can you spend any time with me at all, or
is it too awkward?" He knew it only too well
from his own situation with Elizabeth and the
Barclays.

"I don't think I can." Her eyes were sad as
he kissed her again and she wanted him never
to leave her.

"Then I'll go back to San Francisco. I'll call
you in a few days. And hurry up, will you
please?" he teased. He was unhappy about her
situation but he could live with it for a short
time. It was his fault it had happened in a way,
and although he didn't like it, he didn't con-
demn her for it. It could have been a lot worse.

She could have fallen in love with someone else and gotten married. Hell, she could have had two kids by then. What had happened was unpleasant but at least she still loved him.

He kissed her long and hard before he left, and she couldn't bear the thought of losing him again, but it wouldn't be for long this time. And she knew where he was now. She could call him, and he had promised to call her and tell her how things were progressing in his own life. Once he told Elizabeth, he was planning to be back in California in a few weeks, to start looking for work, and by then she would almost be through with the picture, and, he hoped, would have started solving the problem with Ernie. They had to find a place to live, and there was a lot to think about now. It gave them both hope, as Spencer kissed her again and held her close to him, remembering the sweet perfume of her body.

"I hate to leave you again," he said softly.

"So do I." She smiled. But it wouldn't be long this time, and when they were together again, it would be forever.

"I'll be back soon." He promised as she nodded. They both had a lot to do in the next month, a lot of obstacles to overcome before they could be together.

And then with a last kiss, he left her dressing room and she walked out with him, and stood watching him go with a look of tenderness in her eyes that told the whole story. And as he waved at her, and she waved back, silently so as not to disturb the actors working on the set, neither of them saw Ernie watching from the back of the sound stage.

CHAPTER
30

Spencer went back and checked out of the hotel that afternoon. It wasn't the weekend he had planned, and he was still shocked to realize she was living with someone else, but he had to be fair, he was still living with Elizabeth too. And he knew it was partly his fault that Crystal had given up hope and gotten involved with Ernie. He didn't like it anyway, and he was anxious for her to get out of it. And he was also worried about her contract. He suspected that there was a lot more to it than Ernie had told her.

He flew back to San Francisco that night,

and rented a car, and without knowing where he was going, he started driving north. His thoughts were full of her, and all he could think of was how she had looked when he'd kissed her in the tiny dressing room. All the same feelings between them were still there except that they had gotten stronger.

He reached Napa at ten o'clock, and kept driving after that. He was thinking of stopping at a motel, and then he saw the signs, and knew why he had come that way. He was paying tribute to the past, and the child she had been when he met her. It was eleven when he drove through town, and he stopped outside the ranch. The fence was closed and the house was hidden by the trees, but he wondered if the swing was still there. He hadn't been there in six years. And it had been seven since he first met her.

He stopped at a motel and tried to look the Websters up in the directory, but there was no listing for them, and he no longer remembered where they lived. And he hadn't come here to see them. He had come here for her, and what she had once been. Before Hollywood, before the war, before Elizabeth, and the man Crystal was living with, before all of them . . . when he had first seen her in the white dress at her sister's wedding. It had all been so simple then, at the very beginning.

He sat in the car for a long time and then slowly started it up again. He had his own life to think of now, he had given them both a month. It didn't seem like much now, but it had seemed like a lot that afternoon. He stopped and ate dinner somewhere, in a town he didn't know, and it took him six hours after that to get to Lake Tahoe. He drove over the Donner Pass just as the sun came up, and all he could think of was the girl he'd left at MGM, the woman he loved and was going to marry.

He parked the car, and let himself into the house, and then he tiptoed up the stairs to the bedroom where Elizabeth was sleeping in their bed. And as he undressed, she stirred and glanced at him with a sleepy look.

"You're back?" She was still half asleep.

He nodded, afraid to say more. He was too tired to say anything. And he had promised himself he'd wait until they left Lake Tahoe. "Go back to sleep" was all he said to her, but she sat up in bed, watching him intently.

"I thought you weren't coming back until Sunday."

"I wrapped things up faster than I thought."

Too fast, and not fast enough. He had wanted to spend the weekend with Crystal.

"Where were you?" Elizabeth was studying him as he got undressed and he avoided her eyes as he slipped into bed beside her.

"I told you. Los Angeles. I had some business to take care of."

"And did you?" Her voice was cool, and she was wide awake now.

"More or less. I couldn't see everyone I wanted to, that's why I came back early."

She nodded, not sure that she believed him. She had sensed something different about him for days, ever since he came back in fact, and she wondered what he was up to. "Do you want to talk about it?"

"Not particularly. I've been driving all night." He closed his eyes, hoping that she would stop talking, but she didn't.

"Why didn't you stay at the house in San Francisco?"

"I wanted to get back."

"That was nice of you." He wasn't sure if she was being sarcastic or not, and the last thing he wanted to do was ask her. "Are you feeling better about things yet?" She chatted on as though it were the middle of the afternoon and Spencer groaned as he opened his eyes and looked at her sitting beside him.

"For chrissake, Elizabeth. Why don't we talk about it in the morning?"

"It is morning." The sun was up and the birds had already started singing.

"Yes, I'm feeling better." Much, after seeing Crystal.

"Do you want to talk about it?" She was looking for something, and if she probed long enough she was going to find it.

"Not particularly. There's nothing to talk about." Not yet. Not with their families in rooms all around them. For two weeks they had had no privacy, and he wanted at least that when he told her he wanted to end their marriage.

"I think there's a lot to talk about. I'm not stupid, you know." He suddenly wondered as he sat up next to her if she knew about Crystal. But there was no way she could, unless she had had him followed. "I know things have been bothering you. Your father and I talked about it a few days ago. It's not easy coming home from war. I know that. It hasn't been easy for me either."

He felt sorry for her suddenly, and he wondered how much his father had said. He wished he hadn't gotten involved, and talked to Elizabeth about it. "You've been a hell of a good sport for all these years." He reached for a cigarette, wishing he could say more to her, say that he still loved her. If he ever had. He wasn't even sure of that anymore. His feelings for Crystal had eclipsed everything, and his relationship with Elizabeth had always been so different.

"We'll get used to each other again." She said it gently as she looked at him, and there was gentleness there. It made him feel as though he had betrayed her. And he had, a long time since. He knew for sure now that they should never have gotten married.

"Are you sure you really want to?" He was leading up to something he hadn't wanted to say to her until they left the lake, but she was forcing his hand, and in a minute he was going to have to tell her.

"I think so. That's why I waited for you all this time. I happen to think you're worth it." She smiled and it made him feel worse. His father was right. He did owe her something. But not the rest of his life. That was too much to ask. Too high a price to pay for the years she had waited for him.

"You're a hell of a woman, Elizabeth." But too much so. She was a lot more than he wanted to cope with. She had her own ideas, her own ways, her own house, and her family surrounding her, which he had to contend with. There was no room in the scheme of it for him, or at least that was how he felt. With Crystal he could build a new life. He could do everything for her. He could share the beginnings of her career, start a new life, have kids. And all of that mattered to him. "I don't know what to say to you." He turned to her then, and she saw it all in his face. "I don't think I can go on with this. I don't think we should have ever gotten married."

"It's a little late now, don't you think? After all this time?" She looked angry and hurt, but not surprised. She'd been waiting for this for days. Even before his father had talked to her, she had known it was coming. Judge Hill had told her that Spencer was feeling a little "unbalanced" and she was going to have to be very patient. And as far as she was concerned, she already had been. Three years' worth.

"I've been gone for three years. We had two weeks before that. And we've changed. We both have. I don't want the same things I did. And you have your work. We hardly knew each other when I left, and in the last three years we've become strangers."

"I can't help that. That's just the way it is. But after waiting three years, I'm not going to call it quits now, if that's what you're suggesting." Her eyes were hard as rocks, and he could feel his heart sink as he watched her.

"Why? Why not? Why go on with it? We're only going to make each other unhappy." He was trying to reason with her, but he could see that she didn't want to hear it.

"Not necessarily. We have a lot to offer each other. We always did, I always thought so."

"And I always had doubts. I told you that when we got engaged."

"And I told you I didn't care. We have exactly what we need to make a good marriage. Good careers, bright minds, interesting lives, those are the things that the best marriages are made of."

"Not where I come from. What about love, tenderness, loyalty, children?" But how loyal had he and Crystal been to each other? They were both living with other people. He tried not to think about it as he talked to Elizabeth. But whatever they had, it was more than he and Elizabeth would ever dream of.

"You read too many novels. You've been away from real life for too long, Spencer. Sure, those things are important, but they're the window dressing, not the foundation." But everything she said told him what he already knew. That they were just too different. The same things didn't matter to them. He wanted love. And she wanted big business.

"What do you feel for me?" He turned to her suddenly with a look of anguish. "I mean really? What do you feel when I lie next to you in bed at night? Passion, love, desire, friendship? Or do you feel as lonely as I do?" They had only made love once since he'd been back, and it had been a disaster.

"I feel sorry for you." She looked him in the eye and spoke very coolly. "I think you're looking for something that doesn't exist. You always have been." But what if he told her he had found it? He didn't want to tell her that, though. He wanted to leave her, but there was no need to hurt her unduly. He didn't want that. He just wanted his life back. But it was obvious that she didn't want to give it to him. "I think you're a dreamer. . . . And I think you have to start living in the world around you, the world we live in, Spencer. A world full of important people with important careers. They're all doing useful things, they're not sitting around holding hands with their wives and fawning over their children."

"Then I feel sorry for them, and for you, if that's how you see it."

"You have to pull yourself together, get a

job in Washington, start making friends, seeing the people who count . . ."

"Like the people your father knows?" He cut her off, his eyes beginning to burn with anger. He was sick and tired of them, and their constant search for ever greater "importance." What was important to them didn't matter one whit to him. Especially now, after three years in Korea.

"Yes, like them. What's wrong with them?"

"Nothing. Except that I don't like them."

"You're lucky they even talk to you." She was angry at him too. She was tired of his looking uncomfortable at every party they went to. "You're lucky I married you. And you're even luckier that I'm too smart to divorce you. You're going to make something of yourself one day, and I'm going to see to it that you do it. And one day, Spencer Hill, you'll thank me."

He looked at her and he laughed. He laughed until the tears rolled down his cheeks. She was the most self-centered woman he'd ever met, and she was sure she was right. But she was also a force to contend with.

"What exactly are you planning to make of me, Elizabeth? How about president? Or king? That might be fun . . . actually, I might like that."

"Don't be a fool. You could be anything you wanted to be. Every door in Washington is open to you, right up to the Cabinet, if you play your cards right."

"And if I don't want to play?"

"That's your choice. But I meant what I said. If you want a divorce, I'm not going to give it to you." He hadn't even asked her yet, but he already had his answer.

"Why would you want to stay married if I don't?" He couldn't understand it, but she was very clear about how she felt and she laid it on the line as she got up and looked down at him with an expression of pure iron.

"I'm not going to let you embarrass me after all this time. I waited for you, now you have to pay your dues. The price isn't all that high if you give it some thought. You could do worse." And then, as an afterthought, "Besides, I happen to love you." It might have touched him to hear it if she'd said it differently and a little sooner.

"I'm not sure you know the meaning of the word."

"Maybe not." She looked unmoved. "But in that case, Spencer, you can teach me." And with that, she walked into the bathroom, and locked the door behind her. He heard her run her bath, and half an hour later, she emerged again, looking pristine, in white slacks and an impeccably pressed white silk shirt, white shoes, her pearls clasped around her neck, and a pair of pearl and diamond earrings. She was a pretty girl, but nothing about her touched him or warmed him. "Are you coming down for breakfast or do you want to get some sleep?" They both knew he wouldn't be able to get back to sleep, but he looked awful. The night had taken its toll on him, and the morning hadn't been much better. The news that she wouldn't divorce him put a knife in his heart that was so full of Crystal.

"I'll come down in a while."

"Good. And we're expected at the Houstons' today for lunch. I'm sure you'll be pleased to hear it."

"Thrilled." But in an odd way, he felt relieved after talking to her. At least he no longer had to make the pretense that he could hardly wait to get on with their marriage. She knew where he stood, and unfortunately he also knew where she did. He looked at her again as she prepared to leave the room. "Are you serious, Liz?" His voice was gentle. He wanted to make her see how hopeless it was for them to stay together.

"About what? Staying with you?" He nodded. "Yes, I am."

"Why? Why can't you admit it's all wrong? What's the point of forcing it?"

"I told you, I'm not going to let you make me look like a fool. And besides, it would be an embarrassment to my father."

"That's the worst reason I've ever heard."

"Then think of your own reasons if you want. But I meant it. And I think in the long run we'll both be happy we stuck with it." He couldn't believe she was saying that, but without another word, she left the room and went downstairs for breakfast, as Spencer lay in bed and thought of Crystal.

She had had her own problems that night. She hadn't finished work until ten. One of the klieg lights broke, and a major piece of scenery after that. They had stood around for hours, and it was midnight when she got home, and Ernie was waiting for her.

"What did you do today?" He looked unruffled as he watched her undress. She was bone tired, and she'd been thinking of Spencer all night and what she had to do, and say to Ernie.

"Nothing much. The lights broke, and we got stuck on the set for hours." And they had all complained endlessly about the heat, the long wait and the commissary food for dinner.

"That's all?" He wandered slowly over to where she stood, naked beneath her dressing gown.

"Sure. Why?"

He grabbed a handful of her hair and pulled her head sharply back, wrenching it as hard as he could as she gasped and fought to get away from him. "Don't ever cheat on me!"

"Ernie! . . . I . . ." But the words froze on her lips. She could see in his eyes that he knew Spencer had been at the studio with her. "I had a visit from an old friend . . . that's all . . ." He yanked her hair hard again, and her eyes filled with tears from fear and pain.

"Don't lie to me! It's the guy from Korea, isn't it?" He was smart and the timing was right. He had figured it out, just on a hunch, when the maid told him a man had called, and he went to the set to see if there was anyone there with her. He had arrived just in time to see them disappear into her dressing room. And he had waited a long time before they came out again, looking at each other like long lost lovers.

"Yes . . . yes . . ." She was breathless as he twisted her hair in his hands. "That's who he was . . . I'm sorry . . . I didn't know you'd be upset . . ."

"Stupid bitch." He slapped her hard across

the face and threw her halfway across the room. "If you see him again, or call him, or talk to him, something ugly is going to happen to him. You got that, Miss Purity?"

"Yes . . . Ernie, please . . ." She was horrified. She had never seen that side of him before.

"Now take off your clothes." She gasped at the look on his face, and he wasn't even drunk. But there was a look in his eyes that terrified her as he strode purposefully across the room toward her. He ripped the dressing gown off her back and she stood trembling and naked before him. "And remember one thing, you belong to me now! No one else! Me . . . because I own you! Is that clear?" She nodded, with tears streaming down her cheeks as he slapped her again, and without further ceremony he threw her into a nearby chair and tossed his own dressing gown off as he laughed at the fear in her eyes. "That's right. I'm going to do exactly what I want, because I *own* you." And he took her with such force, such brutality, that this time when she screamed, it wasn't with pleasure but with pain, and when he was through, with a single gesture, he threw her to the floor where she lay sobbing in agony. It was just like what Tom Parker had done, worse in some ways, because she had trusted

Ernie. She should have left with Spencer that afternoon. She knew it now, but it was too late. It was much, much later than she knew, and she was terrified of what he might do to Spencer if he meant what he said. And she wouldn't do anything to risk Spencer. Even if it killed her.

He looked down at her lying there, and laughed as she cried, not daring to look at him. "Get up!" He yanked her up by a handful of hair again, her eyes staring wildly around her in terror. "And if you ever see him again, Crystal Wyatt . . . I'll kill you." He went to bed and she went to the bathroom to throw up, and when she looked in the mirror, the eyes that she saw there were empty. He had given her everything and now he thought he owned her. But one thing was certain, she knew now what would happen if she tried to leave him for Spencer.

CHAPTER
31

Spencer and Elizabeth flew to Washington on September sixth, with the senior Barclays. It had been an agonizing week for him. The strain between them had been killing. But she had gone on, as though nothing were wrong, determined to continue the illusion of their marriage. He didn't know how he was going to get through to her, but in a month, he wanted to be back in California with Crystal. And he was going to broach the subject of a divorce with Elizabeth again the moment they got to Georgetown. Her resistance to the idea had come as a complete surprise to him. He and

Crystal had both been naive about their partners' willingness to give them up, and all Spencer thought about now was how to convince
Elizabeth to divorce him.

But when they arrived in Washington, she
was so proud of the little house, so busy with
her friends, and so busy with her job that he
hardly saw her. She hired a housekeeper to
cook and clean for them, and they seemed to
be invited to every party in town. To Spencer it
seemed almost hopeless. He felt as though he
were drowning in a sea of people, night and
day, and each time he tried to talk to her, she
somehow avoided the subject. And then finally
on the second weekend they were home, he
exploded at her over breakfast. She had just
told him that she had accepted an invitation
for lunch at her parents' that day, and she
thought he might like to play golf with her
father.

"For chrissake, Elizabeth, we can't go on
like this. You can't just go on pretending that
nothing's wrong." For him, nothing had
changed since Lake Tahoe or long before that.

"I told you before how I felt, Spencer. This
is it. For life. You might as well stop fighting it,
and enjoy it." She looked as cool and controlled as she always did and it was driving
him crazy.

He sat down and ran a hand through his hair in the familiar gesture she had not yet come to regard with affection. In truth, it annoyed her. But she was prepared to put up with anything. This was their life, and he was her husband.

"We have to talk." His eyes were unrelenting. She was a decent woman and he appreciated what she had done for him. But this wasn't what he wanted. He knew that now. He was sure of it. And he didn't want a marriage that was all pretense and appearance.

"What do you want to talk about?" Her tone was icy. She was sick of his apparent difficulty in adjusting. As far as she could see, he had everything he wanted. A nice home, a maid to wait on him, an interesting wife with a good job, and important in-laws. But Spencer didn't see it that way. *Not by a long shot.*

"We have to talk about our marriage."

An icy look came into her eyes. She had heard about it before, and she wasn't interested in pursuing the subject. She wasn't going to give him a divorce. He was just going to have to grow up and face it.

"There's nothing to talk about."

"I know," he said ruefully. "That's exactly the problem."

"The problem is that you're still thrashing

around fighting it, and when you stop doing that, things will go a lot better. Look at my parents. Do you think it's always been easy for them? I'm sure it hasn't. They worked it out. So can we, if you'd finally accept what is and get on with it." She looked extremely unsympathetic.

" *'What is'* " for me," he said, and tried to speak calmly to her, "is that I don't consider this a marriage."

"I don't agree with you." She looked angry, but not sad. She was tired of talking about the problem.

"We're not in love with each other. We never were. Doesn't that matter to you?"

"Of course it does. But that will come later." She sounded unconcerned, which made him feel even more crazy.

"When? When do you think that comes, Elizabeth? At sixty-five, like a retirement pension, or a bonus? It's either there at the beginning, or it isn't. And it never was for me. I tried to tell myself that it was, but it wasn't. I wanted out right after we got engaged, and I said so. I let you talk me into this and I was a damn fool, and I knew it. It wasn't fair to you, or to me, and now we're paying the price for your being so goddamn stubborn."

"What price *are* you paying?" She was angry now and it showed, finally. "The price of comfort, of having a wife you can be proud to be married to or a father-in-law who's one of the most important men in the country?"

"I don't give a goddamn about all that, and you know it."

"I'm not so sure of that. Don't you? Why did you marry me, then, if you weren't in love with me?" It was a very good question.

"I told myself I was in love with you. I thought we could make it work, but we can't, and we have to face that."

"*You* face it. *You* deal with it. It's *your* goddamn problem. All you do is whine all the time. Well stop whining and do something about it."

"That's what I want to do, God damn it!" He pounded the table in front of him, and he was tempted to throw something at her. "I want a divorce so I can get us both out of this and start living like a normal human being."

"We're not going anywhere, Spencer. We're married, and that's how it's going to stay. For better or worse, until death do us part. So stop bitching and get used to it. Get off your ass, get a job. Do whatever the hell you want, but understand one thing. I'm not going to divorce you." He felt despair envelop him as he listened to her. All he wanted was to go back to Crystal in California.

"How long do you think we can go on like this?"

"Forever. If we have to. It's up to you how difficult you want to make it."

"Don't you want more than this? I do. I want someone I can talk to. Someone who wants the same things I do. Life, love, and happiness and children." He was almost in tears. "Elizabeth, I want to be happy."

"So do I." She looked unsympathetically at him, and suddenly a thought crossed her mind. She had never thought of it before, but she still remembered the way he had looked at the girl in the nightclub that night after their engagement party in San Francisco, and then his announcement two days later that he didn't want to get married. "Spencer," she looked straight into his eyes, "is there someone else?" But he couldn't tell her that. That wasn't the issue. The real issue was that they had made a mistake and it had to be faced. What happened after that was none of her business.

"No, there isn't." He wasn't going to tell her about that. He didn't want to cloud the issue.

"Are you sure?" She knew him better than he liked to think, but he shook his head, determined to lie to her, about Crystal.

"It isn't important. What I'm saying to you means a lot more than that. This isn't working for either of us, and it isn't going to." But she had come close to a nerve and it showed, and suddenly she knew it.

"It *is* important. I have a right to know if there is someone."

"Would it change anything?" He eyed her carefully.

"I won't give you a divorce if that's what you want to know. But it would tell me something about you. I think all this nonsense you're complaining about is really to cover something else, isn't it?"

"I told you, that's not the issue."

"I don't believe that."

"Elizabeth, be sensible. Please." What could he tell her? That there was another girl? That she was the most beautiful woman he'd ever seen, and he'd been in love with her since she was fourteen? And now they wanted to get married?

"My father wanted to introduce you to some important friends today." She was ignoring everything he had said. "I think we should go."

"For God's sake, we're talking about the rest of our lives. Why won't you listen to reason?"

"Because your idea of reason is divorce,

Spencer. Mine isn't. And I won't let you out of this. It's as simple as that. I'm not going to let you embarrass me publicly. I don't want to be divorced. I want to be married." She had always wanted to be married to him, and she had gotten exactly what she wanted. Almost. But as far as she was concerned, that was all you ever got in life. Almost. It was enough for her, if not for him, and she wasn't going to let him off the hook that easy.

"But do you want to be married like this?"

"Yes." There was no hesitation. "One of my father's friends wanted to offer you a job today. I think you should meet him."

"I'm tired of your father's friends, and your father."

"He's a very important Democrat and it's a government job." She went on as though she hadn't heard him, and Spencer wanted to scream. "And he thinks you could be useful to him."

"I don't want to be useful to anyone right now. Except myself. And you. I want to sort this mess out."

"There is no mess, Spencer. Not as far as I'm concerned. And I'm not going to set you free, so forget it." And as he looked at her, he knew that she meant it. She was never going to agree to divorce him. He was trapped. Perhaps forever.

"You mean that, don't you?"

"Totally." She looked coolly at her watch. "We have to be there at noon. I suggest you get dressed now."

"I'm not a child, Elizabeth. I don't want to be told what to do, when to dress and when to eat, and when to go to a party. I'm a man, and I want to live with a woman who loves me."

"I'm sorry." She stood up and looked at him coldly. He had destroyed any hope of that, but she still wasn't going to let him go. And she was convinced there was another woman. But whoever she was, she wasn't going to get him. "You'll have to make do with this, won't you?" She quietly left the room then, and an hour later she was downstairs in a crisp navy blue suit, and the navy alligator bag and pumps her father had given her for her birthday. And hating himself for giving in to her, Spencer was dressed too. He was wearing a gray suit, and a face that would have been perfect for a funeral.

She chatted with him pleasantly, as though nothing had come between them. He felt as though his life were over. The part that mattered anyway. He felt hopeless. And her father's friend was, predictably, both serious and important. He offered Spencer a job in a gov-

ernment office that would have interested him
if he wanted to stay in Washington, and if he
wanted a job that had come to him essentially
because of the Barclays. But the job that had
been offered him was a good one. It was the
first offer he'd had that interested him, and he
told the man he'd think it over. More to be
polite than because he meant it. All he really
wanted was to talk to Crystal. But when he
called her late that night, when Elizabeth was
in bed, he learned that Crystal had fared no
better. Ernie watched her night and day, and
once or twice she thought he was having her
followed. She was even afraid to talk to Spencer on the phone, but luckily Ernie was out
when Spencer called her. She told him only
that Ernie had threatened her. But in truth she
feared for Spencer's life now. She knew that
Ernie meant business.

Ernie came to the set unexpectedly these
days, sat in her dressing room, monitored her
calls, though she got very few. The only thing
she was allowed to do was to go to work and
go home to Ernie. He didn't beat her up again,
he never raped her, he didn't touch her. He
didn't have to. He just told her he would kill
Spencer. And the day after he had raped her,
he came home with an enormous diamond
necklace. He had smiled at her wickedly and

the card read, "Think of it as a chastity belt. Love, Ernie." But there was no doubt in her mind now what would happen to her if she tried to leave him for Spencer. He would kill them both. Of that she was certain. And he said so.

She knew now what she had to do. She had to let Spencer go, for his sake. She couldn't even tell him why. She was too afraid to tell him the truth, afraid he'd retaliate, or come back to California to try and rescue her from Ernie.

"How's it going out there?" Spencer sounded exhausted when he called. It was after midnight and he was emotionally drained from the strain of trying to convince Elizabeth, unsuccessfully, to divorce him.

"It's been difficult." Crystal spoke in a quiet voice. It was the first time she'd talked to him in days, and tears filled her eyes as she thought of what she'd have to say. But she had to. For his sake.

"That's the understatement of the year, isn't it?" He tried to make light of it but they were both depressed and you could hear it. He had made his first big mistake when he'd decided to go ahead and marry Elizabeth when he knew he didn't love her. He had listened to everyone except himself. And he had thought he was doing it for all the right reasons. He had even tried to convince himself that he did love her, and that his feelings for Crystal were only an infatuation.

"Have you spoken to Elizabeth?"

"Yes. Not that I've gotten anywhere. She absolutely refuses to cooperate, and other than beat her up, or catch her in bed with someone else, I'm not going to have grounds for divorce unless she agrees. But I'm not going to give up. Just give it a while, Crystal, I'll convince her." He didn't know how yet, but he'd have to. But he was in no way prepared for Crystal's next words. They hit him like a wrecker's ball in his guts as he listened.

"You don't need to do that. Ernie and I have been talking it over, and . . ." She almost choked on the words, but forced herself to sound normal. It was the hardest role of her career, but she believed that Spencer's life depended on it, and she had to convince him, no matter what he thought of her after. That was no longer important. She had begun to understand what Ernie's role was in Hollywood. She had heard people talk about him on the set when they'd seen him with her. And rumors of his connections frightened her. There was more to Ernie than met the eye, and there were supposedly dangerous people behind him. And to them, Crystal represented the prospect of a great deal of money. "He thinks it'll hurt my career if I leave him now." She went on, "The publicity could hurt me very badly."

Spencer felt his heart stop as he listened. "What are you saying to me?"

"I'm saying . . ." She forced a cool note into her voice, which was foreign to her. Her voice was normally filled with warmth and passion, just like her singing. "I'm saying that I don't think you should come back out. I'm not ready to make any changes."

"You're staying with him? *Because of what people might say?* Have you gone crazy?"

"No," she sounded so real that it broke her heart to say the words, but better to hurt him like this than to let Ernie do it with his minions. "I think I went a little crazy when I saw you. I couldn't help it . . . it had been so long and . . . I don't know. Maybe I was just playing a part . . . the part of the long-lost lover and the little girl who once loved him." Tears rolled down her cheeks like sheets of rain but her voice was steady.

"Are you telling me you don't love me?"

She swallowed hard, thinking only of him, and not herself, and the empty life that stretched before her. "I think that was all so long ago . . . I think we both got carried away when we saw each other."

"Don't give me that shit! I didn't get 'carried away' by anything. I survived three years of that goddamn ugly little war just to come back to you and tell you I loved you." He was almost shouting at her, and had to remind himself to keep his voice down. Elizabeth was asleep upstairs and he didn't want to wake her. "Maybe I waited too long. Maybe I was a damn fool to do a lot of things. God knows I seem to have screwed everyone's life up, but one thing I can tell you and that was that I was not 'carried away' or playing a part when I saw you. I love you. I'm ready to come out and marry you, as soon as I get this mess settled here, and I want to know what the hell you're really saying."

"I'm saying . . . that it's over." There was an endless silence on both ends, and his voice was deep and raw when he answered.

"Are you serious?" There was a sob in his throat, but he held it fast as he waited.

"Yes." She could barely speak. "Yes, I'm serious. My career is too important to me now . . . and I owe too much to Ernie."

"Is he forcing you to say this to me?" And then a sudden thought. "Is he there?" That would explain everything. She couldn't mean it. He had seen her face, and he knew that she still loved him. At least he had thought so.

"Of course not. He wouldn't force me to say anything." It was a lie on top of all the other lies she had told him to protect him. "I don't want you to come out here. I don't think we should see each other anymore, even as friends. There's no point, Spencer, it's all over."

"I don't know what to say to you." He was crying, but he wouldn't let her hear it. For a moment, he felt as though he had survived the war for nothing.

"Just take care of yourself. And, Spencer . . ."

"What?" He sounded as though someone had died.

"I don't want you to call me."

"I understand. Have a nice life, as they say." He wasn't bitter, he was broken. "But I want you to know something, if you ever need me, I'll be there. All you have to do is call me. And if you change your mind . . ." His voice drifted off as they thought about each other, but she had to kill any hope he had, it was too important.

"I won't." Her face was deathly pale, but he couldn't see that. She had done what she knew she had to, and now all she had left in the world was Ernie. It was a terrifying thought, but she couldn't think of it now. And for these last minutes she could cling to Spencer, even if he didn't know it. She didn't want to hang up yet. She wanted to hear his voice, to listen to him, to be near him for one last moment. "What are you going to do about Elizabeth?" It was something to say, and in truth she had wondered.

"I don't know. She says she won't let me go. Maybe she won't, or maybe she'll get bored with this in time. We certainly don't have a marriage."

"Why does she want you then?" Tears were pouring down her cheeks as she tried to drag out the conversation.

"She doesn't want to lose face. And I think this is all she ever wanted. Someone to play golf with her father, and take to parties." It was an oversimplification but not by much, not by his standards at least. It was certainly nothing like what he had shared with Crystal. And odd as it was, as little time as he had spent with her, he felt as though he knew Crystal better than he knew his wife, or better than he ever would know her. "I don't know what I'm going to do now." Stay in Washington, or go back to New York, walk out on her, or take the job he had just been offered. It didn't matter anymore. He felt like a robot. "Anyway, I guess that's a wrap, as they say . . . or don't they really say that?"

"Yes, they do." She was silent for a minute, aching to tell him that she loved him. She hated the thought of leaving him believing that she no longer loved him. "I guess it is . . . a wrap, I mean."

"Be good to yourself, Crystal . . . take care . . ." And then the words that almost broke her heart as he hung up, "I'll always love you." And then he set down the phone, and sat in the little study Elizabeth had decorated for him, crying like a child who had lost his mother. He sat there and cried for hours, remembering her, savoring the moments they had shared, and trying to believe she knew what she was doing. It was difficult to believe this was what she wanted now, her career instead of him. He knew how important her dreams of Hollywood had been to her, but somehow this seemed unlike her. But he knew he had to respect her wishes now. He owed her that much. All he had to figure out was how to go on living without her.

And in California, Crystal set the phone down with shaking hands. Her whole body felt like ice, and she knew she had done the only thing she could, but she felt as though she had destroyed everything that had ever mattered to her. She had sold her soul unknowingly to an evil man, and now she had to pay the price that she would regret for the rest of her life. And none of it was worth it.

She sat staring into space for a long time, unable to believe that he was really gone. It was as though he had died, and she had killed him. It reminded her of what she felt when Jared died, the emptiness, the guilt, and the loneliness that overwhelmed her.

"What are you looking so cheerful about?" She looked up with a start. She hadn't even heard him walk into the room, but Ernie was standing in front of her, looking angry. "Something wrong?" She shook her head. She didn't even want to speak to him. "Good. Then get dressed. We're going to a premiere tonight. And afterward there are some producers I want to show you off to."

"I can't . . ." She looked up at him with tear-filled eyes. "I don't feel well."

"Sure you do." He poured a drink at the bar and handed it to her. She took a sip and set it down, not feeling any better. Drinks weren't going to help. Nothing would. But Ernie smiled at her with an encouraging look. "You're a good girl. Now go get dressed. We have to leave in half an hour." She looked up at him emptily, and then stood up, and walked slowly toward their bedroom as he watched her. And she didn't know it, but he was pleased with her. He had been listening to her phone call on the machine he kept hidden in his office.

She went out with him that night and there were photographers everywhere. Photographers who took photographs of her looking smashing on Ernie's arm. She was quiet and pale, but no one even noticed. They had arrived late at the premiere, but Ernie didn't care. It only drew a little more attention. He patted her arm as they walked in, and he was happy with her when the producers liked her. She hardly spoke to them, or to him. She was lost in another world, a world that no longer existed. The one she had once shared with Spencer.

CHAPTER
32

By Thanksgiving, Spencer had taken the government job he'd been offered by Justice Barclay's friends. It felt like a sellout, but he knew he had to do something to keep his mind alive. He couldn't go on sitting at home, waiting for something to change. Nothing was going to. Elizabeth wasn't going to let him go, and Crystal had told him she didn't want him to come back to her in California.

But at least he found that he liked the job, much to his surprise, and by Christmas things were settling down, except that he felt as though part of him had died when he gave up

Crystal. It made him plunge into his work, working night and day, and he found that he liked politics more than he had expected.

Washington was exciting and fun, and he would have been happy, were it not for the wasteland of his relationship with Elizabeth. Any hope of establishing a closeness with her had been shattered when he asked her for a divorce. And in the subsequent turmoil, it was obvious that he didn't like her and she didn't trust him. And he felt tied to her now for all the wrong reasons.

She was a lively companion when she wanted to be, she was intelligent and witty and amusing. But their life had changed immeasurably after he told her he didn't love her. It had been a foolish thing to do, but he had been operating from desperation and raw emotion and the hope he had of marrying Crystal. Elizabeth never mentioned it, but he knew she would always hold it against him. Their early passion was all but forgotten now, and although they had begun to make love again, it was with restraint and regret, and a certain bitterness felt by both. But to those who knew them, they seemed like a happy, fulfilled, well-adjusted couple. They played the game well. And their disappointments with each other were kept private. She was pleased about his job, and to her that was most important. His only contact with Crystal was in darkened theaters now. He had gone to see Crystal's first film, one night when Elizabeth was working late, and after they got back from Palm Beach, he read that she was due to star in a big movie.

She wasn't a major star yet, but she was on demand everywhere, and he knew all of the studios who wanted her had to contend with Ernie. She was making a fortune for him and the men he fronted for, which was why he had threatened to kill her if she left him. He had been protecting his investment. The papers said she was due to start her new film in June, and in the meantime, she made news frequently on Ernie's arm, or with well-known stars Ernie set her up with for the publicity they got her. She appeared in the columns regularly, and her face was known to ever-growing numbers.

She was off to a good start, but Spencer shuddered to think what her life was like with Ernie. It made Spencer sick to think about it, and more often than not, he tried not to.

And when she started the movie in June, on location in Palm Springs, Spencer was in Boston with his new boss, lining up political connections. There was a young senator they were talking to, and several others they had meetings with before he went back to Washington. Elizabeth quit her job in the fall. She had decided to go to law school. And she was pleased with Spencer. He was doing well, and her father approved. Spencer was doing exactly what she wanted. And that made her a little more friendly toward him. He hadn't mentioned the divorce again, and she assumed he finally had come to his senses.

And when the phone rang on a cool November afternoon, Elizabeth was still at school, and Spencer had just come in from the office. He hadn't read the afternoon paper yet, and he hadn't heard the news. His heart stopped as he picked up the phone and heard jagged sobbing. The operator had put the call through and all he knew was that it was long-distance. But it was several minutes before he heard her voice, and his heart almost stopped when he realized it was Crystal. It had been over a year since he'd seen her.

"Crystal . . . is that you?"

There was silence at the other end, and only the crackling of the static. For a moment he thought they'd been cut off, and then he heard her again, crying hysterically and saying something he couldn't understand. He wondered if she was hurt, and he was desperate to find her.

"Where are you? Where are you calling

from?" he shouted to no avail, and then he heard her crying again. The only intelligible word she had said so far was his name. The rest was impossible to decipher. He looked at his watch and realized that it was three o'clock in the afternoon in California. "Crystal . . . listen to me . . . try to get a hold on yourself . . . talk to me. What's wrong?" Everything, apparently. And he was ready to cry, too, in desperate frustration. "Crystal! Can you hear me?"

"Yes," it was a low moan as she started to sob again.

"What is it, darling? Where are you?" He had forgotten where he was. All he could think of was the girl on the other end. He wished he could be there to help her, but thank God she had called him. And if that son of a bitch had touched her he was going to kill him.

The crying subsided a little and he heard her take a breath. "Spencer . . . I need you . . ." He closed his eyes as he listened, waiting for the rest of it. "I'm in jail."

His eyes flew open instantly, and his whole body tensed. "For what?"

There was a long pause and a wrenching sob as she almost choked, and then silence again. "For murder."

He felt the room spin around him as he listened. "Are you serious?" He knew she had to be, as a chill ran through him.

"I didn't do it. . . . I swear . . . someone killed Ernie last night . . . in Malibu. . . ." She tried to explain the rest to him, but she was still too upset and he couldn't understand her. Instinctively he grabbed a pencil and started scribbling the little he could understand. She was in the L.A. jail, and they had found his body in the house in Malibu that morning. And then they had come to Beverly Hills and taken her away and booked her for murder.

"Is there any reason why they think it's you?"

"I don't know . . . I don't know . . . we had a fight yesterday on the beach . . . and someone saw us. He hit me," Spencer winced, almost feeling the blow himself, "and I swung at him, but that's all it was . . . . and I left him there last night. He said he was expecting friends, some business associates to talk about a deal. I don't know who they were." He was still making notes as he listened.

"Does anyone else?"

"I don't know."

"What did you fight about?" He was all lawyer as he scribbled.

"The contract again. I wanted to break it.

He's been loaning me out to studios like a car. He makes all the money, and I was tired of it. He didn't even let me decide what movies I wanted to make. He was just using me . . ." She was sobbing again, she had finally understood what he was, but much, much too late. She couldn't get away from him, and she had already lost Spencer. "I hated him . . . but I wouldn't have killed him, Spencer. I swear it."

"Can you prove it? Did anyone see you in Beverly Hills? Did you go anywhere? Call friends?"

"No. No one. Nothing. I had a terrible headache after he hit me on the beach and I went to bed. The maid was off, and I never saw the driver." And he knew that was why they had arrested her. She had a motive and no alibi, and no one to corroborate her story. "Spencer," her voice sounded like a child's again, "I know I shouldn't ask you this . . . you'll probably tell me to go to hell . . . but I have no one else to turn to . . . will you help me?" There was silence on the phone and he heard her blow her nose again. He knew what he had to do. He had known it the moment she'd called him. There was no decision to be made, no choice, he was going out to California.

"I'll be there tomorrow. I'll have to find someone to represent you."

"Can't you do it for me? Oh God, Spencer . . . I'm scared. What if I can't prove I wasn't there?" She sounded like a little girl and his heart went out to her. He was so engrossed in the conversation that he hadn't seen his wife walk in. She was standing in the hall and listening to what he was saying to Crystal.

"Don't worry. We'll prove it. But listen, I'm not a criminal attorney. You should have the best. Don't mess around with this, Crystal . . . please . . ." He would have been too afraid not to do her justice, and there was too much at stake. Her life. And his, indirectly.

"I only want you to do it . . . if you have the time. . . ." She hadn't even thought of that before, but listening to him had calmed her down a little bit and now she had to think of whether or not he would have the time to do it. She assumed he had a job, and maybe he couldn't get away. But that wasn't what he was worried about. He had never been a criminal attorney, no matter how much it fascinated him, or how much he loved her.

"We'll talk about it when I get out there. Do you need anything in the meantime?" He was shouting again. There was static in the connection.

"Yes," she smiled through her tears at her end, "a hacksaw." She laughed damply and he smiled.

"Good girl. We'll get you out of this. Just hang on. I'll be there before you know it. And, Crystal . . ." He smiled thinking of her, and as he did he saw Elizabeth watching him and he knew he couldn't finish the sentence. "I'm glad you called me." So was she, but she felt guilty about it after telling him to leave her alone the year before. But she had no one else to turn to. And she had always loved him.

"I told them you were my lawyer. Is that okay?"

"That's fine. Tell them I just confirmed it. And don't tell them anything else. Nothing! Do you hear me?"

"Yes." But she sounded hesitant. They had already asked her so many questions. They'd been interrogating her all day, until she collapsed in hysterics and then they had finally let her call her attorney.

"I mean it! Don't tell them anything. I want to discuss it all with you first. You got that?"

"Yes." She sounded surer now.

"Good." He was satisfied. "I'll see you tomorrow. We'll get you out of this, just believe that." She thanked him and started to cry again, and a moment later they hung up. He stood looking at the phone for a long moment, and turned to see Elizabeth looking at him.

"What was that all about?"

There was a long moment as their eyes met before he answered. He knew he had to tell her the truth, or most of it. She would have found out anyway once the story hit the papers. Crystal was well known by then, well enough for it to be a big story. "An old friend in trouble in California." He took a breath as she frowned. "I'm going out there tomorrow."

"May I ask why?" Her eyes were cold as she lit a cigarette and watched him.

"I want to see what I can do to help."

"May I ask who the friend is?"

He hesitated for a beat before he answered. "Her name is Crystal Wyatt." The name meant nothing to her but the look in his eyes did.

"I don't believe you've mentioned her before." She sat down carefully on the couch, scarcely taking her eyes off his face. She knew instinctively that this was the woman who had stood between them. "What kind of friend is she, Spencer? An old flame?"

"A little girl I used to know. But she's all grown up now and in a hell of a lot of trouble." He didn't sit down next to her and there might as well have been a wall of ice between them.

"Oh? And what are you planning to do to help her?"

"Defend her possibly, or find her a good lawyer."

"What exactly is she accused of?"

He looked straight into his wife's eyes. "Murder."

There was a long silence in the room, and then she nodded. "I see. That is serious, isn't it? But has it occurred to you, Sir Galahad, that you're not a criminal attorney?"

"I told her that. I'm going to see who I can find to defend her."

"You can do that from here." Her voice was tight as she stubbed out the cigarette.

But Spencer shook his head. "No, I can't." And he knew he had to be there. Just to see her. She had called him in desperation, and he wasn't going to let her down. It was his one chance to help her. Her life was on the line, and no matter what it took, he was willing to do anything for her, even defend the case himself if he had to. "I'm leaving tomorrow morning."

"I wouldn't do that if I were you." There was a thinly veiled threat in her voice as she looked at him. But he was immovable on the subject.

"I have to."

Her voice was strangely calm. "If you go, I'll divorce you." It was what he had wanted a year before, and now she was offering it as a threat. But no matter what she did or said, Spencer knew he was going.

"I'm sorry to hear that."

"Are you?" She was every moment more frigid. "It's what you wanted anyway. And what about Miss Wyatt?" The name was etched in her mind forever. "How would she feel about that?"

"The only thing she feels right now, Elizabeth, is terror." His palms were damp as he faced his wife. They had finally reached the turning point. And it had been a long time coming. "I don't know how long I'll be gone."

"I meant what I said. I don't want to be publicly embarrassed by you making an ass of yourself out there."

"We can talk about it when I get back." The divorce was no longer as crucial.

"I don't think so, Spencer. You'd better give it some serious thought before you go." The silence in the room was so thick you could have cut it with a knife. "I get the feeling you're developing political aspirations, and a divorce won't help you much in that direction."

"That sounds like blackmail."

"Call it what you like. It's something to think about, isn't it?"

"I don't have any choice." He ran his hands through his hair, and there was silver at the temples. He was thirty-five, and he had been in love with Crystal for eight years, and now she needed him. He wasn't going to let her down, no matter what Elizabeth did to him, or threatened. "Elizabeth . . . she needs me."

"Are you in love with her?" But she knew from the look in his eyes that it was a foolish question.

"I was." For the first time, he was honest with her. It was too late not to be. Their marriage had been a mistake from the start. He had never stopped wanting what they didn't have. What he had had all too briefly with Crystal.

"And now?"

"I don't know. I haven't seen her in a long time. But that's not why I'm going. I'm going because she has no one else to turn to."

"How touching." Elizabeth stood up and walked to the stairs that led to their bedroom. "Think about what I said. Before you go. I suggest you call another attorney for her."

But when she was gone, he called the airline and made reservations. He walked upstairs slowly, wondering what would happen to them. But they weren't important now. All that mattered to him was saving Crystal. This was nothing to fool around with. Her life was on the line. But at least she was rid of Ernesto Salvatore. But at what price. He knew she could get the death penalty, or at the very least, a life sentence.

He went upstairs and packed his things, and called his boss to tell him that he had to go to California on a personal matter. He was understanding, and Spencer said he'd call as soon as he knew where things stood, and then he walked into the bedroom, and saw Elizabeth quietly reading the paper. She glanced up at him with a strange look, and as he looked at the newspaper, he saw that she was reading the story of Ernie's murder, and just above it there was a huge publicity photograph of Crystal. She looked far less beautiful than she really was, but she looked striking anyway, in a big hat, and a low-cut dress, and her long pale hair fanned out across her shoulders. Her eyes looked straight out at you, and after a long moment, Elizabeth looked up. There was a strange look on her face. She had seen those eyes before, and she remembered her perfectly as she looked straight at Spencer.

"It's the girl in the nightclub, isn't it?" She had remembered her. It was part of Crystal's appeal. Once one saw her, one never forgot her. And he nodded slowly. The truth was out now. He had lied to her about Crystal right at the beginning, but that had been when he was still telling himself he was in love with Elizabeth Barclay. He nodded slowly as he looked at her, feeling sorrow and regret and guilt. But the marriage had been wrong from the start, and they both knew it. "Funny," Elizabeth mused, "I always thought she was the one. I still remember your face that night. You looked as though you had been hit by lightning."

He smiled then. They were exactly the words he had used so long ago, talking about what he wanted. He had been thinking about her even then, when he had said to Elizabeth in Palm Beach that he wanted to hear thunder and lightning.

"You're going?" She eyed him again.

"Yes."

She nodded and turned off the light. And as he lay in bed beside her, all he could think of that night was Crystal in jail in California.

CHAPTER
33 ————————————————

The gate opened inexorably, with a hideous clanking sound and he was led into a small room with a large window, a battered wooden table and two chairs, and the guard locked the door behind him as he left him. It was a terrifying feeling just being there, and he was momentarily stunned into silence when Crystal was led in, in a blue smock, her arms behind her, locked in handcuffs. Her eyes were wide with terror as she looked at him, and his heart almost broke as they turned the key, freed her hands, and then left her with him. But as her attorney, he didn't even dare to kiss her. All he could do was look at her and feel the same surge of love he had always felt for her, and as her eyes met his, he didn't doubt for a minute that she loved him. The past year seemed to melt away, and he felt powerful beside her.

But he also suspected that the room was bugged and he kept his voice low as he looked at her, and reached for her hand, without telling her any of what he was feeling. She clung tightly to him and her eyes filled with tears. She had missed him so much, and the last year had been a nightmare.

"Are you all right?"

She nodded and sat down, still holding on to him, and he waited a few minutes before asking her any questions. They went over everything, and he was horrified by the story. Salvatore had kept her like a slave, well protected, in the proverbial gilded cage, but she had been his prisoner in recent months and she could only do what he allowed her to. The movies, the parties, the public appearances, the outings. The rest of the time he kept her at home, under careful supervision. And she had fought constantly with him about it. She posed no real threat. There had been no other man in her life since Spencer.

"Did anyone ever see you fight?"

"The maids," she nodded. "The chauffeur."

"Any of his friends?"

"Some. He took most of them to Malibu. He kept his own doings to himself." And she also suspected he saw other women. He had abused her sexually several times in recent months, and given her a black eye that forced her to stay off a movie set for two weeks, and word of it had hit the papers. They had said she had an accident, and her face was too bruised for her to work. She had worked on the sound track instead, now that she had started singing in her movies.

Spencer looked agonized at the tale. "Why didn't you call me?"

"He told me he'd kill you if I ever called you again. He knew who you were that time when he saw you. That's why . . ." She hesitated, "I called you last year and told you it was over. I was afraid for you." She looked at him sadly, knowing the pain she had caused, but his heart soared. She had loved him then, and she had ended it to protect him. His eyes were warm as he smiled at her then and she told him that Ernie had threatened to kill her, too, more than once, particularly recently when she fought him constantly about her contract. "All the money went to him. Everything. All I got was money to buy clothes," like a prostitute with a pimp, but Spencer didn't say that, he just sat and listened, and took notes when she said something he thought was important. He asked her about dates and events and people and places. It had been a terrible time for her, a life built on nightmares. "I used to think I owed him so much. I never understood then what he was doing." She looked up into Spencer's eyes and his heart melted again as he listened. Even more so now that he knew why she had told him not to come back to California. "I guess he always thought he owned me. I was just an object to him. Something he'd bought cheap and made a lot of money from, like a good investment. And at first he always let me think he was doing everything for me." She looked at Spencer bitterly. "I used to feel that I owed him something. But he took everything I had to give, even you." Spencer remembered it only too clearly.

"And then what?"

"We had a lot of fights."

"Publicly?"

"Sometimes." She was honest with him. "I told Hedda once that I was going to break my contract, and find an agent. He almost killed me for that. I think maybe someone else was in on the deal with him, and he was afraid of their reaction. But I never knew, because I never saw my contract again, and I was too stupid to read it the day I signed it." She had even lost touch with Harry and Pearl. Eventually, Salvatore had cut her off from everyone. She was only allowed out to work, and she was getting bigger and better pictures. His investment had done well. Like a prize-winning racehorse . . .

"Did you have a fight with him the night he died?"

"Just the one on the beach I told you about. But that time I hit him back. Hard. I think his ear was bleeding when I went back to the house, but I didn't give a damn. I hated him, Spencer. He was an evil man, and I think he really would have killed me."

"Did anyone see him bleeding? Or see you hit him?"

"A neighbor, I think. He was walking his dog on the beach. And he told the police he had seen me attack Ernie with a stick. But I didn't, I had a piece of driftwood in one hand, and I hit him with the other one." Spencer nodded and made a note, listening to her as a guard walked by the window.

"And then what?"

"I went back to the house, and when he came in he hit me."

"Did it leave a mark?"

She shook her head. "No, not this time.

Most of the time he was careful about that. He didn't want to put me out of work. If I were out of work he and his friends might have lost money."

"Who were they? Do you know?" But she only shook her head. "Then what happened?" He was building the story, carefully. He wanted accurate details when he called an attorney to defend her. He wanted the best there was and it worried him that he had never handled a criminal case before. She needed a lot better than that. And he was going to get her the best.

Crystal sighed and blew her nose on the clean white handkerchief he offered, and she looked up at him gratefully, and took a deep breath as she closed her eyes and tried to remember. "I don't know . . . I walked around in the house . . . we argued for a long time. I broke a lamp."

"How?"

"I threw it at him."

"Did it hit him?"

"No," she smiled ruefully through her tears, "it missed." And then the smile faded. "And then he told me he was expecting someone and he wanted me to go back to the house in Beverly Hills."

"Did he say who?"

She shook her head. "He never did."

"Did anyone see you leave? . . . a neighbor? A servant?"

"There was no one there. We were alone."

"What time did you go?"

"About eight o'clock. I had to be at work the next day. I'd had the day off. But I wanted to get to bed. He said he would spend the night in Malibu. And then . . . I never heard from him again. I thought everything was okay. I left for work at five, the driver took me as usual." She choked on the words then. "And the police came to the set at nine . . . they said . . . they said he was dead. He had been found with five gunshot wounds in his head, and they thought he had died around midnight."

"Did they find the gun?"

She nodded again, looking frightened. "Yes . . . it was washed up on the beach. Someone had tried to get rid of it, but they hadn't thrown it far enough, I guess . . . and there were a woman's footprints on the beach . . . and Spencer . . ." She began to sob. "I swear I didn't kill him."

He squeezed her hands in his own. "Had you ever seen the gun before?"

She nodded. "It was Ernie's. I saw it in his desk a couple of times, but I think eventually he was afraid I'd use it, and I never saw it after that, until . . . until the police showed it to me yesterday morning."

"Isn't there anyone else you know of who could have had it in for him?"

"I don't know . . . I don't know . . .." She had certainly had ample provocation over the past year, but Spencer knew that didn't mean she had killed him. And with the kind of connections he suspected Salvatore had, it could have been anyone. Someone he'd burned in a deal, a woman he had dumped, a man he had cheated at cards, an underling who hated him or even his bosses. But Spencer also knew that whoever it was, if they were part of any underworld, it would all be carefully covered up, and the real killer would never be discovered. They had left Crystal to take the rap. And the noose fitted around her neck to perfection.

Her voice was a whisper in the ugly room. "What do you think will happen?"

He hated to answer her question. If they didn't get her off, she could get life, or worse. He didn't even want to think about it. All he knew was that he couldn't let that happen. "I won't lie to you. It's going to be a tough case. You had the opportunity and the motive, and no alibi. That's a stinking combination. And too many people knew about your troubles with him, hell, anyone would have hated the man. I only wish someone had seen you leave that night, or arrive at the house in Beverly Hills. Are you sure no one did?"

"I don't think so. I can't imagine who."

"Well, give it some thought. And we're going to need a hell of a good investigator on this case." He had already decided to pay for all of it. He knew she didn't have a dime. Salvatore had kept everything from her.

"What are you going to do now?" She looked at him with frightened eyes. She had to go back to her cell, and it terrified her. All the guards had stared at her, and several female inmates had shown considerable interest in their little "movie star," as they called her. Crystal Wyatt was big news in the L.A. jail, and Spencer wanted to get her out as soon as possible. But all his attempts to stand bail for her that afternoon were fruitless. He tried to get the charges reduced to manslaughter, but they called it murder one, and she would have to stay in jail until the trial. She just had to try her best to hold on, he told her, and then he went back to the hotel to make a dozen phone calls. He called two friends from law school, and was given the names of the best criminal lawyers in L.A. But most of them weren't anxious for the case, it sounded open-and-shut to them, and more than one of them implied that a mobster and his babe were just a little too sleazy. He was furious by the time he hung up, and he stood staring around the room. The decision had been made for him, he wouldn't have trusted her to any of them. He was going to take the case himself, he only prayed he would do her justice. They had everything at stake. Her life and their future.

And that night he called Elizabeth and the government office where he worked, and told them he was staying for the trial. His boss was less than pleased, and Elizabeth was furious. He remembered all too clearly the threats she'd made before he left, but none of that mattered now. Crystal's life was on the line, and he was determined to defend it.

"And just exactly how long will that be, Spencer?" she had asked him when he told her he had become the attorney-of-record.

"I don't know yet. She has a right to come to trial in thirty days, and the trial could take weeks. I think I'm here for at least two months, maybe longer." He sighed and stretched out on the couch as they talked. It had been an endless day, and other than getting Crystal's story from her, he had gotten nowhere.

But Elizabeth was furious over the length of

time he was planning to stay in California. "I don't imagine you're planning to come home for Christmas." It was only a month away, and as usual, they were supposed to go to Palm Beach with her parents.

"I didn't think I was still welcome."

"You aren't, but what the hell do you think I'm going to tell my parents?" So that was it. Saving face was still desperately important, rather than saving the marriage. But they had no marriage to save and now he knew the truth about Crystal.

"I don't think you'll have to tell them anything. It's going to be all over the papers for months." Several reporters had flashed his picture when he left the jail, and he expected to see himself in the papers by the next morning.

"Terrific. And your job? I don't suppose you've thought of that." Her father had gotten him that too. It would seem as though he owed him everything, including his daughter.

"I told them I had to take a leave of absence, the government will still be there when I get back, and if they fire me, that's the way it is. I'll have to look for something when I get back, won't I?" If he ever went back. But all of that would have to be sorted out later.

"You make it all sound very easy."

"Well, it's not. But I'm trying to make the

best of a bad situation. The girl's life is in jeopardy, Elizabeth. And I'm not going to turn my back on her."

"I can see why," she hesitated and he sighed, "she might kill you."

"Good night, Elizabeth. I'll call you in a few days."

"Don't. I'll be at school, and I'm going skiing with friends next weekend. And then I'm going to spend Thanksgiving with my parents."

"Give them my love." He was only being half sarcastic but she wasn't amused. He had gone too far, and she had almost decided not to let him come back, even if he wanted to when it was over.

"Go to hell."

"Thank you." At least there he might join Crystal.

He spent days working with her, checking out her story, grilling her and regrilling her, but it was always the same, and by the third day, he knew he believed her. He appeared at several hearings for her, and hired an investigator to check it all out, but it was just what she had said, no one had seen her come and go, and the only witness there was said she had hit him with a stick on the beach, and he even went so far as to say she seemed unmoved when she saw him bleeding. It wasn't a pretty picture for her, none of it. And there was no getting away from the fact that she had had both opportunity and motive, and she couldn't prove her whereabouts the night of the murder.

She grew thinner day by day, and whenever he saw her he thought her eyes looked larger. She seemed stunned by all that had happened, and on Christmas Day it broke his heart to leave her in jail, to share her slice of pressed turkey with the other inmates. They hadn't dared say anything to each other yet about how they felt. But he held her hand before he left, and they both spoke volumes with their eyes. They didn't need the words, they never had. They were at one with each other.

The trial had been set for January ninth, after very few continuances. He was certainly not suggesting any delays. He wanted to get it over with as quickly as possible for her. And the tack they had decided to take was self-defense. It was the only hope she had, and he was going to get as many women as possible on the jury.

He called Elizabeth in Palm Beach on Christmas Eve, and she refused to talk to him. Priscilla Barclay was cool, and she said rather primly that she'd read about him in the papers.

But it was useless to try to explain it. Even more so when he called his parents on Christmas morning.

"What the hell are you doing?" Judge Hill was blunt. "You're not a criminal attorney. You'll lose the case for that girl." But it was precisely what he was afraid of.

"I couldn't get anyone decent to take it on such short notice."

"That's hardly a reason to play games."

"I'm not, Dad. And I'm doing my best."

"Elizabeth can't be pleased."

"She isn't."

"I just don't understand it." His father shook his head in dismay as Spencer wished them a Merry Christmas. And more than once, he had wondered if this was the girl Spencer had mentioned when he came back from Korea. It was only a hunch, but something told him it was, and if that was the case, there was going to be trouble with the Barclays. He wondered if Spencer knew what he was doing. But once or twice, Spencer called him and he gave him what advice he could, off the record. He thought self-defense was the only hope they had, and even that was a slim one.

The jury selection took ten days, but in the end, Spencer got what he wanted. There were seven women and five men, all of whom would cringe at the stories of how Salvatore had abused her. And Spencer even went out and shopped for the clothes she would wear in the courtroom so she would look as she had years before when he met her, innocent and pure. She didn't have to pretend to look frightened, she was terrified as she sat beside him at the defense table. The prosecution's case was direct and blunt and brutal. They painted a picture of a girl who had come to Hollywood to do anything she could to get ahead, including sleeping with a man twice her age, who obviously had less than gentlemanly connections. They didn't try to hide what he was, instead they tried to use it. And the district attorney did it well. He pointed at Crystal across the courtroom. He made her look like a whore, collecting expensive clothes, a greedy life-style, furs, and diamond bracelets. She had done well living with the victim, they pointed out. And so had her career. Thanks to the man she'd murdered in cold blood, she was a minor star, and they listed all the pictures he'd gotten her into, making it sound as though she did nothing to deserve it. They painted a history of violence, a family feud that had left her brother dead and driven her from her home at seventeen, a job in a sleazy nightclub in San Francisco for several years, and then coming to Los Angeles to ensnare anyone she could to help her get ahead. And when he no longer served her purpose, wanting to be free of her contract with him, she killed him.

But Spencer had prepared well, and he hadn't spared a dime in bringing people in to help defend her. Pearl talked of her innocence, her hard work, her good morals. Harry depicted her not like a singer in a sleazy bar, but as a sweet young angel. And Crystal cried as they testified, looking at them gratefully across the courtroom. And the investigator Spencer had hired had unearthed every headwaiter, every maid, every dresser in Hollywood, who had seen Crystal take abuse from Salvatore. There were implications of rape at the house in Malibu, a contract she had never understood, there were beatings and insults and abuse of almost every kind, and Spencer had even talked of her being raped as a child as she stared miserably down at her hands, remembering the scene in the barn with Tom Parker. She was a girl who had been broken again and again, and yet had always survived it, a girl who worked hard, who did well, who never hurt anyone, until Ernie tried to rape her again, until he beat her, and threatened her, and in self-defense she had killed him. There was no point saying that she didn't. He knew he would have lost the case if he tried, so he painted a monster for them instead. A monster who had tried to destroy this girl, with no family, no friends, no one in the world to defend her. And what he said made them hate Ernie for what he had done to her. She took the stand on her own behalf on the last day, and she looked so young and so innocent and so frightened in the plain gray dress she wore, that all of the jurors watched her raptly, and when Spencer finally rested his case, he prayed that he had won them over.

It was a case that almost broke their hearts, but still they deliberated for two days, looking over the evidence, arguing with each other. There were two men who still thought she was guilty of murder one, and as Spencer paced the halls with Crystal waiting for the verdict, he hardly dared to look at her. If he had lost the case, her life was over. It was an agony just being there with her. She seldom spoke, she only looked at him with her huge blue eyes, and when the bailiff called them all inside, her knees were shaking so badly she could hardly walk beside Spencer. The judge told her to stand up, and then he turned to the foreman and asked for the verdict. Crystal closed her eyes and waited. She couldn't even think as she listened. She had been accused of murder in the first degree, and there was no alternative, she was either innocent or guilty. Had she planned it? Had she meant to? Did she know what she was doing when she shot him in cold blood? Or had he threatened her, had she been fighting for her life, had he finally made her snap? If he had, she was innocent, although for the rest of time, the world would believe that she had killed him. She had shrunk at the prospect of that, and insisted to Spencer for weeks that she hadn't killed him, she hadn't even been there when he was shot. But Spencer knew he couldn't touch that. All he could do was create a case that painted her and not Ernie as the victim.

"How do you find the defendant, Mr. Foreman? Guilty or innocent of murder in the first degree?" It was as simple as that in the end, and there was an endless pause as they waited.

The foreman cleared his throat and glanced at her as Spencer tried to read his face. Was he pleased with himself? Or was the jury sorry for what they were about to do? There was no telling. "Innocent, Your Honor." He glanced at Crystal again with a shy smile as the Superior Court judge rapped his gavel, and Crystal fell back into Spencer's arms. She had almost fainted. It was a clear case of self-defense, they

said. She was free. No matter that for the rest
of her life she would carry the stigma of murder. She was free to live her life, and without
thinking, Spencer put his arms around her and
held her. He hadn't dared to touch her in two
months, and now he held her as she cried and
the courtroom went wild around them. Reporters were let in and there were flashbulbs
everywhere, as court was adjourned and Spencer hurried her from the building. He had a car
and driver outside, and they had to force their
way through the crowd. It had been a sensa-
tional case, and whoever had actually done it
was off the hook forever. Crystal had taken the
rap, but she was free. Spencer had done it.

She was still crying in disbelief as they drove
away from the courtroom. She had left her few
belongings in jail. She never wanted to see
them again. She never wanted to see Hollywood or the things Ernie had given her. She
just wanted to go away, and stopping at his
hotel for a few minutes, Spencer packed his
bag, and an hour later they were in a rented
car on their way to San Francisco.

"I can't believe it," she whispered as he sped
north. "I'm free." The world had never looked
so sweet to her. And on a February afternoon
with Spencer at her side, two years after she
had come to Hollywood, she left it.

CHAPTER
34

They were twenty miles out of town, when Spencer stopped the car, and pulled over to the side of the freeway. He just sat and looked at Crystal and suddenly she smiled. It was all over, the nightmare had ended and he'd saved her life, and he grinned and pulled her into his arms with such strength that it took her breath away for a moment.

"My God, Crystal, we did it."

She was laughing and crying all at the same time and she pulled away to look at him and then dived back into his arms again, knowing that she never again wanted to leave them.

"*You* did it. I just sat there being scared out of my mind."

"So was I," he admitted in a whisper as he held her, and then he sat back against the seat and looked at her as he hadn't dared since he'd come to California. But there was no one watching them now. They were finally alone. And he had been watching the mirror ever since they'd left his hotel to be sure that they weren't being followed by reporters. "I've never been so scared in my life." He didn't even want to think about what would have happened if she had been found guilty. But she hadn't. And it was over now. They both needed to catch their breath, and he wanted to spend some time with her and sort their lives out. And then suddenly he laughed. They had been in such a hurry to leave town that he didn't even know where they were going. "Where do you want to go?" Instinctively, he had headed toward San Francisco.

"I don't know." She was still in shock, as she looked at him. Four hours before, her life had still been in danger, and now they had their lives ahead of them. She lifted her face to the winter sun in the simple dress he had bought her. "I just want to sit here and breathe for a minute. I never thought I'd be out here again." He didn't tell her that there were times when he didn't either. He had called his father from the hotel, to tell him he'd won the case, and his father had congratulated him and was looking forward to reading about it in the papers. He had asked Spencer when he was coming back, and he had said he didn't know yet. They both needed time to catch their breath, and it was nice being out of reach of police and reporters. They had driven him crazy throughout the trial, and as she sat back against the seat he asked her if she'd miss it.

"Hollywood?" She thought about it for a while, and then shook her head. "Not really. The work . . . the singing . . . the acting I did. I liked that a lot. But the rest is very empty." And she had paid such a high price for it. She had almost paid with her life, thanks to Ernie. Even in death, he had almost killed her. "I can never go back anyway."

"Why not? You can one day, if you want." But he would have understood if she didn't.

"No, I can't. The morals clause won't let them hire a murderess for a movie." She laughed but it was an empty sound as he started the car again and she glanced out the window. The world had never looked so sweet, and what she noticed most about it was the colors. Everything was so green and so blue and so beautiful, as she looked at Spencer. "I

owe you my life. But I guess you know that."
She touched his hand and moved close to him
on the seat, looking suddenly young again. The
strain was gone, she had let her hair down, and
only her eyes told a tale of utter terror. And
then, as he gently touched her cheek, he leaned
over and kissed her.

"I love you so much. I would have died if
anything had happened to you." She clung to
him like a lost child, and he put an arm around
her and pulled her closer.

"I don't know what I would have done
if . . ." But she couldn't even finish the sentence as he watched the road and held her.

"Don't think of it anymore, Crystal. It's all
over." And as they rode toward San Francisco,
they talked about where she was going. She
hadn't figured that out yet. All she had wanted
was to get as far away from Los Angeles as fast
as she could. She wanted to stop and see Harry
and Pearl, and be with Spencer. They had a lot
to talk about, especially now that he knew that
she had ended it the year before because of
Ernie's threats and not because she didn't love
him.

They arrived in San Francisco at ten o'clock
at night and they went straight to Harry's. But
he'd heard it on the news already. They
hugged and they cried, and he bought them

drinks, and after that Spencer took her to the Fairmont. He booked two rooms, in case someone called the press. They were adjoining and he was pleased to see that. She stood in the doorway and looked at him then, and she felt as though her knees were going to buckle beneath her. He swept her up in his arms and laid her down on the bed. And he held her for hours, rediscovering all that they had both remembered. And when at last she slept, he turned off the light, and she didn't wake before morning. He was waiting for her when she woke up, he had coffee waiting for her, and croissants, and he smiled as she stretched and then slipped back into bed beside her.

"Good morning, Sleeping Beauty. Feeling better?"

He had already called his office, and had a long talk with his boss. What he said didn't come as a surprise, and Spencer wasn't sorry. He felt that the sensation Spencer had caused in the last two months was incompatible with a government job, and that Spencer had become an embarrassment to them. They hoped he would understand, and they were particularly sorry if it was going to upset Justice Barclay. But Spencer had felt a wave of relief wash over him when they told him. He didn't say anything to Crystal about it. He knew she'd be upset for him. And the only other message he had had was a mysterious one from the junior senator from California. And the odd thing was that Spencer didn't even know him.

They lay in bed and talked about the trial again, and over breakfast, he showed her the papers. It was the head story in all the newspapers that day, and Crystal was afraid she'd be recognized if she went out. "It's a hell of a way to get famous." She smiled at him as they shared the croissants and delicious coffee, and he made a suggestion that made her grow pensive. He wanted to drive up to the valley to see Boyd and Hiroko. But Crystal didn't want to go. She knew it would be too painful for her.

"I don't want to see the ranch again." She knew she couldn't have borne it. She was sure Becky was long gone, and Tom, but she thought her mother was still there. And there were too many unhappy memories there for her. But with Spencer next to her, she admitted that it might be different. "What about you?" She looked at him worriedly. "Don't you have to go home?" She knew he hadn't called Elizabeth since they'd gotten to San Francisco. He didn't know what to say. They hadn't spoken to each other in weeks. He had wanted to face that after the trial was over. And now he didn't want to leave Crystal.

"I'm in no hurry." He still hadn't told her he had lost his job. But it was a small price to pay for saving Crystal. They walked along the wharf that afternoon, and she bought a few clothes. She had none of the money she'd earned in L.A. Ernie had absorbed it all, and she had left all her things at the house in Beverly Hills. She didn't want to have them, or own them, or sell them. But she'd have to get a job soon. She couldn't let Spencer support her forever. She was back to where she'd started long before, without a home, or a dime. She'd had more when she'd arrived at Mrs. Castagna's. But she'd had her dream of Hollywood and for a while she had enjoyed it, and at least for now she had Spencer. For a moment, or a day. She knew he'd have to go back to Washington. But she was grateful for every moment they could be together in the meantime. During the trial, they had talked of nothing else. And under the watchful eye of the guards, and with photographers lurking everywhere, he hadn't dared to touch her. But now they had days ahead of them where they could luxuriate in each other.

They went back to the hotel late that afternoon, and after she saw people staring at her in the lobby, she said she wanted to eat dinner in their rooms. Too many people knew who she was now, and most of them for the wrong reasons. They had talked about a lot of things that day, about Washington, his job and his life there. About how much he had come to enjoy politics and the world of government and he admitted to her it surprised him. She talked about the people she'd met in Hollywood, the stars, the hard work. And she said that in spite of Ernie, she had liked it. "I think I would have been good at it one day," she said quietly after he'd ordered dinner for them, and they were sitting cuddled up together in the bathrobes they'd bought that day at I. Magnin. There was a coziness that they shared and a closeness that had survived everything that had come between them.

"You already were good at it before you went there." He still remembered her voice and the way she sang at Harry's. "Maybe when things die down, you can go back someday."

"I don't think I'd want to." Her voice was soft and her eyes sad. "It's a rough world down there." But if not Hollywood, then what? There was nothing else she could do, except sing and act. And she was afraid to show her face now. Everyone would know her. Harry had offered her her old job back that day when she stopped by, but she didn't want it.

"People won't remember the trial forever. It'll fade like yesterday's news," and then he remembered the call from the senator and wondered what he had wanted.

Their dinner came on silver trays, and Spencer watched as she picked at her food. He gently touched her hand and asked her what she was thinking.

She smiled at him, her eyes bright with tears, and then she laughed. "I was just thinking that I'd like to go home. But I don't have one." He laughed too. It was true. She had no place to go, and no one to go home to. Pearl had offered her a room, but Crystal didn't want to impose, and she wasn't sure if she was going to stay in San Francisco. A lot of her plans were going to depend on Spencer.

"Let's go up to the valley for a few days. We don't have to stay. We can stop and see Boyd and Hiroko and then go somewhere else. You need time to think. It's only been two days, Crystal. Let's go up there tomorrow."

She hesitated for a long time, looking at him, and then she nodded. "What about you? You can't hang around, taking care of me forever."

He whispered the words softly to her in the dimly lit room. "I'd like to."

"You have a life in Washington, Spencer, don't you? What's left of it after I dragged you away for three months. I suppose there will be hell to pay." She was thinking of Elizabeth, and she didn't quite understand their arrangement. She wasn't sure of where things stood with them. He never mentioned her, or very seldom. And yet she knew that he was still married. Ernie was gone now, she was free, but Spencer wasn't. The specter of his wife still hung between them, or at least in Crystal's mind it did. Spencer had called her once, and left a message with the maid that he was in San Francisco, but he didn't say that he was at the Fairmont. He wasn't ready to talk to her yet. He just didn't want her to panic if she called the hotel he'd been staying at in L.A. and discovered he'd checked out the day of the verdict. He knew exactly what she'd think, and he didn't want to have to admit or deny it. The way things stood between them now, it was none of her business. He remembered her threat before he left, and wondered if now she would finally agree to divorce him.

He told Crystal then that he'd lost his job, and he said it nonchalantly as she stared at him in horror.

"You didn't!"

"I did!"

"My God! We're both out of work!" She laughed, but she felt desperately guilty. He had told her only that morning how much he liked government and politics and she wondered what he would do now. He told her about the call from the senator then, and she urged him to return the call the next morning. "Would you ever run for office?"

"I might. Or maybe I'll grow up to be a judge like my father." He smiled at her, it all seemed so unimportant now. All that mattered was that she was safe and that they were together. Nothing had changed between them in nine years. He was still haunted by her night and day, and the only thing he knew now was that he didn't want to leave her.

They talked long into the night about his vague political aspirations, her films, and then about things like babies and dogs and Boyd and Hiroko. She was looking forward to seeing them the next morning, despite her qualms about visiting the valley. He had rented another car and they were going to drive up early to see them. She couldn't wait to see Jane. She hadn't seen her since she left San Francisco. She was seven years old now, and probably wouldn't even remember Crystal.

And then finally, they went to bed and made love again, and for long hours of tenderness he held her. And again the years that had separated them melted into moments. It was as though the time they had lost disappeared as they held each other close and slept like peaceful children.

CHAPTER
35

They drove north the next day, and Crystal sat next to him, humming to the radio, lost in her own thoughts, and he smiled at how easy it was to be with her. She made no demands on him, there was no disappointment, no clash of views, no accusations. Inevitably, it made him think of Elizabeth and how different they were. But Crystal was like a dream, always just out of reach, just beyond his fingers, yet always clearly in view, and exactly what he wanted.

They crossed the Golden Gate, and drove north with the sun high in the sky. Everything was green and new, washed by the winter storms that left the hills emerald and sparkling beneath a sky the color of her eyes. She looked peaceful when she looked at him, and they smiled. It was comfortable just being together, they didn't even need to talk as he drove her.

She showed him where to go, and this time he remembered where the Websters lived. Feeling her heart pound, Crystal crossed the tiny garden, and rang the bell. There was a long wait and then a little girl came to the door as tears filled Crystal's eyes.

"Hello." The child looked up at her, and they knew instantly it was Jane. She had her mother's Oriental eyes, and she had dark reddish brown hair, just as she had the day she was born. "Who are you?"

"My name is Crystal, and I'm a friend of your mommy's."

There was no fear in the child's eyes, as Spencer took Crystal's hand. "She's inside making lunch."

"May we come in?" The child nodded and stepped aside, and the room was just as Crystal remembered. Very little had changed. She could tell that they were still poor, but they were rich in the love that they shared. There were photographs of Jane, and Japanese prints Hiroko had brought from Japan with her, the room was clean, full of the few treasures they had. And tears filled Crystal's eyes as she walked the few steps to the kitchen, and stood looking at her friend. Hiroko was singing to herself in Japanese, and she turned, expecting to see Jane. Her eyes grew wide, and with a single gasp, the two women flew into each other's arms.

They held one another and embraced for a long time, the years melting away, just as they had with Spencer. They hadn't seen each other in such a long time, but nothing had changed between them.

"I was so worry about you, Crystal." And then she saw Spencer standing watching them and she smiled to see them together. There was still a photograph of him with Boyd on her wedding day on their kitchen wall. "You look so beautiful!" She kissed her again, as she wiped her tears away. And suddenly they were talking all at once, as Jane stared at them, wondering who they were. Hiroko explained that Crystal had helped bring her into the world, and Spencer listened to the tale he had never heard, and looked with wonder at Crystal.

"There you are," he teased, "you could be a midwife now."

"Don't count on it," she grinned. And she and Hiroko talked endlessly as Spencer and

Jane played. All was well with them. Old Mr. Petersen had died, and left the station to Boyd. Hiroko asked about her movie career, and they talked quietly about the trial. And then they heard a truck roll up, and Boyd hurried in for lunch, wanting to know who was visiting them. He had seen the car. He stopped in the doorway as he came in, and took in the scene, and with a gasp he threw his arms around her, and then he pumped Spencer's hand.

"We've been reading about you." He grinned, relieved to see them both. "I kind of wondered if you'd come up here." Spencer explained that he had driven through two years before, but he hadn't been able to find where they lived. It was off on a back road, and he would have missed it again if Crystal hadn't been there to show him where it was.

Hiroko made them all lunch, while Crystal helped, feeling comfortable, as she always had, in the cozy kitchen. And after a while, Boyd told her all the news. Becky was remarried, and living in Wyoming with two more kids. And then he hesitated, wondering just how much Crystal wanted to hear at that moment.

"Your mom's been real sick," he said quietly. She was the only family Crystal had left. But Crystal didn't want to see her now, and she had already told Spencer she didn't want to see the ranch. It would have been too painful for her, too lonely to see it after these years. It had been six years since she'd left, six years since Jared died, and there was nothing there for her anymore, except her father's grave and Jared's. But she asked Boyd about it anyway, wondering if her mother had moved. "No, she's still there. What's left of it. They sold off the grazing land years ago. There's no cattle left. But I think the vineyards are still going strong, at least that's what I've heard people say. I haven't been there myself in a long time. But I know Dr. Goode's been out there with her a lot. She's been sick since last July," he paused again, glancing at Spencer and then at her. "I don't think she's going to last much longer, Crystal. If that means anything to you now."

And sadly she shook her head. "That's all over for me."

He nodded. He had figured that. "I was going to write to you once or twice, in case you wanted to see her before she dies."

Crystal shook her head, trying to forget her childhood days. They were gone for her now, and so was the ranch. "I don't think there's much point, and I don't think she'd want to see me anyway. I've never heard from her since I left. Is Becky here?" If their mother was dying, she thought she might be visiting from Wyoming.

"She came out over Christmas for a while, my sister said. I didn't see her, though. But she's gone back now." Crystal nodded, relieved somehow to know she wasn't there. Becky meant nothing to her, in truth she never had. The ones she had loved were all dead, except the people she sat talking to in the Websters' front room. And after lunch, they all went for a long walk, before Boyd went back to work. They promised to stop and see him before they drove out of town. Spencer and Crystal hadn't decided where they were going yet. He thought maybe she'd like to visit the wine country, and stay in some small, cozy inn. But when they left Hiroko finally, Spencer took the wrong turn, and suddenly Crystal's face went pale. They were driving along just outside the ranch. He recognized it too, and looked at her with caution.

"Do you want me to stop for a little while? No one would know we were here. If your mom's that sick, I'm sure she's not roaming around." And with an imperceptible nod of her head, she pointed to an overgrown road.

"That goes straight to the river." But he was afraid for the car, and they got out and he took her hand. They walked for a long time, and

Crystal fell silent and stood quietly, when they reached a little clearing, and then he saw three graves there. Jared and her father and her grandmother were buried there, as though waiting for her, and she was quiet as she wiped her eyes. He put an arm around her and as they walked back through the tall grass, he remembered Becky's wedding day, and Crystal standing in her white dress and bare feet, her shoes cast off somewhere, her hair shining like white gold in the sunlight. And then, as they walked, she walked slowly away from him. And she stood looking at the ranch house where she'd been born. It made her think of her father again and it hurt to see it.

"Do you want to go inside? I'll go with you." He was watching her carefully, feeling her pain.

"I don't know what I'd say after all this time."

"Hello is always a nice place to start." She turned and smiled at him.

"Smartass." They laughed, and started to turn away, but suddenly the screen door slammed, and they saw the visiting nurse leave. Dr. Goode was standing just inside the door, and Crystal looked at Spencer for a brief moment. He nodded encouragingly, and she hesitated for a long time, and then walked slowly toward the house that had once been filled with people she had loved, and now only memories that had faded.

"Go on," he whispered the word, and she held his hand, and a moment later she walked slowly up the front steps. Her hands were damp, and Dr. Goode stared at her for a long time, looking at her strangely. He had recognized her and was surprised that she had come. She had been gone for such a long time, and she had left amid so much scandal.

"How did you know?" he asked.

"Know what?" Crystal looked at him, feeling like a child again.

"She'll be gone anytime. She's awake now, if you want to come in." And then suddenly Crystal wondered if the shock would be too much for her after all these years.

"I haven't seen her in six years. I'm not sure she'd want me around at a time like this."

"When people know they're dying it changes things." He spoke quietly, wondering who the man was. "You married now?" She shook her head, and he said nothing more to her. He didn't know where she'd been or what she'd done. He'd been too busy caring for the sick. He had heard she'd gone to Hollywood to be a movie star, but she didn't look like one now. She looked the same to him, a little older, a little thinner maybe, but she was still as pretty as she always had been. "Go on in and say hello to her. She can't do you any harm now." Crystal walked slowly into the kitchen, almost expecting to see her grandmother, but there was no one now. The room was dim, and everything looked old and tired. No loving hands had made repairs in years. It looked as though she'd let everything get run-down, both inside and out. Spencer followed her down the hall to her mother's room, and waited quietly outside, as Crystal knocked and went in. Olivia was lying there and there was almost nothing left of her. She had wasted away, and all that seemed to be left of her were her eyes, staring at Crystal.

"Hello, Mom."

Olivia looked surprised, but not as much as Crystal thought she would. It was as though she knew she'd come, and if she didn't, she didn't care. "How've you been?" There was no mention of the day she'd left, or the pain she had caused her, of Jared's death, or what Tom had done. She was just lying there, looking at her last-born child, and waiting to die and join the others.

"I've been fine." Her mother knew nothing of the trial. She didn't know anything now, and she didn't really care anyway. For months now her world had shrunken to her bedroom.

"I heard you went to Hollywood. Was it true?"

Crystal nodded. "Yes, I did. For a while."

"What are you doing now?"

"Visiting you." She smiled, but there was no answering smile in her mother's eyes, she was much too tired.

"I guess you heard about the ranch. I figured they'd look for you after I died. Becky said Boyd Webster would know where to find you."

"He always did. What about the ranch? Are you going to sell it?"

"That's up to you now. It was always too much for me, but your daddy left it so I couldn't do anything except live here till I died. And then it's yours. Becky was mighty mad for a while. But she's got a good life now. A good man. Did you know that Tom died in Korea?"

"I heard." But her mind was racing over what her mother had just said. She sat down carefully in the rocking chair near the bed, and gingerly reached out for her mother's hand. Olivia didn't object, she just left it there, like a little twig in Crystal's fingers. "What do you mean about the ranch?"

"It's yours. That's how he wanted it. I got tenancy for life, I think they called it, something like that. But after that he wanted you to have all of it. He said you were the only one who ever cared about it." And as she listened, her eyes filled with tears. Her father had left the ranch to her, and they had never said a word. They had let her leave, without telling her that one day the ranch would be hers. "You can even stay in the cottage now, if you want. No one's used it in years. I won't be long," she said, and withdrew her hand. "It'll be yours anytime now."

"Don't talk like that. Is anyone cooking for you?"

"Yeah. Some of the girls from church still come around. I got plenty here, and Dr. Goode comes twice a day, he brings his nurse with him most times." But she closed her eyes then, she was too tired to talk any longer. And as she drifted off to sleep, Crystal stood and looked down at her, the woman who had caused her so much pain, who had never been able to understand her or love her, who had kept the secret from her for all this time. It was hard to feel much for her now, except pity. She was almost gone. And then, all this would be Crystal's. It was incredible. She quietly left the room and found Spencer standing there. She signaled to him to leave, and as they walked outside, she sat down on the front steps and stared at him in amazement.

"You're not going to believe what I just heard."

"She's forgiven you everything." He smiled, and she smiled back.

"No, it's too late for that. She's too sick even to care about all that." She looked out over the fields that were almost hers, and felt a warm surge of love for the land, which was precisely why her father had left it to her. And then she remembered his last words, ". . . don't ever give this up . . . the ranch . . ." And she had felt so guilty when she'd left it. She looked back at Spencer again. "My father left me the ranch when he died, and they never said anything. I guess that's why they hated me so much. Because he left it all to me." She looked as though she was in shock. Seeing her mother again after all these years, and now this. She shook her head and stood up slowly again. "What am I going to do with all of this?"

"Live here, have a good life. It's a beautiful place. Or it was once, and it could be again one day. I bet the vineyards are profitable as hell. And maybe even the corn."

"Spencer," she smiled up at him suddenly. "I'm home."

"Yes, you are," he smiled. "You sure as hell are. And you didn't even want to come here today." They both smiled, and then remembered the woman dying in the house. They walked slowly back to the car, wondering where to go next.

"She said we could stay at the cottage if we want."

"We?" he smiled, "Did she know I was here?"

"No . . . all right . . . she said I could. But I'm sure it's a mess." And she didn't want to be there while her mother was dying. "Let's go away somewhere, and come back here later." He nodded and they walked back to the car. They drove to the gas station then, said good-bye to Boyd and told him they'd be back. And he called them that night at the hotel where they were staying. Crystal had called Hiroko to leave her the number. Her mother had died, shortly after they left. And Crystal sat quietly for a long time, trying to decide what she felt. It wasn't sorrow or loss, or even anger anymore. Almost everything was gone, except a distant memory of the woman she'd known when she was a child. And now the ranch was hers, just as her father had wanted. She had no idea what she'd do with it. But at least she had somewhere to live now.

She and Spencer went back the next day, and two days later her mother was buried with the others. Crystal hesitated for two days while they stayed with Hiroko and Boyd, and then finally decided to move into the main house on the ranch and even stayed in her old room with Spencer. Her old bed was still there, and the floor still creaked just where she remembered it. In an odd way, nothing had changed. And yet everything had, as they walked across the fields at sunset that night, to the place where they had met, and he smiled as he looked down at her. It was strange how life went sometimes. Crystal still couldn't get over it. Only a few days before she'd had nothing in the world, and now she had the ranch her father had left her.

As the sun set, they kissed, and walked back to the house, hand in hand, grateful for the precious moments they had shared, as softly, like a dim memory, Crystal began singing.

CHAPTER
36

Spencer rode over most of the ranch with her the following day. Much of it was overgrown and there were no more ranch hands. Only the vineyards were still halfway well kept, and there were two Mexicans working as they rode past them.

They swam in the stream she had loved as a child, and sat wrapped in blankets afterward, laughing and huddled together, as she sang the songs she had sung with her father. And for a moment she felt guilty, as though she were laughing on her mother's grave, but it wasn't like that. Her mother had been dead to her years before, and the ranch was a final gift from her father.

When they went back to the house, she put the old kettle on, and it brought back visions of her grandmother in her clean white apron. She told Spencer about some of her earliest memories, and he listened raptly. And finally, they talked about Washington, and when he would go back there.

"What about Elizabeth?" They both knew he had to make a decision. But the decision would come of its own if he stayed long enough with Crystal. He couldn't imagine leaving her again, and they both knew he didn't want to. He hadn't seen Elizabeth in three months, and he was almost sure now that with a little pressure from him she'd divorce him. It was too embarrassing for her to have him drop everything in Washington, and stay in California with Crystal. And Crystal wanted him to stay with her, but she wanted the decision to be his. She didn't want him to give up his life in Washington, if it was what he wanted. She had nothing to offer him in comparison to the life he'd lived with Elizabeth and the Barclays. She had learned the day before that the ranch barely supported itself now. She would be able to survive there, but compared to Elizabeth, she had nothing. All she had was her love for him, and all that she had felt for him since Becky's wedding.

He remembered to call the senator back that afternoon, and she washed the dishes while Spencer placed the call. She was listening to the radio, and she looked up when she heard him hang up the phone. She smiled at him, and wiped her hands on the new jeans she'd bought. "What was it?"

He stared at her. Strange things were happening to them. The junior senator from California had been following her trial avidly, and he wanted Spencer to come to work as his aide when he got back to Washington, which he hoped would be soon. He had an important job for him, handling his campaign, and for once, it wasn't even thanks to Justice Barclay.

"Is that what you want?" she asked him after he'd explained. It was a prestigious job and one he knew he'd love, but he didn't want to go back to Washington and leave her. He wanted to be there with her, in the Alexander Valley.

"It would have been just what I wanted six months ago. I would have given my right arm for that." He sat down in one of the old kitchen chairs and she poured him a cup of coffee. "But now, I don't know. I'd rather be here with you." He pulled her down onto his lap and looked at her, still amazed at the senator's offer.

"What did you tell him?" She was watching his face carefully. She needed to know what was best for him and what he really wanted.

"I said I'd call him next week when I got back. He's flying back to Washington tomorrow afternoon. I can't believe he's serious, but he must have been." From disaster they had both earned wondrous blessings. "But where does that leave us? Would you come with me?" He had almost forgotten Elizabeth. Right now only Crystal seemed important.

"That's not the point right now. Where does that leave you is more important." He sipped the steaming brew and looked at her pensively and admitted that it was what he had always wanted. Suddenly the political horizon was opening up to him, but too late, he had Crystal now. He didn't want to lose her again, not even for a job like the one he'd just been offered. But as she listened to him talk about the world of politics, she knew how much he loved it. And she also knew he would do well, with a wife like Elizabeth. But all his bright hopes would die, married to a woman like her, accused of Ernie's murder. The scandal would have finished him, and then what would he have? The life of a farmer. He wasn't cut out for that. He was meant for greater things, and that night when he made love to her, afterward he found her strangely quiet. He wondered what was bothering her, and thought maybe it was the house and her memories of it. It was all so worn out and sad, just as her mother had been before she died. There was an aura of sorrow here, until one went outside, and saw the majesty of the valley.

"What are you thinking about?" He stroked her hair and held her close to him, and she smiled sadly up at him, lying in the narrow bed she had once shared with Becky.

"I was thinking that it's time for you to go back to Washington and face the music." It was the greatest sacrifice she'd ever make, but she knew she had to do it.

He slowly shook his head. "I don't want to leave you again. We've both been through enough. We've earned this."

She lifted herself up on one elbow and looked down at him. "This isn't where you belong, my love. You're meant for greater things than running an old ranch like this." She was sure of it, but he didn't want to hear it.

"And you're not? Don't be ridiculous. Three months ago you were a movie star, and now look at you. You're back here, where you started."

"That's different, Spencer." She kissed the tip of his nose. "That was all make-believe. What you do is important. You could be a great man one day. You might even run for president." But not if she let him stay with her. Not here. Not anywhere, married to a murderess. She could cost him everything. And she wasn't going to let him do it. He had to go back to Elizabeth. She was exactly the kind of wife he needed. "I want you to go back now."

"Why?" He looked at her in amazement. "How can you say that?"

"Because you belong in Washington. You're not finished yet. You have places to go, people to see, ideas yet unborn to share with people who need you. I've had a good time, but that's all it was for me, fun, and at too high a price. I don't want it anymore. You do. That's the difference." She had seen the look in his eyes after he called the senator. She couldn't deprive him of that. And she knew that if she did, one day he might hate her.

"And what do I do? Leave you here? Why don't you come with me?" His eyes pleaded with her.

"To Washington?" She smiled.

"Why not?"

"Because I would destroy you in a minute, no matter how much I love you. Think of what

I'm trailing behind me. I was accused of murder, Spencer. And all the jury said was that I did it in self-defense. They didn't say I didn't do it. Your career would be over the day I arrived in Washington, and you know it."

"I won't go back." He pulled her down next to him and held her close, suddenly afraid that he would lose her.

But she spoke seriously in the dark, and her words frightened him. "I won't let you stay here."

"Why not?"

"Because it would destroy you."

He didn't answer her, and after she fell asleep he lay for a long time, just holding her and listening to her breathe, and he knew that if he left her, he would die, or a part of him would. Forever. But the next day she brought it up again, and she was adamant with him. And in the end, she knew what she had to do. She had to send him away, at any price, even if that meant telling him she didn't love him. In the end, she didn't have to go that far. All she told him was that she wasn't ready to settle down with him. She wanted to be alone on her ranch, no matter how ungrateful that seemed after all he'd done for her. At twenty-four, after all she'd been through, she didn't want to think of marriage. She said she needed to be alone on the ranch but he didn't believe her. It reminded him of when she'd called him a year and a half before and told him she didn't love him, to save him from Ernie.

He looked devastated as they walked back to the house from the stream. "Why do you want to be alone here?"

"I just need to be. That's all. I want to be alone to do my own thing. I have a right to that. Don't I?" He looked wounded to the core, and she had to fight back tears all night as he held her. He argued with her for days, but she held her ground, and after a week of agony she knew she had convinced him. He was going to take the job in Washington, but he insisted he was going to fly back to see her often. She knew the kind of scandal that could create, and she vowed to herself she wouldn't let him. She had to be strong for him. She knew that any hold she kept on him, any contact, any relationship, would destroy him. She was tainted now, and if he had been a different man, it would have been a different story. But his life was ahead of him, and his eyes lit up every time he talked about the new job in Washington with the senator from California. She couldn't rob him of that, or all that might come of it. He could do great things one day, and she wasn't going to be the one to stop him.

She knew he belonged with Elizabeth too, no matter how much he argued with Crystal about it. And as Crystal thought of giving him up to her, she felt like a mother leaving her baby on a doorstep.

He left her late one afternoon, and they kissed long and hard as the sun set behind them. He still wanted her to come with him but she refused till the end. He only agreed to go with the understanding that he'd come back soon, but she knew better. She stood tall and proud, waving at him as though she expected to see him again, but she didn't. She knew she wouldn't let him come back again. It was too dangerous for him and in time she knew he would thank her. She lay on her bed, after he was gone, sobbing as though her heart would break. He was gone again, and no matter how much she loved him, this time it had to be forever. Setting him free had been her final gift to him. It was all she had left to give. He had all the rest, her heart, her soul, her body.

CHAPTER 37

Crystal offered the cottage to Boyd and Hiroko and they moved in in March, after cleaning it up and painting it, and pulling the weeds out of the yard and planting a garden. She had hired two men to tend the corn, and hired new Mexicans to work the vineyard. Boyd still went to his gas station every day, but Hiroko and Crystal worked like slaves to get the ranch house back in shape, with little Jane to help them.

And in April, the sun was already warm, and after scrubbing the walls all day, and then painting them late into the night, Crystal almost fainted. Hiroko helped her into a chair and looked at her with a worried frown. There was something wrong with her, no matter how much Crystal denied it. But the past two months had taken their toll on her, and the trial before that, and worse still the time with Ernie. But the worst of it was the ache she felt for Spencer. He had called several times, but she was vague with him and insisted that he not come back out yet. He was working for the senator, running the campaign from Washington and he loved the job, but he still wanted to come back to see Crystal. She told him somewhat callously that she was seeing someone in town, and that she had the ranch well in hand now. And he was with Elizabeth, who once again in spite of everything had refused to divorce him.

Hiroko put a damp cloth on Crystal's brow and sat down next to her, and insisted that she had to see a doctor.

"Don't be ridiculous. I'm fine. I'm just not used to working this hard anymore." But the ranch was looking clean again, and almost better than it had before. Her father would have been proud of it, and Boyd couldn't believe the changes she'd made in such a short time. She'd been home for two months now.

Three days later, she fainted again, this

time, pulling weeds in her garden, and Jane found her lying there and ran back to the cottage to find her mother. She liked her new home and her new friend, and Crystal had promised to teach her to ride in the summer. But this time, Boyd drove her into town, and dropped her off in front of Dr. Goode's office.

"Get your ass in there, Crystal Wyatt. Or do I have to drag you?"

She grinned at him, it was a warm day, but she was cold and had worn a heavy sweater. He was afraid it was something serious, and it was. Dr. Goode told her in no uncertain terms that she was pregnant. She had stared at him in shocked disbelief, but when she counted back, she knew he was right, and that night she told Hiroko.

"What are you going to do?" Hiroko asked quietly. She knew only too well how much Crystal loved Spencer, and that she had sent him away for his own good, not because she didn't love him.

Crystal looked at her sadly, but there was no doubt in her mind, about the baby or what she wanted. "I'm going to have the baby." It was all she had left of him, and she had a home for the child. It was due in late November. She knew she must have gotten pregnant the first time they made love in San Francisco.

Boyd was stunned when Hiroko told him the news, and Crystal swore him to secrecy, much to his chagrin. He thought she should tell Spencer. But Crystal was adamant. Spencer was well on his way now. And she was going to see that he stayed there.

"You mean you're not going to tell him?"

She shook her head. It was the last thing she would do. She had already cost him one job, and what was happening to him now was much too important. "I'm not going to tell anyone, except you two." She wasn't even going to tell Harry and Pearl. They were part of another life. And she was going to stay in the valley until she had the baby. And as she grew slowly over the summer months, all she could think of was Spencer's child. It was the one great joy in her life . . . her final memory of Spencer.

CHAPTER 38

Crystal had been right. Spencer loved his job. Working for the young senator was exactly what he had wanted. He worked long hours, and the responsibilities on him were enormous. He was suddenly at the hub of the political world, and his legal background stood him in good stead there. He was even thinking about running for Congress himself eventually. But he liked the senator too much to leave him for the moment.

Even Elizabeth was pleased, and it was the only reason why, once again, she had refused to divorce him. In spite of his performance at the trial, and the affair she assumed he'd had, she finally had what she wanted. She was married to "someone important." She'd been furious when he'd come home, and for the first week he'd been back, he scarcely saw her. He was getting ready to move out. With or without Crystal, he knew he could no longer stay married. Being with her had shown him all the more what had been missing with Elizabeth, and he was no longer willing to live without it. He would have preferred being alone, as he told her, when they finally talked about it. And he offered her no lies, no excuses, no explanations.

"It's not good for either of us. You deserve better and so do I." It was the week after he'd taken the job, and after her threats before the trial, and the length of time he'd stayed away afterward, he couldn't believe that she wouldn't divorce him. They had nothing left, and it was an open secret between them that he had spent the last several weeks with Crystal. "I think it's time to call it off." But she was intrigued by his job. It was the first thing he'd done that she thought really had merit. And people were talking about the brilliant job he'd done defending the movie star. Instead of being angry, she was proud, and he realized how little he knew her. It was fame, at any price, that mattered to her, even at the expense of their marriage.

"Why don't we wait a while, Spencer? We've waited this long, we might as well stick it out a little longer." She had looked prim, and she was certainly not feeling romantic. But nor was he. He knew that his days of pretending to himself he loved Elizabeth were long since over. But now he didn't want to play the game. He wanted out, and that was exactly what he told her.

"Why in God's name do you want to continue this, Elizabeth? We're not even friends anymore. Don't you care?" But the truth was, she didn't.

"I like what you're doing these days, Spencer." Being the wife of a senator's aide intrigued her.

"Are you serious?" He was shocked.

"Yes, I am. I'm willing to keep this going, if you are. In fact, I'm not going to let you out." As usual, she was blunt with him. "You owe me this." He was livid.

"For what?"

"You made a fool of me with that girl, and if you think I'm going to divorce you so you can marry her, you're crazy." He didn't tell her that Crystal had sent him back and advised him, for the sake of his career, to stay married.

"I'd like to marry her." He wasn't going to lie to her. "But the truth is, she doesn't want to."

"She's either a fool, or very wise. I'm not sure which."

"She wants to be alone, she says, and she thinks that she would hurt my career."

"She's right. And she's smarter than I thought." She didn't tell him that that told her how much Crystal loved him. Elizabeth wasn't going to champion Crystal's cause to him and she wanted to stay married to Spencer. "Is she going back to Hollywood?"

He shook his head. "No, she went home. That's all over for her."

"And where's home?" She was curious. It seemed wise to know as much as possible about her opponent.

"That's not important."

"Are you going to see her again?" She knew from the look in his eyes that he would if Crystal would let him. But she sensed that something had happened before he came home, and she suspected correctly that Crystal had sent him back. He wouldn't have come otherwise. But now that Elizabeth had him back, she was going to do everything in her power to keep him. "You're a damn fool if you stay involved

with her. And I don't think your senator
would like it."

"That's my problem, not yours." He didn't
want to discuss Crystal with his wife. He was
thinking about her night and day. But when he
called her, she was still adamant about being
alone. She told him their lives were too different, and nothing he said seemed to sway her.

But he was so busy at work that the weeks
seemed to fly by, and in the end he never
moved out and Elizabeth didn't ask him. He
even saw her parents less than he had in the
past, although her father congratulated him on
his new job. And he was pleased for Elizabeth
too. She had been groomed to be the wife of an
important man, and now Spencer could give
her what she wanted.

Spencer never understood why, but he went
on living in the house in Georgetown. He was
always too busy to move, and Elizabeth left
him alone. She went to parties with him, and
helped him entertain, and she had a busy life of
her own, with social activities and friends and
law school. She never complained about the
status quo, and within months, he realized that
being married to her was useful. He felt guilty
for seeing it that way, but Washington was a
strange town, and politics even more so. And it

did him no harm to be married to Justice Barclay's daughter.

By the fall, he'd been working for the senator for six months, and he was so busy, it didn't matter who he was married to. Except for social functions when she was in the room with him somewhere, he never saw her.

He hardly had time to call Crystal anymore and she was always cool when he spoke to her. She said she was fine, and told him about the ranch, but she made it clear that she didn't want to see him. She had sent him home to Elizabeth and Washington and now once again, he was trapped there. It was exactly what she had wanted for him, and what she had instinctively known that he needed.

It was Thanksgiving before he saw his family again. Elizabeth put on a very pretty dinner. His parents came down from New York and stayed with them, and once again his father congratulated himself for urging Spencer to stay married to her during his early days of unrest after Korea. The Barclays were pleased too, and no one asked when they were going to have children, it was obvious how busy they were, and in June Elizabeth would finish law school.

"Imagine that," Spencer's father joked, "two lawyers under one roof. You can start your own law firm." If so, Spencer thought to himself, it would be the only thing they had in common. But Elizabeth gave nothing away, she was as charming and poised as she had ever been, and everyone who met Spencer's wife loved her. There was a bright future ahead of them, and Justice Barclay had suggested that after a reasonable term with the young senator, Spencer look to his own career and run for office. Like Elizabeth, he thought Spencer should run for Congress. But it was too soon for that. Spencer was wrapped up in his job, and he buried himself in his work in order to flee the loneliness of his marriage. At thirty-six, he had gone far. But in the process he had lost what he wanted most . . . not his wife . . . but the girl he had met on the ranch nine years before. He had lost Crystal.

CHAPTER
39 —————————————————

Crystal gave her own Thanksgiving dinner too. She stuffed a turkey, and made homemade cranberries and yams, and tiny ears of corn in the freshly painted kitchen. Hiroko and Boyd came to dinner with Jane, and Boyd smiled at how enormous she was as she sat down with them and Jane said grace. The baby was due any minute. And Boyd knew without asking her again that Spencer knew nothing about his baby. It broke his heart to see the loneliness on her face, but she had been adamant from the first and she stuck by her decision, no matter what it cost her. Boyd thought she still heard from him from time to time. She told them about his rising star in Washington, and the senator's aide, but most of the time she was very quiet.

The ranch house seemed very different now, everything was clean and new and freshly painted. He hardly recognized it as they sat down to dinner at the big oak table in the cozy yellow kitchen. He couldn't even imagine her mother there anymore, and mercifully neither could Crystal. She still thought of her father as she went for long walks. She couldn't ride anymore until after the baby, but she seemed to have enough to do, and she had turned Jared's room into a nursery. It was painted pale blue, with white eyelet curtains.

"What if it's a girl?" Boyd teased that night before they left.

She smiled peacefully at him. "It won't be."

And the next morning when Hiroko came by to check on her, she found her sitting quietly in her room with a look of intense concentration. It stirred a chord of memory, and as she watched, she saw Crystal's face crease with pain.

"The baby is coming, no?"

"Yes." Crystal smiled through her pain, and a moment later she was gripping the arms of her chair. She was unable to speak, and Hiroko ran to get Boyd and told him to call the doctor. They had urged her to go to the hospital months before, but Crystal had said she wanted to have the baby at home. People still knew her face, the movies she had made were still being shown, and more than once people had noticed her in town and stared, wondering if she was the same woman. She wanted no one to know about the baby, no newspapers, no press. The word could not get out. If it did, there would be fresh scandal, and Spencer would know too. She wanted to avoid that at any price. But the price, Boyd and Hiroko knew only too well, could be the baby. They had lost their second child that way, and they would have lost Jane if Crystal hadn't been there. But Dr. Goode said she was healthy and young. There was no reason for a twenty-four-year-old girl not to give birth at home if that was what she wanted.

Boyd called Dr. Goode, and an hour later he came, and by then Crystal could hardly catch her breath between the pains. Her face was drenched with sweat and Hiroko was sitting beside her, holding her hands as Crystal had once done for her. Boyd took Jane outside and let her play in the garden, as Dr. Goode and Hiroko worked, and Crystal labored.

Hiroko came out for a few minutes in the

late afternoon, she looked worried and strained, and she told her husband to go home with their daughter. Dr. Goode had said it might still be hours.

"Nothing yet?" He was worried about their friend. She'd been in labor for a long time and it was hard to imagine that the baby wasn't there yet.

"The doctor say the baby very big." Boyd searched her eyes, remembering their own experience with Jane, but his wife smiled before going back inside again. "Maybe soon." They were the same words she told Crystal a few minutes later as she fought to push the baby out, with Dr. Goode's experienced old hands to help her. He was the same doctor who had refused to come to Hiroko seven and a half years before, or to care for her during her pregnancy because he had lost his own son to the Japanese. But he watched her now, and was touched by her gentleness and compassion and wisdom. She seemed to be lit from within by something deeply warm and kind and religious, and for the briefest of moments he wanted to tell her he was sorry. He knew their second child had died, and wondered if he could have helped them. Hiroko said nothing to him as he watched her, she only encouraged Crystal quietly, letting her squeeze her hands, and crying as the pains came now, longer and harder, but still there was no baby.

"We may have to take her in." He was beginning to consider a cesarean, but Crystal roused herself from her ravaged state and looked at him with such violence he was startled.

"No! I'm staying here!" A year before she had been accused of murder. And all she needed now to complete the picture to end Spencer's career was an illegitimate baby. If anyone even thought it was his, it would be all over the papers by morning. "No! I'll do it myself . . . oh God . . ." Another pain tore through her before she could speak again, and knowing what the doctor wanted to do, she pushed harder. It moved down farther that time, and then she pushed again, and the doctor nodded.

"If you can do a few more of those for me, we might just have a baby here before much longer." She smiled weakly at Hiroko between the pains, and without explaining where he had gone, the doctor went to call his nurse. He warned her that they might need an ambulance at the Wyatt ranch. There was a chance that they might have to take Crystal into the hospital at Napa. He wasn't going to risk her life if it went on for much longer. The nurse promised to stand by, and let the ambulance driver know just in case. And when he went back to her, he saw that she had made a little progress. "Again! . . . that's it . . . push harder now! . . . harder!" She couldn't push any harder, her eyes were almost popping out and her face was red and she strained so hard she almost felt her body explode as there was an enormous pressure, like an express train, tearing through her. She couldn't stop it now, she had to push all the time, as Hiroko watched with eyes filled with wonder. A small red face popped out from between Crystal's legs, with a head full of silky black hair, and he gave an angry cry as Dr. Goode gently turned his shoulders and delivered the rest of him and laid him on his mother's stomach. She was so tired she could barely speak, but she smiled down at him through her tears and then she laughed as she looked at him.

"He's so beautiful . . . oh, he's so beautiful . . ." And even Hiroko saw that he was the image of Spencer. Crystal smiled at the doctor victoriously after he had cut the cord and Hiroko had cleaned her up and wrapped the baby in a clean white blanket. "I told you I could do it myself."

He smiled in answer. "You had me worried for a while. That little man of yours must weigh a good ten pounds." They weighed him on the kitchen scale, and he was right. Spencer's son weighed ten pounds and seven ounces. The doctor handed him back to his mother and she smiled at him again. He was a gift straight from the hand of God, and that was exactly what she called him. Zebediah. Gift of God. It was a strong name for a strong child, born of the love she had carried for so long for his father.

The doctor stayed for a little while as she and the baby slept peacefully. It had been a day of hard work for all of them, and most of all for Crystal. He left the room quietly, and found Hiroko sitting alone in the living room. She offered him a cup of steaming tea, and hesitating for a moment, he took it. It was difficult for him to speak to her even now, but she had earned his respect that day, and in an odd way he was sorry it hadn't come sooner.

"You were a great help to me, Mrs. Webster," he said carefully, and she smiled. She was wise beyond her years. Life hadn't been easy for her, but it had brought her rich blessings, thanks to her husband and Crystal.

"Thank you." She smiled shyly at him, and when he left he solemnly shook her hand. It wasn't an apology, it was too late for that. But it was a first step toward acceptance.

He told his nurse about it the next morning when he went back to his office. It had taken them ten years, but they had finally forgiven her for being Japanese, and come to understand that Hiroko Webster was a good woman. She noticed people looking at her differently after that, and one day when she went to the store with Jane, the woman at the cash register smiled and said hello, after ten years of serving her in silence.

Crystal's baby grew healthy and strong. She was back on her feet remarkably quickly, and when he was a month old, they christened him in the church where her sister had gotten married. He was Zebediah Tad Wyatt, and his godparents were Boyd and Hiroko Webster, and after the service Crystal let little Jane hold him. She struggled with the weight of the sleeping child, and they all laughed, and then she looked up at them with a worried frown, speaking to Crystal and asking a question that brought tears to her eyes.

"Who's going to be his daddy?"

Crystal fought back the tears as she looked down at her, holding the baby that was Spencer's. "I guess he just has me. Maybe that means we'll all have to love him a little more." And one day she wondered if Zeb would ask her the same question.

"Can I be his aunt?"

"Sure you can." The tears slid down Crystal's cheeks as she kissed them both. "Aunt Jane. He's going to love you so much when he's a little bigger." The child looked pleased as she handed Zebediah Wyatt back to his mother.

CHAPTER
40

Four days after Thanksgiving, on November 26, 1956, Zebediah celebrated his first birthday. Ingrid Bergman had made *Anastasia* that year after recovering from just the kind of scandal Crystal was so grateful she had avoided. She was certainly not as well known as the Swedish actress was, but after the murder trial the year before, she would have been the source of fresh scandal, and she was desperately glad she wasn't.

Crystal made Zeb's cake herself, and he chortled happily as he plunged both hands into it, and Jane helped clean him up. She was eight and she adored the child. He was her very favorite playmate.

Hiroko was slowly being accepted now, in tacit ways, by people who had shunned her for a decade. But Jane was still paying the price for her parents' courage, and most of the children she went to school with teased her and called her a half-breed. It made her shy and afraid of them, and wise beyond her years. And with Hiroko's gentle teaching, she was acquiring the gifts of forgiveness and patience. She carried Zeb everywhere she went on the ranch, and she was an enormous help to Crystal, who was busy overseeing everything, and sometimes she even worked in the fields herself. The ranch was doing well and she had sold off a small piece of land to pay for more improvements. But she also knew by then that it was never going to eke out more than a pittance for her. The best she could do was make the ranch support itself, and pay for minimal necessities for herself and Zeb. It was never going to make them rich, or give them even small luxuries, and for months now she'd been worried.

She saw the Websters struggling day by day and she gave them free rent, but like the ranch, the gas station barely broke even. And now she had Zeb to think about. She knew that soon she would have to get a job and put some money away for his future. She knew she wouldn't sell the ranch. She still remembered her father's words, telling her not to sell the ranch, and she wouldn't have no matter what. It was her home, and Zeb's, and now the Websters'.

She didn't say anything about her concerns when Spencer called. He still did from time to time, but fearing he'd hear the baby in the background, she was short with him. And he called less and less often. It only tortured him to hear her voice, and she had told him in no uncertain terms that she didn't want to see him. She was terrified he'd see Zeb, if he came back, and it was a secret she guarded with her life now. She knew that Spencer was doing well, and she read about him once in *Time*, and on occasion even in the local papers.

And by the spring of 1957, the country was enjoying economic prosperity, which seemed to have little to do with the realities of Crystal's life and Crystal knew that she had to do something soon. It had been a hard winter for them, and there was no hiding from it anymore. She had to get a job to earn more money.

Zeb was eighteen months old and running everywhere after Jane. He could hardly wait

for her to come home from school every day.
And on a May afternoon, she and Hiroko were
following them down the dirt road that ran
through the vineyards. She had made the decision the night before, after months of thinking
about it. It was the only thing she knew, and
after two years the scandal had died down. She
knew she had to go back to Hollywood and try
it. Hiroko looked at her with unhappy eyes
when she told her. She had always wondered if
Crystal would go back. And in an odd way it
didn't surprise her. But they would be heartbroken to see her go, she might even sell the
ranch out from under them. But Crystal was
quick to reassure them, and what she said next
overwhelmed Hiroko.

"I want to leave Zeb here with you." She
was watching him follow Jane, as the older
child giggled, and Zeb laughed the belly laugh
that touched his mother's heart. Every moment, every day, he was a constant reminder of
his father.

"You will go to Los Angeles without him?"
Hiroko couldn't believe it.

"I have to. Look what happened to Ingrid
Bergman. It could be years before they let me
back on a picture. They might not anyway.
But it's worth a try. It's the only thing I know
how to do." And she knew she'd been good at

it. She had seen one of her films the year before, and had been intrigued to see herself on the screen. And now at twenty-five, there was a maturity to her looks that seemed to have enhanced her beauty although she didn't know it. She'd be twenty-six that year, and she had a child to think about. But the time to go was now, before she got any older and they forgot her completely. She had lost touch with everyone there, purposely, and now she'd have to start again. But this time she would do it with the hard work, and no easy introductions through a man like Ernie. She would never take favors from anyone again. She had learned that lesson. That night Hiroko told her husband and he was as startled as she had been to hear that Crystal was leaving.

"She's leaving Zeb with us?" Hiroko nodded and Boyd was touched. It was the ultimate sign of how much she trusted them. They knew how desperately Crystal loved her son, and in June, Crystal cried constantly for a week before she left him. It was like tearing her heart from her soul, but she knew she had to do it, for his sake. It was better now than ten years later, and by then it would be too late for her. By Hollywood standards, she wasn't getting any younger.

"What if he forgets me?" she cried softly to

her friend, as Hiroko watched her agonize about leaving him. She wondered if she would be able to do it.

But on a clear day in June, she kissed him for a last time, and stood for a long time on the porch in the morning sun, looking out over her land, feeling the same tug at her heart she always felt when she looked at the earth left to her by her father. She held Zebediah close to her, and smelled the sweetness of his flesh, and then with a strangled sob, she handed him to Hiroko.

"Take good care of him. . . ." He cried and stretched out his arms. He had never been away from her for a single hour since his birth. And now she was leaving him. She had promised to come back as soon as she could, but her finances wouldn't allow her to come back often.

Boyd drove her into town, and watched her get on the bus. She wheeled and hugged him again, her eyes filled with tears as he held her. "Take care of my baby. . . ."

"He'll be all right. Just take care of yourself." He couldn't help but think of the disasters that had befallen her before, but this time she was older and smarter.

She stopped in San Francisco for a day to buy clothes, and she was careful with her purchases. She had to be cautious with the little money she had, and this time she knew exactly what she needed. She bought dresses that showed off her figure without being vulgar, and realized how thin she had gotten working on the ranch. In jeans, she never thought of it, but now she could see how much weight she'd lost, but it only made her legs look longer, her waist smaller, and her bust fuller. She bought hats that accented her face, and high-heeled shoes she could hardly walk in. And she stopped to see Harry and Pearl, and she had dinner with them. She sang for them at the restaurant one night, just to see how it would feel, for old times' sake, and she was surprised she could still do it. But being there again reminded her of the night Spencer had found her there after his engagement. Everything everywhere always reminded her of him. She only hoped that L.A. wouldn't remind her of Ernie.

She arrived in Hollywood the next day, and felt like a forgotten face. No one seemed to notice her as she checked into a cheap hotel. She was just another pretty girl coming to Tinsel Town to be discovered.

She waited one day, to get her bearings, and she called home twice. Zeb was fine, he was eating well, and he had gone back to the big house looking for her, but Jane had followed him and brought him back, and Hiroko insisted that he seemed happy. And on the following morning, with trembling hands, she dialed one of the agents she had met years before. It had been five years since she'd first come to L.A. with Pearl, but this time she knew what she was doing. He gave her an appointment and she went to see him that afternoon, but he was blunt with her.

"I couldn't give you away, if you want to know the truth."

"Why?" Her eyes were wide and sad, but she was still breathtaking as he looked at her. It was a damn shame, but it was the truth. He couldn't use her.

"You killed a guy. This is a funny town. Everyone would do anything they could to anyone, and they've got the ethics of a dog in heat. But when it comes to the morals clause in their contracts, the studios want virgins. They want everyone to stay clean, act nice. You can't be queer, or crazy, or act horny. You get knocked up, you shack up with someone's wife, you kill someone God forbid, and it's all over. Take my advice, sweetheart, go back to where you been for the last two years and forget it."

It was as simple as he said, and she thought of taking his advice. But she had enough money to stay for at least two months, and she wasn't ready to give up yet. She saw three more agents the next week, and they told her the same thing, although in slightly subtler terms. But the message was the same. Her Hollywood career was over. They admitted that her last two movies had been good, and her voice was great, and all of the directors she'd worked with had liked her, but in spite of all of that, the studios wouldn't touch her.

Two weeks after she'd arrived, it was a blisteringly sunny day and she sat wilting in a restaurant drinking lemonade and she saw one of the men she had starred with. He stared at her from afar at first, and then he walked slowly toward her.

"Crystal, is that you?" She nodded and took off her hat, and smiled. He'd been a kind man despite his fame, and he'd been nice to work with.

"Yes. At least I think so. How've you been, Lou?"

"I've been okay. Where the hell have you been all this time?"

"Gone." They both knew why, but he didn't mention the trial or Ernie's murder.

"What are you doing here? Are you working on a picture?" He hadn't heard that she was back in town, he hadn't seen it in the trades, and they'd never been close, but he liked her.

He'd always thought it was too bad that things went wrong for her. She'd been a pro, and he'd always thought she'd make it big one day. But so had Ernie.

She laughed and shook her head. "No, I'm not working." There was a look of resignation in her eyes when she answered him. "No one will touch me."

"The guys play rough here." He had had his own problems over rumors that he was gay. And he had had to marry his lover's sister. Now everything was fine again. No one was willing to accept the truth in Hollywood. You had to play by their rules or forget it. "Who's your agent?"

"Same story."

"Shit." He sat down in an empty chair, wishing he could help her, and then he had a thought. "Have you gone to any of the directors directly? Sometimes that works. If they want you, they twist the right arms, and presto magic, the phone rings and you're working."

She shook her head again. "I think in my case, it may not be quite that simple."

"Look . . . where are you staying?" She told him and he jotted it down on a napkin. "Don't do anything. Don't move. I'll call you." He felt so damn sorry for her as he walked away, he knew how touchy it was, but she didn't expect him to help and she didn't expect him to call her.

She had all but given up two weeks later, and she was aching for Zeb, as the phone rang in her stifling hotel room. It was late July, and she was ready to give up and go home. There was no point staying there through August. But when she answered the phone, it was Lou . . .

"Got a pencil, Crystal? Write this down." He gave her two names, one was a director, and the other a very well-known producer. They made the kind of films that won Academy Awards and she almost laughed at him for suggesting that she call them. "Look, I talked to both of them, they're great guys. The director wasn't sure how much he could do for you, but he wants to try. But Brian Ford told me to be sure to have you call him."

"I don't know, Lou. I think I've given up, but thanks."

"Look," he sounded annoyed, "if you don't call them, you'll embarrass me. I told them you really want to work again. Now do you or don't you?"

"I do . . . but . . . do they know about the trial?"

"Are you kidding?" He laughed ruefully. Sixteen people had told him to tell her to go to hell. They knew. They all did. "Just give it a whirl. What have you got to lose except empty pockets?" He was right, and she called both the next morning. Frank Williams was honest with her, he said it would be nearly impossible for her to find work, but he offered to give her a fresh screen test, and if it was worth anything, she could use it. She decided to do that first, and once they had it, she'd call the producer.

The first screen test they did was weak, she was nervous and felt as though she'd forgotten everything she once knew. But Frank insisted they try again, and this one was better. He stood watching it critically with her and told her what she'd done wrong. She knew she needed a coach again, but she couldn't afford one. She wondered if it was even worthwhile calling Brian Ford. The screen test wasn't great, she was tired and hot, and she had an ugly past behind her. But again for Lou's sake, she called, so that his efforts wouldn't have been for nothing. And at least this way she could tell him that she tried before she went home to her ranch and her baby. She was almost glad it hadn't worked. She couldn't stand being away from him any longer.

Brian Ford's secretary gave her an appointment for the following afternoon, and seemed to know who she was. And the next day, Crystal took a taxi to his office. It was in North Hollywood and she watched the meter nervously. She had forgotten that taxis were that expensive. She'd been in town for exactly five weeks, and her meager funds were dwindling quickly. She was almost afraid to eat some days, and with the heat and missing Zeb, she was never hungry.

The secretary asked her to wait, and it seemed to take forever, and finally she ushered her in. Crystal was wearing a white dress with a long slit in a narrow skirt, and she had brushed her platinum hair until it shone, and for once she had worn it hanging straight down her back as she had done long ago as a child in the summer. She was wearing high-heeled white sandals and she carried gloves, but she wore almost no makeup. She was tired of dressing up, of pretending she was something she wasn't. She wanted to go home and put on her jeans, and this was the last stop. She just wanted to get it over with and go home, and there was some of that in her eyes as the secretary ushered her into Ford's office. It was a huge, beautifully decorated room, with Oscars lined up on a shelf along one wall, a fireplace, a huge glass desk, and a thick gray carpet. As he watched her cross the room, she was aware of a powerful man with snow-white hair, sharp blue eyes, and when he stood up, she saw that he was a giant. He stood six feet five, and he had a deep melodious voice. A long time in the past, he had been an actor. But he had decided early on that other things intrigued him more than learning lines. He had been a director at twenty-five, and ten years later he was producing major movies. And now at fifty-five, he had two decades of film history behind him. He had been making fine films for years, and was respected by everyone. Crystal was sharply aware of what an honor it was that he was even seeing her, which showed only how much respect and affection he had for Lou.

He smiled at her easily, invited her to sit down, offered her a cigarette which she refused, and lighted one himself, narrowing his eyes as he watched her. He looked as though he should have been riding a horse, or walking through the fields as her father had, instead of sitting behind a desk, producing movies. He had none of the glib, shiny ways of the late Ernesto Salvatore. This man was both dignified and important.

"Lou tells me you've had a rough time since you got back." She nodded, she didn't even feel nervous with him. He seemed almost like a father.

"I guess I expected it." And they both knew why, but he was polite enough not to mention it.

"Any luck at all?" He narrowed his eyes in the smoke of his own cigarette, as she shook her head.

"None. I'm going home tomorrow."

"That's too bad. I came up with an idea for you." But she wasn't even sure she cared. Anything she did here would keep her from Zeb, and she had decided that wasn't what she wanted. "We're putting together a new film right now. I'd like to write in a small part for you. Just to get your feet wet again. Nothing big. But it might give us a chance to see what kind of reaction you get."

"Is it a studio film?" She knew by then they wouldn't let her work, no matter how small the part, but he shook his head as he looked at her. Frank Williams had already shown him her test and he liked it.

"No, I'm making it as an independent. They'll handle the distribution for us of course. But they can't say anything about who's in the picture." He had even thought about suggesting a new name for her, but he didn't really want to. No matter what else she'd done,

Crystal Wyatt had begun to be known as a very fine actress. "Do you want to give it some thought? We're not starting till September."

"Would you want me to sign a contract with you?"

He smiled and shook his head again. "Only for this picture. I'm not in the business of owning slaves." She knew then that he knew her history with Ernie, and he was willing to let her work anyway. She felt a wave of gratitude wash over her, and she was tempted to try it.

"Can I think about it for a few days?" But they both knew it was the only chance she'd get. She wasn't being coy with him, she just wanted to decide if leaving Zeb again was worth it.

He shook her hand again, and walked her out, and she felt strangely comfortable with him. Lou had been right. Brian Ford was a nice man and he was opening the door to her to get back into pictures. She lay awake and thought about it all that night, and then she called him back the next morning and accepted his offer. He sounded pleased with the news, and told her he'd send her the contract and the script.

"Have a lawyer check the contract out for you." Again, a far cry from Ernie. "You don't have to be on the set till September fifteenth."

Which was the best news she'd heard all week. She could go home to Zeb for August and half of September. She called Lou and thanked him and got the name of his lawyer who took care of the contract. Then she flew home that afternoon after giving the Ford office her address. And that night she was on the bus back to the valley. She was still touched by how kind Brian Ford had been to her, and as she sat in her kitchen holding her baby in her arms that night, she smiled to herself. It had worked! She'd done it! But the best part was being home with him. For six weeks she ran and played with him, never leaving him for more than a few moments.

Boyd and Hiroko were excited for her, and six weeks later she flew south again. The part was small, but Ford had seen to it that it was a good one. He wanted her to do well. He thought she had talent, and he liked her.

There was an honesty about her that appealed to him, an openness, a warmth, and a quiet courage born of the hard times she'd had. It was a rich addition to her beauty and it gave substance to her acting. And as usual, when he saw the rushes every day, he knew he'd been right. She was good. Very good. He offered her another film after that, and by Christmas, when she went home to Zeb, she had enough money to buy them all decent presents. She had to fly right back again, and she worked hard for him until March, but the second picture was good, and when it came out, the critics loved her. And the past was suddenly forgotten. She was their sweetheart again, only for the right reasons this time. She was a fine actress performing in fine films, made by one of Hollywood's most prestigious producers. There was no sleaze, no pressure, no slimy deals, no underworld. The ghost of Ernie Salvatore had been laid to rest, and Crystal Wyatt had not only survived but triumphed.

Spencer saw her second film alone in Washington one night, and he was stunned to see her in films again. He hadn't called her in months, and he had known nothing of her revived career. He only sat staring at the screen, feeling a dull ache in his heart as he watched her. And the next morning he tried to call her. But the phone at the ranch didn't answer, and he had no idea how to find her in Hollywood. And there was no point calling anyway. She had made herself clear the last time he talked to her. She didn't want him to call her. His own life was full. He was now the senator's most important aide, and he had decided not to run for Congress.

It was early 1959 by then, and Crystal was

starting work on a new picture. She had her own apartment and for the first time she felt secure in her work. The studios all wanted her now, but she liked working independently for Brian Ford. It limited her a little bit, but she loved the quality of the films he made, and he had taught her a lot. And she was making plenty of money. He took her out to dinner now and then, and they were good friends, but he never wanted more from her than she cared to offer. She lived only for her child. She talked to Zeb on the phone every night, and lived to go home to him during the interludes between her pictures.

She was having dinner with Brian at Chasen's one night when he turned to her, and smiled quietly. "Just exactly what is it that you run back to up north all the time?" He had assumed it was a man, because she never got involved with anyone, but she smiled and hesitated before answering. She knew she could trust him though, and feeling unusually expansive, she told him.

"My ranch, and my son. He lives there with old friends of mine while I'm working." Brian Ford frowned as he glanced at her, and then lowered his voice when he spoke again.

"Crystal, were you ever married?" She shook her head, he hadn't thought she was.

"Don't ever tell anyone that. Remember what they did to Ingrid Bergman. They'll run you out of this town so fast, you won't know what hit you."

"I know." She sighed. "That's why I leave him there." Murder they could tolerate, apparently, but not illegitimate children.

"How old is he?" He was curious now, about whose child it was. Maybe that was why she had murdered Ernie, maybe it was something to do with the child. He never asked her about it, and he wouldn't now, but the thought crossed his mind as she answered.

"He's two and a half." Ernie had been dead for three and a half years, and that told him what he wanted to know.

"He's not Ernie's then."

"God, no!" She laughed. "I would have killed myself rather than have his child."

He smiled too. "I can't say I disagree with you. I always felt sorry about your getting involved with him. Someone should have killed him a long time before you did."

"I didn't kill him," she spoke quietly, looking deep into his eyes. "But the only defense we had was to make it look like self-defense. There were no witnesses who saw me leave the house in Malibu, or get home. And the police said I had the motive and the opportunity. But we took the only road open to us at the time. And we won. I guess that's all that matters now." Except that people still thought she'd killed a man, and it still hurt that that was what they thought. In their eyes, she was a murderess. As she thought of it, she realized again that it was remarkable she was working at all. She looked up at him with a gentle smile, her eyes full of the respect she had for him. "Thank you for trusting me. You've taught me an awful lot."

"Those things always work both ways." And then he wondered about the man again. "Does the boy's father live with you on the ranch?" He assumed that that was why she always went back right after a film, not only for the child, but for his father.

But she shook her head quietly. She had made her peace with it. She had been right to let him go. And it always pleased her to hear that Spencer was doing well. He was gone from her life now but she had Zeb for the rest of her life. It was a special gift . . . her little gift from God. "His father left before he was born. He doesn't know about his son."

Brian looked at her long and hard, fresh respect growing for her. "You've had a hell of a hard time." She smiled. Some things she regretted in her life, but never her baby. They talked about her new movie then, and he had other plans, and then he smiled easily as he paid the check. "We're going to get you an Oscar one of these days." But she wasn't dying for that. She was a star again, a big one now. People recognized her everywhere, and people asked for autographs frequently when she went out. They even recognized her now when she went back to the ranch, but she kept a low profile there. She didn't want anyone to discover Zeb and leak it to the press.

Brian took her out again several times after that, and when the film ended, he gave a huge party for the wrap. He asked a few friends to stay and Crystal found herself among them. As they all watched the sun come up there was a Mexican breakfast served to them on his patio, and he talked quietly to her about his sons. Both of them had died in the war, and his marriage had never recovered from it. Eventually he and his wife had divorced and she had gone back to New York. He told Crystal it had changed his life irreparably. He had no desire to marry again, and now she understood why, when she had once invited him to the ranch, he had declined. He knew about Zeb so she had nothing to hide from him, and she wasn't involved with him, she had just wanted to show a kindness to a friend. But seeing her son would have hurt too much. He explained that he didn't even like to be around children anymore, they reminded him too much of his sons. They had both paid a high price for the lives they had, and yet it gave them both greater depth. It showed in the quality of the movies he made, and the way Crystal played her parts.

They talked for hours and after everyone left, he drove her home. She was going back to the ranch again in a few days. And she was planning to stay there for the summer months and start work on a film again in the fall. For the first time it was for another director. But he had encouraged her to do it, saying it would be good for her to change. And he had another project for her after that. It seemed as though the projects they would share stretched on for years. When they arrived at her apartment she invited him upstairs, but he said he was too tired after the long night. He drove away, but late that afternoon he called her. He wondered if she wanted to have dinner before she left town, and she was touched that he had called her.

They went to a restaurant in Glendale, and when they sat at a quiet table in the back, and as he looked at her quietly Crystal thought his eyes looked sad. She wondered what was bothering him and was surprised when he took her hand in his own large one.

"I don't know how to say this to you. I've thought about it for a long time, and somehow it sounds foolish now." She wondered what was troubling him, as she held his hand, and smiled warmly at him. She was deeply fond of the man. He was fifty-seven years old, and she would turn twenty-eight that summer on the ranch, and she was touched that he valued her friendship. "I'd like to spend some time with you when you get back. It's going to be strange watching you work for someone else this time. I'll miss you."

She laughed gently at him. "Of course I'll spend some time with you. And I won't be gone for long. Besides, we're starting work next January on your new film." But he knew she didn't understand what he was saying to her.

"I mean I'd like to go away with you for a few days." She was startled as she looked up at him. He had never said anything like that to her before. "You're the first woman I've really talked to in a long time." He was still amazed he had told her about his sons. He had never told anyone about that in recent years. Much of his spare time he spent alone, gardening, reading quietly, going for long walks, working on new ideas and reading scripts for future productions. In the midst of the chaos of Hollywood, he was a solid, peaceful, solitary man with brains and dignity and distinction.

"Would you like to come up to the ranch?" she invited him again, as she had a long time before. But this time she wondered what would happen. But he smiled at her and shook his head.

"That's your private time. I don't want to intrude on that. We can go somewhere when you get back." And then what? Would they still be friends? She was faintly worried about that, but on the way back to her apartment he set her mind at rest. He wanted very little more from her than he had now. "I'm not saying I'm in love with you, Crystal. I'm not. I don't think I ever could fall in love again. I've had all that. And my life is peaceful now," he smiled at her as they drove through the night. "I don't want children, marriage, obligations, lies. I want a friend I enjoy talking to, someone to be there now and then, but not all the time. I really don't want more than that, and sometimes I think that even as young as you are, you want the same things. You want to work hard, do well, and go back to your ranch at the end of it. Am I right?" She nodded. He had read her well.

"Yes, you are. I've already had everything I wanted in life. A man I loved more than anything, success . . . and now Zeb. That's enough for me." And she had paid for all of it with plenty of heartaches.

"No, it's not enough. One day I'd like to see you with someone you cared about. But right now, selfishly," he smiled, "I'd be pleased if you were content to spend a little time with an old man." The idea of calling him that made her laugh. He looked twenty years younger than he was, or ten anyway. He took good care of himself. He played tennis, swam a lot, seldom stayed up late, and never caroused. She had never heard that he was involved with the latest starlet, or even more established movie stars. She suspected that he was just what he appeared to be, very successful, hardworking, and a hell of a nice man. "When are you coming back?"

"Right after Labor Day." She was starting her new movie shortly after that, and he looked satisfied. He was willing to wait that long and he had no desire to visit her on the ranch in the valley.

He called her a few times that summer when she was gone, sent her some books he thought she'd like, and a wonderful new cowboy hat for her birthday. She turned twenty-eight that year and spent it with Boyd and Hiroko on the ranch. She thought of Brian from time to time, he was so different from the men she had known before. There was no passion, no fire, none of the aching love that she and Spencer had shared, none of the ugliness Ernie had brought into her life, no diamond bracelets, no furs. Only a cowboy hat, and good books, and occasional letters that made her laugh, about the Hollywood scene that never really changed, while pretending to almost every hour, every day. And when she got back to Los Angeles he was waiting for her, just as he had said before the summer. They went to Puerto Vallarta for a few days, and there were none of the disappearances, the mysteries, as when Ernie had gone there to do business with "friends," the friends that had probably murdered him and left her to take the blame and almost go to prison.

The new picture went well, and no one seemed to notice her new relationship. Her involvement with Brian Ford was as quiet as the man himself. She had discovered that he was remotely involved in politics, and gave large sums to the Democrats. He was especially fond of young Jack Kennedy who was running for president that year. And eventually, people began to understand her involvement with Brian.

They never saw Crystal with anyone else. But in Hollywood Brian Ford was sacred. People didn't gossip about him, didn't pry into what he did, and standing in his shadow, the limelight on Crystal seemed to dim, and she liked that. She got more publicity than she needed anyway. Her career was red-hot, but now she was a respected actress. And in April Brian got his wish. Crystal had been thunderstruck by the nomination. And the night of the Academy Awards she sat breathless and staring in her seat as they opened the envelope and called her name. She couldn't believe it. She had won the Academy Award for best actress. And it meant even more to her because it was one of Brian's films. He squeezed her hand as they read her name, and she sat very still for a minute, afraid to move and afraid she had heard wrong. And then she stood up and walked down the aisle, with everyone applauding and the cameras trained on her. She couldn't believe it was happening to her, and everything was a blur as she walked onto the stage and took the Oscar in her trembling hand, and looked out into the audience at where she knew Brian was seated.

"I don't know what to say," she said into the microphone, her voice as husky and musical as it had always been, "I never thought I'd be standing up here, doing this . . . where do

I begin? What do I say? So many people to thank, people who have believed in me. Most important of all, of course, Brian Ford, without whom I'd be picking grapes and corn in a valley far from here. But other people too . . . people who've believed in me for so long . . . a man named Harry who gave me a job singing when I was seventeen," and as she said it, in the restaurant in San Francisco where they were watching her on TV, Harry began to cry openly, ". . . and a very special lady named Pearl, who taught me to dance, and came to Hollywood with me . . . and my father who told me to go out into the world and follow my dreams . . . and all the directors I've worked with who taught me what I know . . . my co-stars on this film . . . and Louis Brown, who introduced me to Brian Ford . . . I owe all of you everything." She held up the Oscar with tears in her eyes. "I owe you this. And also my friends Boyd and Hiroko, who take care of what I love most," and then she paused with a smile, as the tears ran down her cheeks, "and very special thanks to the person who has made me grow, who is everything to me . . . Zeb, whom I love most." She smiled a special smile for him, knowing that he was probably watching. "Thank you all." She saluted them then, and with the Oscar in her hand, went back to her seat as the audience applauded her. They knew how far she'd come, and much of what had happened to her. They knew about the trial, and they had forgiven her. They had accepted her, and given her their ultimate reward. And Brian put an arm around her as she got back to her seat. The tears were still rolling down her cheeks and he gave her a warm hug as she grinned triumphantly at him. "He's a lucky little boy," he whispered to her as the cameras continued to roll and then panned the crowd still applauding. Her fans were pleased, and the people who had heard her say their names were celebrating in their homes. Lou Brown was watching with friends and he was thrilled for her, and Boyd and Hiroko were in shock as they toasted her with sake. Pearl hadn't stopped crying since they'd first called Crystal's name, and Harry was buying drinks for the house with champagne from the Napa Valley. And in Washington, Spencer had stayed home from a dinner party and was in bed with a bad cold. He had sat staring at her, thinking of how far she'd come, and how much he wished he had been there to share it with her. He had been a fool to let her go, to go back to Washington alone, and he wondered sometimes if she had done it purposely. If she had wanted him to go back to Elizabeth and

Washington just to further his career. It was the kind of thing she would have done, but it was too late to change any of it now. He was too deeply entrenched, too involved in politics, and there were other people in her life now. He had seen her hug the man she'd been sitting with. And he assumed of course that he was the much-loved Zeb she mentioned. He was a lucky man, Spencer knew, and he only hoped that he would be good to her. She had looked beautiful on the screen. But he knew another side of her, the side that had helped him achieve his dreams, the side that had shared all her secrets with him . . . the girl he had met when she was a child . . . the woman he'd gone back to the valley with. The woman he had loved more than life itself, and even now, after all this time, he still did. He thought about sending her a telegram, but he didn't know where to send it, and just realizing that made him feel even sadder. He had lost her, she was gone, and she had been the best thing that had ever happened to him. He turned off the TV, and lay in bed for hours that night, thinking of Crystal.

And little Zeb went to bed that night, thinking about her too. He was four and a half years old by then, and he had grinned at the TV as she said his name. "That's my mom!" he announced, and handed his Coke to Jane while he stared at her. He wondered what she was doing there, but Hiroko had told him that she would be home soon.

They were all proud of her, and Brian Ford most of all. They shared a special relationship, and if he had been a younger man and his life had been different before they met, he would have let it go further with her than he was inclined to. What they had suited them both. It was simple and honest and clean. There was no deception, no lies, no commitments, no promises. Just their friendship and the fact that he enjoyed her company. She insisted on buying him dinner that night, and he took her dancing afterward. She said she was still in shock, but Brian wasn't surprised she'd won. She deserved every bit of it, and he was happy because his picture had won too. It was a big night for both of them, and when he left her finally to go home, she sat quietly in her apartment, looking at the Oscar on the table where she'd set it down. It was an amazing tribute to her. An unforgettable night. It was her reward for coming back to Hollywood and doing it right this time, and she thought of her father, as she had earlier . . . and Spencer . . . and Zeb . . . the men she had loved best in her life, and two of them were gone now. But she had Zeb, and one day she would teach him what she had learned from all of them. To be honest, and decent, and work hard, to live well, and love with all your heart, no matter what the price, and never be afraid to follow your dreams, wherever they took you.

CHAPTER
41

The election that year was an exciting one, and with Brian, Crystal got caught up in the excitement of it. He went east once or twice for campaign dinners, while she stayed to work on one of Brian's new films. And he was filled with descriptions of the excitement in Washington when he got back. He was there when Jack Kennedy won, and a new era seemed to have dawned. The days of Camelot, with his pretty wife, their sweet little girl and their brand-new baby boy.

Crystal spent Zeb's fifth birthday with him, and when she got back to Hollywood she was surprised when she got her own invitation to the Inaugural Ball. She would be finished with her current film by then, but she still hesitated to go. There were old ghosts she wanted to avoid in Washington, and she was afraid she might run into Spencer.

"You have to," Brian said. "It's really an honor you can't decline. And this is a special time." He knew that like his time with her, it might never come again. He was pleased for the young senator, and he wanted Crystal to meet them both. He pressed her so hard that in the end she agreed to go with him. It wasn't easy for her deciding to go back. She had read that Spencer had just been appointed one of Kennedy's aides, and she knew he'd be there. But she prayed only that the crowd would be so large they'd never meet. She didn't want to see him again. It had been almost six years and much too long. She didn't want to revive the longing again, and the pain. All she wanted was what she had, her memories of him, and Zeb, waiting for her whenever she could get free from work and go up to the ranch to be with him.

She bought her gown at Giorgio. It was silver and Brian whistled when she showed it to him, and then he laughed. "Well, you've done it, kid. You sure as hell look like a movie star

in that." It was in sharp contrast to the new
First Lady's subtly elegant gowns. But this had
its own elegance, just as Crystal Wyatt did.
The dress sparkled prettily at him, as he smiled
and kissed her hand. He knew that her debut
in presidential circles was going to be a smash.
And it was.

The Inaugural Ball was far more beautiful
than even she had dreamed. There were several parties, and actually two balls, and she
thought the First Lady looked exquisite in her
Oleg Cassini gown. There were crowds of on-
lookers everywhere, and Crystal was recognized and signed hundreds of autographs for
her admirers in the crowd. Brian looked proud
of her in his well-cut dinner jacket. He was
fifty-nine that year, but more rugged-looking
and handsomer than ever before.

"You look pretty good yourself," she had
teased as they dressed at the Statler Hotel. He
had reserved a suite months before, and she
had to admit she was glad she had agreed to go
with him.

Their relationship was still exactly what it
had been from the first, a comfortable companionship and a discreet affair that most people
still hadn't figured out, but those who did kept
very quiet. Crystal was deeply fond of him,
and he met certain needs for her. He was

someone real to talk to in Hollywood, and she often asked his advice about the ranch. And it was physically satisfying certainly, but there was no wild flame, no torment, no passion, no pain. Only the ease of being with a man she both respected and admired.

They went to both of the balls that night, and he introduced her to the President. She was struck by how handsome he was, standing beside his pretty, aristocratic wife. She looked very shy and had been speaking to someone in French, and when she was introduced to Crystal, she told her how much she liked her movies.

They danced late into the night, and it was when Brian went to get her wrap that she saw Spencer at last. He was standing near the door with several of the other men in the Cabinet, he was talking animatedly and laughing with some of the Secret Service men. She started to turn away, feeling a wave of yearning wash over her. She wanted Brian to come back, so they could leave, but he seemed to be taking forever. And as she turned away, the glimmer of her dress in the soft lights caught his eye, and he stopped talking. He excused himself, and a moment later he was standing there, looking down at her, as overwhelmed by her beauty as he had been before. He reached out and touched her arm with a gentle hand, as though to see if she were real. And she was. Almost too much so.

"Crystal . . ." It had been six years. Six long years, filled with hard times and good times, the ranch, and movies, and his baby.

"Hello, Spencer. I thought I'd see you here. Congratulations." Her voice was quiet in the noisy room, but he heard every word she said, and he thought she'd never looked lovelier than she did that night in the silver gown that molded her figure like a veil of ice over the beautiful body he still remembered.

"Thank you. You've come a long way." He smiled. He meant it in more ways than one. The years had made her the big star she had once dreamed of becoming, and now that she was there, she enjoyed it. But it meant nothing compared to what she still felt for him. Just looking at him brought it all back, the joy and the pain, and the lifetime of longing she still felt for him. "Will you be here long?" he asked with casual interest.

"A few days." She was purposely vague, praying he couldn't hear her heartbeat. "I have to get back to California." He nodded, and she wondered if he was still married. And on the other side of the room, Elizabeth was preening in all her glory. Her husband was one of Kennedy's aides. At thirty-one, she had made it. The only woman in the room that she envied was married to the President, but even that dream might come true one day. Anything was possible now. Spencer was an important man, even to the Barclays.

"Where are you staying?"

She hesitated, and then thought it didn't matter anyway. He had his own life now. And she had Brian. "At the Statler."

He nodded, and Brian reappeared with her silver fox. She had no choice but to introduce the two men. Brian knew who he was, but they had never met before, and he wondered how Spencer knew Crystal. Her connection to Brian was obvious, but the look in Spencer's eyes couldn't be ignored. She said good night and they left, and in the limousine Brian found her strangely quiet looking out at the snow falling softly. He didn't say anything to her until they got back to the room, and then he knew he had to ask her.

"How do you know Spencer Hill?" As far as he knew, she'd never been to Washington. He had seen him with Jack Kennedy the year before, and had instantly liked him. He was going to be a big man one day, he already was, and Brian knew how important he was to the young president.

Crystal looked vague as she unzipped her dress, and smiled at him, but her eyes were sad. He saw something there he had never seen in her before, a kind of raw pain that was almost beyond bearing. "I met him years ago, at my sister's wedding. He served in the Pacific with my brother-in-law." And then, turning away, "He defended me at the trial." And suddenly, he knew. He had never been able to figure it out before. He walked slowly toward her and looked down at her with sad eyes.

"He's the boy's father, isn't he?" There was a long pause, and then slowly she nodded, and turned away.

"Does he know?"

She shook her head. "And he never will. It's a long story, but he has his own life, and a good future. Staying with me would have destroyed that for him." She had given him the gift of freedom at the right time, and it was good to know it hadn't been wasted. He had used it well.

"He's still in love with you." Brian sat down heavily as he talked to her. He had known it would come one day, but he was sorry anyway. He had seen Crystal's eyes, and Spencer's.

"Don't be ridiculous. I haven't even seen him in six years until this evening."

But the next morning, when Brian was out

at a political breakfast with friends, Spencer
called her. She felt her heart race as he said her
name, and told herself she was stupid. He
wanted to see her briefly before she left, but
she insisted that she couldn't.

"Crystal, please . . . for old times'
sake . . ." Old times that had given her a
baby.

"I don't think we should. What if some re-
porter saw you? It's not worth it."

"Let me worry about that. Please . . ." He
was begging her, and she wanted to see him
just as badly. But to what end? And even if
Brian was right in suspecting that Spencer still
cared for her, seeing him could only hurt Spencer. She tried to put him off again but he
wouldn't let her do it.

"All right, where?" She sounded nervous.
She was afraid of both the press and Brian. He
was never possessive about her, but she didn't
want to hurt him. Especially now that he
knew. She had seen the sorrow in his eyes the
night before, and she wanted to convince him
that it wasn't worth his worry. Spencer Hill
was no longer in her life. And he never would
be.

Spencer gave her the address of a little bar
he knew, and she promised to meet him there
at four o'clock. Brian was still out, and she

took a taxi instead of the limousine he had left for her. She was afraid that the limo driver might talk to the press, if he recognized her or Spencer.

She wore a big fur hat and a fur coat, and a pair of dark glasses, and he was waiting for her when she got there. There was snow in his hair, which was grayer than the last time she saw him at the ranch. And as she looked at him, she couldn't help but remember the way he had looked the first time they'd met, in his white flannel slacks and his blazer and red tie, his shining black hair and warm smile. He hadn't changed much, but she had. At twenty-eight, the girl she had been at fourteen was all but forgotten.

"Thank you for coming." He reached out and took her hand as they sat down. "I had to see you, Crystal." She smiled, realizing again how like him his son was, the son he had never seen, and never would, the son who gave her life all its meaning, all its joy. "You've done so well," he smiled, "I've seen all your movies."

She laughed, feeling young again. "Who would have thought way back when . . ."

"I remember the first time you told me you wanted to be a movie star." And then, "Do you still have the ranch?"

She nodded, "Boyd and Hiroko live there

with me. I go back whenever I can." . . . to
see your son . . . our baby . . .

"I'd love to get back there sometime." The
thought of it made her tremble. But she knew
that for four years at least he'd be much too
busy even to think of going to the ranch.

And then she dared to ask him the question
she'd wondered the night before. "Are you still
married?" She'd read nothing of a divorce, and
with Kennedy a Catholic she suspected he
wasn't, or he wouldn't have been chosen for
the job he had now.

He nodded pensively. "After a fashion.
There was never anything there, and after I got
back . . . she knew about us. The funny thing
is she didn't care. She wanted to stay married
for her own reasons, which weren't mine. And
now she has what she wants," he smiled and
looked boyish again, "or at least she thinks so.
Just like your being a movie star, her childhood dream was being married to someone important. We go our own ways, but she gives
very nice parties." He sounded not so much
bitter as deeply disappointed. He had given up
the woman he loved, and spent more than ten
years married to a stranger. "I guess we all got
what we wanted, didn't we?" The movie star,
the President's aide, and the wife of someone
important. The only thing missing was what

mattered most. The woman he had loved for fifteen years now. "When do you go back?"

"Tomorrow."

"With Brian Ford?"

"Yes." She looked him squarely in the eye. She knew what he wanted to know, but she didn't want to tell him, and he didn't want to ask. It was all much too painful.

"You've been in some very fine movies."

"Thank you." She smiled gently at him, there was so much she wanted to say and she knew she couldn't.

He laughed again, "I saw you win the Academy Award, I almost cried. You looked beautiful, Crystal . . . you still do . . . nothing ever changes, you just get better and better."

"And older." She laughed. "I can remember when I thought thirty was practically dead." He laughed too. She was still so young and so incredibly lovely. It made him feel a hundred years old and so damn lonely.

They talked for a while and then he looked at his watch. He hated to go, but he knew he had to leave her. He had to be at the White House for dinner at seven o'clock, and he still had to pick Elizabeth up at the house, and change into his dinner jacket before the command performance that night.

"Can I drop you off?" he asked.

"I don't think you should." She was still worried and he smiled at her.

"I think you worry too much. I'm not the President, you know. I'm only an aide. Contrary to what my wife thinks, I'm really not all that important." She slipped into the limousine with him and they drove to the hotel. He didn't ask why she had never married, and she didn't ask why he had never had children. They talked about the ball the night before, and then suddenly the car stopped, and he looked at her dismally and held her hands tightly in his own. "I don't want to leave you again. The last six years without you have been awful." It was what he had wanted to say to her when he called, why he had begged her to see him. He at least wanted her to know that he still loved her.

"Spencer, don't . . . it's too late for us. You've carved out a wonderful spot for yourself. Don't spoil it."

"Don't be foolish. All this could be gone in four years, we won't be. Haven't you learned that yet? Doesn't it mean anything to you that we still feel like this after fifteen years? How long do you want to wait, till I'm ninety?"

She laughed at him, and closing his eyes at the sound of it, he bent toward her and kissed her. She felt breathless kissing him, and when he stopped, her eyes were filled with tears. There was nothing she could say to him. For his own sake, she couldn't give in to him, but she wanted to desperately. And he wasn't making things easy for her.

"If I come to California, will you see me?"

"I . . . no . . . Brian . . . don't . . ."

He asked her bluntly what he had hesitated to before. "Are you living with Ford?"

She shook her head. They had both avoided that, for their own reasons. "No . . . I live by myself. . . ." He smiled happily as he kissed her again, and the driver stood discreetly out in the cold, waiting for them to finish talking.

"I'll call you as soon as I can."

"Spencer! . . ."

He silenced her with a last kiss, and then smiled at her again. "I love you . . . I always will . . . and if you still think you can change that, forget it." They had come too far, resisted it too often, tried too hard, lost and won and lost again. There was no way out of it now. She knew, just as he did, that they belonged together. But stolen moments could cost him everything he'd built and she didn't want that.

She looked at him for a long moment, worried about him and not herself. "Is this really what you want?"

"Yes . . . no matter how little it is, Crystal . . . it's something."

"I love you so much." She whispered it into his neck and then they opened the door and stepped out. She shook his hand, thanked him for the ride, and disappeared into the hotel, still feeling his lips warm on hers, and wondering what would happen.

CHAPTER
42

She and Brian flew back to California the next day, and they were both quiet, as he read and she sat staring out the window. He didn't want to say anything to her yet, but he knew. He had called her all afternoon at the hotel, and when he saw her the night before, he read the whole story in her eyes, and all he wanted was to wish her well and tell her to be careful. They finally talked it over during lunch on the plane, and he sighed as he looked at the star he'd made, but she deserved all the good things that had happened to her. There hadn't been enough good things in her early life, and he prayed for her that there wouldn't be further scandal. This could be a big one for both her and Spencer.

"I want you to know you can always call on me. I will always be your friend," Brian said and Crystal cried as he talked. They had gone to Washington as lovers and friends, and now it was all over. But he had always known the day would come. He had just hoped it would come later rather than sooner. They had had two years of being involved with each other, and he knew he couldn't ask for more than that. He didn't really want more. He had never wanted to marry her. The trouble was, neither did Spencer, he couldn't. He pointed it out to Crystal too, but none of it was news to her. She sighed and blew her nose. It had been a difficult two days in spite of the splendor of the inauguration.

"I know all that, Brian. This has been going on between us for fifteen years." He looked startled.

"Before the boy then?"

"Long before. I've been in love with him since I was fourteen years old."

"Then why the hell didn't you marry him, or didn't he ask you?"

"He did, but never at the right time. It's been a comedy of errors all my life. We found each other again after he got engaged. Then after he got married, he discovered he didn't love her. He went to Korea, and I got mixed up with Ernie, and when he came back, I thought I owed too much to Ernie to leave him then. Isn't that a joke? And then Ernie wouldn't let me go when I wanted to, and Elizabeth wouldn't give him a divorce, and on and on for years, like two crazy people who just can't get away from each other. He asked me to marry him again after the trial, but by then he had political aspirations and a terrific job waiting for him, and a woman accused of murder one is not exactly what anyone needs to win an election. So I ended it, for his sake."

He looked at her with fresh admiration, and guessed the rest. "And then you found out you were pregnant, and you never told him."

She nodded. He had figured it out perfectly. "Not exactly an easy life. And now?"

"I don't know." She and Brian had agreed to end their affair, but that still didn't settle anything with Spencer. It just meant she was free again, but he certainly wasn't, between his wife and his job as a Kennedy aide, he was anything but, and she knew it. "He wants to come out when he can. And then what?"

"I'll tell you what. You'll be fifty years old one day, still in love with a man married to someone else, and waiting for him to show up twice a year. And what if he runs for president one day? Then what? It'll be all over, and how old will you be then? I think you should find some nice young guy to marry you and have more kids, before it's too late." But he wasn't volunteering either, and they both knew he didn't want marriage or more children. He had never wavered on that score, and he had had a vasectomy the year before, which made things easier for Crystal.

But the issue now was Spencer and what would happen next. As her friend, Brian didn't approve, and he thought that she was being foolish. If Spencer couldn't marry her now, she should drop him. But it was easier said than done, and when he turned up in Los Angeles six weeks later, their hours together were filled with all the love and passion they had shared since the beginning. They stayed in her apartment the whole time, and never went out, and two days later he left, leaving a gaping hole in her life, as she waited for him to come back again. But it was another three months before he could get away. It was no way to live, but it was all they had, stolen moments, hidden days, locked away in her apartment, with their secret. As it was, there was constant gossip and guesswork about who she was going out with.

And after a year of seeing Spencer on the sly, she finally started an alleged "affair" with a star she had worked with often, who was gay and equally anxious to keep his secret safe. She also saw Brian from time to time and he always scolded her after asking if she was still seeing Spencer.

Zeb was seven by then and he desperately wanted to come to Hollywood to see her. She relented finally and let him come with the Websters, who were as awed by it as he was. They all went to Disneyland and had a great time. And she promised him he could come back soon, but he was happy to go back to the ranch with the Websters and Jane, whom he frequently referred to as his sister. She was fourteen and as delicately lovely as her mother. Crystal had given them a tour of some of the studios, and she wondered why she hadn't let them come sooner. No one seemed to suspect anything, and Zeb looked nothing like Crystal.

By the summer of 1963, she and Spencer had been seeing each other quietly again for two years, and she was resigned to her fate now. She didn't try to talk him out of it anymore. She knew she couldn't have let him go again. She couldn't live without him, and there seemed to be no need to. No one suspected anything, and Elizabeth didn't care what he did. She was too busy seeing friends, serving on committees, practicing law in her spare time, and giving parties. There was no room in her life for a husband.

And in November, Crystal was working on a film night and day, it was another one of Brian's and a good one. He swore she'd get another Oscar for it, and she was sitting on the set, chatting with the other actors when they heard the news. The President had been shot in Dallas. Her heart thundered in her chest as she ran to an office where someone had a television set to watch the news. At first they thought several of the aides had been shot too, and she watched in horror as they reran the film of his body thrown back in the car, his head on his wife's lap, and then the facade of the hospital where he had been taken. At eleven thirty-five, a.m., California time, the announcer said in a choked voice that the President was dead. His body would be flown to Washington for a state funeral. And they showed his wife's ravaged face, but nothing had been said about Spencer. Crystal's face was white as people began crying around her. And she didn't know whom to call. In desperation, she called Brian's office. He had just heard the news too, and he was crying when she called him.

"I have to know if Spencer is hurt," she said in a choked voice. "Do you know who to call?"

There was a long silence as he thought of what it meant to her. That added to the rest would be one grief too many. "I'll see what I can do, I'll call you right back." But it was hours before he could get through to any of the people he knew at the White House, and she spent all day in a daze, waiting to hear from him. It was nine o'clock that night when he finally called her. Lyndon Johnson had been sworn in by then, and Jack Kennedy was back in Washington as a nation cried, and his wife had stood in her bloodstained suit as they carried him away in his coffin.

When Crystal heard Brian's voice, she began to cry, fearing the news, but he was able to reassure her.

"He's all right, Crystal. He's back in Washington. At the White House." She heard the words as though in a dream and as she put down the phone she lay down and sobbed, for Jack and for Jackie, and for the days of Camelot, gone forever, but also with relief for Spencer, who hadn't been injured.

CHAPTER
43

The funeral was a symphony of pain, with the coffin drawn by a horse-drawn caisson as the two little children stood crying and a little boy saluted his father for the last time. The nation came to a halt as they mourned him. His murderer was shot and the whole world went into shock. It was a time that no one would ever forget, and there was no way Crystal could talk to Spencer. There was no way of knowing how he was, or what was happening to him, and she had no idea if he would stay on to work with Lyndon Johnson. And Brian gave his actors two weeks off. No one had the heart to go back to work. They all needed time to heal, and in deference to the President he had loved, the office was closed in formal mourning.

Crystal flew back to the ranch, and sat there with Boyd and Hiroko watching the news night and day. Even Zeb cried when he saw the funeral on TV, and he and Jane held hands, as they stared at the bereft Kennedy children.

And in Washington, Spencer made a decision. He had been stunned for days, and he had never cried as much in his life. There were heartbroken good-byes, and the bittersweet arrival of the Johnsons. But he knew he couldn't serve anyone as he had JFK. He knew in his heart that he had truly loved him.

The day after the funeral he resigned, wished Lyndon Johnson well, and spent hours crying silently as he packed up his office, and then he went home with his boxes and his books, and his mementos of a man who would be missed forever.

Elizabeth saw him as he came in and she looked shocked. She had gone to the funeral with her father. Spencer had had to go with the rest of the staff.

"What are you doing?" She stood in the living room and stared at him. He looked tired and older than his forty-four years. He felt like an old man with no hopes and no dreams left. And that was why he had done it. He had resigned because he knew the dream was over for him, and he had given up too many other dreams to go on after the death of this one that had meant so much to him.

"I resigned. I'm coming home, Elizabeth."

"But that's crazy." She stared at him. He couldn't do that to her. She knew he was upset, but the presidency would live on, with or without Kennedy. He couldn't just walk out like that. She wouldn't let him. "I don't understand you." She sounded bitter and angry. "You had everyone's dream in the palm of your hand, and you just walked out on it like that?"

"I didn't walk out on it," he said, "it died. It was murdered."

"All right, I know these are difficult times. But Johnson is going to need help too."

But he shook his head and held up a tired hand. "Don't, Elizabeth. It's over. I handed in my resignation this morning. If you want the job, be my guest, I'll be happy to call the President for you."

"Don't be an ass. And now what?" He couldn't even run for office yet, he hadn't laid the groundwork. But he turned to her with a strange smile. He knew exactly what he wanted to do and where he was going from here.

"Now, Elizabeth, we call it a day. It's fourteen years later than it should be. But I, for one, don't want to wake up one morning and be sixty-five and wonder where the hell my life went."

"What the devil does that mean?" The President had been shot, but that didn't mean the end of everything for them too. What was wrong with him? But he was hanging on to the last dream he had, and this time he knew he wouldn't lose it.

"It means I'm leaving. I've been here too long, in a lot of ways. And now it's over for me."

"You mean us?" She refused to understand, but he nodded.

"Precisely. I'm not sure you'd even have noticed if I hadn't told you."

"And just exactly where are you going?" She tried not to show it, but she was frightened.

"I'm going home, wherever that becomes. I'm going away. To California for a start. And to Crystal."

"You're leaving Washington?" She was stunned. He was throwing everything away.

"That's right. I've had the best there is, and now I'm leaving. I'm going to go into private practice somewhere, or maybe local politics on a small scale, but I'm not staying here and I'm not staying married to you. I want a divorce, Elizabeth. And whether you agree or not, that's how it is. I don't need your consent anymore. This is 1963, not 1950."

"You've lost your mind." She sat down on the couch and stared at him. She was thirty-four years old and he was blowing her life all to pieces.

"No," he shook his head sadly. "I think I've found it. We should never have gotten married in the first place, and you know it."

"That's absurd." She looked as ladylike as she always did, in her perfect imitation of the First Lady's style, in her Chanel suit and her pillbox hat. But that was over now too. It all was.

"The only thing that's absurd is that I let you talk me into staying this long. You're still young, you have a whole life ahead of you. You can run for office yourself, if that's what you want. But after what just happened," his voice choked thinking of the man he had loved so dearly, "I don't want it. You can have it all. The excitement, the thrill, the disappointments, the heartbreak."

"You're a coward." She spat the words at him, but it was one thing they both knew he wasn't.

"Maybe. Maybe I'm just tired." And sad. And so goddamn lonely I could cry. And now he wanted to be with Crystal, where he belonged.

"You're going back to her, aren't you?" "Her," the only word she ever used when referring to Crystal.

"Maybe. If she'll have me."

"You're a fool, Spencer. You always were. You're too good for that." But he turned and walked away from her, and he went upstairs to pack his things, for good this time. And when he left the house that night, they both knew it was forever.

"I'll call an attorney when I get to California," he said from the door. It was an odd good-bye to a woman he had lived with for almost fourteen years, but there was nothing left to say to her, and she didn't answer as he closed the door, and drove to a hotel to spend the night before he left for California in the morning.

CHAPTER
44

Spencer called Crystal late that night to tell her his own news. He hadn't called her since before he left for Dallas. But she wasn't home, and he decided to surprise her in L.A. The flight was long, and he was lost in his own thoughts and the only thing that cheered him was seeing her. But there was no one at her apartment, and he decided to find her on the set at the studio where he knew she was working on her new movie.

They had a lot to talk about, and he still hadn't absorbed it all himself. He was free. He had walked out on everything, and he knew it was the right thing. All he wanted to know now was how she felt about it, and he experienced a tremor of terror as he got out of the cab at the studio and walked to the sound stage. What if it was too late for her? If it had gone on too long? If she wouldn't marry him? It was all possible, but unlikely. He knew how deeply she loved him, and how much they meant to each other. It was the one thing he had never really doubted in years.

But the sound stage was empty and he was told that the cast was on a two-week hiatus, in respect for the President. He stood for a long moment, wondering what to do next. And then he knew. He rented a car, and decided not to call her. It was the only place he knew she could be.

The drive took him fourteen hours, but he hadn't wanted to fly. He just wanted to drive along and think of her, and what they would do now. He stopped by the roadside to sleep once when he was too tired to go on, and twice to eat at roadside restaurants. But as the sun came up over the valley, he felt his heart sing, and he felt the spirit of his lost friend somewhere near him. It was an odd time in a strange world, but he knew he had done the right thing. And he arrived at the ranch at seven o'clock in the morning. The sun was high in the sky, but the air was cool. It was a beautiful November day, and there was a little boy running through the fields as he slowed to watch him. For a moment he had thought it was Jane, but as he looked at him, he knew it wasn't. He had shining black hair and he was calling to someone as Spencer got out of the car and watched him. He appeared to be about eight years old, and seeing the stranger looking at him, he stopped and stared, and then he walked slowly toward him.

Spencer never moved as he watched the boy, and as he approached, he almost gasped. He had seen that face before, long, long before, when he was a child himself. It was a face he knew well, his own, it was like seeing his own childhood looking at him as Spencer slowly began to walk toward him. And then suddenly he knew what had happened, and she had never told him.

"Hi!" The boy waved a long, graceful arm, and with tear-filled eyes Spencer stopped. He didn't know what to say to him, he only smiled as the tears rolled slowly down his cheeks, and then he saw Crystal in the distance. She had stopped, terrified to see him there, wanting to call Zeb back to her, but it was too late, and she started running, as though to turn him back. But it was too late, and now all she could see ahead of her was Spencer. He was smiling at the child, and at her, and crying softly she began to walk toward him. He was safe, he'd come home, for a minute or an hour or a day, or however long she'd have him. She saw him walk up to Zeb, and take his hand, and she was still running toward them. It was too late. He knew. Her secret was his now too . . . and Zeb's . . . she reached them just as Spencer lifted him into his arms and she ran to them and held them. He looked down at her, as Zeb stared at them both in fascination.

"I didn't know you were coming." It was the understatement of the century and he laughed at her, unashamed of his own tears.

"There's a lot you didn't tell me, I'd say, Crystal Wyatt."

"You didn't ask." She smiled through her own tears as he kissed her.

"I'll have to remember that next time." Zeb squirmed away then, embarrassed by them, and went running through the vineyards, as she had as a child, and their other children would one day. Spencer took her hand and they walked slowly back to the ranch house as they talked, and the boy watched. And Spencer looked down at her quietly when they reached the steps, and then up into the sky again. It was a sunny winter day . . . but he could have sworn that in the distance he heard thunder and saw lightning, as he kissed her, and the three of them went inside. Home at last. Together.